RUNEBINDER

ALEX R. KAHLER

RUNEBINDER

HARLEQUIN TEEN

ISBN-13: 978-0-373-21263-7

Runebinder

Printed in U.S.A.

for those who never saw themselves as heroes

"And with our greed, a great sin was born unto this world
and like Eve to the apple
that sin shall consume us."

—Caius 8:22
2 P.R. (Post-Resurrection)

PART
1

THE ROAD TO HELL

CHAPTER ONE

IT WAS NOT THE CLEAN KILL HE HAD HOPED FOR.

Tenn raced across the cornfield. Rain seeped through his leather coat and mud squelched up his boots, but he focused on the shadow darting in front of him. Everything else dulled to gray and black and pounding heartbeats.

Gray and black…and red. Too much red.

If he didn't hurry, that red would damn them all.

His prey staggered. Fell. A moment later he dropped to its side, dagger in hand. He didn't want to kill. He didn't want his hands stained red again. But those wants didn't stop him from slicing through its warm, heaving neck.

The buck twitched.

Tenn kept a hand on the deer's flank as its lifeblood throbbed between his fingers. It wouldn't be right to look away, to let the poor creature die alone and cold.

Alone and cold, alone and cold, how many have died alone and cold?

The Sphere of Water raged within his gut. It wanted to revel in the blood. It wanted to drown in red. But he pushed the thoughts and the power away. Now wasn't the time to give in, either to his own weakness or to that glorious strength. His stomach knotted when the deer's rolling eye found his. He almost laughed from revulsion; years ago, he'd been a vegetarian.

"I'm sorry," he whispered as the deer spasmed and fell still. Not that it mattered. Not that those apologies ever mattered—not to the dying, not to the dead. Apologies didn't change the world he lived in, and it didn't change the deeds he'd done.

"Shit." Katherine stopped beside him. "That's a lot of blood."

Tenn glanced up to her and Michael. Their breath came out in clouds, their forms bare shadows in the gloom. He opened his mouth, but the words got caught in his throat.

Three years of killing, three years of bloodshed, and it still turned his stomach. He swallowed and looked away, washing the blood off in a puddle before sliding his dagger back in his boot. Three years of blood on his hands. Three years…

"I thought you said you were a clean shot," Katherine said, turning back to Michael.

Tenn stood. The Sphere of Water still raged, still begged for control. He pushed it farther down. The longer he refused its call, the worse it got.

Michael stepped forward, his shoulders hunched and a bow held loose in hand. He was built like a linebacker, but right then, he looked like a puppy caught pissing on a Persian rug. Five arrows jutted from the deer's hide, and another half dozen were scattered throughout the field.

"I am," Michael said. His words didn't hold much conviction as he gestured to his throat. "Usually. It's just been a while since I had to shoot without magic."

Katherine ignored him. There wasn't time for apologies. She pulled a set of nylon cords from her backpack and handed one to Tenn.

She wrapped one cord around the buck's neck while Tenn tied its hindquarters. Her movements were smooth, well-practiced—her hands were used to dealing with the dead. Like Tenn, she was eighteen. Unlike Tenn, she didn't seem bothered by the buck's sightless glare.

She nudged him. "You okay?"

He nodded, but his nerves were on edge, and the Sphere of Water pulsed in his stomach like a wound. One that desperately wanted to be touched, inflamed. Over a week had passed since he'd been allowed to open to that energy center, that source of pain and power, and like a neglected child, it sat there and wept and begged to be noticed. But they had their orders: no magic. Not until the enemy army arrived.

They needed that tenuous element of surprise.

"We need to hurry," he said. "They're going to smell the blood." He turned to Michael. "And if that happens, it's all on your head."

Had they met before the Resurrection, Michael probably would have shoved Tenn's head into the school toilet just for making eye contact. The guy was a nineteen-year-old tank, with broad shoulders and short brown hair and tattoos from eye to shin. His face was a plane of white scars and black ink. Tenn, on the other hand, was tall and lithe—years of using Water had crafted him a swimmer's build rather than the hulking muscle granted by Earth. He hadn't been at all athletic before being attuned. He'd been a nerd at best, and Michael was clearly used to being respected.

But now, when Tenn spoke, Michael didn't refute. To Michael, at least, Tenn was a superior. The Resurrection had changed almost everything for the worse; this little leveling of the playing field was about the only perk.

Together, they dragged the deer toward the highway. Tenn kept his eyes trained on the fields. He didn't want to see the way the deer's head lolled to one side, its tongue curled out and its eyes wide with static fear.

"We should be okay," Michael said, his voice cutting through the rain like rumbling thunder. "I mean, rain dilutes blood, right? And there's no way anything could hear it through the storm."

"Just shut up and keep your eyes open," Katherine replied.

Yes, there was a chance the rain had diluted the blood and hid the buck's wild cries of pain, but there was also a chance the rain was just helping the blood spread. Tenn wasn't about to test his luck, especially since he'd been sent out with Michael. That alone was a sign the fates weren't on his side.

His hands still felt sticky with blood.

For all his hatred of killing, he felt naked without his quarterstaff, which was lodged in the earth beside the high-way. Katherine had her katanas and Michael had his mace, but physical weapons were barely enough; battles were lost and won by magic now. Without it, they were like lambs to the slaughter.

Not an emboldening thought when lugging a two-hundred-pound sack of meat.

Chills raced across his skin as he peered deeper through the curtains of rain. It wasn't the cold—it was the expectation. The fields appeared devoid of life, corn drooping and swaying in the wind and rain. At least, he thought they were empty.

The storm might have been hiding him and his comrades, but it could also be hiding those he was sworn to kill. Without magic, there was no way to tell. There would be no way to know. A kraven could be out there, hidden in the stalks, just out of sight. Just within arm's reach.

Water sang to him.

Water wanted to help.

Tenn gritted his teeth and focused on the bit of nylon between his palms. The Sphere of Water couldn't *want* things, no more than his kidneys could. It was all in his head. It was stress. They were so close to being done with this damned mission, so close, and that's why Tenn's nerves were on edge. That, and that alone.

He grabbed his bladed staff when they reached the road. Years ago, this would have been like any other quaint Midwestern highway, but now the road leading back was far from pastoral. Cars lay scattered and broken like some kid played God with his Hot Wheels. Shattered glass littered the ground, shards jutting from windows like open jaws. Rust splattered across trucks and semis like bloody stains. Everything, *everything*, was quiet and empty, the only sound coming from the rain and the occasional moan of wind through hollowed cars—a cacophony of and for the dead. No movement. No life.

No bodies.

There were never any bodies. Not in the desecrated cities, not in the wild. Not when there were myriads of creatures to gobble them up, bones and blood and all. Tenn shivered again and looked out to the field.

They unceremoniously dropped the deer atop the small red wagon—the same type he'd dragged around as a kid. The sick sound of flesh thumping on metal was a noise Tenn had grown accustomed to, which almost made it worse. He didn't like relating corpses to his childhood.

How easy it is to get used to dead things.

Tenn nodded to Katherine.

She withdrew one of her katanas and raised it high above her. Then, with a quick slice, she lopped off the deer's head. It fell to the pavement and rolled away, settling in a pool of its own steaming ichor. Tenn turned; its eyes were trained straight on him, and he'd had enough postmortem glares for a lifetime.

"Still seems like a waste to me," Michael said. He threw his bow beside the carcass, not caring if the string got bloody, and picked up the handle. That was the problem with food-scavenging missions—no cars, unless you wanted to scare off prey or attract predators. "I thought the tongue was supposed to be a delicacy."

If not for Michael's usefulness as a pack mule, Tenn would have cursed Derrick for sending him along. The world might have turned on its head in the three years since the Resurrection, when monsters ripped the modern world apart, but Michael was still the same brain-dead jock. Some stereotypes, apparently, were never outgrown.

"What, and risk being followed?" Katherine asked, cleaning her blade with a spare bit of cloth. "Are you a complete fucking moron or just dense?"

Michael shrugged and began pulling the cart down the

highway. Tenn bit back his smirk. At least Katherine was willing to say what he himself was thinking.

"I'm just saying, kravens aren't known for their big brains," Michael said.

Who are you to talk about big brains? Tenn thought. "They think like animals. If they find blood and no body, they'll search for one until they either find a meal or die. And we already have enough on our plate."

They'll search forever. Forever…

Water surged at the thought.

Monsters tear through the city, ripping humans from cars, crashing through houses. Blood puddles like rainwater. He hides behind a hedge, fingers white-knuckled on the gun, blood splattered on his jeans. Not all of it monster blood. How can you tell, when some creatures wear human faces? There's no chance to ask, no chance… He clutches the gun. The useless gun. He opens to Water. He drowns out the screams in the hum of power. This was his home. Once. Now the houses are on fire and the streets are red and black with bloodied bodies and char and I know those bodies, I know those faces. He pushes deeper through Water, lets the Sphere consume him. I have to save them. I have to—

Tenn snapped back, Water's magic crashing from his limbs and back into his gut, where the angry Sphere rested and raged.

"What the hell?" he gasped, his heart hammering in his chest.

"What?" Katherine asked. "Did you see something?"

Tenn shook his head. His thoughts swam from the aftershock of Water and he had no idea how to answer. Water couldn't just dredge up memories like that. Not on its own. Not when he wasn't utilizing it. The Spheres didn't act on their own accord—they were energy centers and nothing more. So how had Water done that? Opened up and dredged up his past... He shook his head again, tried to push down the memories, the screams.

He was just tired. He was losing his grip.

Just tired, and Water was just angry at not being used for so long.

He focused on the cart, on ensuring no blood dripped from the back. He wouldn't give the kravens a Hansel and Gretel–style bread-crumb trail. That, at least, he could control.

The highway cut a straight line through the fields and hills, sharp and bleak and dotted with abandoned cars. Outpost 37 was still a blur on the horizon, several miles and a few hours away. It wavered like a mirage in the rain, a smear of black-inked buildings on pale gray paper. Every step toward the city was a tick against Tenn's nerves. The creaking cart was too loud, the rain too heavy. There was no way they could walk fast enough for his comfort. He wanted to be back and dry and warm, preferably pretending they weren't waiting for battle. Maybe the Prophets were wrong, and the army would miss them entirely. Maybe there *was* no army. Maybe this was all a waste of time, and the worst thing that had happened was that he'd been bored.

Denial had never served him well, but out here, in the freezing cold with no comfort from the Spheres, it was better than reality.

Katherine stopped. She didn't say anything, just stood with her eyes wide and a slight part to her lips.

Shit.

A second later, he heard it. A scream. A *howl*. It sliced through the fields like a scalpel, high-pitched and dragged from the depths of hell.

No living thing could make that noise.

Tenn shielded his eyes and tried to see farther out, but through the rain and the haze all he could see was shifting gray.

The scream was distant. Maybe, if they were lucky...

Michael lowered the cart handle to the ground, slowly, gently, making sure not a sound was made. His mace was in hand the moment he stood. Tenn looked over to Katherine, who had her katanas unsheathed.

"Stay very, very still," Tenn whispered, his knuckles white on his staff. "Maybe they'll pass us by."

"Not likely," Michael muttered, but he held his position.

Seconds passed in silence. Each raindrop froze into his skin, each heartbeat promised devastation.

There was a chance—a small chance—that it was a single kraven. Just one lowly, lonely monster seeking out its next meal. And there was a small chance that the kraven had found the deer's head, taken the bait and was on the run for fear its brothers would discover the bounty.

It was a small chance. Delusional at best.

Silence stretched across Tenn's nerves like a noose. Blood pooled against his gums from a fresh-bitten wound in his cheek. He tried to relax his jaw, tried to breathe slow and deep. In and out. In and out. The silence grew heavier. At least thirty seconds had passed. They would have known if they were spotted by now. He took another deep breath and started to relax his grip.

A second howl split the world, closer this time. And this one wasn't alone. Another voice picked it up, as high and piercing as shattering glass and nails on a chalkboard. He knew the scream of a kraven as well as his own voice, but that didn't mean there weren't other types of Howls out there. The quiet ones were often the deadliest. Without magic or a clear line of sight, he also had no way to estimate how many there were. Could be dozens. Hundreds, even.

It didn't matter. Without magic, even a handful of kravens could be deadly.

Blood thundered in his ears, louder than the rain. He counted his heartbeats in the back of his mind, wondering how many more he had left before his blood stilled. The Sphere of Water roiled in his gut. It could sense the upcoming battle, could feel it in the pulse of the rain—so much blood was about to be shed, and his Sphere yearned to be a part of it.

His Sphere wanted to cause it.

"We're going to die," Katherine said. Her voice was too calm for comfort. Like him, she had faced death a hundred times, and each time had probably felt as final as this. Unlike him, she seemed okay with it. "There are too many."

"You know the orders," Tenn said. *No magic. Even if the orders get us killed.* His eyes flickered to his right arm, to the tattoo he could practically feel burning against his skin. The Hunter's mark—the tattoo that first bound him to Water and, more recently, to Earth. The mark that let him use the Spheres.

Katherine didn't say anything in reply, but he could imagine her nodding her head and accepting her own approaching demise. He wasn't willing to give up so easily. There were still too many lost souls on his conscience to avenge. Some-

how, he was going to make it out of this alive. He owed the
dead that much.

The first kraven broke through the field with a banshee's
scream, and all thoughts vanished in the heat of survival.

Like all the variations of Howls, the kraven had been human
once, though the resemblance was minimal—two legs, two
arms, a torso and head. The conversion process twisted the
host into something beyond a nightmare. Bones jutted like
talons from rotting gray flesh, its spine curved and twisted.
Its eyes were bloodshot, red as meat, and its jaw had snapped
and reformed like the maw of a piranha in a bulbous human
head. The very sight should have been enough to send a sane
man running. If not, the dozen others that appeared close behind it would have.

Before the first kraven even reached the road, Katherine
ran forward, her blades a whirl of silver. Metal met flesh, and
all the fear and anticipation from before washed away.

When he was younger, Tenn had immersed himself in books
and movies of heroic battles. The tales were always gorgeous in
a way—heart-pumping and engaging, filled with quick moves
and dancing blows. Heroes dashed between villains with ease,
always golden, always immortal. Always confident and brave
and beautiful.

The Resurrection taught him that all those stories were
full of shit.

Real battle wasn't pretty. You trained to block and parry
and dodge, yes, but you didn't think about it, didn't focus on
long dancing combinations. You swung. You screamed a lot.
You killed as fast as you could and didn't think about anything
but the feel of flesh giving way under your hands. And if you

were even a hairbreadth too slow, if today just wasn't your day, you were never, ever heard from again.

He gritted his teeth and prayed today wasn't that day.

Tenn lunged forward, meeting a kraven midleap and slicing its body right through the gut. Cold, black blood sprayed out, but Tenn was already slashing another monster before the first corpse fell. Michael was just out of sight beside him, grunting and yelling, the skull-shattering cracks of his mace echoing across the fields like thunder.

But more monsters were coming. The field was thick with beasts, the air alive and hellish with their screams. A shadow darted behind him. He turned just in time to parry the slash of a cleaver. He barely registered his opponent—male, shirtless, whiter than snow and drenched in blood—before counterattacking. The man's head fell to the ground with a wet smack.

"Bloodlings!" Tenn yelled, but even though he screamed it at the top of his lungs, he knew his companions hadn't heard. The world was a living, grinding thing of scarred flesh and teeth and talons, and everywhere he turned he was slashing, dodging, trying to stay alive as the gray tide overtook him. His breath was fire as he fought, as he hacked and screamed his way through the melee. Seconds felt like an eternity, and the damage done to him and his foes was immense. A thousand cuts burned across his skin. A thousand moments he was too slow. A thousand instances he could have died, and a thousand reasons he still might.

A yell broke through the din—masculine, enraged and in pain. Then Michael's voice cut short in a gurgle. Tenn spared a glance over but he couldn't see anything through the kravens scrambling over corpses. Katherine screamed as well, but whether from rage or pain, he wasn't certain.

That's when he realized, in the far-off corner of his mind, that he was going to die. They all were.

His arm went numb from a kraven's bite. His hands were drenched red. And still, the monsters came.

Derrick's voice drifted through his mind as he fell to his knees. *Don't use magic, not under any circumstances. Don't give yourselves away.*

Water and blood seeped through Tenn's jeans, his numb arm limp. He could only stare at the blood and wonder at how quickly this had come, his end. At how easy it was to die. Pain seared across his back as a Howl ripped through his flesh. Blood was everywhere—black blood, red blood, red rain. The Sphere of Water screamed inside of him as his own life spilled forth. Memories rode the current—flashes of his mother and father, the few friends he'd made and lost, his mother's voice and a lullaby he couldn't place. His eyes fluttered. His working hand dropped his staff.

This is how it feels to die, and I will be eaten before they find my corpse.

As another kraven lunged for the kill, mouth wide and broken teeth bared, the Sphere of Water opened unbidden in Tenn's stomach.

Power flooded him, rushing through in a whirlpool of memory and pain, a roar that filled him with a thousand freezing agonies, dragging him down, down, down into the pits of his every despair. Down into the deepest depth of power.

The Sphere connected him to the rain hammering from the sky and the blood pooling on the ground and the pulse in every vein of every creature within a mile. He could feel it. All of it. He felt Katherine a few yards away, her heart throbbing so fast it hurt his own. He felt the Howls, their pulses thick and jagged and starved.

Most of all, he felt *power*. More than he had ever tapped before. The rage, the fear, the anger, the *thirst*. It made his limbs vibrate, made his breath catch, made the rain around him seethe and hum. And in that split second after Water's opening, he wrapped his fingers deep into the torrent and screamed.

The rain shivered. Changed. He twisted the power and twisted the elements and raindrops became ice, became shards sharper than glass, became hammers that lashed from the sky with sickening velocity. His Sphere raged in joy and agony as its power unleashed, as the bloodlust filled his darkening vision and screams filled the air. His screams. Their screams. Blades of ice met flesh, sliced through skin and bone. Ice spilled forth blood, and Water rejoiced as the world drenched itself in crimson.

Power ran through his veins, and this power craved revenge. It was over in seconds.

He felt the Howls die. Felt their blood leave their bodies and pool against the sodden earth. Felt their pain. Felt their final heartbeats. And when every heart had stilled, the power in his chest winked out. He collapsed.

"You're going to do great things," his mom says. She hugs him. Wipes tears from her eyes. "You've already done great things. The moment you came into my life. That was the greatest thing." And he tells himself not to cry. Not here, in front of the dorm. He tells himself he will see her again. "I will always..."

"What do you want to be when you grow up?" Kevin asks.

"A linguist," Tenn replies. "Or a writer."

"You like words?"

"Yes. Words have power."

"Your words do." They go silent, and the stars slide past as they watch from the library. They go silent, and the stars speak for them.

He sees her. He sees her hand. He sees her hand from where he stands in the doorway. It droops from the shed, a finger cocked. Her fingernails red. Fingers red. Red, red—

Tenn curled against himself. Curled against the memories.

Nothing else moved in the world.

Just the rain.

Just his breath.

Just his blood mixing with the dead.

CHAPTER TWO

HE DIDN'T KNOW HOW LONG HE LAY THERE. THE
wind and rain were a constant roar, but their sound was distant compared to the throb of blood in his ears, the roar of
memories in his head.

*His house is empty. Too empty. He walks. The gun is gone. His
hand is covered in blood. Blood, like the blood streaking the walls.
Where is the gun? Where are his parents? He shakes. He walks.
Water roars within him, a tide that drowns the screams outside.
His house is too empty. His house is too silent. He shakes as he
walks and the blood-streaked halls tilt. He shakes, and the back
door swings. He walks, and his silent house bleeds.*

Something brushed his cheek. Frayed nerves snapped to
life, and his eyes fluttered open.

Katherine knelt beside him. Blood stained her skin, and
long gashes webbed across her in leaking lines.

"Are you okay?" she asked. Her voice was angelic, if only
because he had been certain he'd killed her.

Tenn could only nod. There were tears in his eyes. He couldn't force them away. He was hollowed out. Raw. Earlier, he'd wanted to break the world, but the world had broken him.

Even as the memories ebbed, the pain and the sadness lingered in his lungs. Tears leaked from his eyes unchecked.

"You're bleeding," she continued. "Badly."

He tried to sit. His muscles wouldn't cooperate. He felt it then...or rather, he felt the *lack* of feeling. The numbness leaking through his limbs as blood leaked to the soil. His wounds would kill him. Just as her wounds would kill her.

"So are you," he managed. He bit back a sob. The world was spinning. Fading. Fast.

"You've already broken orders," she said, without the slightest hint of sarcasm. "We might as well live to face Derrick's wrath."

Tenn closed his eyes and reached deep into the pit of his pelvis, to the place where the Sphere of Earth rested. It was the second and last Sphere he'd been attuned to. He coaxed it awake and sank his focus into the rich soil of it, to the heavy power that rooted him to the earth. Energy filled him with green light, with the warm, calming sap of gravity and flesh.

He didn't open his eyes. He couldn't. Just as he couldn't move his arm to meet hers, to start healing. His fingers twitched, and she placed her bloodied hand in his. Energy connected, a snap of power, and slowly, painfully, he began his work.

She winced as flesh knitted itself back together. There was no shortcut—he had to heal each wound one at a time. If his connection to Earth had taught him anything, it was that dying was easy; healing was the painful part.

"So like you," she muttered. "Healing me before yourself."

He laughed. It hurt like hell, but he didn't let his concentration break. Even when something warm dribbled from his lips.

"You're the pretty one," he whispered, and choked down a sob of pain or despair, he couldn't tell which.

When her wounds had closed, he turned his attention to himself. Arcs of fire lanced across his skin, seared through his bones. He didn't grimace. This pain, this physical hurt, couldn't hold a candle to the hell that Water had dragged him through. This was just a reminder that he was still alive.

After what seemed like hours, he closed off to Earth.

The Spheres all had a backlash as unique as their power, but Earth's was, in many ways, the most dangerous. Earth was like a drug: when you were on it, you felt invincible, high, *immortal*. The moment it left you, you were sharply reminded just how weak and mortal and close to death you truly were.

His limbs, though healed, shook as he forced himself to sitting. His heart raced and his stomach wanted to eat itself, but at least he hadn't used so much that he passed out. Or lost a chunk of hair. Again. He just hoped that nothing would break when he moved.

Together, the two of them hoisted each other up to standing. Katherine wouldn't meet his gaze; she stared out at the creatures littering the ground around them. Limbs and carcasses were splayed everywhere and, even with the rain, the stink was atrocious. Blood pooled dark and thick like an oil spill.

"Michael?" he asked.

She shook her head and continued looking off into the distance. The rain hid whatever tears she might be shedding. He bit back an apology; apologies wouldn't bring the guy back.

Idiot or no, he had still been their companion. He was still important.

For a while, they stood there, looking out over the massacre. Tenn's heartbeat didn't slow, but it was no longer just the blowback of Earth. It was the fear. The fear of what he'd done, or what Water had done. He'd jeopardized their mission by using magic.

Rather, the magic had used *him*. How? And where the hell had that power come from?

"How did you do that?" Katherine asked.

He started, wondered if he'd spoken aloud. Then he realized that of course she would ask that, because no one could use that much magic and live. At least, no one he'd ever met.

"I don't know," he replied. His voice rasped.

"You killed them. All of them."

"I know."

He wondered if Michael had still been alive when he called down the power. Pain wrenched in his chest at the thought. If he'd killed Michael by accident…

"Did I—"

"He was already dead," Katherine whispered. "I saw him go down."

That shouldn't have been the relief that it was. It almost made him feel worse.

She looked at him, but her eyes quickly flicked away.

"I've never seen that much power," she said. "How are you still standing?"

"I don't know," he said again. He felt like a broken recording. "Did you know…"

He shook his head. "I was ready to die."

"Me, too," she said, and went silent.

Despite the fact that they needed to move, despite the cold and the scent and the bodies, they stood there in silence and let the minutes drip by. Tenn tried to gather his thoughts, tried to create an argument that would hold up against Derrick's inevitable tirade. He failed. He couldn't stop looking at Katherine, at the old blood trickling down her face and the small quiver in her fingertips. What did she think of him, after what had happened? What would she say to the others?

Tenn looked back to the bodies. Michael was under there, somewhere. He deserved a better burial than this.

"We need to burn them," Tenn said. "In case…"

In case they attract attention. In case any are still alive. In case others come along and devour Michael's corpse…

She looked at him, and maybe it was his imagination, but that look was different. Like she wasn't certain who or what she was staring at. She didn't speak, just nodded tersely, and light flickered in her chest as she opened to the Sphere of Fire. Heat shimmered around her, made sweat break out across his skin. Then, with tendrils of flame snaking around her fingertips, she lashed out.

The fields erupted into flame. Tenn hid behind his arm as the world around him roared with heat and anger. Katherine screamed as bodies caught fire, as rain sizzled and the earth cracked. She screamed and cursed until the roar of flames drowned her out.

Fire was the Sphere of passion and hate. It pulled from the heart, just as it burned it apart.

It lasted only a minute. But when the power died down, the fields were nothing more than smoldering ash and steam.

He put a hand on her shoulder, trying not to wince from the heat of her skin.

"Don't touch me!" she snapped. "I'll fucking kill you."

He stepped back.

This was why he didn't get along with Fire users. After using their powers, they were unstable at best.

Then she started to laugh. He took another step back.

"Sorry," she said through the laughter. She sniffed and wiped a tear from her eye. "It's gone," she continued. "The fucking deer. It's gone. They ate it."

Tenn turned to the road. She was right. Hell, there was nothing on the road anymore save for the burned-out scraps of cars and pools of the dead that streamed like magma.

"Michael would be so pissed," Katherine said. She giggled. Then her laughs choked into a sob. "We should have let him eat the tongue."

The walk back to base was long and silent. Tenn ate some jerky from their packs, but it didn't assuage the hunger gnawing at his bones. That, he knew, would take hours and a few days of rest to overcome, just like the waves of sadness that kept washing over him. He didn't stop scanning the fields, but both he and Katherine kept their Spheres closed off. Katherine didn't ask him any more questions; somehow that made things worse. He was asking them all himself, and he didn't have an answer.

How had Water opened like that? The Spheres weren't sentient, they were just energy centers. Everyone had them, but only those who were attuned could use each particular Sphere. Even then, it required training and concentration to get them to influence the outside world. Magic wasn't just something that *happened*; it was something you had to force. So how had Water taken over? As though it were a reflex, as though the Sphere itself hadn't wanted to die. And where the hell had that *power* come from? It should have been beyond him, should have drained him entirely. Yet here he was. Alive.

What the hell is wrong with me?

Everything. Everything.

For the first time since he'd been attuned to Water, he was scared. Not of the monsters. Not of the world outside. But of the power that rested within him. The power that seemed to be scratching for control.

Only one thing was certain, and it wasn't a truth he wanted to think about. The Howls they'd faced weren't the army his troop had been warned about. It had been a roaming band, one of the thousands scattered throughout the uninhabited swathes of America.

That meant there was still another, bigger fight left.

They reached Outpost 37 before nightfall. Home sweet home. Once, it had probably been some quaint touristy harbor town. Now the scattered houses along its perimeter were empty. Whole lots were charred to piles of ash, while other homes were unscathed save for shattered windows or scratched facades. Lawns entangled forgotten toys, and fences lay like dominoes. Everything had that sick old stench of antiquity, like a sodden vintage store. Even here, though, there were no bodies or bones, no scavenging birds or mice. The Howls were efficient, if only because they were hungry.

Cities were often the emptiest. After all, what was a city to a flesh-craving beast besides a buffet?

It wasn't just the Howls that had destroyed the town. Necromancers had done their own part, and the Hunters that fought against them probably hadn't helped. Lake Michigan swallowed half of the buildings, and a small hill erupted through another city block, the houses there toppled and tossed. Much had changed in the chaos of the Resurrection—whole cities burned or buried, mountains collapsed or created. Magic had altered the face of the country in more ways than one.

The world didn't like being manipulated. At times, it seemed, the very planet fought back.

Katherine said nothing as they trudged through the streets, stepping over rusted bikes and piles of old refuse, dodging craters and overturned cars. Both her swords were clean and bared, and Tenn's grip on his staff was just as tight as hers. No matter that the rest of their troop was only a hundred yards away—anything could have happened in their absence.

Every time Tenn walked through the base, he was reminded that they hadn't been stationed here to thrive. Nothing in this shell of a town hinted at humanity—the storefronts were shattered and looted, the houses razed. There was no music, no industry, no trace of civilian life. No real reason to wake up in the morning, save to fight.

Shadows shifted over the rubble, and he jerked his staff to the ready. Then the shape stepped into the road: a small fox, its ribs horribly pronounced with hunger. The creature didn't flinch as he and Katherine walked past. It watched them intently before finally turning and slinking back into an alley.

When houses gave way to the broad downtown avenue, his nerves calmed. Their hotel rose up from the buildings on the other side, one of the few structures still intact. Uprooted trees stretched like black veins across the concrete. Marble slabs and pillars of other structures tumbled across the road in piles of white bone. Only the hotel stood strong and seemingly deserted, the clean red brick and white marble an anachronism in the destruction surrounding it.

Something moved and Tenn turned on the spot, ready for the attack. A girl in black stepped out from the crumbling post office.

"Audrey," he said. He lowered his staff.

"Jesus H.," she said. There were two daggers in her hands, the kris blades glinting like wolves' teeth. "I thought... We thought you were in trouble. Derrick's had us on high alert since noon." She looked between them, and it seemed to click then that Michael was missing. Her voice became a whisper, and her shoulders slumped. "What happened? I've never felt that much power. It was like a bomb going off."

Tenn's pulse began to race. If the troop had felt their use of magic all the way back here, there was no way the necromancers had missed it. There was no way Derrick would let him live for his insubordination.

"Where's Derrick?" Tenn asked. The last thing he wanted was to admit what he'd done. Not when he wasn't certain himself. He didn't want to face their commander, either, but it would be easier to get it over with than wait in fear.

Audrey nodded to the hotel. "His office," she said. "He's meeting with the captains now. Everyone else has been stationed in the field in case..."

"In case we brought anything back," Katherine finished.

"Yeah."

"How pissed is he?" Tenn asked.

Audrey gave a small grin, though it was more forced than anything.

"Well, *I* wouldn't go near him. Though maybe he's cooled down by now."

"Right," Tenn said.

He'd have rather faced another bloodling.

Their base was depressing even during good days. Today definitely wasn't a good day. The rain wasn't helping.

Outpost 37 hadn't been built to house civilians, but to act as a buffer between Outer Chicago and the wild lands beyond. Wild lands that were inhabited by necromancers—mages who bowed in service to the Dark Lady, the Goddess of Death— and the Howls they created and controlled. There were other settlements and other outposts scattered across the States, many of which Tenn had bounced between after the Resurrection. Hunters had no say in where they were stationed to fight the forces of the Dark Lady. They went where the battle was. And, frankly, the battle was everywhere.

Outpost 37 was home to him and maybe thirty other Hunters. For now.

These were the trenches. Those stationed here would fight until they died, and their bodies would burn or be tossed in the lake, and a fresh batch of Hunters from Outer Chicago would come in to take their place. Or they were transferred to die in service somewhere else.

Being a Hunter wasn't glorious. But it did mean you were fighting back, trying to return the world to what it once was, rather than sitting around waiting to be eaten. After every- thing he'd seen during the Resurrection, joining the Hunters was honestly the only way forward. Revenge was the only reason he could live with himself.

A few Hunters mingled in the hotel lobby. Maybe *mingling* was the wrong word; they were clearly all waiting for the alarm to sound. Their weapons were at hand, and though a few were reading musty paperbacks and another group was playing cards, there was a tension in the room that belied the apparent ease. Tenn nodded at those who looked up, waiting for them to ask about what had happened in the field. About what *he'd* done in the field. But they said nothing. Even the new recruits—easy to spot, from the lack of scars and the life in their eyes—knew better. *Someone* had fucked up, and since Tenn had been in charge of the food-scouting mission, it was on his shoulders no matter what.

He looked down and continued up the emergency stairwell to the top floor.

"What the hell happened out there?"

The words were out of Derrick's mouth before Tenn closed the door behind him.

Whereas the rest of the encampment was cold and dark, this suite was warm and brilliantly lit, albeit far from welcoming. Flames danced across every surface, fires fueled by magic alone. It should have been beautiful, but it just set Tenn's hair on end. The Sphere of Fire burned brightly in Derrick's chest and his eyes darted with agitation. That was never a good sign.

Derrick himself stood behind a grand mahogany desk, its surface coated in papers and maps and weapons. He was tall, commanding, his Mohawked hair burnt-red and his skin traced with scars.

"I didn't mean to—" Tenn began, but Derrick cut him off.

"What do you mean, *you didn't mean to?*" He stepped around the desk, hands clenched tight into fists. Small sparks flickered around his skin. "I felt your fucking magic all the way out here!"

Tenn wasn't about to point out that *none* of them should be using magic and that Derrick was betraying his own orders, but he knew that the amount Derrick channeled wasn't enough to give them away, and, frankly, Tenn didn't think Derrick would appreciate the reminder.

"We were surrounded," he said, lowering his eyes. "There were dozens of kravens. We wouldn't have made it."

"Then you should have died."

Derrick's voice was so terse, so fully void of emotion, that Tenn barely realized it sounded more like a command than anything else. It was a stab in the gut. Water churned over. *You should have died, you should have died—your life is worth nothing, and neither is your death.*

"I meant to," he said. His words sounded small. "But Water took over."

"The Spheres don't control you. You control the Spheres."

It was ironic, seeing as Fire users were notorious for the tempers their chosen Sphere gave them. But it was a phrase they'd all learned during training. It might not be true, but the meaning was clear: you didn't give in. Ever.

"Not this time," Tenn said. He looked up then, just in time to see something new flicker across Derrick's features. Fear. "Water took over. It... I don't know. It *killed* them. Every last one."

"You aren't that powerful," Derrick said, his voice muted. It wasn't a dig; it was fact.

Tenn didn't have anything to say to that.

"I should have you killed for this," Derrick said. He stood up straighter, as though taking more control of himself and the situation. "You jeopardized the safety of everyone in this troop. Because of you, we have lost the element of surprise."

This outpost has been here for over a year. We lost that element a long time ago. But Tenn didn't say that. Of course he didn't say that. Outposts always changed locations. Keeping one in place had been a new tactic, decided by the higher-ups of Outer Chicago itself. If it was expected that base locations changed, having one stay put would be a surprise to the necromancers and the Howls. So long as it kept a low profile. So long as it wasn't compromised.

"I'm sorry," Tenn said.

"Tell that to your comrades who are going to die tomorrow."

Tenn's eyes shot up.

"Tomorrow?"

Derrick turned and walked back toward the desk.

"Our scouts have spotted them. The armies are moving. They will be here by sunrise."

A lump of dread twisted in Tenn's stomach.

"We need every fighter we have," Derrick continued. "So I won't kill you. Not tonight. I'll let the necromancers do that in the morning."

There wasn't the slightest hint of humor or mockery in Derrick's voice.

Tenn bowed his head and turned from the room.

It wasn't until he was halfway down the stairs that he realized he hadn't even mentioned that Michael was dead.

It didn't matter. In the morning, thanks to him, they all would be.

CHAPTER THREE

THE RAIN TURNED TO A DRIZZLE AS THE NIGHT BORE on. Tenn stood on the hotel roof, watching water pool and stream below. The hotel offered the best view in town—quite literally—and without magic to guide their sight, they needed all the vantage they could get. There was a small, guttering torch on the ground, the only source of light in the darkness. Beyond, everything was dark and sifting and slick with rain.

He knew that Derrick hadn't sent him up here out of necessity. He was up here for punishment. Far from the glory of battle. And, being so high up, he'd be the first thing the necromancers could target.

Tenn turned at the sound of footsteps. Katherine. She'd been chosen as the other lookout, probably on some sort of probation because of him. He wondered if this was the worst of her punishment for not killing him in the field.

"We need to talk," she said.

He didn't answer, just tightened his grip on his staff and

stared out into the dark. His stomach flipped over, and once more the thought flickered through his head, *What is wrong with me?*

"What happened out there—"

"There's nothing more to talk about."

"I wanted to thank you."

Tenn's internal tirade silenced. He turned to her. Firelight flickered over her face, but even in the shadows he could feel her eyes trained on him.

"What?"

"You saved my life. You avenged Michael's death. So…thank you." She brushed a strand of hair from her face and looked toward the darkness. "Don't make me say it again."

"I…"

But there wasn't anything else for him to say. He hadn't tried to save them. He hadn't *wanted* to save them. Something else had taken control.

She sighed and walked over to the edge of the roof.

"Derrick is an asshole," she said. She glanced at Tenn. "And I think he's scared of you."

He frowned. "What?"

She didn't look at him, just kept staring out at the shifting rain and shadows.

"Everyone felt it. That much power… Hell, I was there, and even *I* don't believe it." She paused, took a breath. "It should have killed you."

"I know."

"What did it feel like?"

It wasn't the question he expected.

"Honestly…it was terrible. I've never felt so much pain."

She nodded to herself.

"Fire can be like that, sometimes. It burns through you. But it feels good, in a way. All that pain makes you feel alive. Even if it does nearly kill you."

"Yeah."

Except it wasn't like that. Not really. Fire was about rage. Water just felt like drowning in misery. And delighting in it.

"Are you hungry?" she asked. Again, not the question he expected.

"Yeah." His stomach rumbled with the thought. Derrick had sent him up here immediately after their meeting, and Earth was still ravenous. "Starving."

"I'll grab you something from the storeroom. I think they have Twinkies down there."

She walked over and patted him on the shoulder.

He wanted to ask her something, anything. He wanted to talk, to have someone help him understand how the impossible had happened. Instead, he stayed silent. He knew she wouldn't have any answers, and he didn't want her thinking he was crazy as well as dangerous.

She left, the roof door slamming loudly behind her, and he went back to his watch.

It was nearly impossible to see anything in the darkness, but he was out here to sense more than see. Necromancers would use magic to lead the Howls in their army. Most turned to the Goddess of Death for power or immortality, to be on the winning side of this constant battle. There really wasn't a middle ground—either you used magic to fight the Howls, or you used magic to create them.

Tenn figured they were all insane. The Dark Lady was just a

myth. The trouble was that the necromancers took the idea of her seriously. Their cult was what had caused the Resurrection—the day the first Howl was created. Tenn never quite understood the event's name—*Resurrection*—since Howls could only be created from the living.

Really, it didn't matter if She was real or not. Her followers were dangerous either way.

Footsteps sloshed through the puddles behind him. He didn't turn around, assuming Katherine had taken the stairs at a run.

"Beautiful night, isn't it, Tenn?"

It wasn't Katherine. It wasn't any voice he knew.

He spun around, staff raised and ready.

The man in front of him was a stranger. Despite the freezing rain, he wore dark jeans and a thin white shirt unbuttoned to his waist. The fabric clung to his body like some romance-cover model, accentuating his perfectly chiseled chest and stomach, his smooth olive skin. Chin-length black hair hung in loose waves and twined over his ears. Everything about the man screamed sex and desire and danger, from his broad shoulders to his low-slung jeans. Even his copper eyes glinted seduction. Tenn's heart raced, but whether from fear or something else, he couldn't be sure.

"Who are you?" Tenn asked. He took a half step back, then realized he was already too close to the edge. Thunder rolled overhead; he could barely hear it over the thunder in his own blood. "How did you get up here?"

The stranger cocked his head to the side, the smile never slipping, as though he were examining a plaything. Or a tasty appetizer.

"How civil." He ran a hand through his hair, and even that

movement seemed perfectly executed. His voice was low and husky, a bedroom murmur. "He asks not what, but who."

In the blink of an eye, he stood an inch before Tenn, his face so close their lips nearly touched. Copper irises filled Tenn's vision. The guy's heat sent sweat dripping down his skin.

"My name, young Tenn, is Tomás." His voice made Tenn's heart beat with lust.

The name rang a bell Tenn didn't want to recognize, a tone tolling destruction. He knew he should push the stranger away, should use the staff lodged between them to force a retreat, but he couldn't budge. Tomás was still as stone and just as immovable. He burned like a radiator; rain hissed and steamed, and Tenn's skin seared with the nearness. The heat. He should push him away. But the heat…the *heat*…it made him want to draw Tomás closer.

Something clicked in the far corners of his mind, and Tenn knew precisely what he was facing and just how screwed he was.

"*Incubus*," Tenn hissed through clenched teeth.

Tomás's eyes narrowed. "What did you call me?" The words dripped venom.

The copper eyes. The heat. The perfect seduction. Tomás was a Howl birthed from the Sphere of Fire, a demon craving human warmth. And like all incubi and succubi—their female counterparts—they preferred feeding through more lascivious acts.

"You're…an incubus." Even before the words left his lips, he knew it was the wrong thing to say. Tomás's eyes sparked red.

"Incubus?" His composure cracked. Model became monster, and Tenn's desire turned to fear. "You dare call me incubus? Monster? Demon?" Tomás grabbed a fistful of Tenn's hair and yanked his head back. Where Tomás's flesh touched his, Tenn's skin turned to ice.

"I am more than any incubus, little mouse," Tomás whispered. His lips just brushed the nape of Tenn's neck, sending ice and flame across his skin. "And you would do well to remember this."

He let go, and Tenn stumbled, nearly careening off the roof's edge. When he steadied himself, Tomás was a step back, hands clasped behind him and an insidious smile slashed across his perfect face.

"The army is coming," he said. His words were calm, and a frightening juxtaposition to the rage that seemed to lurk within. "They will be here before dawn. You cannot stop them. If I were you—and I'm most assuredly grateful I am not—I would be gone before they arrive."

Tenn tried to catch his breath. He hadn't realized just how fast his heart was pounding, just how much he wanted to run. But whether he wanted to run away from or toward Tomás, he couldn't tell. *Fucking incubus.* They were renowned for their ability to draw desire from their victims. He couldn't believe he was falling for it.

"Why are you telling me this?" he asked.

Howls didn't reason. They didn't talk or tell you their names. Howls killed. The fact that Tomás didn't follow any of these rules scared the shit out of Tenn.

Again, Tomás's head cocked to the side. The grin didn't slip and, for a moment, he just stood there, considering, as rain dripped down his delectably disheveled hair. Tenn kept his focus on the man's eyes; he couldn't be trusted to let them wander anywhere else. It already took all of his concentration to keep his thoughts focused, to not imagine what the man would look like naked, or how they would feel pressed against each other.

His pulse doubled every time he considered it.

"Because," Tomás finally said, "my sister, Leanna, has an interest in you. And what she desires, I, too, covet."

That name rang a bell, this one louder than the first. Leanna was the Kin who controlled America. The one who ran the Farms and dictated where the necromancers attacked. For many, she was an embodiment of the Dark Lady herself.

Tomás's name clicked into place.

Tomás was also one of the Kin, one of the six most powerful Howls in the world—the direct descendants or creations of the Dark Lady. They were the ones who ran the world now; the monsters who had humanity under their thumbs. Tenn's eyes widened.

"Bingo," Tomás said. "Tell the boy what he's won."

"What the hell?" Katherine yelled. The roof door slammed shut.

Tenn looked past Tomás at Katherine, who was holding a covered plate. The next moment, Tomás was beside her, a single hand around her neck.

The plate fell to the ground and shattered.

"You will be inspired, I think, to tell others you have seen me." Tomás didn't raise his voice, but it still cut through the rain, as if aimed for Tenn's ears alone. "Perhaps to warn them of my presence. Perhaps to try and save yourself. That would be a *very* bad decision."

Tomás barely moved, but the crack that resonated said enough.

He let go, and Katherine crumpled to the roof, her neck crushed.

Tomás stepped forward, not even looking at Katherine. Tenn wanted to throw up. Bile twisted in his stomach, but with Tomás's every step toward him, the sensation faded, replaced by a growing desire to pull the man closer, to tear the world down and bathe in blood and flame. Tenn forced down the imagery. Or tried to.

"I have marked you, Tenn. I will follow you everywhere you go. And if you so much as speak my name aloud—" he was now so close that Tenn's skin burned "—I will kill everyone you tell. Slowly. In front of you. I will make you wish I let you die."

He smiled sadistically. Tenn couldn't take his eyes off Katherine's limp body. Tomás had killed her, not by draining her heat, but by snapping her neck. He'd killed for the hell of it.

Until now, Tenn had thought Howls only killed for food.

"What do you want from me? Why?" Tenn's voice shook, but it still carried. That was enough.

"I want you to do your job," Tomás said. His grin widened. Any larger, and it would split his face. "A job you are proving more than capable of doing—killing the minions of the Dark Lady."

Thunder crackled overhead. Tomás burst into giggles.

"Oh, She is watching. Yes, She is." He looked up into the sky and raised his hands. "But what do I care, Mother? What do I care, when you are dead dead dead?" He hopped around when he said it. One rotation, and he snapped back to attention, calmly staring at Tenn with his head tilted to the side.

"You will help me. But you cannot do that if you stay. Your friends cannot beat this army, Tenn. Not when the army is coming for *you*."

Tenn opened his mouth to speak, heart thudding with Tomás's final statement, but Tomás was there again, faster than lightning, faster than anything human. One hand gripped Tenn's jaw. The other snaked behind his waist, pulling their hips close. Tenn couldn't help the moan in the back of his throat. Tomás very clearly noticed.

"Run along, little mouse." He bit Tenn's lower lip. Fear and shock and desire pulsed through Tenn's chest. When Tomás let go, it took all of Tenn's control not to bite back. "Run before the monsters get here. I want to make sure you live long enough to play with."

Then he was gone.

Tenn staggered at the sudden loss and fell to his knees. Once again, he couldn't stop staring at Katherine's body. He could no longer hear his thoughts in the drowning silence and rain. Gingerly, he touched his own neck, feeling Tomás's handprint burning ice-hot. He hunched over and heaved.

He cowered there, curled over in the rain, his knuckles dug into the concrete.

He waited for Tomás to reappear.

He waited for Katherine to wake up, for it all to have been a dream.

He waited.

Katherine stayed dead.

The nightmare stayed reality.

And on the horizon, he felt a surge of power flare.

CHAPTER FOUR

FOR THE BRIEFEST MOMENT, TENN THOUGHT IT WAS the enemy attacking.

There was no one else out there—at least, no one from his troop—that could use that much power. A power that was racing toward the outpost, strobing against the sky like lightning.

Tomás had barely been gone a minute and Katherine was dead and what the hell was going on that everything was falling to shit so quickly?

He jumped up and ran to the edge of the hotel, ready to send out a signal, ready to scream that they were under attack, when he realized the power was coming from the west. From Outer Chicago. And there was no way the enemy could be coming from there. Not when Outer Chicago was ringed with outposts like his to keep it safe.

Light flared as the door burst open, and Derrick ran up beside Tenn, followed by two younger recruits. Fire flickered to life all around the edge of the roof, casting garish shadows and splays of light over the crew. Whether the fire was for defense or a beacon or just from Derrick's anger, Tenn wasn't sure.

Derrick didn't even look at Katherine's body. He was too trained on the sky. The others, though, they lingered. Kneeled at her side. Tenn looked away.

They would say he did that, too. They would say he killed her to hide the evidence of his treason in the field.

"Commander…" Tenn began, not knowing what to say, but Derrick cut him short.

"They're here," Derrick muttered.

"The army, sir?" one of the recruits asked.

Derrick glared back at him.

"No, idiot. The fucking cavalry."

That's when Derrick noticed Katherine.

He turned back to Tenn. Tenn had seen his commander angry before, but never like this. Derrick's jaw was tight, and full flames swirled around his hands and from the burning Sphere of Fire in his chest.

"What the hell have you done?" he seethed.

Tenn didn't get the chance to answer.

Lightning flashed above them as a gust of wind buffeted the roof, sending Tenn to his knees.

He blinked away the afterglow, his ears ringing with thunder.

There were three of them—two guys and a girl—all in pale clothes and white trench coats, all emanating more power than Tenn had felt in his lifetime…save for what he'd wielded that afternoon.

The blond-haired guy stepped forward. A broadsword was strapped to his back, and his pale, angular face bore a dozen half-healed scars. Something about that face made Tenn's heart flip, almost with recognition, but he was positive he'd never seen him before in his life. The man didn't speak at first, his arms in front of his chest. He looked like he was assessing their value.

He looked like he didn't enjoy what he saw.

"Outpost 37," he said. "I'm Jarrett, captain commander of Outer Chicago. I've been sent here to handle the rest of this mission." His eyes looked over all of them again. Maybe it was Tenn's imagination, but they seemed to linger on him.

"And one of you has fucked up."

"This is madness," Derrick said, chasing behind Jarrett. Tenn and the others followed them down the steps. The other newcomers were silent, ghosting behind them all. Easy to forget, if not for the shivers they sent down Tenn's spine every time their cold eyes raked over him.

"What do you expect when your orders are disobeyed so flagrantly?" Jarrett replied. He was taking the steps two at a time, his pale undercut glowing red in the light of Derrick's angry fires.

Even with fear lodged in his gut—surely this would get him discharged or killed or worse—Tenn was mildly impressed that Jarrett knew the word *flagrantly*.

"This is my outpost and my troop. You can't just waltz in here and—"

Jarrett stopped and spun, and before Derrick could blink, Jarrett had him pinned against the wall, one hand to Derrick's chest and the other holding a dagger to Derrick's neck.

"This outpost is owned and run by Outer Chicago," Jarrett

said. There wasn't the slightest hint of emotion in his voice, which almost seemed worse than Derrick's anger. "And that means we own and run *you*. You screwed up, commander. *That is why we are here*. So I suggest you take your cocky attitude and shove it somewhere dark and quiet, because the army is nearly here. And, quite frankly, I'm more than happy to throw you out there as bloodbait. I can promise you that Cassandra won't give a damn if you're gone." He resheathed the dagger and patted the side of Derrick's face, smiling. "Understood?"

He stepped back, turned and continued down the steps until they reached the bottom floor. Derrick seethed silently behind him, fires flickering in and out. Once in the lobby, Jarrett gestured to the strangers he brought with him.

"Devon, Dreya, go secure the perimeter. I want troops every hundred yards. Keep them tight and close to base. You know the drill."

The two strangers nodded in unison. Tenn had to believe they were related, despite the contrast in their appearance. They were both tall and lithe and angular. But the girl was paler than ivory, with long willowy fingers and silvered hair that reached her waist; paired with the white coat and faded jeans and sweater she wore, she looked like a specter. Even her blue eyes were nearly gray. But the boy—her brother—was darker than night, with choppy black hair and a burgundy scarf wrapped around his face, leaving only his blue eyes bare. So blue…it must have been their use of Air. Tenn tried not to stare. He'd seen plenty of people subtly changed from the element they used, himself included, but he'd never seen transformations so distinct. Neither seemed to carry weapons, which meant their magic was impossibly powerful.

The pair strode toward the hotel exit. Then Air opened in their throats, and they flew off into the night.

"You don't need to change our formation," Derrick said when they were out of sight. "I already have scouts in position."

"We don't *need* scouts," Jarrett said. "We know the army is coming. And they know where we are. We need our ranks close. Otherwise, our fighters will be swallowed up one by one."

Derrick said nothing.

"And you," Jarrett said, turning his attention to Tenn. "What are you?"

It wasn't so strange a question. Not anymore.

"Earth and Water. Sir."

"That one's a fuckup," Derrick interjected. "Nearly cost us the whole mission this afternoon, which is probably why you're here. Went against orders."

Jarrett eyed Tenn up and down, a hint of...something...in his pale eyes. "He doesn't seem the insubordinate type. What happened?"

"He—"

"I was asking *him*," Jarrett said quietly. Why was his voice so familiar? "What happened today, soldier?"

"I used magic. Against orders."

Jarrett's eyebrows furrowed.

"And why did you do that?"

"I didn't," Tenn said. "It...it used me."

"He's clearly crazy," Derrick said, "or just trying to save his own a—"

The Sphere of Air opened in Jarrett's throat, harsh and pale blue, and a second later Derrick slammed against the wall. Jarrett didn't even gesture or take his eyes off Tenn.

"What's your name?" Jarrett asked.

"Tenn."

Jarrett's eyes narrowed.

"And you say your Sphere...what? Acted against your will? Used itself?"

A lump lodged in Tenn's throat, but he forced himself to speak.

"We were surrounded. Only two of us left. I was prepared to die. I swear. But Water just...took over. Before I could stop it..." Tenn took a deep breath. Saying it again felt like insanity. "It killed every single Howl surrounding us. In a heartbeat. Before I could try to stop it."

Jarrett didn't say anything. Not for a long time. And whether Derrick was silent out of newfound respect or some sort of invisible gag, Tenn couldn't say. Tenn didn't care. He couldn't take his gaze off Jarrett. Not because he was scared—though he was, definitely—but because there was something about the way Jarrett looked at him that sent electricity through his veins. Like Jarrett knew his secrets.

It should have made him feel like he was being appraised. Instead, he felt, in that moment, like the center of Jarrett's universe.

He couldn't say he didn't enjoy it.

"Is this the first time it's happened, Tenn?" Jarrett asked. Just hearing Jarrett say his name sent another course of energy through his veins. It was nothing like what he'd felt around Tomás, but the intensity was just as sharp.

"Yes. Sir."

"Call me Jarrett," he replied. He lowered his voice. "When this is over...we'll talk again. At length." He looked Tenn up and down. "I want you to stay out of the fight. The reports say you don't have many healers out here, so we'll need all the Earth mages we can get. And if your Spheres *are* acting up, I think it's best you stay out of battle."

Jarrett patted him on the shoulder and left. Derrick slumped down from the wall, rubbing his throat. He didn't approach Tenn, but the glare he shot over was enough.

"You killed her, didn't you?" he rasped. "You killed her, and now you've damned all of us."

He spat on the ground.

"You're no better than a fucking Howl."

He walked out, and all light went with him.

There, in the darkness, Tenn began to wonder if it would have been better if he'd died.

It was sometime past midnight. The troop was assembled and the orders had been given. Tenn was back on the roof of the hotel, most of the troop stationed to the city or field beyond. Katherine's body had been...removed. He didn't ask where, or by whom. No one told him. No one told him anything.

Especially not the two Hunters he'd been stationed with.

Devon and Dreya stood farther back. They'd been there when he arrived, and when he tried to introduce himself, they stared at him like he was speaking a different language. He shrunk under Dreya's hawk-like glare and didn't try speaking to them again.

The rain pounded down harder now, but he barely felt it. It was a perk of being attuned to Water, though it didn't necessarily make up for the emotional backlash. You took what you could get. Like Tenn, the cold and the rain didn't seem to bother the newcomers. He looked back to them. They stood on opposite sides of the roof, both open to Air as they scanned the sky.

Neither of the twins spoke as they stood there, waiting. Minutes churned to hours. The night deepened. His nerves sharpened to daggers with every drop of rain. He wasn't just waiting. He was waiting to die.

No. He was waiting for something else to go horribly wrong.

He stiffened when Dreya walked up next to him. She stood by his shoulder, staring out at the abandoned town. She was almost a head shorter than him, though she seemed much taller.

"You say that Water used you," she said. Her voice was soft, barely carrying over the rain, but it was perfectly enunciated.

He nodded.

"That should not be possible," she continued.

"I know."

She didn't say anything for a while, so he took that as his opportunity.

"Why are you here?"

"Because you need us."

It was not the response he expected. She had to be lying—they were clearly here because of him, to take him away. They were just guarding him to ensure he didn't escape.

"Then why just the three of you? If you're here to stop the army, why didn't they send more?"

She laughed. It was high, and childish, and completely belied her serious demeanor.

"We are more than enough, Tenn," she said. "Besides, the

Prophets did not send us here to save your army. They sent us to save *you*."

He couldn't speak. The fear in his chest prevented it. The Prophets were a group of mages dedicated to understanding the fifth and elusive Sphere of Maya—the one Sphere you couldn't attune to by choice. *It* had to choose *you*. No one had seen the Prophets, no one knew how to contact them, but many battles were won or prevented by their guidance. Tenn didn't know how anyone learned what the Prophets decreed. He'd never wanted to ask.

The future wasn't something he wanted to know too much about.

"You are being noticed," Dreya whispered. She reached out and touched his neck. Right where Tomás had gripped his throat before. "That is a very dangerous thing."

Fire blossomed on the horizon, a red stain on night's canvas. He didn't have a chance to speak.

"That is the first line," Dreya said. In this new light, her damp hair glinted rose. "The army is near."

Tenn closed his eyes and took a deep breath. He'd spent the last week waiting for the executioner's ax to fall, and here it was, at last.

Dreya walked back to her brother, who stood with his hands clenched at his sides, his eyes narrowed. The red on the horizon seeped closer, the whole town illuminated in its ghostly light. Tenn could sense the magic even from here. Somewhere out there, the necromancers were pulling out their big guns and spurring their undead army with fire and fear. Tenn counted the seconds in his head, like counting the space between lightning and thunder. He counted the seconds until death arrived.

Deep in the pit of his stomach, the Sphere of Water simmered. It knew battle was coming, and it was excited.

Flames leaped higher, burning through the fields and stretching to the clouds above. The wall of flame burned white-hot, speeding toward the city in a ravenous wave. Years ago, magic had turned the tides of war. It was no longer the most powerful who walked away from battle, but the quickest. He prayed his comrades in the field had shielded themselves. He prayed that he would get out of here alive, that Water wouldn't destroy him.

The fire splashed closer, only a mile away. Its roar chilled his bones, and its heat threatened to melt him.

And then, behind him, the twins began to sing.

The sound sent chills up his spine, and he turned and glanced at them, the fire momentarily forgotten. The twins stood there, heads tilted back and hands outstretched. Three Spheres blazed in them like ghostly lights—the slow blue of Water in their stomachs, the fierce red of Fire in their chests and the swirling vortex of pale blue and yellow Air in their throats. Everyone had all five Spheres, but you had to be attuned to them individually to use them, and each consecutive attuning was more difficult. Most mages could only handle one Sphere. Two at most. To split your concentration to three Spheres was nearly impossible. To be so powerfully trained in them...it made what Tenn's Sphere did that afternoon feel small in comparison.

It also explained their appearance. Overuse of Air would account for Dreya's paleness. But Devon...he must have primarily been a Fire mage.

Air flared in the twins' throats and lightning crackled across the sky, a pulse of blue light that shattered in a dome above them, spiderwebbing down to the earth. Tenn looked to the field just in time to see the necromancer's fire billow closer, only seconds away. He winced.

Fire hit the invisible shield, burned across it with all the power of hell before flaring out into nothing. He blinked hard, tried to get the sear of fire from his eyes. When his vision cleared, he saw the army.

They swarmed across the land, a black tide that screamed and howled like demons. More fires roared around them, but none broke past the twins' shield. Yet.

Jarrett had commanded him to stay back; he hadn't commanded him to stay out of the fight.

Since he couldn't trust Water, Tenn opened to Earth.

Power surged in his pelvis, pulling down through the concrete of the high rise, rooting him to the soil. He could sense the flesh of every creature for a mile, could taste their decaying feet on the earth as they ran. The Howls were hungry. Their empty, ulcerated stomachs burned with his; their need for flesh brought bile to his throat. It sickened him, but the power of Earth kept him rooted.

It would always keep him rooted.

Then, against his bidding, Water flared to life, and his head swam as the traitorous Sphere pulled him under.

"We're so proud of you," Mom says, hugging him one last time. They stand outside the dormitory, Dad idling the car in the street. Dad never likes goodbyes; one quick hug had been enough for him. "You're going to be great."

Tenn takes a deep breath. Tears burn behind his eyes, and he wants so badly to tell her to take him back home, to lie and say he doesn't want to learn about the Spheres and magic, even though a week ago it was all he could think about. The buildings are too big, the other kids too loud. Home is too far away, and no magic, no power, could be worth this much hurt.

"I love you," she says. One more hug. He inhales the scent of her, the perfume that lingers against his clothes. She is shaking. She's trying not to cry. That makes it harder to keep his own emotions in check. It's always been hard to keep his emotions in check. "I'll see you soon. Over winter break."

He tries to stem his tears while she turns and walks back to the car. The dorm-mother shuffles up behind him and puts her hand on his shoulder. "It's okay, son," she says. "You'll see her again before you know it."

He knows it's a lie.

He knows it's a lie.

And there's nothing he can say to bring her back.

"Shut up!" he screamed.

His words ripped through the memory and slammed him—throbbing and raw—back to the battle, back to the roof of the hotel and the screams of the monsters now crashing against the shield. He knelt on the ground, hands pressed to his head. The memory pulsed in his ears like a migraine and tears ran down his face like the rain. What the hell was happening? The visions were becoming stronger. Water was gaining control. Sobs welled up in the back of his throat, but a scream from outside the barrier cut them short.

He pushed down the sadness, buried it deep under Earth, forced Water away with a wrench of willpower.

He was in charge. Not the Spheres.

He grabbed his staff from where it had clattered to the ground and pushed himself to standing. Then he reached his senses deep into Earth and pushed the power out.

The ground rippled. Just outside the shield and beyond his comrades, a wave of soil burst up and spilled out, sending Howls and their human slave drivers stumbling. It was a small act of magic, but Earth sapped him fast. Too fast. He leaned heavily against his staff as hunger gnawed at his stomach and his knees shook. If he used much more, he'd drain himself completely.

Lightning flashed down outside the shield like the spears of angry gods, piercing Howls and necromancers and filling his ears with thunder. More fires raged, these spurred by the powers of his friends, flames hungry for undead flesh. The sky swirled faster as great funnel clouds sank from the heavens and roared across the plains. He could feel the power of his comrades, could feel the magic racing through the air as they struggled to hold their ground. It was enough magic to level cities.

The army still came.

He wondered if their power was enough.

Electric-blue cracks spiked along the shield where Howls threw themselves upon it. He gripped his staff tighter. He wanted to be out there. Water wanted to fight. Even now, tired from Earth, he wanted to be close to the blood. More cracks lanced over the shield. He gritted his teeth. If they could just kill off enough before…

Devon gasped.

The shield above them shattered with the sound of breaking glass, blue sparks raining down like snowflakes. Screams pierced the night as the shield collapsed and the hordes of Howls broke through.

"What happened?" Tenn yelled. He ran over to Dreya's side, to where she cradled her unconscious brother. The town around him erupted in flames, the earth shaking with magical tremors. *This* magic, he knew, wasn't fighting for his side.

Dreya's eyes were wide.

"Someone drained him," she whispered. "He's been tapped."

Tenn's thoughts spun with the impossibility. *Someone tried to drain his Spheres. Someone tried to turn him into a Howl. That shouldn't be possible, not from so far away.*

Dreya glanced up. Her eyes covered over in shadow. She didn't flinch when someone screamed below them. The Howls weren't just coming...they were here.

Power surged and the hotel shuddered.

"Shit," Tenn hissed. He ran to the edge and glanced down. Howls filled the streets, swarmed like ants around a person he could only guess was one of his own.

The Hunter's screams were cut short.

"We have to get out of here," he yelled.

The hotel lurched again, magic laced through its very foundations. Necromancers were trying to raze the whole city. He glanced over to Dreya, who still knelt beside her brother with her hands on his chest.

"Dreya, we can't stay here." A wail came from the streets below him. If it was human or undead, he couldn't tell. "We need an escape route."

She looked up from her brother; he expected her to wallow, but her gaze was sharp.

"That I can give," she said. She closed her eyes, and Air blazed in her throat.

Wind tore through the streets. It whipped up rubble and shoved cars, bashed through windows and shattered bones. Tenn shielded his eyes as it screamed past him, as the Howls below were swept up and tossed about like crumpled paper, splatting against buildings, crashing through trucks. He didn't watch for long. He ran over to the twins and pulled Devon to standing. Dreya still channeled Air, still cleared the streets of Howls, but she helped drag Devon toward the fire escape.

It wasn't any safer down there, but at least they wouldn't die in a building collapse.

They rushed down the fire escape and into the back alley. The street was clear, wind screaming like a banshee. Tenn kept his eyes narrowed, tried to see through the dirt and rain and debris that swarmed around him like wasps. He needed to keep Devon out of harm's way. If another necromancer came along and tapped him again, he'd die. Or worse, he'd become a Howl. Tenn couldn't let that happen. He needed to get them someplace safe. But where in this hell could be considered *safe*?

They ran through the crumbling, burning streets. Kravens and bloodlings darted about, but the dust and debris from Dreya's windstorm kept him and his comrades hidden. Elsewhere, he heard the screams and clashes of combat. Blood hammered in Tenn's ears. Water wanted to fight; Water was tired of running. It felt the pain and agony ripping through the fabric of the city, and it wanted to respond. It wanted to create more hurt. He kept a tight rein on the power, forced it down, but he knew if he stayed here, he wouldn't be able to hold it down forever.

The temptation to unleash its power sang sweet in his ears.

The streets opened up ahead of them as they neared the shore. If he could get them there, maybe they could defend themselves. At least they couldn't be surrounded, with the lake at their back. Buildings thinned out into smaller shops, the streets widening into long boulevards of abandoned benches and torn trees. Waves crashed and seethed, but at least here, for now, there were no Howls. He helped lay Devon on the ground.

Fire roared behind them, and their hotel crashed down with a tremor that shook him to his bones.

"I have to go back," Tenn said, looking between the two of them. His heart hammered and his breath burned.

"No," she said. Her voice was breathy from exertion, and her pale eyes seemed unfocused. "We have our orders. We are to keep you safe."

"I'm not going to stand by and watch my troop get killed."

Dreya must have seen something in his expression. Her resolve cracked.

"As you wish. I will support you," she said. Her Spheres burned brighter as a tornado funneled down in the heart of the city. It roared like a demon, hungry and feral. He knew Air, being the most ethereal of the Spheres, was easier to wield, but how was she still channeling so much power? "Just make sure you make it back alive."

Tenn didn't hesitate. He ran back into the flames.

If hell was a city, it would have been this one.

Tenn raced through the burning buildings, Water writhing in his gut, Earth filling his limbs with momentum. Even the bricks were on fire, everything shadow and flame. Ash fell down with the rain, coating his sodden body in gray. Everything was crumbling, burning, roaring with despair. He skidded to a halt at an alley thronged with kravens, their misshapen bodies burning and bleeding even as their hunger drove them onward. As one, their heads snapped to face him, jagged mouths open and dripping disease. It was only then that he realized they were crouched over the broken body of a Hunter. All that was left of the corpse was cloth and snapped bones.

The monsters screamed.

Water screamed back.

Tenn gave in to the siren song, and Water dragged him down with delight. Magic beat a battle drum through his veins as he let the power free.

He ran to meet the monsters head-on. He spun, slashed, danced with the pulse of Water. Battle might not have been graceful, but Water made it ecstasy. Blood sprayed through the air like oil, made his black clothes blacker. Water laughed, and he laughed, too.

Kravens fell around him like cards, crumpling headless into heaps. Talons slashed his skin, sent fire racing across his flesh, but Water delighted in the pain. He drowned in power, drenched himself in glory. Dozens fell, and dozens more came, drawn by the screams and the scent of blood. Water was a torrent of agony in his veins, and even that pain was bliss.

Something appeared over the writhing mass of bodies, a shape more humanoid than the monsters. The kravens went still, their prey momentarily forgotten. Tenn's lungs screamed from exertion. Water wanted more—more blood, more bliss— but he didn't attack. He stood, transfixed, surrounded by corpses, the buildings on both sides of the alley burning and crumbling, everything black and red and ashen. The silhouette stalked closer, slowly, and that's when Tenn realized the flames bent around the figure—not away from, but *toward*. The remaining kravens hunched over as if kneeling, scuttling back toward the shadows and away.

What the hell?

All heat drained from the world the moment the shape resolved itself. Well, *herself*.

She wore a long white dress, splotches of black and crimson seeping up the hem. In her bloody hands was a glass mason jar. A flickering flame hovered within.

"Hello, Tenn," she said. How her voice carried over the roar of destruction, he wasn't sure. It took a moment, through the haze of Water, to realize there was no way she should know his name. "Leanna will be so delighted when I bring her your body."

Fire opened within her, and the jar blazed red-hot.

Cold lanced through his chest, his heart screaming with ice and agony. His grip on Water and Earth shattered. He crumpled atop corpses and screamed as wave after wave of freezing pain shot through him, all aimed at his heart. All aimed at draining energy from his Sphere of Fire. His back arched. His jaw clenched in a rictus.

The agony stretched on forever. He felt everything, *everything*. Rage and hatred, passion and desire—they coursed through his burning, freezing heart in a deluge. He couldn't stop screaming, couldn't stop the fist from tightening around his chest. Everything turned to ice. Everything threatened to burn his world away. And he knew...he knew that this was how he would die.

He would become a Howl.

An incubus.

Then, suddenly, it stopped.

Heat flooded through his body as he fell limp to the ground. His muscles relaxed, heavy and wet and shaking with new-found warmth. A hand closed on his shoulder. He flinched aside.

"Tenn," a voice called. Masculine, familiar. His eyes cleared. Jarrett stared down at him, his face bloody and eyes tight with worry. "It's okay," he whispered. "It's me. You're safe."

"What…" Tenn croaked. His throat was raw.

"Shh," Jarrett said. "She's gone. Can you walk?"

Tenn's body gave another involuntary shiver. He shifted and tried to sit up; he failed. That was answer enough.

Jarrett lifted him to his feet. Tenn ached with cold and heat, every nerve tingling like he'd plunged from ice water into a sauna and back again. The world around them burned, but he barely felt it. For the moment, Tenn could only focus on the warmth of Jarrett, the solidity of the arms wrapped tight around his body.

"Come on," Jarrett said. "We're regrouping."

With Jarrett still supporting him, Tenn hobbled through the streets. His foot kicked something. He glanced down and saw it was the woman's head.

"What was…what was she?" he asked.

"A necromancer," Jarrett said through clenched teeth.

Tenn wanted to speak up, to tell Jarrett that this had been a setup: Leanna was actively hunting for him. *My sister Leanna has an interest in you*, Tomás had said. If Tenn was wise, he would give up now. Or he would beg Jarrett for help.

Then he remembered Katherine's limp body, and Tomás's heavy promise. Another shudder ripped through his body as chills raced down his spine. He looked up to one of the few remaining buildings and swore he saw a shadow standing there, the barest silhouette of Tomás. Watching. Always watching. Waiting for him to speak up. Waiting for another reason to kill.

Tenn kept his mouth shut.

CHAPTER FIVE

THE TWINS AND A HALF DOZEN OTHER HUNTERS waited by the shore. Devon was conscious, but he crouched on the ground with his head in his hands, looking at no one. The sky was a hazy pink from the flames, and Tenn felt the magic of Dreya's barrier the moment he walked through. Regrouping. *Right.* It felt more like gathering for the slaughter. Storms stretched across the black horizon, arcs of lightning flickering over the endless water. How much of that was magic? How much was just nature being pissed?

Dark shadows oozed from the city as kravens and other nightmarish creatures swarmed the boulevard. Dreya's shield was thin at best. Judging from the strain in her features, she couldn't hold on much longer.

Jarrett helped Tenn sit down on one of the benches. A few other dirtied Hunters were there, but no one seemed too heavily injured. He prayed that this wasn't all that was left of their troop. Not only because that was a lot of deaths, but because there were many more Howls to kill.

And because, in some unknown, twisted way, those comrades were dying and bleeding because of him.

An explosion rent through the air. Light burst from the city, followed by a tremor so great he nearly toppled from the bench. But it wasn't the mushroom cloud billowing into the air or the scent of brimstone that made them cower—it was the power, the sheer force of magic, that ripped through the town like a bomb.

Tenn had seen power in his life, but never had he seen magic as great as that. Even the twins paled in comparison.

They stared in silence as the smoke cleared, weapons raised and pulses speeding. Air glowed brighter in Dreya's throat as she reinforced the shield. There was a note in her eyes that scared Tenn more than anything else: fear. Something told him it wasn't an emotion she experienced often.

"What the...?" Derrick whispered, Fire sparking around his bared sword.

A shape floated out from the ruins. The silhouette soared high above the crumbling towers and burning storefronts. Then a glint of light, a breath of power, as the stranger's Spheres came into focus: Earth, Fire and Air. The energy radiating from them made Tenn's frozen skin drip sweat.

"Shit," Jarrett cursed. He looked to the troop. They were broken, bruised, barely able to strike the lesser Howls now spreading across the boulevard. Fear was plain on everyone's faces. Even Derrick's. Whoever this enemy was, they were far outmatched.

"We need to run," Jarrett said. "We can't fight this. Not now."

Laughter cut over the sounds of fire.

"Run?" came a man's voice. The figure above the city floated closer. "I wouldn't do that if I were you. You'd be *so* easy to follow."

In the blink of an eye, the figure stood before them, barely a dozen feet away. The movement reminded Tenn of Tomás, and the thought made his stomach churn. But this man was definitely not the incubus. This man was tall and sharp, wearing an immaculate black pinstripe suit. His gray hair was combed back, and his goatee was the color of ash. Every inch of him was sleek and strong, a sharp contradiction to the destruction around him.

He reached out his free hand and tentatively stroked the surface of Dreya's shield. It crackled under his touch, flurries of sparkling energy trailing to the ground with a hiss.

"So charming," he mused as he watched the sparks fall. "And so naive to think a magic so simple could protect him from me."

With the press of his finger, he brought the whole shield down in a cascade of sparks. Dreya gasped, hands going to her throat as Air winked out. The man smiled directly at Tenn. That look poured ice down Tenn's veins, and he knew that none of them would leave here alive.

"Who are you?" Jarrett asked. He took a step forward, his sword held at the ready. Air burned in his throat, but he didn't make any move to attack. Tenn couldn't help but notice the slight shake in his hand.

"My name is Matthias," the man answered. He gave a curt nod. "And I have come for the boy." He pointed to Tenn. Tenn took a half step back.

"You can't have him," Jarrett said. Despite everything, Tenn's stomach flipped at the resolve in Jarrett's voice.

Matthias grinned. "Oh, I think you'll find you're much mistaken. My mistress desires him, and I shall bring him to her with or without your cooperation."

"Mistress?"

"Leanna." Matthias's words dripped poison. The hole in Tenn's stomach grew wider.

"Never," Jarrett said. He didn't take his eyes off the man, but Tenn knew the body language well. Jarrett was preparing himself for one last stand.

Tenn wouldn't let him fight alone, not when it wasn't even his fight. He tightened his grip on his staff. Dreya's hand clamped down on his arm before he could move forward. She gave a slight shake of her head, her eyes never leaving Matthias.

"Let's let him decide that, shall we?" Matthias asked. He winked at Tenn. "After all, who better to decide the worth of his own life? Is it worth, say, one other?"

He waved his hand, like he was batting away a fly. Fire flared brighter in his chest.

Derrick didn't even have time to scream.

Fire burst from his chest and lips, curling around him and hollowing him out so that—in less than a heartbeat—he was nothing more than a shell of ash. His sword clattered to the ground, dropping from his paper fingers. The rest of him collapsed in a cascade of soot.

Tenn cried out. Dreya's hand tightened, kept him from running forward. Derrick had been an ass, but he had been alive. He'd been worth keeping alive.

"You bastard!" Jarrett yelled. He launched forward; Matthias held up a hand, and Jarrett stopped in his tracks, seemingly held in place.

"Now, now," he said. "Let's not be too hasty. After all, I highly doubt Tenn would like any more deaths to weigh on his soul." He looked at Tenn, his smile deepening. "Personally, I would have thought Mommy and Daddy were enough."

The words were a punch to Tenn's gut. He stumbled back and felt another set of hands holding him up. He barely had time to register the twins flanking him before Water stirred in his stomach, dragged at him with cold fingers. *Mom, Dad, where are you?* It took everything he had to force the bloody memory down.

"You aren't taking him," Jarrett said. His voice was deadly low.

"Your choice, Tenn," Matthias said, as though he hadn't heard Jarrett's warning. He gestured to the rest of the troop. "You have seven more chances to come willingly."

There was no way in hell Tenn was going to let anyone die for him. He wasn't worth it.

"Okay," he said. "I'll go."

But before he could shake off the twins to join Matthias, Jarrett lunged into action.

Tenn yelled, but Matthias just brushed Jarrett aside with a wave of his hand. Jarrett skittered to the ground at Tenn's feet. The rest of the troop rallied immediately, running toward Matthias with weapons raised and magic blazing.

Before Tenn could join the fight, before he could keep these idiots from dying for him—*him*, worthless, meaningless him—someone pulled him back toward the waves. Fog descended over the boulevard, broken only by muffled shouts and flares of fire. Then he was plunged beneath the waves, and everything went cold and black.

They raced beneath the waves of the lake. Magic wrapped around them, pushing them through the water at breakneck speed. Tenn's lungs burned as they rocketed away from the shore, heading deeper and deeper into the depths of the lake, far out of Matthias's sight. He couldn't see anything through the darkness, couldn't tell how deep they were diving. But he could feel the cold pressure of the water, the endless expanse of the lake, as his own magic-fueled senses stretched out. Dreya's hands were still tight on his arm; he tried to fight her off. He had to get back to them. Had to save them. Had to keep them from killing themselves over him. But Dreya's hands were a vise, the magic and water pressing him tight to her. Try as he might, he couldn't break free. His lungs and limbs burned with the effort.

When he couldn't take any more, he took a frantic breath. Air filled his lungs. He didn't even bother to be surprised.

He gave up the struggle.

Deep in the darkest pits of his heart, he knew it was already too late. His comrades were dead or Howls now. Matthias wouldn't have delayed the slaughter. If anything, Tenn's leaving probably hurried it.

The only consolation was the tingle of magic nearby. The slight halo of energy that ringed the others who fled beside him. The hazy halo of blue emanating from Devon: Water and Air, just like Dreya. And just like Dreya, he carried another. He could sense the shape of the figure with Water's power. Jarrett.

It shouldn't have made his heart warm, but it did.

He expected the dark water to erupt into flame, expected Matthias to drop down into the depths and kill them. Matthias had to be close behind. He had to be following them, enraged, and Tenn could only imagine what would happen to them when they were caught. The ash of Derrick's body still seemed to cling to Tenn's lungs, making him want to gag. Derrick's image stuttered like a broken movie reel, shadowed by the flares in the fog, the silhouettes of his comrades as they fought against Matthias. As they died for him.

Because of him.

Seconds turned to minutes. Minutes ebbed to hours. Tenn lost track of how long they fled, and the depths gave no hint of the time. There was nothing to distract him from the memories, from the smell of his comrades' burning flesh. Nothing to distract him as Water regurgitated the battle scenes, meshed them with all the horrors of the past few years. Every once in a while, his attention would flick back to the water surging around them. Back to the hands holding him tight.

Back to the awareness that Jarrett was nearby. Safe.

Why did that make him feel better?

Why did it keep reminding him of a past he'd tried so hard to forget?

After what felt like days, the water around them lightened. The sun must have been rising; they were still so deep he couldn't see more than a tinge to the black. A tinge that illuminated great shapes below them. The Sphere of Water filled in the rest. Massive blocks stretched through the darkness like shipwrecks, forms of concrete and steel. Some glinted slightly in the sun. Others were dark, pitted and cavernous.

He jolted as they abruptly changed course. Dreya dragged him up, away from the structures below, and in seconds, they plunged into the air. Only a few moments of weightlessness, the shock of light after so much dark, and then they landed on top of a crumbling concrete slab. For a while, he just lay there, gasping, as the water pooled and cold air soaked to his bones. He couldn't focus on what was happening. Couldn't force his mind to kick-start and work again. All he could do was focus on the cold and his breath and the pain. Every muscle in Tenn's body ached, but he didn't open to Earth. He wanted to feel the hurt. After everything that had just been sacrificed for him, it was the least he could do.

He closed his eyes, let his focus drift in and out. Shreds of conversation drifted through his clouded mind. Finally, he forced himself to sitting and looked around, wincing from the effort. The morning was cold and clear, the sun streaking across the horizon. Beautiful, if not for the nightmare still plaguing him. No land in sight. Just sparkling waves and broken plinths rising from the surf. Things clicked with a disgusting snap. He knew precisely where they were. This was all that was left of Chicago. And the water had once been Lake Michigan.

"What the hell are we doing here?" he asked.

The twins stood farther off, conferring with Jarrett. All of them were dry. Tenn very much was not.

Jarrett looked over and the twins went silent.

He knew the three of them could kill him in an instant, knew it was *them* who should be questioning him. But the pain in his heart was too much. Water raged. He let it. It was easier than thinking about what he'd done. Easier than thinking about the deaths. Or Tomás. "What the hell is going on?"

Tenn stood as he spoke, realizing he'd lost his staff somewhere along the way, and tried not to sway too much when he did so. Everything was quiet and pastoral, save for the lulling wash of waves. He wanted to scream. Scream because it was too picturesque, too quiet, and his comrades were either dead or dying and here he was, alive and well, for absolutely no reason. He wanted to get back to them. He had to. He had to give himself up.

Jarrett stepped forward and reached out.

"Tenn, let me explain."

"No. No, don't touch me. Tell me why you were sent."

"You know why we're here," Jarrett said slowly. As though Tenn had lost his mind in the battle. "We were sent to protect your troop."

"Bullshit!" Tenn yelled. Water pulsed in his gut, and waves crashed higher against the building. Shakily, he pushed the power away. He couldn't trust himself with it. "If you were just sent to protect us, why didn't you stay with them? Why did you…?" He could barely force down the tears. *Why did you save me? Why didn't you save everyone else? Why am I here, when the rest of them are dead?*

Jarrett looked back to the twins. Dreya shrugged. Devon studiously looked away. When he turned back to Tenn, Jarrett wore an expression Tenn couldn't place.

"You have to understand, Tenn. We're just trying to protect you."

Tenn shook his head. "Why? Why me? Why didn't you save everyone else? You *could* have saved everyone else."

"We could not," Dreya said. She stepped forward. Devon moved at her side. A shadow. "We would not have had the strength to carry so many. To do so would have risked us all. We would have been followed."

"But why me?" *I'm no one. I'm worth nothing.*

"Because we were sent to find you," Jarrett said.

Hearing him say it was a kick in the stomach.

"Why?"

Jarrett opened his mouth, but Dreya put a hand on his shoulder and stepped forward.

"You are being targeted by the Kin," she said.

Tenn's heart lurched to his throat. Did she know about Tomás?

"Dreya, don't—" Jarrett began, but she waved her hand and continued, anyway.

"It is not a statement you wish to hear. Any sane man would feel the same. But it is the truth. The Kin desire you, and they will stop at nothing to take you. That is why we were sent."

He went silent. Having the Kin after him wasn't a shock after all that had happened. The shock was that others knew about it. The shock was that these three had let the rest of his troop die for it. For *him*.

"You should have let Matthias take me," Tenn whispered. "I'm not worth their lives."

"Do you really think Matthias would have let us go?" Jarrett asked. Suddenly, there was a hand under Tenn's chin; Jarrett tilted Tenn's head up to meet his gaze. "Matthias is a necromancer, Tenn. He would have taken you and killed the rest of us, anyway. At least this way... At least now you're safe."

Tenn wanted to look away, but he couldn't. Jarrett's gaze held him, as surely as Jarrett's touch sent flames racing through his chest.

"Why? What makes me special? Why do they want me?" Jarrett grinned.

"That's what we're trying to figure out by keeping you alive. The Prophets told us to protect you. Personally, I'd guess it's tied to your Spheres acting up. I've never heard of that happening before."

Tenn couldn't take his eyes off Jarrett's. They were so warm. So familiar. He was acutely aware of Jarrett's fingers under his chin, of their closeness, of the warmth Jarrett gave. A warmth, and a confidence. He could have stayed there forever. Instead, he pushed the warmth away and stepped back, letting Water slosh through his veins in a cold curse.

He hated himself. For being alive when the rest of his troop was dead. For being the reason his troop was dead. But mostly, he hated himself because, right then, he *didn't* hate himself. There was something about being in Jarrett's gravity that made him feel alive. That made the last few years of bloodshed and regret fade away.

Something clanked beneath Jarrett's coat as Tenn stepped away.

"What's that?" Tenn asked, pulled from his thoughts.

"Something I picked up," he said.

Jarrett pulled the object from inside his pocket. Tenn gasped and stepped back. It was the jar the necromancer had held, the one with the flickering flame.

"Why—"

"I thought it might come in handy," Jarrett said.

The twins stepped forward, peering over Jarrett's shoulder silently. But Tenn wasn't watching them. He couldn't take his eyes off the jar.

At first, he thought it was badly scratched, but the more he stared at it, the more the markings that flickered in the sun and from the inner fire became, well, if not legible, at least uniform. Definitely symbols. Harsh and angular. They seemed to whisper in his head, like reading a foreign language he could almost place. *The weight of a void, the dark center of a star, the raging heat of space, consuming, consuming...*

"What?" Jarrett asked.

Tenn looked up. He didn't realize he'd been moving his lips.

"Can you read them?" Dreya asked.

Tenn stepped back and looked away. "No. I just... No."

He caught the twins looking at Jarrett. He caught Jarrett's furrowed brow. He caught the slightly stronger glow coming from within the jar. Or maybe it was just the sun.

"It sounded like you were reading it," Jarrett ventured.

"No. I was just making it up."

Jarrett's next words were slow. Confused. "Are you—"

"We should be moving," Dreya interrupted.

Jarrett seemed to snap back to reality. He looked to Dreya, shoving the jar back inside his pocket.

The moment it was hidden, the whispers in Tenn's mind quieted. He hadn't even realized they were still there.

"Are you recharged?" Jarrett asked.

"Not fully," she said. "But we do not have time to waste. Especially if you are carrying that."

"Where are we going?" Tenn asked. Jarrett was still looking at him curiously, like he wanted to ask him a thousand questions. Questions, he knew, that had nothing to do with the symbol-covered jar.

"Outer Chicago," Jarrett replied. His words were still guarded.

Tenn looked to Dreya. He could feel the warmth of Jarrett's gaze. It lingered in his chest, thawing the cold places. And sending a dozen more questions racing through his brain.

"Why?" he asked.

Dreya sighed. She kept looking to the horizon, to the way they'd come from. "Outer Chicago is safe. Mostly."

Did she mean that he would be safe there? Or that keeping him there would make it safe for others? Either way, Tenn knew he didn't have a choice. He couldn't turn them down even if he wanted to. But the truth was, he didn't want to fight them, and not just because of Jarrett. Tenn had planned to spend the rest of his short life wandering between outposts, fighting the undead until he died for a cause. But now, knowing that he was a danger to those around him...

Or were they just bringing him back so they could experiment on him? He looked from Jarrett to Dreya to her silent brother, Devon. Tenn wanted to believe they were on his side. He couldn't afford that luxury.

The truth was, though, it didn't matter what their motives were: he had one of his own. He didn't have anyone left to fight for, but what he *did* have was an ax to grind. If what was happening to him—the strangeness of Water, the attraction of the Kin—could be used against the Howls, he would embrace it. If only so he could use it against those who had destroyed his life.

"Let's go, then," he said. He opened to Water. Memories flooded to the surface—Derrick, curling into flame; his bedroom, dripping blood—but he was ready for them. He grappled them down with a well-practiced hand. "But I'm not letting you drag me there."

"He has spark," Jarrett mused.

"And you have no tact," Dreya replied.

She opened to Water. Devon opened at the same time. He felt the twins wrap their power around Jarrett, the barest flicker of blue in the sun.

Jarrett just chuckled and leaped over the building, swandiving into the lake. Dreya followed close behind.

Devon, however, stood there for a moment, hands crossed at his chest and his eyebrows furrowed.

"You still hear them, don't you?" His voice was gruffer than Tenn expected.

"Who?"

"The dead."

Tenn's blood went cold. He could only nod.

"I hear them, too. Every day. Sometimes, I wonder if I'm even me anymore. Or just all the dead I carry around."

Devon shook his head, then tightened the scarf around his face and leaped into the water.

Tenn walked over to the edge. Stared down into the waves. They were already jetting off, cutting beneath the waves like spears of light. Devon's words lingered, curled around the base of his skull. The last thing he wondered before jumping in was if Jarrett and the rest would save him, or if they'd just be three more names on the list of the dead he carried on his soul.

CHAPTER SIX

IT WAS LATE AFTERNOON BY THE TIME THEY REACHED the shores of Outer Chicago. The water grew shallower, until they were able to trudge up through the waves toward the shore. The lake lapped at the highway stretching before them, slowly eating at the asphalt, turning it to sand and stone. He wondered if the destruction had been intentional—some necromancer trying to drown the whole city—or if it was just the Earth rebelling, eating itself alive to escape the madness magic had wrought. The aftershocks of the Resurrection had struck deep, and humans weren't the only ones to receive the blowback.

Dreya slumped heavily against Jarrett as they made their way into the sprawling suburb. She had used the last of her magic to drain the water from their clothes. Devon held her hand.

Both of them were crying.

Gray clouds streaked through the slate blue sky, and the horizon was heavy with the promise of rain. Tenn glanced up and shuddered. Late December in the Midwest and still no snow—another reminder of how much they'd fucked everything up. The summer had been unbearably hot and dry, and it seemed to be continuing into the winter here, too.

If the servants of the Dark Lady didn't kill them all, then Mother Nature would pick up the slack.

None of them spoke as they made their way through the abandoned streets. The air was still and perfectly silent, save for the twins' occasional muffled sobs. After the roar of battle and water in his ears, the hush made Tenn's head ring, like he'd stepped from a crowded school dance into the night air. This was the type of silence that always, always, foretold disaster.

He focused instead on the city, or what was left of it. They'd already passed over the ruins of Chicago, and this was all that remained of the once-thriving metropolis. Countless streets of empty houses, broken and gaping like corpses, all stretched out in a disrupted grid. The place looked like something out of a disaster movie: browned yards tangled with faded clothes and toys, overturned cars and pileups at every intersection, charred houses, and craters carved into the concrete. Even three years later, death and absence hung in the place like a ghost. He expected to hear the wails of the dead, to smell the smoke of burning bodies, a scent other than rain. Hundreds of thousands of people had tried to escape the city during the Resurrection.

Hundreds of thousands of people had failed.

But even here, there were no bodies. The necromancers had turned those they could into Howls, while the rest were devoured by the loved ones that had been turned. The cities were always the worst.

He shuddered and forced down the bile in the back of his throat.

"Did you ever come here?" Jarrett asked, breaking the silence. "Before..."

Tenn nodded. "I went to school nearby."

"Silveron?"

Tenn's heart hitched with the name and Water pulsed with recognition. Too many memories were attached to it. Too many ghosts. He nodded again. He couldn't get any words out around the pain.

"I did, too."

Tenn looked to Jarrett, opened his mouth to ask more. How had he not recognized Jarrett? Why hadn't he said anything earlier? But Jarrett gestured, and around the corner Tenn saw what was left of true human civilization.

A smooth, black-earth wall rose from the street, stretching four stories above the pavement. Its surface glinted in the dull light like obsidian, impossibly slick and impossible to scale. Great metal spikes stuck out from the highest ramparts, all angled down to impale anything dumb enough to try climbing over. It stretched beyond eyesight, cutting through the remains of the suburb in a protective ring.

When the four approached, Jarrett called out in a loud, clear voice.

"I am Jarrett Townsend, commander of Troop Omega, requesting permission to enter."

Something shifted on the high wall. A figure peered over the top.

"Are you untouched?" the guard called.

As one, the three of them opened to their Spheres. Jarrett glanced at Tenn and quirked an eyebrow; abashed, Tenn opened only to Earth. He didn't want to risk Water, not after so much use.

The guard disappeared from sight and, moments later, a chunk of the wall in front of them shivered. Like the waves of a mirage, the stone faded from sight, revealing a large door of rusted steel and heavy girders. It slowly parted with a shrill scream and the rumble of machinery.

They slipped through before the entrance fully opened.

"Welcome back, commander," the guard said. She couldn't have been older than fifteen, yet she carried a bow and arrow and sword, and her face was crossed with scars. She nodded deferentially to the twins, but when her eyes caught on Tenn, suspicion clouded her face. "You found him?"

Jarrett nodded. Tenn's stomach lurched; how many people knew him?

"I knew I would," Jarrett said.

The guard didn't linger. She was already turning a great gear that slid the entry shut behind them. Apparently, he was worth noticing, but not much beyond that. At least it saved him from answering any questions.

In stark contrast to outside, the town within the stronghold's walls was packed and thriving, like some modern re-invention of a Renaissance fair. Houses had been converted to apartments. Apartments had been built upon and converted into multilevel units. Laundry stretched from roof to roof, flapping like flags above stalls selling the last of the season's fruits and vegetables. He inhaled deep. There was even the scent of baked bread. Three years had passed, and with the Resurrection had come the fall of modern man: no more smartphones,

no more internet, no more technology. All of it had been rendered useless with the onslaught of magic. But here, in Outer
Chicago, humanity actually seemed to be doing more than
holding on. It seemed to be crawling forward.

His cheerfulness cut short when he stepped in a pile of crap.
He glanced down, nose instantly wrinkling, and wondered if
it was human or dog. He hadn't seen a dog in years.

"Careful where you step," Jarrett muttered. He didn't seem
amused.

Even though they were surrounded by people, and even
though the guard had very clearly known them, no one in the
city met their eye. People walked about in a crazy mismatch
of fashion: high-end coats and shabby jeans, dresses layered
with parkas, piles of jewelry amid rags. Like they'd just raided
whatever shops they could, and had been stuck with it ever
since. The citizens all milled or argued or hurried past. They
talked to each other, but it felt like Tenn and his comrades
were invisible.

Someone elbowed him in the side as they rushed past. Tenn
started, but Jarrett's hand was on his shoulder before he could
react.

"Don't bother," Jarrett said, his voice still a low grumble. He
was watching the crowd with outright animosity. "To them,
we're as bad as the Howls. We keep them alive, but we still
use the magic that put them here."

Tenn kept his head down and his eyes peeled after that,
feeling the weight of the city press against his shoulders. He'd
experienced this before, in smaller communes. Hunters used
magic; civilians didn't. And even though Hunters fought off
the Howls and the necromancers, even though Hunters were

sworn to defy the servants of the Dark Lady, they were still viewed as the cause of the Resurrection. With so much spite concentrated in one spot, he was surprised there wasn't a riot.

He wanted to scream at them as his group pushed their way through the crowd. He wanted to yell at them just how many good men and women had died to keep them all safe, the names and faces that would go unmourned, unburied. Worse, he wanted to tell them about the Farms, where unturned humans were kept as cattle, and how much worse their lives could be. But he didn't. He feared what speaking up would do. There might not be a riot now, but he knew the desire for vengeance like a bad taste in the air.

Water churned in Tenn's stomach, twisting with guilt and fear. Water wanted to show them all, too. There was so much pain in this city, and it resonated in Tenn's gut like a minor key. He kept the power forced down. Was it even safe for him to be here? Even without Matthias and the Kin, he could barely trust himself with Water's urgings. Maybe these people had been right all along...maybe he *was* a danger.

He glanced at Devon, heard the guy's words filter through his head. *Sometimes, I wonder if I'm even me anymore...*

What the hell am I?

The only thing keeping him grounded was Jarrett's hand on his shoulder. The guy's grip was strong. Heavy. For an Air user, he had a weight, a presence, that snared all of Tenn's senses like a sun.

Right before they rounded the block, Jarrett leaned in and whispered into Tenn's ear, "Whatever you do, don't kill him. The council looks down on that sort of thing. Even if it's Caius."

Chills raced down Tenn's neck at the feeling of Jarrett's breath on his skin. It didn't take him long to figure out what he was talking about.

A man stood on a pedestal in the center of the street. He wore a faded three-piece suit that barely covered his potbelly, his messy gray hair unsuccessfully slicked back with grease. He reminded Tenn of Matthias, albeit much less refined. Despite the man's ragged appearance, he still had a crowd. It was the only part of the city that didn't seem to be moving. People crowded around the dais like sheep as he spoke, his words cutting above the din of the city around them.

Whatever rant or sermon he had been on cut short when Tenn and the others rounded the corner. The man sneered over at them from his perch, causing more than one head to turn. Their venom was palpable.

Water seethed.

"So, the child army returns," the man said. He had the voice of a man who used to smoke a pack or twelve a day.

Adult mages existed, but were rare; for some reason, kids seemed more adept at attuning to and using the Spheres than adults. Although Matthias seemed to be a terrifying exception to the rule. As it was, very few people lived beyond their twenties: if you could wield magic and fight, you would probably die in battle. And if you couldn't fight, you were probably already a Howl, or food for one.

"How many have we lost today, friends? How many souls have you handed over to Satan?"

"Ignore him," Jarrett whispered. He took Tenn's arm and guided them around the crowd. Small picket signs had been thrust into the grass.

Magic Is Sin
The End Has Come

Classic. Tenn had seen those since before the Resurrection, in the scant months between magic becoming mainstream and magic fucking everything up. Hell, the signs still littered the highways, more common than bodies.

Tenn envied the twins; they walked on as though completely oblivious to the world around them. Or maybe it wasn't that. Maybe they just hadn't deemed the outer world *worth* noticing. It was a skill Tenn wished he could employ, especially right now.

"Oh, look," Caius said. "God must have been on a break today, friends. He let the queer live."

Jarrett grunted under his breath and said nothing, but his hand tightened on Tenn's arm, anyway.

"It's not worth it," Jarrett said, dragging him on.

Tenn made sure to kick over a God Still Hates Fags poster on the way.

Behind Caius was a reinforced building that Tenn figured was the guild. The place looked like a multistory gym, though the windows were sealed and the street in front was covered in metal spikes. The only people who walked in and out were clearly Hunters—not many others wore all black and carried medieval weapons. They made their way past the blockades. Jarrett still hadn't let go of Tenn's arm. Dreya and Devon walked side by side, silent and smooth as ghosts.

Inside, the lobby still held the smell of a gym—the hint of bleach, the tang of rubber, the aftertaste of sweat. It felt strange walking in, dressed in leather coats and scuffed boots when, not four years ago, the place would have been crawling with soccer moms in spandex and bodybuilders with protein shakes. Now, the foyer was relatively empty. There was only a single guard behind the front desk. He gave them a perfunctory nod before going back to reading his book.

Jarrett led them through. Tenn still wanted to ask about Silveron, but something in Jarrett's silence said that it wasn't the time.

The back hall was flanked by workout rooms. A small group of Hunters was sparring in one room. The other was still filled with free weights and machines. Orbs of flame hovered in the corners, fueled by a Fire mage currently doing handstand push-ups. The light glimmered off metal and iron, everything within surprisingly well-maintained. It didn't take much to figure out why the place was spotless: boredom didn't kill, but it meant you were wasting time. If you weren't fighting or eating or sleeping, you were training whatever way you could. Tenn knew the routine well.

The hall darkened farther in, ending with a set of stairs. The only light came from a few torches guttering along the walls. For being so big, why was there no electricity in this place? Even some of the smaller outposts he'd been in had had power. Some, at least.

"Let us know what you discover," Dreya said. "We will be in our room."

Jarrett nodded. Without even glancing at Tenn, the twins walked downstairs. Jarrett and Tenn watched them go.

"Well," Jarrett said. "I guess I'll show you to your room."

"My room?" He'd spent the last few years living in communal barracks. The idea of having his own room...that wasn't a notion he'd harbored since before leaving for Silveron.

"Yeah. Unless you want to share." Jarrett winked at him, then continued on down the hall.

"Why are you doing that?" Tenn asked as he followed. He wasn't certain where the words came from. Maybe it was just the exhaustion of the last few days—he was tired of feeling like he was being played with.

"Doing what?"

"Flirting with me." Despite the initial confidence, his words died into nearly a whisper. He expected Jarrett to laugh. Or to say he hadn't been.

"Because you're cute," Jarrett replied. "In a quiet, emo sort of way."

Tenn immediately regretted asking. Not because he didn't like the honesty, but because it had been years since he'd even considered hitting on someone, let alone having them do it back. He felt the blush rising back on his cheeks. Not just because of what Jarrett said—something in the forwardness reminded him way too much of Tomás.

"Who are you?" Tenn asked. He had to stay on the offensive. Couldn't let himself start asking the questions he hadn't let himself consider in years.

"I'm Jarrett Townsend, captain commander—"

"Who are you really? I never met anyone named Jarrett. Not at Silveron."

Jarrett paused and studied him for a moment. They were only inches apart. The way his eyes seemed to bore into him... Tenn's heart couldn't beat any faster if it tried.

"Before the Resurrection..." Jarrett sighed and looked away.

"Before all that shit, before I became this—" he gestured at himself, still not catching Tenn's eye "—before either of us were what we are...you were called Jeremy. And I was Kevin."

Tenn gasped at hearing his old name. And Kevin...he remembered that name. He couldn't forget it.

Jarrett smiled at his shock.

"Yeah. I hit on you once before—I'm glad you seem to remember. Surprise."

CHAPTER SEVEN

"YOU... I DON'T..." I HAVEN'T HEARD THOSE NAMES in years.

Jarrett's grin didn't slip, but it took on a darker cast.

"I know," he said. He lowered his voice. "I thought I recognized you when we met, but I wasn't sure. But when you said Silveron... Well, we've both changed a lot."

Tenn nodded, thoughts slowly congealing into something he could recognize.

Kevin.

Memories blurred. He'd done so well at hiding the past from himself, he could barely recognize the life that slowly swirled to the surface.

Kevin had been in the year ahead of him. They'd crossed paths a few times. Had taken a world history class together.

Water surged...

"Do you want to grab something to eat?" Kevin asks.

Tenn looks up from his homework, his stomach rumbling at the thought.

"I'll take that as a yes," Kevin replies.

Light rain drifts outside the window, blinking in the lantern light like the butterflies awakening in his stomach. Tenn had been able to keep them silent, wrapped up in wars and dates and political figures he knew he'd forget the week after the exam.

His skin tingles as the papers before him flutter and the history book slams shut.

"You're not supposed to use magic outside the classroom," Tenn says, but he can't help the smile that fights its way to his lips as he looks at Kevin. The Sphere of Air swirls light blue and yellow in Kevin's throat, illuminating the planes of his chin and collarbones. Tenn goes back to packing up his notes. He doesn't want Kevin to notice his stare, because then he'd clearly know everything that Tenn had been thinking. And wanting.

"I do what I want," Kevin says. He shoves his own papers sloppily into his bag. "It's easier to beg forgiveness than ask permission."

Tenn keeps his head turned. Damn it, now he's blushing. But if Kevin notices, he doesn't say anything as he pulls on his coat.

They head toward the on-campus café. Tenn glances at Kevin, then opens to Water. It pulls at him, but he's getting the hang of it. After two months of sitting by the lake in class and trying to manipulate the waves, even this little bit of magic feels like a victory. He focuses, and arcs the rain around them.

Kevin smiles and pats him on the shoulder. Warmth floods through Tenn's chest.

"See?" Kevin says. "A little magic never hurt anybody."

Tenn stumbled as Water sloshed off. Jarrett's hands were there, steadying him, keeping him balanced. But his hands couldn't force away the memory, the roar of Water in Tenn's ears, the after-cries of the thousands of other memories that bubbled alongside that one. He'd hoped that leaving the field and the bloodshed would help, but...

When will it stop?

"What was that?" Jarrett asked.

Tenn couldn't answer at first; he studied Jarrett's face, compared it to the boy he barely remembered. Three years of fighting and magic had definitely taken their toll—this new incarnation was taller, more muscled, his skin paled by magic and scarred by bloodshed.

"Water," he finally said. "Sometimes it... Sometimes it dredges up memories."

Jarrett nodded slowly, studying him, his hands still steadying Tenn's arms.

"Are you okay?"

Dozens had asked Tenn that over the last few years, normally during or after battle. Never had he actually felt like the other person wanted an honest answer.

"I don't know anymore," Tenn replied.

A Hunter walked past them, saluting Jarrett. Jarrett just nodded. His hands didn't leave Tenn. The fact that he wasn't hiding this closeness sent another wash of heat through Tenn.

"How did you know it was me?" Tenn asked.

Water and war had changed him, too. He'd watched the transformation in the mirror over the last few years—the new scars, the dark circles under his eyes, the gauntness that never seemed to fade no matter how much he rested or ate. He didn't think he looked anything like the boy he once was. He sure as hell didn't feel like it.

"You stood out back then," he said, squeezing Tenn's shoulders. "And you stand out now." He actually reached up and brushed the side of Tenn's face, tracing a scar with the back of his fingers. Tenn nearly collapsed at the softness of that touch. "It takes more than a few scars to hide that."

Jarrett's seriousness was replaced with a grin.

"Besides, you're just as gloomy as you always were." He took a half step back. "Who'd have thought we'd meet again out here, at the end of the world?"

Tenn shook his head. It was still swimming. His skin burned and tingled from Jarrett's touch, and he wanted nothing more than to close the space between them, if only to be held, if only to connect to a part of his past that wasn't covered in blood. A part of his past that suddenly, like a flare of light in the dark, felt like it could beckon toward a different future.

But he didn't.

He doubted he ever could.

"Why'd you change your name?" Jarrett asked.

Tenn snapped back to the present, felt his treacherous face flush. The question was enough to slam him back into his body, though. It was enough to make him stop thinking of something better and focus on everything that had happened since.

"Because," he replied. It was all Jarrett would get. At least for now. "Why did you?"

Jarrett shrugged. "I thought it sounded more commanding than 'Kevin.'" He sighed. "Speaking of... I need to go talk to Cassandra. She'll have learned we made it back, and she's going to want to know that I found you."

Suddenly, the past seemed entirely unimportant. In the weight of what was happening—Tomás and Leanna and Matthias— having this small connection seemed insubstantial.

"You still haven't told me why you came after me," Tenn said. He tried to steel his voice. Water made it waver.

Jarrett hesitated. It was clear he didn't want to continue talking. At least not about this. It was a trait Air users seemed to have in common—the moment things became emotional, they drifted.

"I already told you," Jarrett said. "The Prophets sent us."

Just like that, it was like a wall slid between them, all in the name of duty.

Anger boiled within Tenn; how could the guy act non-chalant right now? They'd just witnessed a few dozen Hunters get murdered, had just confronted the most powerful necro-mancer Tenn had ever encountered. Not to mention that Water still hadn't calmed down, and they still didn't have an answer as to why.

"How can you be so calm about it? Matthias is still out there. People died. They died for *me.*"

"Thousands of people die every day," Jarrett said. His voice was cold, distant, and Air glowed faintly in his throat. "That's the world we live in. That's the world we're trying to change. Four years ago, all I could think of was going to college and get-ting high and playing video games. Now I'm in charge of one of the largest human outposts in America. I've sent hundreds of my comrades to die, and I'll probably send hundreds more." He closed his eyes. When he spoke again, his words were softer, almost a whisper. "If Leanna wants you, you're dangerous— either to us, or to them. Either way, I'm going to keep you from them. It gives me a purpose—that's why I'm calm."

Tenn couldn't even begin to process what Jarrett was say-ing. It was all bullshit. He didn't believe in any Chosen One prophecy. He didn't hold the key to ending the Kin's reign. He was a fighter, and only because he had to be. Only because *not* fighting had cost him everything.

"But why me?" Tenn asked, deflated. He hadn't actually meant to say it, but the words spilled out against his will.

Jarrett studied him for a moment before answering.

"I don't know," he finally said. "But I plan on keeping you around long enough to find out."

Jarrett continued down the hall, and Tenn followed close behind. His head was spinning. He was in Outer Chicago, standing beside the city's second-in-command. He'd been pursued by Howls and necromancers and, now, the most powerful mage alive. In a way, it sounded like a fairy tale.

So why did it feel like a nightmare?

"All our rooms are underground," Jarrett said, leading him through a tunnel that definitely hadn't been part of the building's original construction. The walls here were bare stone, smooth and shining and dotted with doors; Tenn knew Earth magic when he saw it, and this place had been carved out by Earth mages. Flickering lamps dotted the walls, making the entire place feel like some archaic dungeon. "Hopefully you're not claustrophobic. We had to put some apartments up top for the Air mages." Jarrett looked back and grinned—apparently, the seriousness from before had passed. "We're not so good with being buried alive."

Jarrett stopped and opened a door, gesturing inside. "Home sweet home."

It was stupid, but despite everything, seeing the room sent a small wave of relief through him. Inside, lit by a hurricane lamp, was a single large bed, a sink and a dresser. Just one of each. Which meant he wouldn't have to sleep with a dozen others snoring or yelling in their dreams. And, if he was being honest, a space this far underground made him feel safe. Secure. Ever since last year, when he'd been attuned to Earth, the closer he was to the soil, the happier he felt.

"What am I doing here? I can't just sit around and wait for them to find me."

"No one's going to find you here, Tenn. I promise you that." Jarrett reached out and put a hand on Tenn's shoulder. Once more, the current connected, and Tenn found himself wanting to lean into the gravity. "I'm going to go talk to Cassandra. She's the one in charge. Once we figure out our next move, you'll be the first to know."

Tenn bit his lip.

"Hey," Jarrett said. He moved his hand to Tenn's cheek. "Don't worry. I'm looking after you. I won't let anything hurt you."

Tenn wanted to say he'd been looking after himself just fine. He wanted to feel a fire of indignation. But the way Jarrett was looking at him…it didn't make him feel like he was being talked down to. It made him feel kind of nice. To not have to be the only one watching his back. To know that he didn't have to figure this out on his own.

"Thanks," Tenn finally managed.

"Of course. I'll come find you after the meeting's done. Bathroom and showers are down the hall. Rest up. You've earned it."

When Jarrett left, though, Tenn didn't feel like showering. Didn't feel like taking a break. Because the moment Jarrett walked away, Tenn's thoughts and doubts returned.

And then, all he could think about was how much he felt like bait.

* * *

The room was simple, clean—smooth earthen walls that shone like marble, a worn Oriental rug, a few lamps and candles and a large bed. It had made him feel guilty at first, having his own space down here while the rest of the city seemed to live all squashed together, then he'd remembered the news from New Orleans: a civilian had helped smuggle his fiancée-turned-bloodling into a camp, sure that she would never, ever kill like the other monsters. The ensuing bloodbath had been proof enough that Hunters and civilians needed to be kept apart. Hunters were few and far between, even when they weren't being murdered in their own beds. Not to mention, Tenn had a sinking feeling that Caius and his ilk would be more than happy to do "God's good work" in the dead of night.

He sat on the bed in the suffocating silence and stared at the wall.

It was all he could do to keep Water from taking control. It roiled beneath the surface, a constant hum in his ears, a baritone tinnitus. His stomach rumbled. He needed to eat. And sleep. But he had no clue where to get food and he had a terrible fear that if he let go for one second, if he let himself drift, Water would open and drown them all before he could control it.

What the hell was he doing here? How was he supposed to be a threat to the Kin when he couldn't even keep his powers under control? In less than a day, everything had turned on its head. He hadn't thought that was possible anymore—the Resurrection had pretty much fucked everything up beyond compare.

"Lost in thought, Tenn?"

Tenn's heart leaped to his throat as he jumped to his feet; he knew that voice in the deepest corner of his darkest desires. *Tomás.*

The incubus seemed to glow in the lamplight. Or maybe that's just how he always looked. He leaned against the door, one foot propped against the wood in a pose that reminded Tenn of an old cowboy poster. The fact that Tomás was wearing snakeskin boots helped, though Tenn had never seen a cowboy go about in skintight black jeans and no shirt. He couldn't keep his eyes from wandering over the curve of Tomás's lips, the arch of his collarbones, the perfect V of his torso. Tenn was used to seeing bodies carved from use or magic, honed for a purpose. But this was different. Tomás's body was crafted to be desired.

Then again, for an incubus, that was a weapon all on its own.

"How did you get in here?" Tenn asked. His voice caught in his throat. It wasn't just from the fear of being trapped with a Howl. He hated the fact that desire rose within him. He hated that he *didn't* hate it. It made him feel warm.

It made him feel alive.

"Oh, I come and go where I please." Tomás pushed himself away from the door and sauntered toward Tenn. Every step closer seemed to raise the room's temperature. He burned like a radiator, which meant he must have fed recently. Tenn wondered who they'd find dead and frozen in the morning. "I'm glad to see you made it back alive."

Another step, and he was only a foot away.

Tomás reached out and caressed Tenn's cheek. Tenn tried not to flinch. He tried not to pull the demon closer.

"Though I am a bit saddened you didn't heed my advice," Tomás whispered. His words were frighteningly delicate, on the verge of shattering. "I told you to run."

Tenn tried to hold on to his senses. He tried to turn the desire into rage.

"I'm not going to take advice from an incubus."

Instantly they were both on the bed, Tenn on his back and Tomás crouched on top of him. Tomás's knees pinned Tenn's arms to his sides. The Howl's copper eyes blazed gold and his hands clamped against Tenn's neck.

"I told you not to call me that," Tomás seethed. He shook his head, as though trying to drown some inner voice. When he looked back at Tenn, he cocked his head to the side and smiled. There wasn't the slightest bit of kindness in those perfect white teeth. He released the pressure on Tenn's throat. Slightly.

"It seems he is not good at following directions." Tomás shifted his grip, released one hand to drag a finger along Tenn's jaw and toward his collarbones. He leaned in close, until their cheeks were brushing. Tomás's breath in Tenn's ear was a sensation Tenn never knew he could want so badly. "Perhaps he *wants* to be punished?"

Tomás's hand continued trailing down, a nail snagging on Tenn's shirt, slowly ripping it open. Tenn writhed under that touch, his pulse throbbing. Twin voices screamed in his head. One—the sane one—wanted to escape. The other...well, the other part wanted to pull Tomás closer and show him just who was going to be punished.

He forced the thoughts away. He had to remain in control.

Of all the goddamned things in this world, he could at least have some control over his urges.

"Why are you doing this?" he managed, pissed at how breathy his voice had suddenly become.

Tomás paused. Tenn wanted to pull the man closer, wanted to force his hand lower.

"I have already told you," Tomás finally said. "What my sister Leanna covets, I, too, desire."

"But why? Why me? Why now?"

Tomás sat up, his hands lingering on Tenn's chest. "You are special, Tenn. Powerful in ways that are only just awakening, in ways only *I* can help you understand. That is why I want you. And why she wants you. You hold a power that could prove very useful to us."

"I would never help you."

Tomás chuckled. He dug his nails into Tenn's hip, and Tenn's back arched in pleasure and pain.

"I think you'll find that you will want to help me," Tomás said. "In fact, I think you would give me anything I desire."

His fingers clenched tighter. All Tenn could do was moan.

When Tomás finally let go, Tenn collapsed to the bed, shaking.

"Yes, I believe you will play our game quite well. Leanna was right to place her focus on you."

Tenn's thoughts swam. He had to stay focused. This was a *Howl*. This was the *enemy*.

"Why don't you just bring me to her, then, if she wants me so badly?"

Tomás considered a moment, stroking Tenn's hip absent-mindedly. Tenn didn't want it to stop.

"Because I would much rather let my sister work for her prize," Tomás finally said. He leaned in and licked Tenn's collarbone. Frostbite burned with ecstasy.

"I'm not your prize," Tenn gasped.

Tomás practically purred.

"Oh, but you are. You are the greatest prize of all. But I am okay sharing you. For now." Tomás leaned back and looked him in the eyes. All taunting was gone, replaced with cold calculation. "There are two types of men in this world, Tenn. Those who will use you openly, and those who will use you under false pretenses. But do not for one second think that you are not being used." He ran his fingers through Tenn's hair. "You may think you are safe here, you may think you have found someone who sees you for who you are, but he was sent to collect you. He will always see you as an object. A duty."

It shouldn't have worked, but it still made Tenn's heart sink. Mainly because he had already been thinking the same thing. Even if Jarrett was a link to his past, he had still been sent after Tenn for another, hidden purpose.

"And you see me differently?" Tenn asked.

"Of course not," Tomás replied. "But you will have a lot more fun under my care, that I can promise you." He leaned in and whispered in Tenn's ear, sending heat and desire flooding through his veins. "He is using you, my pet. As am I. But at least, with me, you will always know where you stand...or kneel. And I will ensure you relish it."

Tenn didn't even realize Tomás's hand was inside his jeans until the man's hand clenched, and ecstasy and flame burned through him. But the moment the wave hit, it was over, and

Tomás stood by the wall, hands behind his back and a studious look on his face.

"That is but a taste of what I could give you. An eternity of pleasure. Of power. Or you could spend it here. With them. Miserable and manipulated."

Tenn managed to grab on to his senses.

"What about Leanna?"

Tomás just smiled.

"Leanna won't be in the picture forever. Not with you around." His face shifted, once more becoming grave. "Do not let your petty feelings control you. Ask the boy why he sought you, when he returns. Ask him, before you claim that *I'm* the monster."

There was a flicker of power, the briefest twist of Air in his throat, and then Tomás was gone.

Tenn collapsed back on the bed, panting, the ceiling spinning slowly as his body burned and shivered in turn.

Despite Tomás's earlier threats, despite knowing the Howl would carry through on killing everyone he told, Tenn knew he should run from the room. He should tell the compound that a Kin was here. That he wasn't safe. Or he should simply run from the room and never look back. Death followed him, and Death had many faces.

As his breathing slowed and his thoughts became his again, he did none of those things.

Not because he was scared of Tomás's wrath, but because, around Tomás, he felt alive in ways he never had before.

He didn't want to push that away. Not just yet.

CHAPTER EIGHT

TENN SAT IN THE BRANCHES OF A WILLOW TREE; ITS long limbs dipped into the lake stretched out below. Across the water, glinting like stars scattered across the sky, warm windows shone with the promise of home. He brought his knees closer to his chest and stared out. He'd come here, to the Academy, to learn about magic. He hadn't known at the time that the biggest lesson he'd learn was loss and the heavy absence of *home*.

The lake was where he'd spent most days over the last month or so training. Ever since he'd been attuned to Water, he'd come out here with a small handful of other classmates to practice connecting to the waves, all from the warmth of their small lakeside pagoda. The hours were long and boring—staring at the water, trying to *feel* it in his veins, trying to stretch and manipulate it like a limb. But it wasn't the practice that was getting to him—it was the Sphere itself. Water seemed to have a life of its own. He'd been to the guidance counselor weekly since the attuning, thinking he'd developed schizophrenia or depression or bipolar disorder. He couldn't sleep, couldn't stop falling prey to visions of his early childhood: all the family fights he hadn't consciously remembered, all the time sitting alone in his room and wishing elementary school would grant him at least one friend. All the tears he'd shed or hidden. The counselor assured him it was normal. That was just what Water brought up for people.

That might have been nice to know beforehand, he'd thought at the time, but he knew it wouldn't have changed anything. They didn't have a choice in which Sphere they were attuned to. After the testing period, they were all paired up to their optimal match and given the tattoo that connected them to the magic. *Your magical mark*, his professor had said.

The Mark of the Beast, the protest signs along the road warned.

Tenn pushed those images away. The protesters scared him more than the power, even if Water did seem to set everything on edge. But the fact that the overly emotional Sphere had been considered his best fit made him question his own stability…and that wasn't something he wanted to be worrying about.

At least it might have explained all the emotions that had bubbled up around that boy in his history class. Kevin. It wasn't the first guy he'd crushed on, but it *was* the first time he'd let himself realize it. The first time he let himself imagine it going somewhere. Kevin just had this presence, this calmness, to him. And when he smiled…*ugh*. Tenn hated just how much he loved it when Kevin smiled.

It didn't help that the guy was crazy smart and cute, in all the ways Tenn felt he was not.

"So this is what you dream, Tenn?"

Tenn jerked around, nearly falling out of the tree.

A man stood on the shore a few yards away. He was unfamiliar—pin-striped black suit, slicked gray hair. The man didn't belong here. But then again, neither did he. He glanced down at his hands. They were worn—calloused and scarred, hands used to battle and bloodshed. And he wasn't in school uniform; he wore the ragged blacks of a Hunter.

"What are you doing here?" Tenn asked.

He half expected the dream to fade, now that he was aware he was, in fact, dreaming, but it didn't. Somehow, that was worse.

He tried opening to the Spheres, and nothing happened. It was as if he'd never been attuned. He couldn't even feel them.

He was facing the man who'd killed his comrades, and he could do nothing about it.

"I'm just observing," Matthias answered. He took a step closer. His feet didn't leave an impression in the sand. "After all, someone whom Leanna so actively seeks must surely be an interesting specimen." He chuckled to himself. "I must say, I am so far unimpressed. All you seem to be good at is running away and letting others die in your place."

It was a blow to Tenn's gut. The tree around him seemed to shudder from the pain, from the sudden wind that howled through the branches, screaming like Tenn's fallen comrades.

"Get out of my dream." Tenn stood up on the thick branch. He wanted to fight. He wanted to prove that he didn't just run. But he had no weapon and no magic—what good was he against the man who had killed Derrick with a snap of his fingers?

Matthias didn't answer. Instead, he sauntered closer to the tree.

"Why do you dream of this night?" he asked. "Why is this so tender in your heart?"

Tenn said nothing. Matthias glanced out to the horizon. Above them, the stars began winking out with small flares.

"Ahh," Matthias said as recognition dawned. "I see."

More stars blinked out. Even the lights on the horizon faded as the dream twisted into nightmare, as the wind picked up and the howls became inhuman.

The sky dripped darkness.

"This is the night before the Dark Lady began her work."

Tenn shivered. The Dark Lady: the woman who had created Leanna and Tomás and the other four Kin, the woman who vanished off the face of the earth once her work was done—some said killed, others said in hiding. She was the woman who had set the world ablaze—follow her, and you would have immortality. Destroy for her, and She would grant a new life.

The Resurrection occurred when She turned the first human into a Howl. It had been impossible to miss—every television station, every radio channel, every website and social media outlet, all of them had been hijacked. All of them had aired the same footage, at the same time, on repeat. It was the first human turned into a new form. That was the day monsters and twisted magic became mainstream and the necromancers began their attacks.

The day that Tenn realized his life as he knew it was over.

Matthias's next words were low, the mockery gone. He

looked at Tenn as though he knew the most intimate details of his soul. Like he'd been following his every step. His every thought.

"This is the night before the world was damned. The last night you had a home."

Tenn said nothing. He didn't move, just stood among the branches and watched the lights wink out, one by one, as the screams grew louder.

"She's not gone, you know," Matthias said, his calm words piercing the din. "Not really. My goddess, She still lives. And She stirs."

The words made Tenn's limbs go cold. He gripped a branch until he felt blood drip between his fingers.

"I don't believe in your goddess," he whispered.

"But She believes in you," Matthias said. "And in the end, that is all that matters."

All the lights winked out, save for two red eyes on the horizon. The Dark Lady smiled in the depths of the darkness. She purred.

Then She swallowed Tenn whole.

Tenn woke screaming. The sheets were tangled at his feet, and the hurricane lamp burned low on the nightstand, casting shadows throughout the room.

He was alone.

His heart raced as he looked around the room. He had the worst feeling that he was being watched, but neither Tomás nor Matthias lurked in the corners. Or—he thought, with a certain sense of disappointment—Jarrett. He flopped back on the bed.

For a long time he just lay there, trying to calm the furious racing of his heart, the staccato of his breath, wondering if someone would come in and ask if he was okay. He could still feel those red eyes on him, and every second that ticked by made him feel more and more alone. With every blink, he expected to see her, the Dark Lady, watching him from the shadows. Matthias's words echoed in his skull: *She believes in you.*

A few years ago he'd barely been a presence in whatever outpost he'd been stationed. Now, every force of the Dark Lady was after him.

His thoughts drifted. What had Tomás meant about Jarrett? Hell, what had the incubus meant about anything?

Water surged in his stomach. It didn't want to be toyed with; it wanted to be in control. Tomás and Jarrett thought they had the power, but Water wanted to prove otherwise. If only he would let go. If only...

"Damn it." If he stayed in here, he'd probably flood the whole compound.

Tenn pushed himself out of bed and followed the copper pipes hanging in the corridor toward the bathroom, watching the walls change from smooth earth to moldy tile. A shower wouldn't fix everything, but it would definitely help. At least it would get him out of the room and keep his mind off things.

The showers were clearly part of the original gym, and Tenn highly doubted that they'd have hot water—not many places did anymore—but when he walked over to a stall and slipped out of his ragged clothes, he discovered that they had hot water in excess. He stepped under the spray and felt his muscles unknot and his stress melt away. He sighed and pressed his forehead to the cool tile wall, watching the water drip down his limbs.

His eyes caught on his Hunter's mark.

He'd received it after undergoing all the preliminary tests at Silveron: the written exams, the consultations, even the strange free-association art projects. The series of concentric circles and strange symbols had seemed like a badge of honor at first, some sort of badassery on an otherwise-boring kid like himself. He'd definitely been the youngest from his hometown to get a tattoo, let alone one that connected him to a Sphere of magic. But now, as he stared at the crossing lines, at the circles and symbols he'd researched and realized were variations on Celtic and Norse—and many unknown—runes, the whole thing felt like a curse. It whispered to him, the symbols murmuring of power. Of servitude. He wanted to scratch it off his skin. Wanted to burn the ink from his flesh.

Not that that would help. He'd seen comrades lose limbs. They could still use magic.

Once you were attuned, there was no turning back.

He really wished they would have told him that at the Academy.

Tenn couldn't help but wonder about Jarrett, about why he had such a tug on him. Maybe it was just the connection to his past. Jarrett was probably the only living person who knew him from *before*. Who knew him as Jeremy, and not a name he now bore out of necessity. He wanted so badly to corner Jarrett, to ask him about what he remembered from childhood, from before he became a weapon. He wanted to figure out why he still felt the pull toward him. Why, after three years apart, after barely even knowing the guy at school, there was a part of Tenn that still spiraled toward him. That still wanted to be in his orbit.

He'd barely thought of Kevin, or Jarrett, or whatever he wanted to call himself, after they'd parted ways. There hadn't been time. And, honestly, he'd figured Kevin—like the rest of his classmates—had been killed by the Howls.

Now, he was traveling with a reminder of the future he could never have.

He'd spent the last few years running away from it. He'd tried so hard to become something else. But here was Jarrett, holding up the mirror and reminding him that he hadn't run fast enough.

Tenn closed his eyes, let a finger on his free hand trace the slight raised lines of his mark. Water bubbled at the touch.

He couldn't run fast enough. *I can't run fast enough.*

Before he could stop it, Water boiled over.

"Mom, Dad? Are you home?"

It's too much to hope for; he knows it before opening the front door. But he holds on to that flickering light, anyway. It had led him here by bus and on foot, across miles and miles of highway crawling with dead bodies and not-so-dead bodies. The thought of the monsters he'd had to avoid to get there makes his stomach lurch. The thought of what he'd had to do when he couldn't hide made it worse. The news had said things were bad. He'd had no clue just how bad they were until leaving Silveron.

Thankfully, Water filled in the blanks when it came to fighting. He may have wanted to run; the Sphere, however, wanted to seek out blood.

Maybe that wasn't something to be thankful for. He wasn't a killer. He wasn't a killer.

He only wants to save them.

Has to save them.

The house feels empty, and he knows it is in the pit of his gut. Not just empty. His house is hollowed, like someone stepped in and ripped out its heart.

He steps into the upstairs hall. His heart thuds in his chest and Water churns memories in his gut.

"No," he whispers. "No."

Blood smears across the walls in long streaks, straight to their bedroom. Straight to the closed door he'd knocked on every Christmas morning. Straight to the clean, bloodless door.

"No," he repeats. He wants to run. He wants to turn around and never look back. But Water leads him forward, pulls him by his gut. It can't be theirs, he thinks. It can't be.

He presses his hand to the door.

It swings in on silent hinges, the only sound his blood in his ears.

It's empty.

"Mom?" he calls quietly. "Dad?"

Their bed is made, the quilt from his grandma folded neatly at the foot. The windows are closed. Blinds open. It's sunny. It shouldn't be sunny. There should be clouds and storms and screaming. But it's quiet. His whole damn town had been quiet. It was worse than the screams. Far worse.

He walks over to the nightstand and the photo sitting there, under the lamp.

He and his dad at Christmas. He'd been four when it was taken. They're surrounded by crinkly wrapping paper, with a fire roaring in the hearth behind them. He can see his mother's slippered foot at the bottom of the frame—she was always the one taking the photos. She'd sent him a box of them his second week at Silveron, complete with homemade cookies and confetti.

He sits down on the bed and picks up the picture, stares at his dad's smile.

Then his heavy heart sinks.

There, in the corner, is a tiny smudge of blood.

Outside, a gust of wind slams the shed door. He starts. Looks up. Another gust, another slam—

"Tenn? Are you in there?"

Tenn opened his eyes, Water sloshing away with the sound of slamming doors. His heart was ice in his chest, though the shower was still scalding.

"Yeah," he called. His voice was rough and his lips were salty. How long had he been standing there? How long had he been crying?

"You have been summoned," Dreya said.

He wiped his eyes and peeked around the curtain. Dreya stood in the doorway in a new pair of faded jeans and a fluffy white knit sweater. Where she got fresh, mended clothes in a world of disrepair was beyond him. Maybe she had a stash from her travels. Her hair hung over her shoulders in waves, almost disappearing against the pale shirt. She was doing that hawk-gaze thing, which didn't make him feel any more comfortable about being naked. It was like she could see through the curtain and into his thoughts.

"What?" he asked.

"Cassandra, our commander. She has summoned you." A hesitation. "All of us. We are having a meeting. The entire guild."

"A meeting?" The way she said it made him think the worst.

"Yes."

He took a deep breath.

"It's about what happened to us, isn't it?"

She nodded.

"Shit."

"I suggest you hurry," she said. She gestured to a chair, which had a new set of clothes and a towel folded neatly on top. "I altered these for you. I hope they are to your liking." She shook her head, as though realizing it didn't really matter. "Cassandra called the meeting ten minutes ago, but we couldn't find you. You're already late."

With that, she turned and left. Tenn shut off the water and grabbed the towel. He hadn't even been here a day before drawing attention to himself. He'd been hoping to have a bit longer before they threw him out.

CHAPTER NINE

TENN WISHED HE'D HAD A MOMENT TO RELISH THE
fact that he was wearing the first new clothes he'd had since joining the Hunters—up until now, he'd been given hand-me-downs
from the dead. New recruits rarely got anything better. His new
clothes were black, but the jeans were slim and fit perfectly, and
the long-sleeved shirt was snug. It was the coat, however, that
made him want to stop and stare at himself—it was perfectly
tailored and, like the white ones worn by the twins, covered in
belts and buckles. Far above and beyond the guild standards he'd
grown used to. Dreya must have been a seamstress or something
in a previous life.

Dreya was waiting for him outside the bathroom, her arms
crossed and her eyes closed. Devon was at her side, just as silent
as always. She looked Tenn up and down the moment he was
out, gave a quick nod and then headed down the hall. Devon
followed close behind. Tenn didn't even have the chance to
thank her for the clothes, or ask how she'd known his size.

He wanted to ask them something, anything, to get them talking about who they were, and where they trained. If they were as powerful as they seemed, they had to know more about magic than him. He'd seen them both use Water, so maybe they knew how to control it. Maybe they knew how to control the visions, the flashes of power. At the very least, he hoped they knew how to keep it from controlling *them*. But the urgency with which they walked told him that now wasn't the time.

It would probably *never* be the time.

The meeting took place in an old basketball court. By the time Tenn and the twins got there, it was already well under way. He knew it was all in his head, but he felt like everyone looked at him when he entered the room. Like they could tell he was new.

Like they could tell he was the cause of all this... Whatever "all this" was.

The twins edged past the open double doors and stood in the shadow of the bleachers, and Tenn followed close at their sides.

He assumed it was Cassandra pacing in the center—the command she radiated was more than enough to convince him she was the leader. She was in her late twenties, with dark ebony skin and long black braids that nearly reached her waist. The Sphere of Earth pulsed slow and green in her hips, the faintest trace of a glow. Most Earth mages Tenn knew were stocky, grounded, but not Cassandra. She was tall and stunning, with a perfect hourglass figure. She wore all black, from her knee-high leather boots and tight black leather pants, to her skintight top barely concealed by a sheer coat. It wasn't an outfit meant for battle. That confidence alone spoke volumes of her power.

"Our forces are dwindling," she was saying.

Her voice was powerful, and it carried throughout the gym. Dreya had made it sound like the whole of the guild was there, but the bleachers were barely half-full. He'd heard stories of Outer Chicago, and how great its fighting forces were. If this was all they had left...

"Our hold on civilization is slipping. Leanna is pushing her forces east. Already we've received reports of her armies as close as Des Moines." She paused under one of the brilliant balls of fire floating high above. "We can barely hold on to the little land we *do* control, let alone try and topple Leanna's compound. No previous attempts have proved successful. America is dying. Every day, another guild or outpost falls and another Farm takes its place. If we don't do something fast, our great nation will be left to the Howls."

A murmur rumbled through the bleachers, and Tenn didn't need to be among the troop to know the gist. None of this was new information, but it wasn't something anyone wanted to hear. Even *he* had heard the horror stories of attempted conquests—the Hunters who made it back from raids on Leanna's compound and could barely speak through their shock; whole armies, wasted in a heartbeat from magic or hordes of higher-Sphere Howls. Even attempting to liberate the Farms had proven useless—the necromancers learned to protect their prized stock, and too many Hunters had fallen for the few innocents that had been saved.

He hadn't heard of an attempted attack on Leanna or any other Kin in over a year. His stomach dropped at the idea of how this could relate to him.

"Which is why," she continued, walking out of sight. Tenn stepped closer, so he could see her over the stands. "I have asked you all here." She gestured to the shadows at the side of the space. "Jarrett, if you please."

Jarrett walked out next to her, his boots echoing in the otherwise-silent room. He wasn't in his field attire, and he looked like the Resurrection had never happened—ripped blue jeans, black combat boots and a gray T-shirt with a logo that had faded beyond recognition. Even from here, Tenn could see the intricate lines of Jarrett's Hunter's mark on his right forearm.

The sight of him made Tenn's pulse race. He tried to find a trace of the boy he used to know. He tried, but every time he thought back to Silveron, Water surged with dangerous abandon.

It wasn't Jarrett's appearance that brought everyone to a deeper silence. It was the object he gingerly placed in Cassandra's hands. Tenn's dread doubled at the sight of it.

A small glass jar, with a curl of flame hovering within.

Cassandra raised it high above her head like Lady Liberty with her torch. Even from here, he could feel the wrongness, hear the whispers he could only describe as evil. Even from here, it made his Hunter's mark tingle with goose bumps.

"This," she said, "is the weapon used against us. This is the Dark Lady's greatest secret, the one her minions have died to preserve and protect from us. Until now." She smiled at Jarrett. Her grin reminded Tenn of a feral cat. "Now we have insight into their dark magic, and with that knowledge we can finally turn the tide of this war."

Tenn wasn't watching Cassandra as intently as the rest of

the troop. He was watching Jarrett. And Jarrett looked terribly uncomfortable. He must have known what would come next. Tenn did, too. His chest constricted from the memory of it.

"But first, a demonstration. Sam and Maria, if you please."

Two Hunters from the front row came forward. The girl had a strong, lean figure and dark hair that curled past her shoulders. Sam was about the same height, with spiked brown hair and a goatee.

"Maria," Cassandra said, holding out the jar, "if you would take this for a moment."

Maria took it without hesitating. She held the jar in one hand, staring at the flame with a small smile. Cassandra told them to face off. That was when fear began to show on Sam's face. Especially because Maria was still staring at the jar, the flame reflecting in her eyes.

Cassandra didn't seem to notice, or she just didn't care. "When I say so, channel a thread of Fire into the jar. I want you to focus on Sam while doing so. When I say stop, you stop. Understood?"

Maria didn't say anything.

"Maria—"

The girl looked up.

"Yeah. Got it. Go easy on him." She smiled at Sam, who took a step back.

He didn't have time to reconsider.

"Go."

Fire opened in Maria's chest. The flame within the jar burned brighter and the symbols on the glass flared to life. Sam cried out as his back arched and Tenn could *see* his Sphere being tapped, could see the tendrils of heat and energy spiral-

ing from Sam's chest and into the ever-burning jar. That wasn't
what made Tenn's skin go cold, though—it was the voice, the
whisper, the harshest female rasp: *drain, devour, be mine.* Tenn
clenched his fists as the voice hissed in his head, seethed with
steam and hatred. He felt himself falling. Falling. Twisting into
that burning void.

He felt the Dark Lady's nails scraping within his head. Calling him. Demanding him.

Listen. Be mine. Be mine.

And then, like a switch, it stopped.

Dreya's hand was on his shoulder, and Devon looked at him
with concern in his eyes. Tenn realized he'd fallen to his knees.
His breath burned in his chest and he feared he'd screamed.
But the show was still going on center stage. Sam clutched his
own chest, his eyes angry and trained on Maria, who was already handing the jar to Cassandra and walking away.

Only the twins seemed to have noticed Tenn's collapse.

Well, them and Jarrett, whose eyes bore into him.

"What the hell was that?" someone called out as Tenn
pushed to his feet.

"That, comrades," Cassandra said, "is how the necromancers
have been creating the Howls. This is how they are able to
drain a human's Sphere past the point of depletion." She traced
the jar's surface with a finger, the line of symbols seeming to
glow under her touch. "They're using runes. Runes we've never
seen before. And if we can understand them, there may be a
way of combating them. Perhaps disabling them. Perhaps even
reversing the process."

The gym had been silent up until then, but that statement
started an uproar of conversation.

Reverse the process?

For years, they'd been trained to believe that the only way to eradicate the Howls was to kill them—even if the host had been human, even if they'd been someone you knew. This wasn't just a revelation or a way forward: this was a tragedy. How many people had Hunters killed in the name of defying the Dark Lady? How many died when they could have been returned to normal?

The thought made Tenn want to throw up. All that blood. *All that blood.* And the only way he'd been able to handle it had been the thought that it was the only way...

Jarrett opened to Air, and when he spoke, his voice cut through the general din of the room.

"Silence," he called. The troop hushed immediately. Even Tenn's inner monologue snapped off.

"There is much we do not know," Cassandra said. "But trust me, we are going to find out. Tomorrow, a few of our finest will be sent out into the field. Our sources know of those who might have insight into the runes. We are making it our prerogative to seek them out. Those selected will receive their orders by nightfall."

She took a deep breath and surveyed them all.

"Remember this moment, comrades. This is the day we cease being the hunted. This is the moment we take back what they have stolen. This is the moment we remake our world."

The crowd broke into applause.

Tenn couldn't join in.

If they had found the language of the Dark Lady, what did it mean when She was speaking directly to him?

* * *

"A word, Dreya?"

He and the twins had waited in the hall to meet with Jarrett. He hadn't expected Cassandra to pause by their side as she left. Up close, he could smell the spice of her perfume—a rarity, anymore. Her green eyes looked only at him. If Dreya's gaze felt like being stared down by a hawk, hers felt like being inspected by a goddess.

"I would like to speak with you." Her eyes flickered from him to Dreya. "All three of you. I'll meet you in your room in five minutes."

She didn't give anyone a chance to respond. She was gone down the hall before anyone could get a word in. Devon and Dreya exchanged another look. Tenn really wished they'd stop doing that and talk like normal people; it just meant he stood there in silence while they shared some secret language. It didn't help that Jarrett never came through the doors they were haunting. When the gym was cleared, Tenn and the twins returned to their room.

"What do you think this is about?" Tenn asked when the door closed behind him. He didn't expect Dreya to answer; he just knew if he was silent anymore, Water would take control.

Dreya leaned against the wall, and Devon took a chair. They did another long look exchange, leaving him to his thoughts. The room was exactly like his—sparse and clean, with a wardrobe and flickering hurricane lamps—though there were two small beds, rather than just one.

"I cannot say," Dreya said. Her voice made him jump. "We are reaching into territories we should know nothing about."

"What do you mean?"

She didn't answer the question. Instead, she peered at him with that intense look again.

"What happened to you back there?" she asked.

He'd hoped she'd forgotten, or passed it off as stress. Of course she wouldn't—she already knew to keep an eye on him for...irregularities.

He opened his mouth, not sure if he would tell the truth or make something up, but the door opened behind him and Jarrett and Cassandra entered, saving him from having to answer.

Cassandra strode into the center of the room like it was her own and looked them over, weighing them, judging them. Jarrett stayed in the corner. Tenn knew he should be focusing on Cassandra, but his eyes kept looking back to Jarrett. Cataloging the way the man stood. The scars and planes of his face that hid the boy he'd known as Kevin. The slight gray in his pale blond hair, from magic or stress, Tenn couldn't tell. Somehow, though, the years of fighting didn't seem to weigh on Jarrett the same way they did on Tenn—Jarrett stood tall, light. Something about him defied the darkness of the Resurrection. Something about him made Tenn feel like things could be okay.

Until Cassandra started speaking. Then his heart fell from his throat to his feet.

"Let me get to the point. In light of recent developments, I'm afraid I must send you back out into the field." Her gaze narrowed on the twins. "I hear you know how to find the Witches."

The silence that answered was deafening. Fire flickered in Devon's chest, just for a moment, but that was enough to make

Tenn take a half step back. The guy seemed like a ticking time bomb. He could practically hear Devon's teeth grinding.

"How did...?" Dreya started with obvious surprise. Then she looked at Jarrett, and her mask slipped back into place. But colder. "You swore you would say nothing."

Jarrett looked down to the floor. "These are dark days, Dreya. I had no choice."

The glare Dreya cast between Jarrett and Cassandra could level mountains.

"Our ties to the clans have been severed," Dreya said, her voice flat and an octave lower than normal. "We cannot help you."

"I am not *asking* for your help," Cassandra replied. She stepped forward. Even with her hands in her pockets, she spoke like she was brandishing a weapon. "I am *telling* you. If you know how to find the clans, if you have even the slightest *inkling* of an idea, you are bound by duty to do so."

Dreya pushed herself from the wall. Air flickered in her throat, and her hair billowed in the sudden breeze. Devon wasn't able to hold back his agitation anymore; sparks flared around his fingertips where they clenched the chair, sending the scent of burning wood through the room. Tenn's skin went cold. He didn't want to see what would happen if the twins tried to mutiny. He doubted he'd get out alive. Even Jarrett stared at them with a hint of fear.

"You know of our agreement," Dreya said, her voice still taut. "We are not bound by the laws of your guild. We are not governed by your *commands*. We fight those battles which *we* deem necessary. And this is not our battle. You know not what you ask."

"Are you so naive?" Cassandra demanded. The two were barely inches apart. In her high-heeled boots, Cassandra towered over Dreya by a good foot, but Dreya was far from cowering. Hell, Tenn expected her to hover. Cassandra opened to Earth, and somehow, just being open to the Sphere gave her a presence, a solidity, that said she would not be toppled. "Do you truly believe this battle ends with you? If you fail to aid us, how many lives do you think we'll lose? I'm not speaking dozens or hundreds or even thousands. Millions will die, Dreya. Because we. Are. Losing. And you…you will be responsible for those deaths. Are you really comfortable with more innocent blood on your hands?"

Dreya gasped. Air winked out, and she took a step back, her eyes darting between Jarrett and Cassandra with a look that tore at Tenn's heart. Betrayal. Pure and utter betrayal. She looked like a little girl who'd just been told Santa wasn't real.

"We cannot," she said after a moment's hesitation. Her voice was soft, tinged with hurt. "Our ties are severed. There is no way—"

"We'll do it."

The room silenced in an instant, all tension gone like a snapped violin string. As one, they turned to Devon, who was studiously looking everywhere but into the eyes of those he'd spoken to.

"What?" Dreya asked. More hurt in her voice, with another layer of betrayal.

"I said we'll do it," he said. His voice was muffled and husky through his burgundy scarf. Fire still flickered in his chest, sending waves of heat that made sweat break out on Tenn's otherwise-freezing skin. Devon looked at Dreya and they stared at each other for a long moment. Dreya seemed to wilt further under her brother's stare. Finally, she sighed and nodded, settling back against the wall and hiding her face behind her silvery hair.

"We know how to find them," Devon continued. He didn't stand up, despite the resolve in his voice. If anything, he seemed to sink lower in his chair. "But whether or not they'll help us, I can't say." Then, almost to himself, he muttered, "They have every reason not to."

"That's more like it," Cassandra said. She nodded, and Earth faded out. Her expression wasn't smug, but it was close. Tenn could tell from that one look that she wasn't the type who was ever denied anything. "You'll leave tonight. I don't want anyone to know it's you leaving. Jarrett tells me there's reason to believe you might be targeted.

"You have your orders," she said, looking back to Jarrett. "I don't expect you to return until they've been fulfilled."

He nodded.

She walked toward the door and put her hand on the knob. Before opening it, however, she turned around.

"More than you know is riding on your shoulders. If you fail, there will be no point in coming back. You'll have already damned us."

Then she opened the door and was gone.

They stood there in the silence for a good minute before Jarrett finally spoke.

"Right. We'll meet at the south tower at five to midnight, right before the guard changes. We'll have to fly out."

That got Tenn's attention. He'd always heard that non-Air users couldn't fly, but neither of the twins seemed to catch what he said. Dreya was still slumped against the wall, watching her brother with wary eyes. Devon stared at Jarrett, his blue eyes intense and his hands knuckled white in his lap.

"You should not have told her," Devon finally said. "We trusted you."

"We need your help," Jarrett said. "Things are... Things are changing. The *world* is changing. And if we don't find a way to fight back, we're going to be destroyed. I know what I'm asking you, but it's nothing I wouldn't do myself. We have to protect what's important. No matter the cost."

Tenn could have sworn Jarrett's gaze flicked to him when he said it.

Devon closed his eyes and took a deep, ragged breath. Fire burned out, and a little more tension bled from the room.

"We will see you before midnight," Dreya said. She pushed herself from the wall and put a hand on Devon's shoulder. Without another word, Devon stood and followed her from the room. They didn't even seem to care that they were leaving Jarrett and Tenn alone in their space.

Jarrett walked over to the bed and sat. Tenn hesitated, then sank down next to him.

"What was that all about?" Tenn asked.

"Politics," Jarrett said with a sigh. "The joys of being in command. Sometimes the good of humanity means fucking over the ones you care about. Here's hoping it wasn't a total loss." He looked at Tenn. "As I said, easier to beg forgiveness than ask permission."

Tenn's heart stuttered. Jarrett remembered that night of studying together. Did that mean he reminisced about Tenn, too?

"But who are the Witches?" Tenn asked, trying to focus on the matter at hand. "Why are we going after them?"

"They're a group. A religion, maybe. Honestly, I don't really know. I'd barely heard of them before this. They pretty much avoid the outside world. But rumor has it they're the ones who discovered how to use runes and magic. If they know about these—" he brushed Tenn's tattoo, flooding heat through Tenn's veins "—maybe they know about the ones the necromancers use. Maybe they know enough to reverse them."

Jarrett shifted, and suddenly Tenn felt the heat of Jarrett's arm near his back, reaching out behind Tenn, in an almost-embrace. Heat flared in Tenn's chest as he glanced over, and Jarrett looked back, not breaking his gaze.

"Tell me a story," he said.

"What do you mean?"

"I'm about to head out into the field with you again. I also just lied through my teeth to keep you from being imprisoned. I need a distraction." He gave a small smile. "Besides, you once told me you were good with words."

Despite the compliment, fire turned to fear.

"What do you mean, you lied? About what?"

"Cassandra didn't know about you specifically, only that the Prophets needed us to investigate. If she'd found out that your magic was acting up, she'd probably have you stuck in a cell for testing. So, tell me a story. Consider it repayment."

Tenn could only think about Cassandra, and the curious looks she gave him. Did she believe he was the cause of this? And if so…would he actually make it out of there tonight?

He tried to shake the questions from his head and focus

on Jarrett. Jarrett, who inspired an altogether different sort of anxiety.

"What do you want to know?"

"Everything. But we can start with where you're from. I don't think you ever told me."

"What's it matter?" Tenn asked, his walls instantly slamming back up. "Everyone from there's dead."

Jarrett went silent. He didn't try to negate Tenn's statement or push him into answering.

"Then tell me what you dreamed of being when you were a kid," he said after a few moments had passed. "What did you want your life to be, before all this?"

"I try not to think about it. Not when I know it can't be."

Jarrett brought his arm closer, touched the small of Tenn's back.

"Why else do you think we're fighting?" Jarrett asked. "I believe it can be. Someday. We can rebuild. But you have to have a dream to get there."

Tenn looked to Jarrett. In all the years of fighting and fear, there'd never been a discussion like this—the question of what might come next. Of what the world *could* look like. Could it ever go back to the way it had been, to the way he'd dreamed? Getting a job and having a husband and living in a cabin in the woods, making art and raising kids and having a herd of golden Labs? Those were dreams he'd kept tightly locked away. They hurt too much to think about. They suffocated in the gray and the rain of this reality.

"Honestly," Tenn said, "I gave up on that after Silveron. I'm not fighting to rebuild anymore. I'm fighting to make peace."

"We *all* are. Tell me what peace would look like to you, then."

Tenn wanted to ignore the question. He wanted to push Jarrett away and go back to his room and ignore this, all of this, because it was making pain twist in his chest, and he didn't know if he wanted to rage or cry.

But he realized there was another force. One that made him want to talk. Jarrett seemed to honestly believe that things could change for the better. He didn't seem to hold on to the past as a reminder of what he'd lost—he held on as a blueprint of what he could one day create.

Jarrett chuckled and flopped back on the mattress to stare at the ceiling.

"What?" Tenn asked, bristling all over again.

"You," Jarrett said. "You haven't changed one bit."

"What do you mean?"

Jarrett's smile both pissed him off and sent another wave of heat through him. Maybe Tomás wasn't the only one who made Tenn feel alive. Though with Jarrett, the excitement wasn't from danger, but from the promise of something bigger. A thread that ran from his past into an unknown future.

"You're still moody. You still worry about what everyone else thinks." Another chuckle. "Still cute, too."

Tenn blushed. It had been a long time since anyone had called him that.

"What was it like for you?" Tenn asked quietly, trying to change the subject. "After Silveron. Where did you go?"

The mirth cut short in an instant.

"It was hell," Jarrett whispered. He stared at the ceiling, lost in his own past. "I went straight home. All the way to Florida." He laughed, this time without any humor. "Half the state was already underwater by then. I was too late to save…" He trailed off. "I was too late."

"Me, too," Tenn replied, his voice soft. The barbs had dulled at the pain in Jarrett's voice. He knew it well.

"But we're here," Jarrett said. He shifted again, brought his arm to Tenn's waist. Then, before Tenn could realize what was about to happen, Jarrett gently reached up and pulled him down, bringing Tenn's head to rest against his chest.

Tenn froze. It was the moment he'd wanted so badly at Silveron. Three years too late.

But then he heard Jarrett's heartbeat. Felt the thud in his ears, the slight vibration against his body. His tension began to dissolve.

"I didn't think I would see you again," Jarrett said, his words so quiet Tenn would have missed them were he not against his chest. Tenn brought his arm over Jarrett's waist, pulled himself closer to the warmth. He almost expected Jarrett to flinch back. Instead, Jarrett brought him closer.

Tenn didn't reply, just nodded against Jarrett's chest. He didn't want to speak. He didn't want the moment to end—the heartbeat, the warmth, the closeness.

"What happened after?" Jarrett asked gently. He paused. "Actually, no. Let's talk about Silveron. What do you remember?"

"How bad Chinese night in the cafeteria was."

Jarrett laughed. It shook Tenn's head and made him smile.

"Christ, yeah. That was terrible. My clothes always smelled like soy sauce for a week."

Tenn chuckled. Then, softly, "I remember you."

Jarrett made a noise that was almost a purr.

"I'm hard to forget," he said. He paused. "I remember you, too." Tenn's heart wouldn't stop flipping, and he was worried if this went on much longer Jarrett would notice and worry.

"What do you miss?" Tenn asked. It was a dangerous question and they both knew it. Hopefully, though, the lighthearted tone would continue.

"Everything," Jarrett replied. "Watching movies in the dorm at night. Music. I even miss the classes, sometimes. Learning something that wasn't just how to stay alive. Junk food... pizza, burgers. Soda. All food, really." He laughed. "Well, except Chinese nights."

Tenn laughed.

"I'd kill for ice cream," he said.

Jarrett moaned and pulled Tenn in, rocking slightly.

"Ugh, don't mention that. I would kill for a milk shake."

"I think you still owe me one," Tenn said, smiling into Jarrett's chest even as tears threatened to prick his eyes. "For helping you study."

Jarrett went silent. Only for a second.

"I do indeed," he whispered. He tightened his hug. "I do indeed."

CHAPTER TEN

TENN DIDN'T KNOW HOW LONG THEY LAY THERE on a stranger's bed, staring at the shadows on the ceiling and talking.

Discussing the things they missed should have set Water off. Talking about the past should have sent him drowning in misery and regret. But, for some reason, the Sphere stayed closed. The memories stayed peaceful. For the first time in nearly four years, Tenn talked about what he missed, and what might have been, and what he would like to be, and Water stayed silent. The fact made him curl even tighter to Jarrett, made his heart warm even more. Jarrett was the ward against the terrible memories. Jarrett was the calm silence after years of inner howling.

Jarrett was warmth.

They talked until they ran out of words and the lamps ran out of fuel. It had to have been a few hours. And there, in the darkness, they stayed, Jarrett's hand on Tenn's hip, Tenn's head on Jarrett's chest. Tenn listened to the rise and fall of Jarrett's breathing, though he wasn't asleep. It was nice, though, to have a moment of quiet. To just exist. It felt like the way life used to be. The way life could have been.

Tenn's pulse began to race. They were alone in the dark, and he was realizing he wanted more than anything else to reach up and kiss Jarrett, to lean against him fully, to see how their bodies matched. It wasn't just lust, though, making his blood sing. It was something else. Something that tugged from his chest. Something that wanted to connect on a deeper level.

He hadn't wanted that since Silveron.

Jarrett clearly felt it, too. He shifted his body slightly, curling in toward Tenn. He wrapped his other arm around Tenn's back. He nuzzled his scruffy chin against Tenn's forehead.

"I didn't think I would ever feel this again," Jarrett whispered.

"Neither did I," Tenn replied.

Then Jarrett kissed the top of Tenn's forehead.

"I want this to last forever," he said. "But it's getting late. I need to go check in on a few things before we go."

It ached, that statement. Tenn hugged him closer.

"This is dangerous," Tenn said.

"I know," Jarrett replied. "And I don't care."

Another kiss on the top of the head. Then he slowly unwound himself from Tenn's limbs. Every movement was slow. Every movement was agony.

This was why there was no room for love in this world. Loving always meant leaving. And leaving meant potentially never coming back.

Jarrett opened to Air, and Tenn didn't have to ask to know it was so Jarrett could sense his way around the room. Tenn opened to Earth so he could do the same, the whole place opening out to his senses like sonar. He couldn't *see* the room, any more than he could without Earth, but he could feel it. Much like he could feel his toes or fingers in the dark, the walls were simply a part of him.

"I probably won't have time to meet up again," Jarrett said as he walked to the door. "Even though I'd like to. Feel free to take a nap in here if you want—I doubt the twins would mind. Or, I don't know, explore what's left of the city."

The thought of exploring both excited and scared Tenn—there was no way in hell he could fall asleep after cuddling with Jarrett. His nerves were on fire, and besides, he didn't want to sleep through their escape. In a way, he almost didn't want to see the truths of Outer Chicago. He preferred his fantasy of the place, where everything was clean and happy and possible. He preferred thinking the two of them could have a future here. Or somewhere better than here. The reality outside these walls wasn't one he wanted to face.

Jarrett paused in the doorway, like he wanted to say something more.

"Midnight, then," he said finally. He chuckled. "I don't think I've ever been so excited to start a mission before."

Tenn laughed, as well. It was short-lived. Now that Jarrett was about to leave, he was reminded of everything he was about to do, and everything he didn't yet know.

"Midnight," Tenn said.

He felt Jarrett move, and then he was close again, wrapping Tenn in a quick hug.

"I'm glad I found you," Jarrett whispered in his ear. He kissed Tenn's cheek and left.

* * *

Tenn lasted about five minutes in the room before anxiety got the better of him. He kept waiting for Tomás to appear, to threaten him again. Tenn had been so, so close to telling Jarrett about the Kin. Then he'd remembered the sound of Katherine's neck snapping, and the desire snapped with it. Now, without Jarrett there to keep the thoughts and demons—figuratively and potentially literally—at bay, his imagination was getting the better of him.

He kept open to Earth as he walked, using the element to map out the guild in his head. The place was a lot smaller than he imagined—just the gym and maybe a block or two of underground tunnels and rooms. The stories had made this place out to be a bastion of hope, the crowning gem of the resistance. This was where dreams were remade, where humanity held on and thrived.

The truth was pretty damn depressing.

He managed to walk past the kitchens and grabbed some bread and cheese and a carrot, scarfing them down while making his way outside. He felt naked without having a weapon in his hand as he left the building. But he was safe in here.

Tomás's face flickered through his mind.

Maybe *safe* was a relative term.

The night was calm and clear, the sky scattered with stars and a gibbous moon. He half expected one of the guards to call out, demanding to know where he was going at this time of night, but no one stopped him as he walked down the street. No one seemed to be out. The town was eerily quiet.

Moonlight glinted off puddles covering the cracked streets, litter fluttering against chain-link fences like tiny ghosts. Al-

though debris was everywhere, the place smelled a little better. The rain must have washed away the decay that seemed
to linger here, the stench of a thousand humans slowly decom-
posing as they fought to stay alive. His foot hit something, and
his heart stopped as a can skittered across the street. *So much
for being inconspicuous.*

"Who's there?" grunted a man's voice. He knew that voice,
even though he'd only heard it once. Once was enough.

"Caius," he muttered under his breath, his blood immediately set to boiling. He didn't stop walking, though. He wasn't
going to let a religious nutjob ruin his only night here.

Something hit the ground in front of him. The bastard was
throwing things at him.

"I asked you a question," Caius called. He kept his voice
down, but there was a sense that if Tenn didn't stop, this would
get ugly real fast. He paused.

"Oh," Caius said. The preacher shuffled closer. He smelled
distinctly of whiskey. "It's you. The newest recruit."

"Yes," Tenn said. His jaw was clenched. "What do you want?"

Caius shrugged. He was still in his suit, his hair mussed from
sleep, or lack thereof.

"Just to talk, Hunter. Just to talk." There was a slight slur
to his words.

"I don't have time."

He took a step, and Caius's arm reached out and stopped
him in his tracks.

"Make time," Caius grated. He let go of Tenn's arm and
stood back, brushing himself off. It was futile—the dust was
as much a part of his suit as the fabric.

Tenn really didn't want to stand around with this guy. He

distrusted the religious fanatics on principle alone. He'd seen the posters in the year or so before the Resurrection, when magic was a new discovery. Magic had always been seen as the devil's work, and many people died because of it. But not at the hands of the mages or the monsters.

Apparently, burning people at the stake hadn't died out with the Puritan times. A new Church had formed in direct opposition to magic and the Dark Lady, a faith devoted to ridding the world of darkness and evil. One whose methods overshadowed the whole "love thy neighbor" thing.

The last thing Tenn wanted was to make a scene. Caius's sheep were probably close at hand, ready to tear him apart. And Cassandra wanted this to be a quiet exit.

"You have two minutes."

Caius sighed. "Impatient, impatient." He took a hand-rolled cigarette from his pocket and brought it to his lips. From another pocket came a matchbook; he flipped it open, struck a match and lit his cigarette in one well-practiced movement. "That's what got us into this mess." He took a long drag and exhaled slowly. The smoke wafted up into the moonlight like a shade.

"What are you talking about?"

Caius's breath might have smelled like the bottom of a whiskey barrel, but his hands didn't shake and his eyes never left Tenn's face.

"The Dark Lady," Caius said. He spit, then took another drag. "She was human once. She was impatient, too."

"I don't have time to listen to your myths."

"They aren't myths," Caius said, the smoke seething from his lips. "I know. I knew her."

Tenn paused. The man could be out of his mind—it

wouldn't have surprised him, especially since he was probably drinking homemade moonshine—or just being a dick. But Caius wasn't throwing slurs or railing against him. He seemed conversational. Rational. Except for the Dark Lady bit. No one from the Church would claim they knew the goddess that destroyed mankind. At least, not unless they were boasting that they were the ones who killed her.

"I know what you think of me," Caius said. He gestured to his filthy suit. "I wasn't always like this."

"None of us were."

Caius chuckled. "Of course, of course. You weren't always doing the devil's work. Might even say you were tricked into it. Too bad you're going to hell for it."

Tenn sighed. On that track again. It was time to go, then. "I need to—"

"Listen. For once in your godforsaken life, that's what you need to do." Caius flicked the cigarette to the ground. "Why do you think I'm here, huh? Why am I in a devil-controlled colony when there are perfectly good septs a hundred miles away? Do you think I like living among sinners and sheep?"

He had a point. Most of the old priests lived in the Church-controlled septs, the religious safe havens. They wouldn't think of stepping foot in a place controlled by mages and Hunters, who were no better in their eyes than the monsters roaming outside.

"I figured you were like everyone else. You were here because you didn't have a choice."

"You're right," Caius said. "But not for the reasons you think. I knew things, things the Church never wanted me to know, and they tried to kill me. Sent their Inquisition my way in hopes of silencing me. So I came here. But soon, they'll find me. And when they do, their deepest secrets will die with me."

"I don't understand," Tenn said.

"You will," Caius replied.

He stepped closer, so close Tenn could smell the rot of the man's teeth.

"There's a darkness stirring in the world, Tenn. A darkness that fills even the holiest of men's hearts. It started years ago, in the heart of the light. You think you know hell, think you've seen death and destruction, but you know nothing. Not compared to the evils yet to come."

Tenn backed up. How did Caius know his name?

"What secrets?"

"You aren't ready for them," Caius said, still whispering. "Once you know, you'll have the whole of the Church with a dagger at your back. But you *will* know. God told me. You'll know soon why the first Howl was born."

Caius cleared his throat and looked around.

"Now, I believe you had somewhere to go."

"I..."

"I'm tired of you wasting my time, Hunter," Caius said, even louder. "I've got no use for heathens." He spat at Tenn's feet and walked away, staggering slightly.

Tenn watched him go for a moment. He couldn't force down the chills that raced over his skin.

How many people in this godforsaken world knew him?

Tenn spent the next hour wandering, his nerves steeled for another confrontation. But the world was eerily silent—even in the outposts, there had been noise: the crackle of fires, the murmur of voices. Here, there was just the still air and glimmering sidewalks, everything wet and reflective, slick as nightmare.

These had been the suburbs of Chicago, but three years had changed them. The great wall circled the entire compound, and the houses closest to it were dilapidated and charred. But when he opened to Earth, he found they were still inhabited. Judging from the smell, well…they either hadn't been cleaned, or no one ever left them, even after death. The thought made him wonder what they did with the dead. He didn't see a grave-yard, and the lake was still a mile or so away. Maybe cremation? He glanced at the wall, and the few ladders and ramps on this side leading to the top. He hoped cremation. He'd seen far too many commanders leave their dead for the Howls.

Closer in, away from the danger, the houses were nicer. They were still overcrowded, but at least these had been kept up. Some even still had all their windows.

Despite this—or because of it—those were the streets Tenn avoided. They felt too much like before the Resurrection. If he ignored the twisted streetlamps, or the makeshift sheds and yurts built on front lawns, he could almost pretend this place had never been tainted by magic or monsters. The streets were clean and wide, the cars gone—probably to be used as bar-riers outside, or locked eternally in the standstill traffic that clogged every highway in America, creating a veritable buffet for the undead. Mailboxes gaped for letters that would never come and hedges were neatly trimmed. The quaintness set his nerves on edge.

So he stayed near the town center, where the buildings were cramped and the laundry fluttered overhead like ghosts and everything had an air of ruin and despair. Shops were boarded up for the night, outdoor stalls were emptied of produce, litter clogged gutters. He hated to admit that those were the streets that felt the most normal. He hated how they made him almost feel safe.

The idea of safety sent another thought through his head. Without a weapon, he felt naked. He wasn't as powerful as the twins, who didn't seem to need a blade to feel safe. Magic always exhausted him. Power always ran out. And when the magic was gone, he was defenseless.

He passed by what was clearly the dump, or junkyard, or some mix of the two: a large lot that had probably once been for parking, but was now filled with trash metal and twisted bicycles and the overpowering scent of rot. He didn't want to wonder what was decaying deep within the pile. He opened to Earth and used it to seek out something suitable. Finally, he found it—a piece of steel pipe a few feet long, thankfully along the perimeter of the mess. He wrenched it free and examined it under the moonlight.

It was heavy, and covered in rust, and bent in a few places. But it was the right size, and with a little work...

One of the hardest parts of the Resurrection was adjusting to the weaponry required to survive. Guns and nukes and the rest were obsolete, and the typical zombie-killer flair of nailed baseball bats and chain saws didn't hold up to hordes of monsters. Weapons could be twisted by any mage. Bullets could be stopped, bombs disarmed. The only way to make a weapon your own was to infuse it with your own blood and magic.

He pushed through Earth, rooted down into the soil and through the pole in his hand.

Metal shivered and melted and reformed, rust sloughing off like snakeskin as the staff elongated, became smooth. He twisted the power and twisted the pole, made it sleek and straight, its weight even. He pulled a blade from each end, each curved and sharp as a crescent moon. He ran his thumb along the top blade, let it slice into his skin, the blade so sharp he barely felt it. Blood trickled down, and he used the power to absorb it into the metal, threading it through the staff and blades, until every inch of it was infused with his lifeblood. Another twist of power, and silver steel turned black.

He closed off to Earth and examined the weapon in the moonlight. It was nearly identical to his old staff, and when he spun it the blades whistled their familiar call through the air. But something about this one felt different. Something about it seemed to signal a new life. For a moment, the thought thrilled him. Then he remembered everything his new life entailed, and the excitement cut off, sharp as the blade he wielded.

The twins were already at the south tower when he arrived. It was clearly a new construct, made of magic-churned earth and bristling with steel spikes. It towered above the encircling wall, accessible only by a staircase that spiraled its way up through the center. The twins stood at the edge of the roof, their white coats glowing in the moonlight. Dreya's coat was especially embellished, covered in more belts and buckles than seemed necessary. Devon's coat was darker than his sister's, like a cloud on the edge of a storm. The clean lines made him look like a military commander, though the burgundy scarf made him look like a commander with a cold.

"You guys look nice," Tenn said. He didn't know what else to say. "New coats?"

Tenn expected coldness from them, but to his surprise, Dreya smiled, the merest tilt of her lips. That was enough. Apparently, still being a newcomer had its merits.

"Has Jarrett been here?" he asked.

Hopefully she couldn't see the blush that rose to his cheeks as he asked.

Devon shook his head, but it was Dreya who answered. "No. But I have no doubt he will be here soon. It is still early, and he is still covering our tracks."

Tenn nodded and walked to the edge of the tower, staring out at what lay beyond the safety wall of the colony. The streets of the abandoned suburb were almost beautiful like this. Up here, away from the threat of, well, dismemberment and eventual death, it was easy to imagine how this place would have been years ago—families all asleep in their houses, dogs barking now and again in the yards. Easy to imagine, if you ignored the crashed cars and magic-pitted streets and the glitter of glass that swept across the debris-filled lawns.

"Do you ever think we'll get it back?" Tenn asked, thinking of his earlier conversation with Jarrett. He hadn't meant to say it aloud.

"This world?" Dreya asked. She stepped up beside him and put her hands on the steel banister that kept them from plummeting. The ground was a long, long way down.

She didn't say anything for a while. Tenn knew from her expression that she wasn't dismissing the question, but mentally debating the possibility. A small part of him yearned for her to say what he knew she wouldn't. That lie would give him hope, the hope that someday he could entertain the idea of a boyfriend, or a husband, or a home. The hope that maybe Jarrett—back after so many years apart—would be the one to signal it. The thought made his heart ache and Water boil.

"I do not think so," she finally said. Her words were barely more than a whisper. "But I wish... I wish it could be."

She exhaled deeply. "But wishes do not change anything."

"What are we wishing for?" Jarrett asked. He stepped up behind them, his sword strapped to his back and another bag of provisions in hand. He was back in his blacks—wool coat, black boots, black combats. The only color was a light-blue knit hat pulled down over his ears. It made him look like a Nordic elf. One into heavy metal.

Dreya, of course, said nothing. Tenn wondered if she was actually embarrassed.

"Everything set?" Tenn asked, doing what he could to cover the silence. Jarrett just raised an eyebrow.

"Yeah." He set his bag beside the others. "I double-checked to make sure the changeover was still at the same time. Midnight. On the dot."

"I still do not like this plan," Dreya said. She looked at Tenn. "This will kill him."

Jarrett bit his lip before catching himself.

"It's dangerous," he admitted. "But Cassandra insisted we don't just walk out. She'd rather someone know magic was in use than have us identified. Over is the only way."

Tenn turned and looked over the railing. The cars looked like toys. It would be a very long way to fall.

"What do you mean, kill me?" he asked. He couldn't cut his eyes from the ground far, far below.

Jarrett sighed and stepped up behind him, putting his hands on Tenn's shoulders. The motion felt so easy, so familiar...

"It won't kill you," he said. "It's just...well, we can fly because we're attuned to Air. For anyone else, it's like being caught in a tornado."

"That is an understatement," Dreya said. "Do not try to soften the reality. For him, it will not be flying. The winds that bear him will rip him apart."

"No," Jarrett said. "We'll stick close, shield him with our bodies. And, Tenn, stay open to Earth. Keep healing yourself."

Behind them, deep in the heart of the town, a bell began to chime. Midnight. Jarrett scooped up the bags and handed them over.

"No time for discussion," he said, slinging one on his back. "They change on the tenth ring."

Tenn pulled on his own bag, and the twins crowded close, each wrapping their arms around his waist. He felt like a sandwich. Jarrett took off his hat and shoved it over Tenn's head before wrapping him in an embrace. Tenn closed his eyes—despite everything, all he could focus on was Jarrett's scent, the musk and far-off fragrance of soap. He wanted to lean forward into that embrace forever.

"Close your eyes," Jarrett murmured into his ear. "It'll be over soon. And whatever you do, *don't stop healing.*"

Then the tenth chime rang, and the three of them opened to Air. The other two chimes were lost to the roar of thunder.

CHAPTER ELEVEN

IN THE CORNER OF HIS MIND, TENN KNEW THIS WAS
suicide. He could feel the invisible shield surrounding the compound flicker when control passed over to another Air mage.

Then they were beyond it.

That was all he could sense. Everything else was a roar of
wind in his ears and the flare of pain in his flesh. Even with
the twins and Jarrett clinging to him tightly, every minuscule
piece of exposed skin screamed as the wind tried to tear him
apart. He bit his tongue to keep from screaming, too. Earth
flooded his body with magic as chunks of flesh shot into the
night, only to be replaced and torn off again. It seemed to last
an eternity, the pain and the screams and the wind.

Then he felt Earth connect to the sudden ground beneath
his feet. The wind stopped.

Flesh knit itself together one final, searing time as the twins
stepped away. Jarrett kept a firm grip on him.

"Are you okay?" he asked. His voice was a little breathy, and his chest moved fast. Only the twins seemed unfazed by the experience; they stared at the horizon, Air glowing in their throats as they scanned.

Tenn nodded and the world swayed with that movement. If not for Jarrett's firm grip, he would have fallen over.

"Never again," he said, his lips cracking from Earth's drain. He let go of the Sphere; his stomach rumbled in protest.

He fought down the bile that rose in his throat and wiped away his tears—from pain or the wind, he wasn't certain. All he knew was that he'd used far too much magic lately. He needed to sleep. He needed to recharge.

The four of them were covered in Tenn's blood, white clothes stained crimson, Jarrett and his blacks oily and slick. A momentary pang of guilt flooded him before he was able to remind himself that flying hadn't been his choice. Before he could feel too guilty, Dreya opened to Water and pulled the blood from their clothes. Blood could be controlled by a Water mage only once it was outside of a living body; otherwise, bodies were protected against manipulation unless direct contact was made.

"We must go," Dreya said when their clothes were cleaned. "The guards will have felt that much magic. They will send a search party soon."

It was only then that Tenn realized they weren't in the suburbs surrounding Outer Chicago, but in the middle of a highway that shot like a silver arrow through the night. He glanced over his shoulder. The city was barely a glimmer in the distance. But Dreya was right; that much magic would have triggered an alarm. How was she still able to talk? Jarrett still seemed to be recovering, his breath fast and his eyes darting, but she was fine.

"Where are we going?" Tenn asked. Here they were, in the dead of night, in the middle of the monsters, with no plan. At least, none that he knew of. They needed to move fast. Even if the Hunters didn't send scouts, there were still Howls and rogue necromancers to contend with.

"The Witches," Jarrett said. Tenn couldn't tell if it was condescending or not.

"Where are they?" he asked.

"This way," Dreya said. She walked off, leaving him no choice but to follow.

"Where?" Tenn asked again. He refused to budge, even though Jarrett cast him a bewildered glare.

He almost expected them to leave him there, but Dreya stopped and looked back.

"We cannot tell you."

"Can't, or won't?" Maybe it was the pain of flight, but Tomás's words fired through his brain. Why were they dragging him along on this mission? Why had they come to him in the first place? "I'm sick of being led along like a dog."

He expected Jarrett to speak up, but it was Dreya who replied.

"Won't," she said. She sighed. "If we tell you, and you are captured, and tortured, you may reveal their location. We swore we would protect their safety and their secrets. We cannot risk that by telling you where they are." She looked to Jarrett, and her sad expression turned razor-sharp. "Some vows, at least, we must uphold."

Jarrett bit his lip, but he didn't say anything, and neither did Dreya. She turned and continued on.

Tenn considered not moving. He considered turning around and wandering off into the night.

"Don't do this," Jarrett whispered.

Tenn stared at him.

"Do what?" He watched Dreya and Devon walk on; neither looked back.

"This isn't the fight you want," Jarrett replied.

"I don't want a fight. I want answers."

"I know," Jarrett said. He put a hand on Tenn's shoulder. Tenn hated himself for it, but that one movement weakened his resolve. "I want answers, too. For both of us. Whatever's happening with this—" his hand moved from Tenn's shoulder to his stomach, to where Water churned over with wanting "—affects both of us. The Witches are said to have discovered magic. They trained those two." He nodded to the twins. "If anyone will have answers, it's them."

Tenn knew he should be asking more questions. He should keep the inner fire going. But he couldn't get his thoughts in gear—they were spinning on Jarrett's statement. *This affects both of us.* Both of them. Together.

Maybe Jarrett wasn't trying to use him like Tomás had said. Like Tomás was. Maybe Jarrett was trying to work toward a mutual future.

Tenn nodded, and Jarrett pulled him in for a quick hug, kissing him gently on the neck.

"We'll figure this out. I promise."

He pulled away and walked on before Tenn could get used to the closeness. The absence was stronger than anything Jarrett could have said to convince him—it tugged Tenn onward, and he knew then that he would follow Jarrett wherever he went.

They trudged on in silence until the night was deep and the city was barely a memory behind them. Moonlight filtered down from the clear sky, making everything glow silver and ink-black. They hadn't come across a single soul since they'd left the compound. The night seemed longer and emptier than it should have—just endless road and fields and abandoned cars. The sight of the fields reminded him way too much of Michael's death. How had that only been a day ago? It felt like the entire world had changed.

Minutes dragged to hours and the cold went from cool to piercing. There were a thousand questions Tenn wanted to ask—who were the Witches, how did the twins know about them and where the hell were they going?—but he kept quiet. The questions he truly wanted answers for were the ones he couldn't voice, the ones he was terrified to know. Tomás and Matthias were out there, still hunting him. And he still had no idea why.

Devon and Dreya paused by the side of an old SUV. It didn't stand out from any of the other vehicles they'd passed, save for the fact that all its windows were intact.

The twins exchanged another look. Devon shrugged.

"Devon thinks... He thinks he can drive this," Dreya said.

Fire and Water flickered in Devon's body as he peered intently through the windows, his hands tracing the glass like a kid ogling a candy-store window.

"Drive it?" Jarrett said. "Good luck getting it to start."

Tenn remembered the cold mornings of his childhood and his mother's frantic attempts to get the car running so she could get him to school on time. Memory made his heart clench, but he stayed focused on the present. The last time this SUV had been used was probably three years ago. Minimum.

"The tank is full," Dreya said. "The battery is dead, but Devon can change that. He is good with cars. They were his fascination as a child."

Jarrett raised an eyebrow. If Devon was paying them any attention, he didn't show it.

"Tenn?" Dreya said. "The doors, if you please."

"Um, okay." He opened to Earth and pushed his senses through the various mechanisms, finally finding the locks on each of the doors. He twisted the metal and rendered the locks obsolete. Crude, but it got the job done.

"Everyone in," Dreya said. She walked around to the passenger's side and got in without waiting for an answer.

"Beats walking," Jarrett said with a shrug. He opened the door for Tenn and then slid in, throwing their gear in the trunk.

"Have you done this before?" Jarrett asked when they were inside.

Devon nodded. "Once," came his muffled reply.

Tenn didn't want to know what Devon was doing. Fire and Water and Air were glowing in his body, and that was enough to give Tenn a hint. Strange noises came from the engine. The truck shuddered.

"The oil is bad," Dreya said. "He is purifying it. And charging the battery."

"I didn't realize you could do that," Jarrett said.

"At its base, Fire is energy."

"So why don't you have electricity in Outer Chicago?" Tenn asked.

"Ask Cassandra," Dreya said. Tenn couldn't see her face, but he could tell from her voice that there was a smirk on her lips. "Other guilds have electricity. So far, hers is the only one we have visited without it. I think she prefers the appeal of living in the Dark Ages."

"Not surprising," Jarrett muttered.

Tenn sank back in the seat, and Jarrett put his arm across Tenn's shoulders.

He tensed for a moment. Even though they'd spent a few hours earlier curled against each other, this felt foreign. This felt too normal. Too good. He waited for Jarrett to shift, to retract his arm. He didn't. So Tenn decided to go with it. Tenn snuggled in close, absorbing Jarrett's warmth. If he closed his eyes, he could pretend they were just in the back of a car on a cool winter's night, about to drive with friends to the movies or out to eat. He could pretend there were no monsters and no magic—just an empty road and warmth on the horizon. If he ignored the pops and hisses coming from the engine, that is. He didn't ask if Devon *really* knew what he was doing. He didn't want to know.

Finally, with the crunch of gears and a rumble, the SUV shuddered to life. Devon looked back at the two of them. Although his mouth was covered by his scarf, his eyes grinned with a distinct *told-you-so* look.

"Damn, boy," Jarrett said. "If only we'd known about your skills sooner. You could have been the official bus driver."

Devon chuckled and turned back to the front. With a shift of gears, they were off.

To say it was strange was an understatement. Tenn hadn't been in a car since...well, since he'd fled from the Academy. He'd never expected to have the experience again. He stayed nestled against Jarrett and watched the world streak by outside the window. Devon turned the heat up.

"What are you thinking?" Jarrett asked. He ran his fingers through Tenn's hair.

Tenn shook his head. It was way too easy to get used to this closeness. Way too dangerous to think this was possible.

If he let himself think either of those things, he'd just want it more.

"Nothing. It's just...this is weird. I mean, it's just so...normal."

He didn't just mean the car ride. He meant Jarrett, the way that being around each other felt natural, every movement and touch one of memory and not new territory.

Jarrett felt like home. All of this did.

"I know," was all Jarrett said. Then they both went back to staring out the windows, lost in their own thoughts.

A few miles in, Devon turned on the radio. No stations played, of course—just static. It's not like they were expecting some magical mystery signal from a Howl-free country or something. That shit only happened in bad zombie flicks. There was a CD in the player, and Devon switched over to it. Tenn jumped as heavy metal blared through the speakers. Devon turned it down.

The world had changed entirely. Tenn knew that. But here, in the car, snuggled against Jarrett, he could almost let himself believe otherwise. He could almost forget about the Howls and the necromancers and the monsters that seemed to stalk his bedside. He could almost forget the blood staining his hands and heart. If he tried, he could almost let himself believe that this was a life they could have again—driving around with friends, listening to music, going somewhere for enjoyment rather than necessity. He could almost believe there'd be a house at the end and a family to invite over for dinner.

He could almost believe that everything would be okay.

He could pretend.

That lie... That lie was the only thing that made life worth fighting for.

He closed his eyes, and sleep found him immediately.

CHAPTER TWELVE

HE STOOD AT THE WINDOW IN HIS ROOM, LOOKing out at the familiar geometry of the streetlamp and garage and backyard, the three-story house across the alley and the giant pine tree at its side. His hand trailed across the curtains. He couldn't sleep. It was well past midnight, and his parents had been in bed for hours. A part of him didn't want to be awake, didn't want to be waiting with this sickness in his stomach. The other part of him wanted to take it all in, every single last second he had here. Tomorrow, he left for Silveron. Tomorrow, he left everything he'd ever known behind. Not that there was much to say goodbye to. Most of his friends had stopped talking to him the moment he'd mentioned his acceptance—whether from anger or jealousy, he wasn't certain.

Even his dad had been against the decision. *Thirteen is too young to leave home*, Tenn had heard him telling Mom. She'd put up a fight. She always would.

Apparently, a few of his friends thought that magic was the

devil's work, and if so, what did that make him? He'd spent the last weeks of summer vacation here, in his room, alone, watching TV and waiting. It was supposed to be an exciting time—that's what all the pamphlets said. Instead, he felt miserable. His summer hadn't been filled with video games and pizza, no more talk of what the coming school year would bring. At least, no more days of that for him; his friends had kept up the tradition without him.

The photos they'd scattered on social media like intoxicating bread crumbs were proof enough of what he was missing.

Behind him, the room was cluttered with packed boxes and suitcases. He'd tried to pack light, but his mom wouldn't have it. She'd thrown in extra blankets and sweaters and socks, and even filled a box with emergency supplies—cookies, granola bars, instant noodles—just in case the cafeteria food was gross. Tenn's stomach turned. It was the little gestures like that that made leaving so hard—the idea that someone loved him so much, the idea that he was willingly leaving that behind. Most kids his age wouldn't have thought twice about it. Then again, most kids probably didn't think they needed to leave home to find themselves. His only consolation was that it was just for a few months.

Just a few months.

Even then, though, he knew he'd never come back. Not as the person he was. He'd come back and be able to use magic, and that would set him apart farther than anything else. He'd entertained the idea of showing off to his friends, making things fly or lighting candles or walking on water.

What was the point in even thinking that when he didn't have friends to return to?

He took a deep breath and went back to his bed, sat down on the covers and stared at the open suitcase in the corner, filled with all his new uniform clothes. It wasn't robes. He'd almost hoped it would be, fulfilling some childish wizarding fantasy. The uniforms didn't even look British. Just generic gray collared shirts and black slacks they'd gotten from the same store he got all his clothes.

He wasn't even able to convince himself to bring his stuffed owl. He had a feeling the other kids would think it was stupid. Magic was no longer for the geeky. Magic was a career move. Magic was humanity's way forward.

He glanced up into the mirror above his dresser and yelped.

With a crash like a wave, reality came back. He wasn't thirteen, he wasn't leaving for Silveron in the morning and he definitely wasn't meant to be here. His heart raced; if he was here, that meant… He pushed himself from the bed.

"Going somewhere?"

Tenn turned around and faced the man standing in the shadows.

"Get out," he whispered. Matthias just laughed. That's when he noticed that Matthias was holding something in his hand. A book.

No, not a book. His journal. His heart dropped, doubled over with the feeling of betrayal, of being laid bare. Matthias caught his glance and smiled. He stepped from the shadows and into the moonlight.

"You're making this too easy," Matthias said. "Going out into the field again? It's almost like you want to be found."

"Stay away from us," Tenn said. The glint in Matthias's eyes made him realize his mistake a second too late.

"Us? They're forcing bodyguards on you now? How embarrassing." He tossed the journal into the air and caught it. "Stupid, too, when one considers the rather mortal implications of being by your side." He opened to a page. "It would seem that those close to you often meet rather untimely demises."

"Shut up," Tenn said. He didn't move to attack; he knew there was no point. Not in a dream. Not without any weapon, magical or material.

"'I'm worried about leaving,'" Matthias read in a mocking, childlike voice. "'What if something happens to Mom and Dad when I'm away? I know I can't protect them, anyway, but I don't know what I'd do if something bad happened. How do I know I'm not saying goodbye forever? I don't want to go. I know I can't stay here, not if I want to really live my life. But I don't want to leave them behind. It feels like leaving them is the end. Like if I'm gone, something bad will happen. I don't want to lose them. I already feel like I've lost everyone else.'"

Matthias closed the journal and looked up at him. Tenn felt hollowed out from having his words read back.

"How does it feel, Tenn?" he asked smoothly. "How does it feel to know that every one of your deepest fears came true? And that you were the cause of them?"

"I..."

"You will come to me," Matthias said. "You are weak. You think you're strong, that your training has made you hard, but deep inside, you're still a lost little boy crying for his mother."

"Shut up," Tenn said. There were tears in his eyes. Why wasn't the dream ending? Why couldn't he wake up?

"When will you understand? More will die because of you. Even the friends who keep you safe—either I will kill them, or you will." He honestly looked concerned. Like he was talking someone off a cliff. Then his mouth quirked into a smile. "You're dangerous, Tenn. To yourself, and to others. That is why Leanna wants you. You need her guidance. You need her help, before you kill everyone."

"I'll die before I serve her," Tenn whispered. He tried to build the fire inside him, tried to steel his voice, but being here, being back in this room, hearing those words... He didn't have the resolve. He was weak. He was empty. He could never run far enough from this place to be anything beyond what he was—lost, scared, confused. Just like Matthias knew him to be.

"No," Matthias said. "I know you, Tenn. I've seen into your heart. You won't die. Not yet. You're too cowardly for that, and Leanna wishes for you to be brought to her alive. You are safe, so long as you do not defy me. But your friends? They are not so important to my mistress. They will die first. Then, when you have no one left to harm with your *protection*, you will come to her, begging for forgiveness."

Tenn looked at Matthias.

"If you hurt them, any of them, I'll kill you."

Matthias just laughed and dropped the journal at Tenn's feet.

"Perhaps," he said. "But the threat of death means nothing to one like me." He leaned in close and whispered into Tenn's ear. "Either come to me or do not. I'll find you no matter what. And when I do, I will kill them. One by one. And you will watch them scream."

His fingers dug into Tenn's shoulder. Pain coursed through him, and the dark room bled black.

* * *

Cold sweat coated Tenn's skin when he woke, and for a moment, he had no clue where he was. Then he blinked and realized the rumbling was from the car and the warm pillow beneath his head was Jarrett's lap. He looked up into Jarrett's face. He was sound asleep and peaceful.

"Bad dreams?" Dreya asked, peering back to face him. She was still in the passenger seat, Devon behind the wheel.

"I guess you could say that," he replied. He slowly forced himself up to sitting, every joint in his tired body reminding him that he was not built to be sleeping in the backseat of a car.

"You mumbled," Devon said. Which, in Tenn's opinion, was a rather ironic thing to say.

"Sorry," he replied instead.

Matthias's words dug into his skull. He hadn't seen that old journal since Silveron, but he knew deep in his gut that the words were true. What did that mean? Had Matthias found the journal? Or was the man able to claw into Tenn's past and read every line of his memory? His chest constricted; if Matthias could read Tenn's mind, whatever he learned would be fed right back to Leanna.

Tenn looked to Jarrett. He hadn't had anything or anyone in his life he'd worried about losing since he'd found his parents torn apart in the garden shed. Not until now.

"It's Matthias," Tenn whispered.

Devon immediately swerved, and Dreya's head jerked back. Jarrett mumbled in his sleep.

"Not here!" Tenn said, fervent but quietly. Devon let out an audible sigh. "He… He's in my dreams."

There was a long silence. Tenn immediately regretted his

decision. He fully expected Devon to turn the car around, or for them to kick him out. If Matthias was in his dreams, none of what they said was private.

"For how long?" Dreya finally asked.

"Just a few days. Just after…after Water…"

She swallowed.

"Then we must be more careful," she said. "If he is watching…"

He caught the subtext; she was grateful she hadn't said where they were going. And she was wondering just how deep they'd gotten.

"Can you stop it?" Tenn asked. He hated how his voice cracked.

Neither of them answered. That was answer enough.

"It's getting worse, isn't it?" Dreya asked after a while. It was barely above a whisper. "Water. It is growing stronger. More violent."

Tenn nodded, wondering how much he'd said in his sleep, or how much she felt from her own attunement to the Sphere.

"We thought the end had come with the Resurrection," she said gravely. "Now I am not so sure. The world feels once more like it did before the Howls came. An ending is coming. Even the Spheres are calling out to it."

In spite of the heat pumping through the vents, he shivered.

"Does this have to do with the Witches? With our mission?"

She nodded.

"In a sense." Her words were slow, picked carefully to not give too much away. "The Witches are tied to the very fabric of the world. They understand the Spheres on a level deeper than most. For them, magic is a religion, a way of life, rather than a tool to kill. They were the first to know of the Spheres, and look what the rest of the world did with their discovery. Since then, they have hidden themselves, lest their knowledge be bastardized again."

They hit a bump that Tenn prayed wasn't a body. Jarrett snorted himself awake and looked around, eyes immediately wide.

"What was that?" he asked.

"Pothole," Devon replied.

Jarrett opened his mouth like he was going to ask more, then thought better of it.

"Did I miss anything?" he asked instead.

"Just scenery," Dreya replied. She looked back to him. Her eyes flickered to Tenn—would she mention Matthias to him? Should Tenn? "It is almost morning. And we are on half a tank."

Jarrett nodded. "Let's stop soon, then. You guys need to sleep, and I don't know how to drive." He looked to Tenn. "Do you?"

Tenn shook his head. He was supposed to get his learner's permit the summer after his first year at Silveron. Like so many things, that had never come to pass.

"That settles it," Jarrett said. "We'll stop at dawn. Find a strip of cars so we can transfer, get a few hours of sleep. Then we're off again. Matthias won't even know we've been here."

Tenn cringed.

Matthias would always know where they were. So long as Tenn was around, none of them were safe.

Tenn had become used to thwarted plans, so when they stopped by an abandoned traffic jam a little after sunrise, he expected the worst. Jarrett scouted the area with Air while they sat in the parked car, the engine rumbling and the CD still on repeat.

"All clear," Jarrett said, Air winking out in his throat. Devon turned off the ignition, and the sudden silence was deafening.

"Are you sure this is smart?" Tenn asked. Now that he knew Matthias was on his heels, rest was the last thing on his mind. No matter how much his body and Spheres craved it. The Spheres normally gave the body power as energy centers, much like chakras were said to do in Eastern philosophy, but when they were used too deeply, they needed rest or nourishment to recover.

Not even magic was abundant in this world.

"There's nothing around for miles," Jarrett replied. "I'll take first watch. Gods know I got enough sleep—I forgot how easily driving knocks me out. You guys rest. You need it."

The twins didn't need any more coaxing, even with the knowledge of Matthias's watchful eye. It seemed like nothing could disturb them. They both reclined their seats and curled onto their sides. Like true warriors used to the road, they were asleep in moments.

"You, too, Tenn," Jarrett said. "You've barely slept at all the last few days."

"I'm not tired," Tenn said. His yawn betrayed him.

"Like hell," Jarrett replied. He smiled.

Tenn wanted to tell him about Matthias haunting his dreams. He wanted to say he didn't feel safe, that it was better for everyone if he stayed awake, but before he could say any of that, Jarrett had gently pulled him down, resting Tenn's head once more in his lap. Jarrett ran his fingers through Tenn's hair. Chills curled down his skin while heat flowed in his chest.

"Don't worry," Jarrett whispered, looking right into Tenn's eyes. Tenn could stare at those blue eyes for eternity. "I'll protect you."

And maybe it was stupid, but that was enough. Tenn closed his eyes and said nothing.

He knew Jarrett couldn't protect him from Matthias, but there was a comfort in Jarrett believing he could.

He'd let them both hold on to that dream for as long as possible.

CHAPTER THIRTEEN

TENN DIDN'T DREAM. BY THE TIME HE WOKE, THE sky had darkened to slate gray, and the twins had already prepared a scant dinner of warm tea and biscuits. Tenn wolfed it down; it wasn't enough to assuage Earth, but it was something. By the time they were on the road again, he was beginning to feel more human.

They switched SUVs and drove for a few more hours, navigating around stopped cars and overturned semis, while a new collection of CDs played. Finally, they passed into Michigan. The sky outside had gone from gray to pitch-black almost as swiftly as his mood had when they saw the welcome sign.

Then it began to snow.

Slow, at first—big thick flakes that drifted slowly in the evening haze. Then more, heavier flecks of white streaking like falling stars in their headlamps. With every mile, the snow grew thicker. With every mile, the ground cover became worse. Clearly this wasn't the first snow this area had seen and, without plows, the road quickly became treacherous. Devon slowed the car, but even that wasn't enough to keep him from slipping around on the asphalt like a drunken teenager. He managed to avoid the stopped cars that hulked like igloos. Tenn gripped his fists tight to his lap, tried to keep his breathing calm and his jaw relaxed. After everything they'd been through, he would have found it terribly humorous if he died in a car crash.

Devon slowed the car to a crawl. Tenn wanted to beg the guy to clear the snow with Fire or even Air, but to use magic out here would give them away quicker than the dull thrum of their engine.

Tenn kept his eyes on the horizon, on the trees that loomed pitch-black in the deepening dark.

The headlights caught on a graffiti'd billboard. He knew it before the words resolved through the swathes of snow.

Silveron Academy
Empowering Youth
for an Empowered Future

Water surged at the sign, at the familiar crest, at the pictures of campus. Water surged, and even though he wrestled it down, he couldn't keep it from spilling between his fingers.

"Your father and I went to school around here," Mom says.

Dad had stayed back home—couldn't get the day off work— so it's just the two of them heading up to Michigan to check out Silveron. He still can't believe his mother had not only agreed to let him apply, but had offered to drive him the eight hours to check it out when he was accepted.

Hell, he still can't believe he was accepted.

He doubts he will ever forget seeing that large white envelope on the kitchen counter, his name printed in royal blue. He will never forget the feeling of his heart in his throat and his hands shaking as he opened the envelope and pulled out the letter. Congratulations! You have been accepted to Silveron Academy. Together, we will create a magical future.

A magical future.

So why does he feel—even now, even as they drive—like he's giving something else up? He's supposed to be excited...and he is. He just didn't realize how excited he could be while feeling terrified at the same time.

He stares out the passenger window as the cornfields roll into evergreen forests and the air stops smelling like pollution and starts to smell, well, green. It makes his heart swell a little bit. It's also a reminder that even the scents here will be new and different.

"You're going to love it out here," Mom says. *She reaches over and puts a hand on his shoulder.*

"Mom?" *he asks. His voice sounds small in the silent car. Why does it sound so small? He has the opportunity to learn magic.*

"Yeah, sweetie?"

"Do you think I'm making the wrong decision?"

She glances over at him, then looks back to the road. She doesn't take her hand away.

"I think you're making the best possible decision you can." *She pauses, considering her words. He glances at her and tries to memorize the lines of her face, the way the light catches on her hair in the sunset. Even now, it makes him miss her.* "There's nothing back home for you. This is your chance to make something big *out of your life. I know you. You'd never forgive yourself if you let it pass by. You're meant for bigger things."*

He sighs. Bigger things. He can't think of anything bigger than being one of the first students at Silveron, being among the first to learn how to use magic. It's the opportunity of a lifetime, the promise of an exciting career and a ticket out of his backwoods town. He knows she's right: there isn't anything back home for him.

Besides, this is his chance to make her proud. That, perhaps, is the most important thing of all.

I will do something great with my life, he thinks. That will make this worth it.

He goes back to staring out the window. He tries to find the stirrings of excitement he'd had at discovering his acceptance. Instead, he finds only the fear. He knows he will accept Silveron's offer. He knows he will spend his high school years here.

He knows that whatever they find when they reach the Academy will be his future. He just hopes it's one worth the struggle.

With a furious wrench, Tenn pushed Water back down into submission. It seemed to squirm against his concentration. Silveron was still a hundred miles and a few hours away, but that didn't calm the memories. The closer they got to that cursed Academy, the more Water wanted out. It recognized home. It recognized the beginning of his pain. He gritted his teeth and didn't relax until the Sphere finally died down.

"You okay?" Jarrett asked, squeezing Tenn's thigh.

"Yeah," he said. "Just…memories."

Jarrett nodded like he understood, but Tenn knew he didn't. Jarrett was an Air user: for him, memories and emotions weren't tactile things. That wasn't what scared him, though. He'd thought that Jarrett's presence could calm Water's raging, but Water wasn't giving in. He should have known it wouldn't be that easy.

"We are going to have to park soon," Dreya said. "We are nearly out of gas, and the roads are becoming impassible."

Jarrett nodded.

"Any towns nearby?"

"Yes." Air glowed faintly in her throat as she searched—just enough to see, but not enough to be seen from far away. "We will come to one in a few minutes. It is deserted."

"Good. Let's find a place there and settle in for the night. No use being outside in the snow if we don't have to."

Dreya nodded and turned back to quietly confer with Devon. They pulled off at the next exit and drove into town.

Tenn couldn't see anything in the darkness, just the snow slashing through their headlamps, so he opened to Earth and pushed his senses out like sonar. The place was small, barely a handful of houses and commercial buildings. *Podunk*, his mother would have called it. Much like his own hometown.

They pulled to a stop in front of an old farmhouse at the end of a winding drive, the tangled path and fading facade illuminated in the headlights. The house was huge—three stories tall with peeling whitewashed siding and large picture windows. A wraparound porch stuck out from the front, complete with broken rocking chairs and a swing. Something about it made Tenn's gut twist: a familiarity, a call. Even though he was positive he'd never been there before.

"This'll work," Jarrett said. Air glowed in his throat as well, and Tenn had no doubt he was scanning the interior, making sure the place really was as abandoned as expected. The fact that they hadn't run into any wayward Howls was unusual.

The cold must have driven them to shelter, whatever that was to the undead, and he couldn't imagine any necromancers traipsing around in this weather.

The first snow. When Tenn was younger, it would have been cause to run around outside, catching snowflakes on his tongue. He'd long since outgrown that, but staring at the snow-coated house through the beams of their headlights brought a little bit back. Some trace of antiquity, of perfection, even if his gut was saying the place was eerie. If not for the obvious disrepair, the scene could have been from a greeting card.

Devon killed the engine and they got out, grabbed their things and then trudged through the snow up to the front door. Tiny orbs of light hovered around Devon as he opened to Fire, snow hissing against their glow. Everything was white and black, and it made Tenn feel like they were in some vintage fairy-tale film. Or noir horror.

The front porch creaked under their combined weight. Definitely noir horror.

Jarrett pushed the door open, the hinges shrill, the only sounds beyond the gusting wind. The air inside smelled stale from years of neglect.

As they walked in, Devon shot lights into every room, upstairs and down. Dreya and Jarrett went off to investigate the kitchen and bedrooms and to scavenge for provisions, while Tenn stalked down another hall alone. In here, sheltered from the wind and snow, he could hear every shudder of the house, every throb of his blood. He paused by a door, listening to whistling on the other side. Pressing his hand to the ice-encrusted knob, he opened the door and stepped inside.

Immediately, he knew he didn't want to be in there. He'd

never really liked abandoned places. To him, they smelled like ghosts. This room especially. Mainly because it howled like one.

Two orbs of light hovered up near the crystal chandelier, making everything in the dining room a pallid grayscale. The air was even colder: with the great picture windows in the far wall shattered, a frigid breeze gusted in, billowing the long drapes in perfect horror-story undulations. What he had first mistaken for ice on the carpet was actually shards of glass, all glittering in the half-light like crystal knives. Everything was broken or flung about, from the overturned dining table to the chairs reduced to kindling to the plates and cups dashed to pieces as fine as snow.

His fingers shook, and not from the cold. The air in here just felt *wrong*. Like it carried the rawness of an old wound, a scab peeled back from flesh.

Almost against his will, his fingers trailed along the overturned table.

Water uncurled in a wave.

"What the hell is that?" the woman asks. "James, did you hear that?"

Screams pierce the night. All close. Too close. Screams, and the thunder of gunshots.

The man's eyes are wide as he looks from his wife and kids to the window, to the flashes of light that last far too long for lightning or rifles.

"Stay here," he says, his voice frantic. He pushes himself from the table, toppling his chair, and runs to the hall. The woman stands and gathers her two sons, pulling them back to the wall.

Their wide eyes reflect the light and chaos outside, but in here, they are so silent they can hear the rapid flutter of their breath.

The man is back in a moment. He holds a shotgun.

"Get to the basement," he says. "Quick."

They turn. The basement is safety. It's where they've gone for tornado sirens. It's where they can escape.

But before they can move, something crashes through the window, sends glass screaming through the room. They flinch. Cower. It isn't a brick or bomb landing before them. It's a human. He stands slowly, unfolding himself until he towers above them all. Save for his height, there's nothing to make him stand out—faded blue jeans, old flannel. Eighteen, maybe. But his eyes...

His eyes keep them from running. They are the most piercing blue.

Those eyes stop the breath in their throats.

"Good evening," he says calmly, as though he hasn't just crashed through a window. The mother pulls her boys close, and it is only now that she realizes the boy hasn't been cut by his entrance. The husband moves in front of his family. A shepherd, vainly trying to defend his flock. "I thought I might join you for dinner."

"Get out," the husband says. His words waver. Outside, another scream rips through the air, cut off with a gurgle that makes the youngest boy shudder. "Whatever the hell you are, get out."

The intruder smiles.

"That is no way to treat a guest." His voice has a slow, Southern drawl. Charming. And dangerous.

The stranger steps forward.

The man shoots.

The blast from the gun is too loud for the room, too awful for the place they've quietly made their home. The echo is the nail in the coffin, the trumpet blaring that their quiet life is dead.

Blood splatters across their carpet, across the drapes. The boy staggers. Clutches his hands to his chest. But he only falters for a moment. When he looks from his bloody hands to the husband, his smile is gone. His eyes glow like the hottest part of a flame.

The man had raised his children to be decent and God-fearing, but the evil that cracks through the boy's face is a force no faith can withstand. The man tries to reload. He knows he has damned them all, and already he is praying for forgiveness.

Salvation.

The boy snarls as his blood drips to the floor in deafening pats. His wound is already smaller. His flesh knits itself together, bloody and raw. When he speaks, the drawl is gone, replaced with a grit from the bowels of Hades.

"And here I was going to be merciful."

The boy inhales.

It is like plummeting into the farthest reaches of space.

The man drops his gun and reaches for his throat, choking and gagging as his eyes bulge and his family falls beside him. They can't even cry out as their lungs collapse. As the intruder pulls the air from their chests with a single breath.

The boy smiles again. There is blood in that smile. And hunger. He steps over to them. Just out of reach of their clawing hands, their rigid fingers. He smiles his demon smile and pulls the youngest child to his feet.

"I think I deserve dessert first, don't you?" he asks, looking down at the father. He wants the father to understand. He wants the father to suffer the most. He pulls the boy's face close to his and *inhales. The kid's eyes widen and roll back, bulging; his skin pales, and turns blue. His gasp is a rattle, a gurgle of bleeding lungs.*

One long, last breath, and the child is dead.

The demon drops him to the ground.

"You will watch them die, old man," he says, kneeling before the husband. His eyes dart to the rest of his family. "One by one." Another flash of light outside, and the boy hesitates. Looks back to the engulfing darkness outside. "Actually, no." He reaches out and runs a finger on the man's jaw. "I think I will let you kill them. How does that sound?" He stands and walks to the window, calls out to the night beyond. "Matthias! I have a new convert!"

The demon turns. The hole in his chest has closed.

"Oh, we are about to have some fun. At least, I am."

Someone slapped Tenn's face, jarring the scene from his head.

Memories swirled in Tenn's skull as Water slowly released its grip, sloshing back into silence in the pit of his stomach. His ears rang with the echo of gunshots and screams. So many screams. *Matthias. Matthias is coming.*

"Are you okay?" Jarrett asked. "You look like you've seen a ghost."

It was only then that the room swam back into focus. Pain lanced through his hands where he'd fallen on shards of window. His blood had turned the stained carpet crimson. He shook his head and forced himself up to sitting. He focused on his breath, on being here. Present. There were no bodies in the room. No screams or gunshots outside the window. Just him and Jarrett in the dining room. Tenn opened to Earth and pushed the power through his palms, healing the lacerations as pieces of glass plopped into the chilling blood like tears.

"What was that?" Tenn asked. He raised a shaky hand to his head. The ringing was worse, along with that train-coming-down-the-tracks vibration that always signaled a migraine. When he looked at Jarrett, the guy faded in and out of focus.

"What are you—"

"We heard a crash," Dreya said, skidding into the room. Her eyes took in the scene in one quick sweep. "What happened?"

Tenn closed his eyes. The lights in the room were so *bright*. "I saw...something." The scene played itself out over and over behind his eyelids. It wasn't just a vision. He had been there, standing in the corner, watching the family die. He could hear them gasping. He could *feel* their panic, their dying emotions. He was there. They were here. It didn't feel like the past at all.

"What did you see?" Dreya asked. Her voice was closer. He didn't open his eyes, but he heard her kneel down beside him, her jeans crunching in the glass. She put one hand on the back of his neck. Her touch was cool and tingled with magic.

"I saw them die," he whispered. "The family that lived here. I saw them get attacked by a Breathless One. And then he called out for Matthias."

Jarrett was on his feet in a second.

"Here?"

"No. I mean, yes. But not now. It was like a vision...but stronger. Water opened up, and I saw it. No. I was *there*. I felt them. All of it. I felt them gagging for air."

"Emotional transference," Dreya whispered.

Whatever magic she'd been working had done its job. The pain in Tenn's temples subsided. He opened his eyes and squinted. The twins were lost in a silent conversation, staring at each other as though their expressions could convey stories.

He desperately wanted to know what they were thinking, just as much as he never wanted to know.

"What?" Jarrett and Tenn asked at the same time.

Again, another glance between the twins. When Dreya spoke, she didn't look away from her brother. Devon's eyes were furrowed with concern, and he kept looking over to Tenn like he was a newfound threat.

"Emotional transference," she repeated. She sighed. "It's rare. Very rare. But sometimes, if you use a Sphere for long enough, it becomes sensitive to the external world. Normally, the Spheres respond to inner triggers—emotional responses, like fight or flight. Or they are willed into use through training. But if a Sphere is sensitive enough, it can pick up triggers embedded in the nature of things. Strong emotions, from memories ingrained in the wood of a place." She trailed her finger along the same dusty path he had. If she saw anything, she didn't show it.

"How do you know this?" Tenn asked. "They never taught that at Silveron."

Then again, there was a lot he hadn't learned at Silveron. Maybe because the training was cut short. Maybe because his teachers didn't actually know.

"Because we get it, too, at times," she said. She sounded sad. "Fire and Water, they're emotional Spheres. They resonate highly with the pain and anger in the world. You're just able to tune into it more than most."

"How do I control it?"

Dreya shrugged. "You don't. Any more than you can control your inner workings. When the world wants to speak to you, it will use whatever tools it has. And Water is the most vicious tool of all."

"Can I stop it?" he asked.

"Yes," she said.

"How?"

It was Devon who responded.

"You die."

CHAPTER FOURTEEN

TENN SAT ON A STOOL IN THE CORNER OF THE kitchen while Jarrett cooked. Pretty much everything in the house had expired, but they'd managed to find some canned carrots and dried beans that still looked good. Dreya sat at the island in the center of the room, idly chopping a few wild onions and fueling the fire simmering under the large cook pot Jarrett was stirring. Devon had gone out into the night— who knows where—and no one had questioned him. Tenn had a feeling Dreya knew precisely where her brother was at all times, and that was enough for him.

He still couldn't force out the memory of the family's last moments. There was no telling what other horrors he would have seen if Jarrett hadn't snapped him out of it. Matthias had been here, in this very house. Almost like he was hunting Tenn's past.

He shuddered.

He'd never encountered a Breathless One in real life, but

the memory had been enough to tell him he never wanted to. Kravens were the most common Howl, the Sphere of Earth being the quickest to deplete. From there, the Howls got more deadly, more humanoid and thankfully more rare. He'd encountered a fair number of bloodlings in the field. Tomás had been his first incubus. But a Breathless One…a creature who could kill crowds with a single inhalation…that was the stuff of nightmares. His lungs still burned with the trace of memory.

At least no necromancer had learned how to tap into the Sphere of Maya. He couldn't even imagine what sort of Howl that would breed.

For a while he could only sit there, imagining the rest of his life like this—falling apart whenever he stepped into a room touched by tragedy, reliving every nightmare. The States were scabbed with pain and hatred. There was no way he could manage if this emotional transference shit kept happening.

Still, if the twins could do it, so could he. *You're not as strong as they are*, Water hissed within him. *You'll succumb eventually.*

He pushed the dark thoughts from his head and focused on Jarrett, who had taken off his coat and was dancing around the kitchen with his long white sleeves pushed up to his biceps. More scars laced his pale forearms, crossed over his single tattoo. Every once in a while, Jarrett would glance over and smile. Every time, Tenn blushed and looked away. He was already dreaming of Jarrett in their own kitchen, making coffee and reading the paper. It was a beautiful image, even if it was an impossibility.

Then again, maybe Jarrett was right. Maybe he *did* have to envision a better future. Maybe it *did* make everything else more manageable.

The strangest part was the ease with which Tenn could visualize that future. Even before the Resurrection, he'd been a fatalist: couldn't imagine reaching his next birthday, or what college would look like. A few of those fears had been realized, sure. So why was it so simple to build a warm and happy home for him and Jarrett in his head now? Jarrett, whom he barely knew? Water usually curled doubt and questions through his gut, but even it was quiet. He might not know if Jarrett was right for him, but Jarrett was here, in this kitchen, and that had to mean something. Something that a cold, desperate part of Tenn wanted badly to discover.

The near silence of the kitchen felt comfortable and calming—the sound of simmering soup, the chop of metal on wood. After everything that had happened, this alone threw him for the biggest loop. This was all so normal, so fucking *familiar*, that it hurt worse than any stab wound. They'd driven here in a car and, sure, they'd used magic to get the car running, and even now Dreya's chest was glowing red with the thin flicker of flame she funneled into the stove's burner, but it was so easy—the normalcy, the ability to forget that at any moment another Howl might burst through the window and try to kill them just as it had in Tenn's vision. They all knew the world was no longer safe, but this felt safe. It felt like nothing could possibly be wrong in the world. And that was the most dangerous thing of all.

While Tenn was lost in his thoughts, Jarrett came over holding a wooden spoon.

"Try it," he offered.

Tenn took a sip and smiled. "You make an excellent housewife," he said. He hadn't meant to say the words he'd been imagining, but Jarrett—rather than freaking out—just smiled.

"Always knew that was my calling in life." Jarrett moved back to the stove and said, "Dinner will be ready soon. Is Devon nearby?"

Dreya nodded. She was reading a cookbook she'd found on the shelf. It was the last thing Tenn would ever expect to see her reading. She seemed more like the Foucault and Kierkegaard type, not that Tenn had ever actually read either of them. He'd been too busy studying magic to focus on literature.

"He's just outside rummaging. He'll be in soon."

Sure enough, Devon returned a few minutes later, carrying a few sacks of stolen goods that clunked when he set them down.

"Food," he said. "And clothes."

"Good work," Jarrett said. He ladled out a few porcelain bowls of soup and passed them around the island. No one suggested eating in the dining room. Tenn doubted any of them would go in there again.

"You seem quite happy, all things considered," Dreya said to Jarrett, one eyebrow raised. She took a delicate sip of her soup.

Jarrett just shrugged.

"It's not very often I get to spend a day without having to kill something. I count every one of those days as a blessing."

"The day is not over yet," Dreya said.

Tenn fully expected the dinner to be held in silence—after all, the twins were far from talkative and Tenn was a close runner-up—but Jarrett managed to get everyone talking and laughing. Even Devon.

Later, Jarrett found a bottle of whiskey and spent a good

twenty minutes teaching them how to drink it (*A drop of water at most. No mixers, no ice. Take a sip on the tip of your tongue first. Let the flavors blossom. Then drink in earnest.*) and by the time the bottle was halfway gone, Devon was in tears on the ground, laughing his ass off over a joke Tenn had been too tipsy to follow. Dreya started singing, opening to Air, and she made the spoons and napkins dance around the room erratically, her hiccups making them fall. It looked like some strange Disney montage. Tenn hadn't laughed so much or so hard in his life. There hadn't been time. He leaned against Jarrett, with Jarrett's arm slung over his shoulders.

Life felt warm and golden. Life felt possible.

They sat around the table for hours, telling stories of life before the Resurrection. Well, Jarrett and Tenn did. Jarrett told them about growing up near the beach in St. Augustine, Florida. Days surfing, nights spent riding around. He talked about Silveron, about all the trouble he'd gotten into. Tenn chimed in on occasion to add details about professors or the color of the dorm hallways or when sign-in was. At times, it became their own little conversation—just like on the bed before—but the twins didn't seem to mind. Dreya watched with excited, glossy eyes. Even Devon muttered that he wished he'd gone to school there.

Sometimes, when Jarrett would quiet, Tenn would pick up the slack. He talked about growing up in Iowa. He talked about his dying town, about playing video games with friends. About nights spent watching horror movies and drinking too much soda, and days hungover on sugar and junk food. About staring out at the Mississippi at two in the morning, watching the stars slowly scratch across the sky. He talked about why he'd decided to go to Silveron—to find something new, to do something big with his life. And because he always wanted to be a wizard.

He talked about a life that he'd forgotten he actually had.

Eventually, Dreya told stories about the places she'd traveled with her adopted, fashion-designer mother. Devon chipped in details—the hotels they stayed in, the dinners they had—but for the most part, he stayed silent, giggling to himself and sending small flares of fire dancing into the air. She spoke of visiting beautiful fabric shops in New York and Milan, of making her first dress at the age of eight and jumping into cosplay immediately after. She said she always had the best costumes—not because she was good, but because her mother always helped. *I did, too,* Devon chirped in at one point. Dreya had just smiled and patted him on the shoulder and went back to talking about her dreams of being a major designer. And chemist. Because even as a kid she had been keenly interested in the nature of things.

She made it sound grand, all of it. Like she had been the player in some beautiful story. Which made Tenn wonder—albeit hazily—what had happened to her in the interim to turn her into a battle-hardened warrior? She didn't speak of magic or her training or the Witches. Not once. And Tenn was perfectly fine with it staying that way.

The night wore on, and Devon fell asleep in his chair, signaled by a napkin catching ablaze from a wayward spark of his.

Dreya smiled and shook her head, looking over to her brother through her pale white hair.

"It was the hardest on him," she whispered, her smile dropping, becoming forced. "I hope you understand that. It was the hardest on him. And I don't want him to experience it again."

Jarrett's mirth slipped, as well.

"You know it wouldn't… I wouldn't have done it. If I didn't have to."

She nodded. "I know."

Tenn looked between them. What were they talking about?

"You should sleep," Jarrett said. "We all should."

Silently, Dreya stood and looped Devon's arm over her shoulders. It was such a tender movement; it made Tenn's heart break. What did it feel like to have someone you wanted to protect? Someone whose life meant more than your own?

Jarrett stood and helped her move the mumbling Devon. Tenn watched him. The way Jarrett bent and moved, the small ways his face changed depending on his thoughts… Tenn already felt he could trace Jarrett's image in memory.

Maybe Tenn was starting to understand again what it meant to have someone he didn't want to lose.

He followed the three of them up the stairs, though he diverted and went into one of the smaller bedrooms. It was dark, and now that the flickering lights in the hall had faded, he had to navigate by Earth and feel alone. There were teddy bears along on bookshelf. A pile of clothes in the closet. A bed, made tight and neat like a hotel. It made him smile. He sat down; the bed reminded him of how his mom had made her bed. Tears welled up in his eyes.

"You okay?" Jarrett asked.

Tenn sniffed and wiped away the tears. Amazingly, Water didn't rage—especially strange, since Tenn wasn't forcing it into submission.

"Yeah," Tenn replied. For the most part, he actually meant it.

Jarrett sat down next to him. In the frigid room, Jarrett's heat was like a furnace.

"You're freezing," Jarrett said. He rubbed his hand along Tenn's back. Tenn practically purred.

"I run cold."

Jarrett sighed, like there was something deep weighing on his mind. When he spoke, though, he kept his voice light.

"So what do you think? Want to move to a city or the country?"

It was so absurd Tenn laughed aloud.

"What's so funny?" Jarrett asked.

"Sorry," he replied, but chuckles still built up in the back of his throat.

"I'm serious," Jarrett said. "I figured you'd be more of a country boy. And besides, every Earth user I know prefers staying away from large groups of people."

Tenn nuzzled his face against Jarrett's shoulder.

"Yeah, I think I'd like that," he admitted. "A place in the middle of the woods, maybe by a stream. Nothing too fancy, of course... I just need a fireplace and some trees and I'm happy."

"Dog or cat?"

"Both."

He never thought he'd have this conversation again. Tenn had only had a few friends at the Academy, but he and one girl—Amanda—would go out for lunch every once in a while and chat about their dream houses. He'd always had this beautiful log cabin in mind.

This was the first time he'd let himself dare believe that he could one day occupy it along with someone else.

"I'd love a wolfhound myself," Jarrett mused. "Don't know where you'd get one anymore, though."

Tenn didn't want to wonder if there were any more wolfhounds left in the world, so he pushed the conversation down a different path.

"What about you? City or country?"

"Oh, I'd be okay with the country. So long as it was near enough to a city. Culture and all."

Tenn laughed.

"Yeah," he said, "can't miss out on all those concerts and museums."

"Hey, art's important," Jarrett said. "Art and love are what we fight for."

Tenn sealed his lips. *Fight for* was just a reminder that this little fantasy was just that—a fantasy. There'd never be a cabin in the woods or an apartment in the city, no black-tie affairs at the symphony or fancy dinner parties.

It made him sink a little lower.

"Hey," Jarrett said, noticing the swift decline. He shifted a bit. "Don't go down there."

"Sorry," Tenn replied. "It's just…"

Jarrett nodded, their foreheads pressing together. "I know," he said. "But no matter what the future looks like, I'm still going to fight for it. So long as it includes you."

Then he leaned in a bit farther and kissed Tenn on the lips.

Tenn was still swirling down in the cesspool of his thoughts, but that kiss was a buoy, a tie to dry land. It filled him with hope, with light, and it made the world golden again, gilded in a way that lasted longer than his intoxication.

And he knew, so long as he had Jarrett, that thread would always be there. There'd always be a way out. A way forward.

The war would always be worth winning.

CHAPTER FIFTEEN

TENN WOKE WELL BEFORE DAWN, WHEN THE SKY
outside was just starting to turn blue with light. His heart
raced, but he couldn't remember his dreams or why he'd woken
up with sweat drenching his skin. Jarrett sprawled out beside
him, his breath deep and regular. Despite the fear racing in
his chest, the last few hours bled through his memory in a
golden hum. There had never been any question about Jarrett sharing his bed. Just as there had never been a question
as to what would happen.

He lay there for a few seconds, watching Jarrett breathe,
watching his bare chest rise and fall, letting his own nightmarish heart settle. Tenn reached over, gently traced a scar on
Jarrett's pec, let his fingers memorize the guy's smooth skin, his
heat. Jarrett mumbled something and curled over, toward Tenn.
Tenn let himself be swept up, encircled. Jarrett even smelled
like home, in a way he couldn't quite place. He kissed Jarrett's
muscled forearm. Somehow, that brought to mind Tomás.

He knew the Kin would be back. He knew he was still a target. But he wasn't as afraid, not anymore. He wasn't alone. And, frankly, he had someone that put even the incubus to shame.

Someday, though, he would have to tell Jarrett about Tomás. He would *have* to. He just wanted to ensure he was ready—he had to be able to kill the incubus before Tomás could kill anyone else. It made him burn inside, this secret, but at least he knew it was keeping the others safe.

Still, something tugged at the edge of his consciousness. Something that sounded like fading screams.

He uncurled himself from Jarrett's arms, then pushed himself out of bed and wrapped a fallen quilt around his shoulders before padding over to the window as silently as possible. Moonlight peeked out from the clouds. Everything glowed silver in those patches of moonlight, gently covered with snow—the farmhouses, the gas station, the trees. Straight out of a painting.

He readjusted the quilt and began to turn from the window when something shifted in the corner of his vision.

A shadow darted between the trees.

Tenn opened to Earth. Blood thundered in his ears as he searched...and found it. He'd hoped it was an animal—maybe a deer or a raccoon.

It wasn't.

It was humanoid. Broken and bent.

"Kravens!" he yelled.

Jarrett woke in an instant. Tenn leaped over to the bed and threw on his clothes. Jarrett was right behind him.

Tenn wanted to scream as they thundered through the

house, rousing the twins and trying to get their hazy brains into action. This wasn't supposed to happen. Not like this. Not this soon. He just wanted one night with Jarrett. One goddamned night of calm and warmth before the blood had to fall again. Tenn grabbed his staff from the hall and raced up the stairs to the roof. Blood pounded in his ears. He wanted to scream. He wanted to make the Howls pay for ruining the last few hours of perfection. Outside, the screams of the Dark Lady's horde pierced the pastoral night.

"How many?" Dreya asked.

They stood on a rooftop balcony, one of those stargazing platforms no one ever really used. The frozen air made their breath come out in tiny clouds. All four of them were open to their Spheres. Tenn knew perfectly well that she could sense that they were surrounded. She was just trying to make conversation while they waited for the enemy to attack. The fact that the beasts were just out there biding their time made Tenn's hair stand on end. The Howls were waiting, moonlight making their gray, twisted bodies even more ghastly. Howls didn't wait. Not unless they were under strict order.

"Hundreds," Jarrett said. "We're surrounded."

Tenn's dream filtered into his thoughts, a terrible déjà vu. *"It's almost like you want to be found..."* Matthias's warning chilled its way up Tenn's already frozen spine, sending a new wave of shivers across his skin.

He'll never give up, Tenn thought. He looked to his companions. *He'll never give up, and you'll all suffer for it.*

"Why aren't they attacking?" Jarrett asked.

"Because it's not an attack," Tenn said. "It's a safeguard."

The Howls stared up at the rooftop like grotesque marble statues. He could smell the rot of their flesh even from here.

"He doesn't want us to flee," Tenn continued. The others didn't ask who he was talking about. They knew. "He's coming back for me."

As if to accentuate the point, the kravens below them began to part. Someone else moved out there, a darker shadow in the silvered landscape coming steadily toward them.

"And so we meet again," Matthias called. It echoed through the air, amplified by magic. Tenn could see the Spheres burning in Matthias's body, glowing brighter the closer he got. Other flickers of power manifested around them. Each one sent another wave of dread through him. The Spheres of the encroaching necromancers burned like gas lamps in the shadows. Dozens of them.

"As you can see," Matthias said, "we have you completely surrounded. There will be no easy escape like last time."

His feet crunched up the snowy drive, until he was only a few yards away from the SUV.

"Stop right there," Jarrett said. He pushed a bit of power through the air and a gust of snow kicked up around Matthias, sending him back a few steps. Matthias chuckled. The laugh was colder than ice.

"You have guts," the man said. Tenn could see him clearly now: just as dapper as ever. Just as deadly. "And soon, my minions will feast on them."

"What do you want?" Jarrett asked, clearly trying to bide time and figure out an escape.

"I think you know what I want," Matthias said. "Hand over the boy and I'll make sure they kill you quickly. You defied me when I was prepared to let you live. I do not like being defied. This is my final mercy."

"Fuck your mercy," Jarrett hissed. "You aren't getting him."

Tenn put a hand on Jarrett's shoulder. His stomach was twisting double time. "Jarrett, don't. I'm going. This ends to-night."

Jarrett turned his fury on him and pushed off his hand. Air burned in his throat, and Tenn knew the guy he fell for was gone for the moment, replaced by a machine of cold calculation and ferocity.

"Like hell you will. I'm not letting you go. Not without a fight."

"If you two are done with your lovers' quarrel," Matthias said, "I believe Tenn and I have some unfinished business."

Resolve settled itself into Tenn's bones. If he went down there, maybe the others could escape. Maybe he could distract Matthias long enough to leave that window open. He looked at Jarrett and felt tears burn in the back of his eyes. He wouldn't let Jarrett die for him. Not today.

Jarrett took his hand.

"We fight together," Jarrett whispered. He wasn't looking at Tenn. He was looking at the twins.

"I wouldn't recommend—" Matthias began, but the scream of a storm cut him short.

The world erupted in white.

Power swirled from the twins, snow raging in an instantaneous blizzard, the moon blacked out in a breath.

"We have to get out of here," Jarrett yelled through the roar of snow. The house stood in the eye of the storm, the sky above them clear of clouds. It was only a matter of seconds before the necromancers would launch a counterattack, before Matthias regained his bearings and brought hell raining down on them.

"There's no way," Tenn said. "He'll follow us. He'll always follow us. I have to give myself up."

"This is all very touching," came Matthias's voice. Light flared in the heart of the blizzard, a strobe that floated up into the air. Matthias was silhouetted inside it, the storm raging around him. "But if that is the best you can do, I'm afraid you are wasting your time."

Snow turned to flame.

Dreya and Devon gasped as the magic was wrenched from their control. The world was red, and hot, and screaming, burning like the devil's beating heart.

"I have to end this," Tenn said.

"No," Jarrett said. He glanced to the twins. "I do."

He leaned in close and kissed Tenn fiercely on the lips.

Then he pushed Tenn away and, in a gust of power, rose into the air. Devon grabbed Tenn's arms as he screamed, but Jarrett wasn't listening. He shot forward, his Sphere blazing bright, wreathing him in power that burned like a comet. Straight toward Matthias.

"No!" Tenn screamed. He struggled against Devon, reached deep into Earth and made the whole world shudder. Water howled inside of him. He saw the two figures meet in the haze of fire, Jarrett glowing brighter than the sun, Matthias burning with equal fervor. They met in the space of a heartbeat, and when they collided, the world flashed white.

Then the twins surrounded him, wrapped their arms tight as they sandwiched themselves against him, and the world was replaced by screaming wind. Screaming wind and pain.

They flew.

Tenn struggled, or at least he tried, but the twins bound tight to him and something stronger held him in place, a barrier of Air that kept him still. Earth kicked in, some reflex he didn't know he had, knitting his flesh back together. He didn't want it to. He wanted the wind to tear him apart. He wanted to hurt.

He could do nothing but struggle.

The scream of wind was over in a heartbeat, and then they were on the ground, and the twins were pulling him forward. Running. Running. His limbs were numb and his brain was dead and it was the three of them, running in the snow, in the night, as the twins gasped and pulled him along and he stumbled drunkenly between them. He didn't want to run. He had to go back. He had to go back.

They wouldn't let him.

Jarrett.

Jarrett...

Moments later they were in a car. A huge SUV. They threw Tenn in the backseat and Devon jumped in the front and they were moving. Driving through the silent night. It was only then that the magic gagging Tenn vanished. Only then that he could force himself to sitting in the cold, hellish backseat.

Just him in the backseat.

"Take me back!" he screamed. Earth was still open, and when he yelled he lashed with power. The ground rumbled, making the car sway and veer. Still Devon raced forward.

Dreya turned and slapped him. Hard.

"Quiet!" she yelled. Air flared and wrapped around his

throat, stilling the words in his lungs. Her chest was heaving and tears raced down her eyes.

"He is gone, Tenn," she said. She didn't break eye contact. A single tear fell down her face. "As he knew would happen. As he *planned*."

Tenn struggled against the invisible bonds around him. Another flare of power, and another tremor vibrated through the car. This one weaker. Things weren't clicking. Things weren't clicking.

She didn't raise her hand again. She barely raised her voice.

"He knew you were being chased," she said steadily. "We had planned for this." She gestured to the SUV. "We had this escape route ready. In case." She swallowed. But she still didn't look away. "In case Jarrett needed to get you out of there. He knew this would happen. And he knew he would die to keep you safe."

Why me? Tenn wanted to ask. He couldn't speak, even though she'd released his gag. His words were snarled in tears.

"Keep quiet. Do not use magic." Her words were so quiet. Distant. Like she was repeating something Jarrett had told her. "We must keep you alive, no matter the cost. Do not let Jarrett's death be in vain."

The hum of the truck was quiet. Too quiet. Things weren't clicking.

Then, suddenly, things *were* clicking.

Jarrett had died to save him.

Jarrett had died to save him.

Tenn's world inked to black and fell away.

Jarrett was dead.

Jarrett was dead.

Jarrett is dead.

"We have turned our backs on the gods
and the gods
as one
have turned their backs on us."

—Rhiannon's Diary.
I.P.R.

PART
2

THE DEVIL'S MINIONS

CHAPTER SIXTEEN

DO NOT LET HIS DEATH BE IN VAIN.

Those words kept Tenn silent as they sped through the night. Devon veered back and forth through the snow, through the storm, but Tenn was past caring if they crashed or made it through. Air glowed in the twins' throats, both to guide them and to gust the snow away. It was enough magic to be followed. It was enough to be seen by Matthias.

Tenn didn't care about that. Let Matthias follow them; he had nothing left.

Jarrett had died to save him.

Jarrett had *known* he would die to keep Tenn safe.

Tenn could barely convince himself that Jarrett was a future he could have.

Jarrett had known Tenn was worth sacrificing his own future over.

The thoughts sloshed in his head as the SUV drove through the night. He didn't even try to hold Water down. He didn't need to; the Sphere didn't need to do a damned thing to drag him down into despair. He was there. Sinking. He was there, because Jarrett was not.

What could Water show him that would outmatch this?

He didn't know how long they drove. Hours, maybe. Maybe only a few minutes. The sun rose and the world was filtered gray and dark and his insides felt the same. He wanted the twins to say something. *Anything.* They didn't. And that meant he couldn't say anything, either. This wasn't a world for mourning the dead; he would get no comfort from either of them, and he knew that. But he wanted it. He wanted someone to acknowledge the loss that gaped in the car like a wound. Did they expect him to just follow along now? Not that he really had any other choice. He would keep ambling forward until he died.

Tears ran down his cheeks as he slumped against the window and watched the gray world go by.

Twelve hours ago he'd been snuggled in the backseat with Jarrett.

Twelve hours ago he'd thought he could have a future.

Now, he had nothing.

Eventually, the tears ran out and he could only slouch and watch and wait with cold dread for Matthias to come. Because, eventually, Matthias would come. In Tenn's dreams, and now his reality, Matthias was always waiting.

He couldn't even be *angry* at Matthias.

What use was revenge when he no longer had a future to fight for?

This was the world they lived in: it was always spelled out that, eventually, one of them would die. If anything, the whole situation just felt inevitable.

And, if he was being terribly honest, it was almost a relief. He'd now experienced the worst. There was no need to wait for the ax to fall anymore.

He tried to quell the thought. Tried to figure out if it was Water talking or his depression. Eventually, he decided it didn't really matter. Water was a part of him. So were all the terrible thoughts he ever tried to hide away.

They weren't made better by the scenery. The snow lessened as they drove, and the open expanse of fields quickly turned to thick pine forests. But that wasn't what kicked his numb heart into gear. It was the sign they passed that made him want to jump from the car.

Silveron Academy
for the Magical Arts
40 Miles Ahead

Maybe he'd been kidding himself about the worst already happening.

The green sign was pockmarked with bullet holes. Below it was a sign he'd become all too familiar with in the days before the Resurrection.

Magic Users
Are the
Devil's Minions

Howls weren't the first monsters spawned by the Spheres. The protesters had almost been worse.

Tenn had never heard of a Howl barricading children in

a school for magic and burning it down. That had been in Texas, two weeks after his classes at Silveron began. A week after that, an academy in Georgia had to close after a fanatic blew up half a dorm. His school had never suffered the same fate, but that didn't mean the locals enjoyed having a school of sinners so close to their homes. Protesters continually lined the front gate, and the school received a multitude of threats. And Tenn received anxious calls from his parents every week, making sure he felt safe, making sure he didn't want to go home.

Tenn hadn't realized, when he applied, that the first and last time he would be allowed to leave the campus was after the first Howl was born.

The fear in his chest was a nice change from the numbness. Another inevitability. Of course they would be passing by his old school. Of course.

He slid down in his seat and closed his eyes. He didn't expect to fall asleep. He didn't want to fall under, didn't want to cave to Matthias's gloating, but the hum of the car overtook him, and the stress of the last few hours finally gave way to exhaustion.

Sleep came on ragged wings, carrying with it a silence as deep as death.

The last thing he thought before he was dragged under was Jarrett's face.

I'm sorry, he mouthed to the darkness. *I'm sorry.*

He didn't dream of Matthias.

But he didn't know if that made him feel better or worse.

"Now, now, Tenn, crying won't help anyone," Tomás said,

reclining on the leather armchair. "If you want revenge, you'll have to take it."

Tenn's thoughts slurred with his emotions. He was dreaming, he knew he was dreaming, and he'd experienced enough of these to feel a sort of indifference. It was just a dream. Of *course* Tomás would find a way to infiltrate them.

"Fuck off," Tenn said. He was on an armchair across from the Howl, and manacles secured Tenn to the leather.

Tomás just smiled and adjusted his pose, the leather creaking under his skin.

"You're hurt," Tomás said. His voice dripped saccharine. "I understand that. But let's be honest—we both knew Jarrett was just using you. Why do you think he even showed up at your outpost? Everything he said was a lie, Tenn. He only told you those things so you wouldn't leave him. So he could do his duty. So he could interfere with your destiny. But now, he is out of the picture for good."

Tenn wanted to burst to his feet, to rage against the incubus, but the chains held him in place. He struggled for a second, until he saw that it was only making Tomás smile.

"Don't stop on my account," the incubus said. "You're giving me so many ideas."

"Don't you dare," Tenn whispered. "Don't you dare say his name."

"Did I hit a nerve?" Tomás asked, a grin still splashed across his face.

"I'll kill you," Tenn said. Red filled his vision—red overlaid with Jarrett's face moments before he leaped. "You did this to me. You're the reason he's dead!"

Tomás was there in a second, kneeling on the arms of the chair, one hand on Tenn's thigh and the other gripping his neck.

Tomás leaned in and whispered into Tenn's ear. "Don't fuck with me, Tenn. I've kept you alive because I like you, but that doesn't mean I'll tolerate such rudeness. I had no hand in your lover's death, pain me as that does. I've saved your ass more times than I care to count. Don't make me regret it."

"I'd rather die than have you help me again," Tenn gasped. "A Howl that thinks he's a king is still a Howl."

Tomás blazed heat. It burned and seared and froze Tenn's skin as Tomás screamed in his ear. "How dare you call me that!"

He dug his fingers into Tenn's leg. Fire seared up Tenn's thigh, but that was nothing compared to his fear of the incubus himself. Tomás seemed unhinged. The air around him quivered and glowed red like a hellish mirage. His lips pulled back in a sneer, his canines bared and more pronounced than normal. His clothes and hair seemed to billow in the storm of his rage.

"You're still a monster," Tenn said, trying to keep his voice from shaking. "Look at yourself."

And then, just like that, the aura around Tomás disappeared, the flame in his eyes winked out.

"He thinks I'm a monster," Tomás whispered. "A monster. I'm a *monster*." He looked at Tenn, then at the blood dripping down Tenn's thigh. "I hurt you." He shook his head, backed away and stared at the wall. "No, he deserved to be hurt. He dared insult me." Another shake of the head, a flicker of red aura. "He deserved pain." His entire body shuddered this time, like something was trying to escape. When he looked back to Tenn, his face was carefully composed, perfectly arranged.

"I'm sorry," he said. He clutched one hand to the side of his face. "Sometimes. Sometimes it's hard to..." He shook his head. "We can't fight what we are, Tenn. Not forever. Not even you. We're a lot alike, you know. You burn. You burn even brighter than me." He reached out and touched Tenn's heart. The Sphere of Fire flared under Tomás's fingertip, making Tenn's breath catch. Tenn had never been attuned to the Sphere, and feeling it burn in his chest was both foreign and familiar. "You'll burn the whole world, given half the chance." He removed his finger and sat back, staring at Tenn like a sad specimen. Tenn's whole body ached for that touch, for the hate and passion that seemed to ooze from Tomás's skin. It filled the void Jarrett had left, brought sensation to the parts of him he had written off as numb.

"Why. Are. You. Here?" Tenn asked, biting hard on each word to keep his body in control. Even in a dream, he wouldn't let the Howl overtake him. He wouldn't give Tomás that satisfaction.

A confused look passed over Tomás's face, as though he wasn't so certain of that himself. It passed in a heartbeat as the perfect mold of composure slipped back into place.

"I am here..." he said, his words their usual purr. He leaned a bit closer, putting his weight on one hand like a prowling cat. "Because I know what you want. You want revenge."

"I want Jarrett back," Tenn said.

"We can't always get what we want!" Tomás snapped, another flare of energy whirling and settling around him. He squeezed his eyes shut and took a deep breath. Tenn waited, tense, vaguely wondering what would happen if Tomás killed him in the dream.

"I am here," he said again, his eyes still closed, "because I can help you fight back. I know how to reach Leanna. I know her weaknesses. You can't get your *lover* back. I know how that feels, Tenn, to lose the man of your dreams. I would rip off the head of whoever did that to me." He smirked, the tone of condolence fading. "I *did* actually. It felt amazing."

"Why would you help me?" Tenn asked.

"I have my reasons," Tomás said quietly, as though those reasons were of the utmost secrecy. "Jarrett would have wanted this, you know. He would have wanted you to avenge him. Do you think, if roles were reversed, he would have let your killer live?"

Anger roiled through Tenn's veins. A hundred curses whipped across his tongue—*you didn't know him, don't ever mention him, he was too good*—but if the roles had been reversed, Jarrett would never have stopped looking for Matthias. Not until every Howl and necromancer had paid for what they'd done. At least, if Jarrett cared about him as much as he said he did...

Tomás seemed to read his thoughts. His sneer widened, and he crept a few inches closer. Heat coursed through Tenn's body as images floated through his mind—tearing Matthias limb from limb, stabbing the unknown Leanna through the chest, letting all the rage and hatred burn over, destroy the world. Tomás's visage seemed to echo over all of it, like some heathen god of destruction.

"Yes," Tomás hissed. "That's the fire. Jarrett deserves your anger. Your retribution. Fight for him."

Tenn shook his head against the visions of blood. It was harder, in the grasp of a dream. Like swimming through quicksand.

"What do you want from me? From this?"

Tomás was on top of him now, his hands on the chair's arms and his face only inches away. His copper-flecked eyes glinted in the candlelight.

"Let's just say Leanna and I have a score to settle. You help me kill her, and I'll help you get your revenge. We both get what we want." Tomás leaned in, gently brushed Tenn's cheek with his own. Goose bumps tingled under that touch. Tenn moaned and tried not to lean in. "And, if you're like me, you want a lot. It's about time we got what we wanted, wouldn't you agree?"

His eyes burned into Tenn's when he leaned back. In that moment, Tenn couldn't decide if he wanted to rip the man apart, rip off his clothes or both.

Tenn nodded. He couldn't be certain what would come out if he opened his mouth.

"I thought you would see things my way."

Tenn didn't ask why Tomás wanted to kill his own sister. He didn't ask why Tomás didn't just do it himself. He didn't care, so long as Leanna ended up dead. So long as she died at Tenn's hand.

"What do you want me to do?" Tenn asked, his words breathy with anticipation. Excitement over the prospect of killing Leanna. Excitement over the nearness of the incubus.

Tomás's grin spoke volumes. "So many things," he replied. "But for now, just keep moving forward. I cannot play with you if you are dead."

Tenn nodded. Tomás leaned in.

"I know you mourn his loss, but soon you will rule at my side as king."

Tomás kissed Tenn's neck. Desire curled in the back of Tenn's throat, heady and hot.

"I will show you all the pleasures of the world," Tomás cooed. "Just as soon as you have proven yourself worthy."

He bit Tenn's earlobe, a shot of adrenaline to Tenn's heart and, the moment the sensation faded, Tomás was gone.

"We will be safe here."

Dreya's voice cut through the fog of his dream.

"What?" he mumbled. He forced himself up. His throat was dry—had he been screaming in his sleep?

"We must stop soon. We are nearly out of gas, and we must regroup."

He glanced around. It was impossible to tell where they were, surrounded by endless trees and snow-covered signs. But something in the way Dreya spoke had his nerves on edge. It was like she was scared of admitting more.

"How much farther?"

"The Witches should be near," she said, "but we cannot risk bringing attention to them or ourselves. Not right now. Especially not if the Witches have moved on...that would leave us too vulnerable. We must find a place that is safe and let Matthias pass us by."

They passed another road sign.

Silveron

Left Ahead

"No," Tenn muttered, but Dreya cut him off.

"You say Matthias has been in your dreams, yes?" she asked. She looked back to him. "Then he knows you would avoid this place. He knows how much it pains you. It is the last place he would expect you to go."

Tenn didn't want to stop again. He didn't want to have time to think about what had happened. He didn't want to see the halls that he and Jarrett had walked down, the place that marked both the beginning and the end of their future. But he knew from the look in Dreya's eyes that he wasn't being asked his opinion.

Dreya turned back to the front and Devon turned the car up the drive. Tenn wrapped himself tighter in his coat. He wanted to feel bad about pushing the two of them away, but that would require feeling something.

Right then, he felt nothing at all.

CHAPTER SEVENTEEN

THE ROAD THAT LED TO SILVERON QUICKLY CHANGED from concrete to gravel, the grit crunching like snapped bones beneath the snow. Branches stretched overhead like black veins, pulsing memories into the twilight and bleeding through his mind. How often had this path haunted him? All the dreams of death and destruction, the final flight from this place. All the times he returned in his sleep, drifting like a ghost through the rooms of his past. And now, here he was, driving that very path. It didn't feel any more real than the dreams.

They rounded the corner and there it was: Silveron spread out before them like an admissions photograph, everything snow-covered and pristine in the dying winter light. The buildings were the typical New England flair, everything wooden and white. Long two-story buildings for classrooms, a steepled clock tower jutting from the central library, wide swathes of open lawns dotted with benches and shrubs. Charming. Unassuming. As though looking like any small college was a part of its defense.

Before it all stood the great wrought-iron gates that barbed up like talons through the white. "Silveron Academy" wove itself through the top arch, gilded in chipped gold. He'd passed through those gates twice during his time as a student. Once, when his parents dropped him off, and last, when the school was evacuated mere hours after the Resurrection was televised.

His gut turned over as they passed under the arch.

He hated how much it felt like coming home. It just made the empty backseat seem emptier. He'd never considered coming back here with Jarrett, but coming back here *without* Jarrett felt like torture.

He bit his lip and tried to keep from breaking down.

Somehow, the school was still immaculate, as impressive and imposing as the first day he'd stepped foot there. The lawns were clean and blanketed with fluffy snow, the windows intact and the roofs perfectly dusted with frost. All that was missing was the warmth of inner fires and lights. But there was an emptiness to the place, too. A hunger. It drew them in and promised to never let go.

Devon parked just inside the gate and the three of them got out. Tenn stared up at the sky, a few stray flecks of snow falling on his face.

"I am sorry," Dreya said. She stood beside him, so pale in this light that she could fade out against the snow.

He didn't know what she was apologizing for. Whether over Jarrett or bringing him here, it didn't really matter.

"Why can't we just go to them?" Tenn asked. "The Witches. If they're close, why do we have to stay here?"

"Because they might be dead," Devon said. He walked over to them, snowflakes catching on the fibers of his scarf, making him look festive despite his words. "Witches keep to the wilderness, which means we have to go to the wilderness to find them. That means we would be in the open at night. It could be a trap." He stepped closer, and Fire flickered in his chest, sending a small shiver through Tenn; just knowing Devon was under Fire's spell made him nervous. "I am too drained to fight off Matthias. As is my sister. And you cannot control your own powers. So we will stay here. Where it is safe. Where we can rest. And when *we* are ready to move on, we will."

Dreya didn't seem to breathe. She stared at her brother with a slight part to her lips.

"I didn't ask you to get involved," Tenn said. It was barely a whisper—Devon's words cut deeper than they should have. Devon was right: Tenn was a burden. If the two of them couldn't fight, he had no chance. "I didn't want anyone to die."

"But they did," Devon said. He looked Tenn right in the eyes when he said it. "Many people have died. Some to keep you safe, others as part of this unending war. If there is a chance— any chance—that you can end it, or make their lives worth something, you will see it out. To do anything less would be a disgrace." He wrapped the scarf tighter around his neck. "Now. Lead on."

Dreya looked from her brother to Tenn and shrugged.

Tenn thought she might come to his aid, but her silence said it all. Devon was right. Tenn had to keep moving forward. There was never time for weakness, and now least of all. He shoved his doubts down and led them toward the dorms. If they expected a vocal tour, they would be disappointed.

The only consolation Tenn could find as they made their way through the maze of sidewalks was that his classmates had all gotten out. There was no sign of battle here, no sign of bloodshed. There had never been any victims here to devour. But it also put him on edge: nowhere else in the world was a landscape so untouched, especially not one inhabited by humans. Why had the Howls—or, hell, the Church—avoided this place?

Behind the beautiful facade of normal buildings were the true structures that set Silveron apart. He led them toward his dorm, past the field of stones used for Earth practice, around a tall stone tower that had been reserved for Air. The Fire bunker was farther down the path, near the lake where he'd spent the vast majority of his time. Tenn nearly jumped when something shifted on one of the benches. Then the light caught, and he realized it was just a fox, ribs pronounced and eyes wide.

"She watches," Dreya whispered.

Tenn's heart leaped into his chest.

"Who?"

The fox stared at them, its eyes seemingly too intelligent.

"The Violet Sage," she whispered.

"Who?" Tenn repeated.

But Dreya shook her head, and he knew that he would get no more from her. The dorm, one of only four on campus, housed the underclassmen. It was stone and wood and two stories tall, flanked by massive oaks that had long since lost their leaves. Like the other buildings, the windows here were intact. The glass front door was closed and whole, the lawn in front devoid of the clutter and chaos he'd grown so used to seeing. He gripped his staff tighter and walked up the front steps. A twist of Earth and the lock broke. The door creaked open, the noise far too loud in the otherwise-silent air. More chills curled down his spine. Everything about this place felt haunted, and it wasn't just the memories warring behind his thoughts.

Ghosts of history swirled inside the lobby. He saw the vending machine that had saved him on more than one early morning of skipped breakfast and sleeping in. Over there, the wooden cubbies that had served as their mailboxes. And in front of them, the front desk he'd lingered by more nights than not, hoping to catch sight of Jarrett on his way back to his room. Tenn nearly dropped to his knees as the full weight of his past slugged him in the stomach.

If not for this place, he never would have learned magic. He never would have met Jarrett. He probably wouldn't have survived the first few days of the Resurrection.

He owed this place everything.

Yet he also felt like this place had taken everything away. And here it was again.

"This was my dorm," he said. His words echoed in the lobby. "The last time I was here…"

The last time I was here, my friends were running out the door with their bags half-packed because the monsters had been set loose. The last time I was here, I thought the end had come. The last time I was here, Jarrett and I were just kids. Now one of us is dead.

Why couldn't it have been me?

He glanced around, surveying the empty lobby, trying to keep his thoughts or Water from getting the upper hand.

"If you want to rest for the night, we can stay here."

Dreya nodded. Neither she nor Devon moved. He didn't

want to take command, but it was becoming clear they expected as much. At least in here.

A part of him wanted to take them to the opposite wing, to some random stranger's room so he wouldn't have to feel like he was stepping into his old life, but there was another part, a masochistic part, that wanted to see his old bed. He'd dreamed of this place more often than he could count. He wanted to lay those nightmares to rest, one way or another.

Besides, Jarrett had lived in the opposite hall. He wasn't as masochistic as that.

So he led them upstairs and down the hall, toward a room near the fire escape in case they needed a quick getaway. All the doors along the hall were closed but unlocked, their faux wood surfaces glinting in Devon's light. A few still had the construction paper signs the RA had made before they arrived. The rest of the signs littered the floor like faded leaves. It felt like being in a crypt, like every one of those closed doors and fallen signs was a testament to a life unlived. He pushed open a door—the one across from his own—and held it for them.

"This work?"

He knew he shouldn't be short with them, but he couldn't find room for eloquence.

Dreya peered inside. Thin light filtered through the curtains, but Devon opened to Fire and sent more lights through. When he stepped inside, Dreya shrugged again.

"It will do."

But she didn't head inside. She stood there in the entry and stared at Tenn.

"You should eat something," she said finally. "You will need your strength."

She had a bag slung on her back she'd pulled out of the SUV. Apparently, they hadn't been lying about planning ahead. It made Tenn feel even worse. His stomach rumbled with the thought of food: even the small amounts of Earth he'd been using had drained him.

"Maybe later. I…I think I need to sleep."

Clearly, Dreya knew he was lying. He'd never been good at that. But she didn't question. She probably figured he'd already been through enough.

Tenn glanced over her shoulder to Devon, who sat on the bed and stared out the window.

"Why?" Tenn asked.

"Why?" she repeated.

He looked to her. It was so hard to keep his voice from shaking, to keep himself standing.

"Why did you come after me? The three of you. Why?"

"The Prophets," she said.

He shook his head in agitation. The urgings of the Prophets had saved more than one outpost Tenn had been stationed in. But that didn't mean he trusted them. Anyone who used Maya was a wild card. It was the one element you couldn't just attune to, the only one that was supposed to be mildly sentient.

Maya was the godsphere, the power of spirit. *It* chose *you.*

"But why you three?" he asked. "Anyone could have come. Why did it have to be you?"

He wanted to say *him.* He could tell from the look in her eyes that Dreya knew it, too.

"We were chosen by name," Dreya said. Her words were small. Clearly, she didn't like being singled out by the Prophets, either. "We had no choice. 'Find the boy that Water weeps for. His words will shape the world.'"

Cold settled in Tenn's chest.

"What does it mean?" he asked.

She shrugged. "We have no way of asking them. And I hear the Prophets don't interpret, only relay what Maya whispers." She looked back to her brother. There was no way he wasn't hearing this, but he ignored them entirely. "We can only hope that the Witches will know something of this."

"And if they don't?"

She hesitated.

"Then we find someone who does."

He nodded. He knew it was a lie—if the Witches didn't know, who would? It's not like they had any hope of finding the Prophets.

"Tomorrow, then," he whispered.

She reached out and patted him on the shoulder. "Tomorrow."

The moment their door was closed, he felt the emptiness around and within him contract. He pressed his forehead to his old door, squeezed his eyes tight. He felt the dorm breathe around him, felt the throb of blood in his ears as Water roiled with memory—his classmates, dragging a mattress into the hall and jumping around after sign-in; him, carrying his first care package from his parents back to his room, opening it while listening to music and dreaming of family; the day of the Resurrection, when they were dragged from their rooms and told they would need to return to their homes and defend their loved ones.

And Jarrett. The night they'd studied together, when Jarrett led him back to his room.

Tenn had wanted so badly to invite Jarrett over to watch a movie. He'd planned on it.

He'd never gotten the nerve, and never got the chance. How different would his life have been if he'd made a move back then? If they'd fallen for each other? If they'd spent this whole time fighting at each other's side?

They were thoughts he shouldn't have allowed himself to have. But there, it was impossible to keep them down. They were living, breathing things. They had teeth.

He pressed his hand to the cold doorknob. Then, before he could tell himself this was a horrible idea, he opened the door.

History washed over him in a waft of dust and desertion. The faintest light filtered through the window opposite him, casting heavy shadows on everything within. He didn't need light or magic to see. His body knew every corner of this place—the cinder-block walls, the wooden shelves, the desk with his computer still sitting on it. He stepped slowly inside and felt the bile rise in his throat. Moonlight shone in from a space in the clouds. Photos still lined his wall—him and his few friends making sand castles by the lake or eating lunch at the mall; his family at Thanksgiving; the tree outside his old bedroom window.

He collapsed to his knees.

His heart was on fire, every fiber of that muscle tearing itself apart. He gripped his head in his hands and sobbed on the floor, tears pooling in the dust. Memories ripped through him, but it wasn't Water at work. The Sphere didn't need to do anything. The real wounds were all there—the pain, the history. This is where he'd lain awake for hours, wondering if Jarrett actually liked him. Wondering if *anyone* would like him. So much time wasted to worry. He would never get it back.

He curled in on himself, wishing death would take him. The fire from before, the burning desire for revenge, snuffed out. What point was revenge if there was no one to come home to? What was the point of pushing forward when everything he loved, everything he worked for, was continually ripped away from him? He couldn't find any answers, and he couldn't find any drive. All that was here was the dust of his past. The memory of what wouldn't be.

He forced himself to kneeling and stared at his hands as they pressed into the linoleum. His hands were worn. Long, thin fingers, crossed with scars. They didn't fit into this place. Neither did he.

He pushed himself up, grabbing the chair for support. He was about to make his way to bed when he stopped; something caught his eye.

The dust on his desk was lit up by the moon, a pale sheen of uniform gray. Save for one small patch.

Words had been written in the dust, a fingertip's scrawl.

Three words, in a script he didn't recognize.

Welcome home, Jeremy

CHAPTER EIGHTEEN

HE STARED AT THE HANDWRITING FOR WHAT FELT like hours, every throb of his blood the tick of a clock. He didn't recognize the script, but he knew without a doubt that it was Matthias's. Tomás would have just appeared in briefs and a smile to torment him. It wasn't the fact that the writing was recent that made his heart clench but, instead, what it entailed. Matthias knew his name. Matthias knew his history. Matthias knew more about him than Tenn had given him credit for.

Which meant Matthias would be back. He expected Tenn to return here.

They *weren't* safe.

He brushed the dust and the handwriting away.

Water resonated.

"We have to go!" his roommate yells. Greg shoves clothes into his backpack, but he's barely paying attention to what he grabs. Tenn watches five pairs of socks and a scarf and two tank tops go into the bag.

Tenn can't move.

If he moves, he'll have to believe this is real.

He'd thought it was a joke, at first. Some part of their training. Handling emergencies or something like that. It started with a news clip on repeat, one that had taken over every single TV station, every radio signal, every internet channel: a woman in black in the middle of a basement somewhere, a man chained to a chair in front of her, marks covering his body. A grim smile was on his face like he wanted to be there. Like he volunteered.

The woman said that the time had come for a new savior. And she was the one to herald them in.

Them. Not him. Them.

Tenn had watched on the dorm TV with his classmates as she opened to Earth. As the man screamed and shook in the chair, as his body arched and snapped and bones shot from flesh and blood oozed down skin and then the screaming stopped. Changed. Became a howl that pierced Tenn to the core as the man's face contorted and elongated and his jaw cracked and his teeth gouged and when it was over, when it was finally over, he was no longer a man.

"I give you the new era," the woman said. She stepped forward. She wore black, but her face was pale. Almost angelic.

Blood splattered her cheeks.

"Join me," she said. "Join me, and know eternity. Defy me, and not even death will release you from my wrath."

The footage had cut off, repeated itself for at least an hour. But then the repetition stopped, and new footage appeared. Live footage. People running through the streets, screaming as monsters chased them. As mages set fire to buildings or boiled lakes or called down storms. It was coordinated. It had been planned.

The moment it started, the war was already won.

"Jeremy!" Greg calls. "Get off your ass and pack!"

Head reeling with memory of the footage, Tenn stands and be-gins slowly putting things in his bag. This is all just a dream, he tells himself. This is all just a joke. Water simmers in his gut, as if responding to something far away. The Sphere had been acting up the last week. It had been harder to control. More volatile. Had it felt the wrongness in the world?

Was that even a thing that was possible?

Someone knocks on the door and opens it before Tenn can say anything. He hopes it's Kevin, but it's just Mark, their RA.

"Bus leaves in twenty," Mark says. Then he's off to the next room.

Tenn thought it was strange that they were evacuating the school. There were gates here. And people who used magic. That had to mean it was safe, right?

"Do you want to get left behind?" Greg asks as he pushes out the door. He looks Tenn up and down. "God. At this rate you'll be the first to get eaten."

Then he leaves, before Tenn has a chance to respond or even comprehend. Eaten. That's a legitimate threat now.

He looks at the photo on his desk of his family. Reaches to take it, then thinks better. It would be safer here. He'll find them. Soon. He'll find them, and he'll bring them back here. Where it's safe.

Of all places in this world, Silveron has to be safe.

Tenn barely felt Water transition from a memory to a pull. It sloshed around in his gut and his mind, dragging not only his memories back, but his body forward. *Safe. Something has to be safe.*

But Water knew better. Water resonated with the pain, and

embedded deep within the foundations of the school was a burning, nagging shadow of something terrible. Something inhuman. And that sense, that wrongness, twined itself around Tenn's heart. Water echoed the monster's hymn, and Tenn's body had no choice but to march to its cadence. It tugged him forward. It told him to obey.

He left his quarterstaff in the room and slid out the door. A small part of him was dimly aware of how silent the hall was, how loud his footsteps were on the tile. But the twins didn't stir. He had meant to tell them something. Something about the safety of this place, but Water was louder in his head than his own thoughts. He could only move with the tide, a stick caught in the stream.

He didn't stop at the lobby. He continued down into the basement, toward the room where the laundry machines and Ping-Pong tables were. The room was more than just a lounge. Doors lined every wall, and behind them was a series of tunnels that linked to every building on campus. He could practically feel the ghosts of his classmates here, but the perception was dim, lost under the crashing of his mutinous Sphere. He slipped through the lounge like a sleepwalker, past sofas and tables littered with magazines, and made his way to a door at the far end. It opened silently under his touch, the hall beyond stagnant with dead air.

The door at the other end of the long hall was locked. Water roared like rapids.

A flick of Earth, and the lock crumbled. When he stepped inside, Water stabbed him with agony, a pierce that coiled through his guts and made his eyes flutter. The walls in here breathed pain. And that pain, that crippling hurt, drew him forward and filled him with a new sort of ecstasy. A different sort of hunger.

In a small corner of his mind, he knew the room should have been like many of the other downstairs lounges, with sofas and tables and bookshelves. But this room looked like a kitchen. Knives dangled from grids on the ceiling and steel bowls piled on every surface. Rows of metal tables were meticulously arranged side by side in the middle of the room, more knives and bowls artfully displayed on top. Stacks of wood or metal were piled along the walls in pyramids. Tenn didn't need light to know that there was no dust in here. He could sense it—the cleanliness, the almost sterile scent in the otherwise-stale air. And yet, despite the order, he knew the walls should be bleeding. They were screaming curses through his veins. He pitched forward. The door slammed shut behind him.

That's when he noticed the body.

It was the mouth of the whirlpool, and Water left him no choice but to fall toward it. The slumped corpse against the wall dragged him forward, tugged at Water with a hook he had no desire to escape. It was male. Older. The flesh tight over sharp bones. Tenn dropped at the body's side, his head spinning, spinning. *I shouldn't, I shouldn't—I need to get out of here, I need—* Water drowned the fear. It sang a horrible ecstasy. The body was wearing a suit, a wool suit. Tenn's fingers brushed the rough fabric. His hand pulled itself toward the body's face. Fingertips brushed dead skin. Water screamed.

"Dmitri," she says. "You love me, right?"

He nods, though he doesn't mean it. Of course he can't mean it. Not after this.

"And you see the good I'm doing, yes?"

He nods again. It's all he can do, really; it's impossible to talk through the gag, and the ropes tying his wrists to the chair are strong. He'd given up struggling hours ago. The walls are thick down here. Even if he could have screamed, no one would have heard him. Even if he managed to escape these bonds, there was nowhere for him to run. The whole faculty has gone insane.

Get the kids out. Get the kids out. Those had been his last words, before Helena pulled him down here. Those had been his last words, and he didn't know if anyone had heeded him.

Helena pushes herself away from the desk. Her black hair is pulled back in a ponytail, and she wears the pencil skirt and white blouse that he'd always joked made her look like a sexy librarian. He isn't joking now. And neither is she.

She holds a scalpel from one of the art studios. It's already covered in his blood. His skin burns with cold and pain, his blood dripping in slow rivulets to the sterile tiles below. She hadn't hesitated the slightest bit when she'd brought the blade to his flesh. Not the first time. And not the second or twentieth.

She leans in close, her green eyes blazing.

"Then you understand why I must do this." Her eyes flash to the blade in her hand. She isn't a Howl—one of the monsters that had been kept out of sight of society until yesterday. He knows that much. She's worse. He'd watched her slow progression toward madness and power. And like everyone else at the Academy, he'd done nothing to stop it.

Hell, he might have encouraged it.

He'd been on the admissions board, and had handpicked the students she used for subjects. He'd found fuel for her madness. So much of this was his fault...

"I've studied the words of the Dark Lady. I know her secrets.

And I think," she says, leaning in, like this is some intimate secret and not his death sentence, "I think I can become just like her. I could become a goddess."

The Sphere of Water courses in her stomach. You're unstable, he wants to say. The Spheres have made you crazy. But there was no logic with her, no reasoning. Not anymore.

"With these runes, I can keep you sane. I know the science. The base creatures, they lose their minds. Only those of Water or Fire or Air have sentience, but even that is fragile. But I know. I know how to keep you mine. I know how to give you power."

He can't scream as she pushes the blade into his skin, scratching marks along his arms and chest that he can't see and can't comprehend. Runes to bind you to me, she'd said. Runes to make you like the Kin. Runes to let you keep your magic. There had been tears in her eyes the first time she'd made a cut, unflinching as she'd been.

Not anymore.

Now she's smiling, his blood staining her lips a deeper crimson as her scalpel licks him again.

Tenn surfaced from the flood, barely able to gasp as Water's grip loosened and reality crashed against the waves. His thoughts were dim, congealing. He knew those people. Dmitri had been his biology teacher. And Helena…he knew her all too well.

She had been Silveron's president.

Dmitri's body twitched beneath his hand, breath escaping in a hiss from long-silent lips. A voice inside of Tenn screamed, begged him to run from the Howl at his fingertips, the Howl that was slowly coming back to life, but Water bellowed louder. Water wanted to help Dmitri, wanted to mirror his pain.

Water won.

"Please," Steven cries. "Please don't do this."

The boy squirms on the table, but the ropes hold him strong. Helena stands beside Dmitri, watching him work, watching as he sobs with hunger and hatred.

She hands him the knife.

"Do it," she whispers into his ear. "My love, my slave." She kisses the back of his neck.

Dmitri's hand trembles as he brings the knife down. He can feel Steven's pulse without touching him, can hear his heartbeat echoing his own. The water, the water—it's all he can sense, all he can taste. His throat burns with hunger, with need. He'd heard that higher-Sphere Howls could control their hunger, could remain sentient. Helena swore the runes she carved into him would make him like a Kin, would let him keep his mind, his emotions, his identity.

She lied.

The runes only make him more aware of what he does. Of the hunger he has no control over.

Steven struggles as Dmitri slowly lowers the blade. It feels like a blessing, like the most intimate of touches. It makes Dmitri's bloodlust rise—that increase in pulse, the terrified patter of the boy's heart. He barely hears the boy scream as the blade pierces through flesh, shallow first, then deep as the hunger takes over. Red fills Dmitri's vision. Red fills his lips. His starving Sphere sings, and hunger becomes ecstasy.

Tenn jolted back, surfacing with a gasp. Dmitri pulled him closer. Tenn couldn't have pulled away; he didn't want to pull away. Water throbbed inside of him. Everything felt slower, drugged.

Dmitri brought Tenn's hand to his cracked lips. Tenn didn't

flinch when the bloodling's teeth sliced into his flesh. Water, Water, Water was all. Dmitri drank, and Tenn fell under the waves.

"Dmitri, please," Helena whimpers.

"Dmitri is dead, you made sure of that," he hisses. *She struggles against the bonds holding her to the table, but the knots hold strong. She taught him those knots, and he was nothing if not a fast learner.*

Everything rages inside of him. Every hurt and hate, every regret. Every hunger. Every guilty drop of blood. Her fault. All her fault. Make her pay for what she did.

"Don't worry," he says, leaning in close. *"I've had practice. I can keep you alive forever if I like. Just like you showed me."*

He digs a finger into her forearm, his nail burrowing deep. Blood pools within the depression. She screams. Tears fall down her face as he leans in and licks up her blood. Her blood, like poison, like honey.

Her blood, like power.

"Stop," Tenn whispered.

Water fluttered inside of him now, a thin stream siphoning through a tunnel. It didn't hurt, that loss. He didn't hurt. Nothing hurt, not even as Dmitri's teeth dug into his wrist, warmth spilling across his skin. The numbness was a beautiful release. It was freedom.

Tenn slumped down on top of Dmitri. It felt like falling on bones.

"Quiet, kids, quiet now," Dmitri says. *But they won't stop screaming. They won't stop crying.*

Blood everywhere. On hands and knees, cleaning every drop, licking every drop. But still hungry, so hungry. Not enough blood.

Never enough blood. They're crying blood. The water is never enough. Never enough.

"Shut up!" he yells. They sit in the corner, crying. He runs over to them, smashes in their skulls, but they're still crying. He kicks their bones, scatters them like sticks, but they won't stop. "Shut up, shut up, shut up."

He bangs on the door. Locked. Helena had locked it behind her. She's in the corner, too, sitting by herself. She isn't crying. She's stuck with him. Forever. My love, my slave.

He crawls over to her. So hungry. She'd brought down the last of the students—those who were kept behind—ages ago. Weeks. Months. Years. She brought the last. And when that wasn't enough, he took her.

"Speak up," he hisses at her. He picks up her skull, stares into her empty eyes. "Speak up."

Her mouth is open, skin taut, but she doesn't say anything.

She'd stopped talking weeks ago.

But not the blood.

Her blood still screams, still sings in his bones. She is still with him.

She will never get away.

When he gets away, he will make them pay. He will devour—

Water stopped.

Tenn floated, warm, his arm tingling with pain and pleasure. Red. Warm and wet and red.

"Saving your ass grows tiresome," Tomás whispered into his ear. A warm hand stroked his face, chilling the spilled blood to frost. Everything was red.

Red, red and black.

CHAPTER NINETEEN

"WHAT HAVE YOU DONE?"

Dreya's voice pulsed through the darkness, a wash against the red staining his inner eyelids. He wanted to float there, lost in emptiness, but there was a hand on his skin now, a tingle of magic that swept through his bones. The energy filled his insides with fire and ice. His eyes fluttered open as a shiver racked his body, a shiver that sent lances of pain through his arm.

It took a few moments for the scene to focus.

Dreya knelt by his side, one hand on his chest. Devon stood behind her like a sentinel. Both of them stared down at him, awash in pale white light that filtered from an orb hovering above Devon's head. The room took even longer to come into view. First the floor, smeared with what looked like black oil, glinting in the light, then the sensation, the wetness, the softness beneath him. His arm gave another twinge. He looked back and nearly yelped.

Dmitri was there, slumped against the wall, his jaw gaping on broken hinges. Dmitri, looking so much more alive than when Tenn came down here. His flesh was full, his chin dripping Tenn's blood. Much more alive, save for the butcher knife firmly embedded in his neck. Blood slowly dripped off the handle and onto Tenn's shoulder. *Pat, pat, pat.* Tenn tried to jerk away.

"He's dead," Dreya said. She forced Tenn to stay still. "It's okay."

Water was a slow thrum in his gut. It ached, but the damned Sphere seemed to enjoy it. He remembered kneeling there, remembered placing his hand on the corpse's skin...then the rest flooded back in a smear of pain. He had willingly knelt there and let Dmitri feed off him, all while...what? He relived Dmitri's own painful past?

What the hell had Water done to him?

Perfect crescent moon gashes were etched deep into his flesh, his bones just visible through the mess of muscle. Before he could lose any more blood, he opened to Earth and sealed off the wounds. The scars welled up pink as flesh knitted itself together. Shivers racked through him the moment he closed off to the Sphere; somehow, he felt even weaker than before.

"You lost a lot of blood," Dreya said. "You are lucky you did not bleed out." Her magic flooded him, burning through his veins and spurring his marrow to produce more blood. He shivered uncontrollably, but he'd rather she did this than have to do it himself.

Earth might leave him weak, but there was no way he would trust Water. Not now. How was she able to use it without succumbing to the terrors of this place? How was she not seeing what he had seen?

Tenn looked back to Dmitri, to the knife embedded in his throat. The voice he heard before fainting filtered through his ears. *Saving your ass grows tiresome.* Tomás had been here. Tomás had saved his life.

"What the hell were you doing down here?" Devon asked. He nodded to the broken Howl. "It could have killed you."

"Water," he said. The words left his mouth in a dry croak. "I don't... I don't know why. Water pulled me down here. It took over. Again." He clutched his head in his hands and closed his eyes, tried to drown out the new memories that interlaced with his. He had *been* there. He had *worn* Dmitri's skin. "I *felt* it," he said. "I saw his memories. How he died. What he did." He trailed off. The memories burned. The blood of his classmates was a sharp tang in his mouth.

He knew it wasn't his doing, but Dmitri's sins felt like they were his own now. The blood he'd tasted danced in his veins.

"That is more than transference," Dreya whispered.

Tenn nodded slowly. His fingers dug into his hair, tried to press the images out.

"I have never heard of this," she continued. "Places resonate and Spheres answer, but they do not compel you toward death. They do not make you live another's life."

"I don't care what it is," Tenn said. He opened his eyes. "I just want it to stop."

"You can't stop it," Devon said. He knelt down, Fire flickering in his throat. "But maybe...maybe the Witches can help you control it."

Tenn didn't answer. He just dug his head back into his

palms and tried to force out the memories. *Control it.* Right. The Sphere was controlling *him.* He just hoped he could turn the tables before it killed him.

The twins helped him limp through the halls and up the steps. His stomach burned with hunger, and every muscle in his body felt like it had been pressed through a meat grinder. He wanted to lie down and sleep for eternity, but he knew that wasn't going to be a possibility. They weren't safe here. Once he told them about the message on the desk, it hadn't taken long for them to decide that, even if it risked everything, they would find the Witches tonight.

Dreya didn't leave his side while Devon retrieved their things. Without speaking, she magically drew the blood from his clothes. He watched impassively as the gore trickled down his jeans and across the floor before evaporating into nothing. There was a look in her eyes that told him she was keeping silent for a purpose. She was calculating. It wasn't until Devon returned to the lobby that he realized what she was trying to figure out.

"How did we not feel that bloodling?" she asked.

"It was dead," Tenn said. He nearly lost his appetite just thinking about it. "At least, until..." *Until I fed it my own blood.*

"But how?" she asked. She glanced at him, but her gaze wasn't accusatory. She was curious. "Bloodlings aren't able to compel their victims. They can't hide from magic. I searched every inch of this place. We should have felt it, just as we should have felt it drawing you in."

He didn't want to remember, but it was too easy to sift back through those moments. Dmitri's life and death were as firm in his mind as his own history. Maybe even stronger.

"He wasn't like other bloodlings," Tenn said.

Dreya raised an eyebrow.

"Runes," Tenn continued. "The necromancer who turned him...she covered him in runes before actually draining his Sphere. She said they would make him stronger. That they would let him keep his mind and his magic. She wanted to make him like the Kin." Even just saying the words sent memories coursing through his mind. He tried to squash them down and keep talking. "I don't think it worked, though. The runes turned him into something different. Gave him power. But not like the Kin."

"That is the key," Dreya whispered. She shared a glance with her brother. "I saw the marks on the bloodling's neck, but there was too much blood." She pushed herself to standing. "I must go investigate." Another glance to Devon, who nodded solemnly in return. Then she left.

"What do you think it means?" Tenn asked. He didn't think Devon would respond. The guy just stared past him, eyes fixed on something out of sight. When he finally spoke, his words made Tenn jump.

"There is more to this than anyone will say," Devon said. "The language of the runes should have been lost when the Dark Lady died. If her words are being spoken once more..." He focused on Tenn. "We're as good as dead."

They left soon after Dreya returned from her study of Dmitri. Her expression was stormy as they trudged down the path that led away from Silveron.

"What did you find?" Tenn asked.

"Nothing good," she replied. Her words were clipped—he knew she wanted to keep it at that. But after what he'd experienced, he couldn't let it lie.

"How did he come back to life?" he asked. "Was it the runes? I've never seen a Howl covered in marks like that."

With kravens it was impossible to tell, what with their twisted bodies and warped skin—Earth wasn't kind to its hosts when inverted. But he'd killed his fair share of bloodlings. None of them had those marks.

Dreya shook her head. "I have never seen runes like that before. I can only guess…"

"Then guess," Tenn said. He didn't mean to sound so angry, but he *had* almost been killed by a creature that should have been nothing more than a corpse.

"The runes were clearly meant to give the creature power," Dreya said. "And it worked. Howls die out if they cannot feed, albeit slowly. Perhaps the necromancer wanted to make him like the Kin, but she failed. She made him into something else. Something almost immortal."

"Until we killed it."

"But perhaps, if you had never appeared, it never would have truly died. It was kept alive by magic alone. Perhaps that magic is what kept him hidden from us. And what drew you to him. Water pulled."

He shuddered. Water had definitely gotten him into this mess. But that didn't answer the question of what had gone wrong in Dmitri's conversion or what the runes actually *did*. He'd seen so much of Tomás's skin, and there hadn't been a single rune or tattoo. So how had the Kin been created? If

Dmitri was a failure, but still close to immortal, what did that mean about the Kin themselves?

The silence stretched between them the full length of the night. The fields and forests they trekked through were empty, and the only light came from a few dim flares that hovered around them like fireflies. Every second he expected to see a fire on the horizon, for Matthias to appear in a blaze of flame and turn his friends to ash.

Which was why, when he saw the dim light in the distance, his throat constricted with dread.

But the light didn't flicker like fire. Wasn't warm. It glowed white and steady like a city. But there were no cities out here. Nor any farms. This part of America had been abandoned because of winters too cold and summers too harsh, the weather itself sharpened by the claws of the Resurrection.

"A sept," Dreya whispered.

"What the hell is a sept doing this close to the Academy?" Tenn asked, gut in his chest.

The septs were the only other established human communes besides guilds. Septs, however, were created and ruled by the Church, and were formed even before the Resurrection. He had no idea how the places managed to survive the undead hordes, no matter how high their walls. Without the magic they deemed as evil, they should have gone under in the first few weeks. It's not like they could rely on guns or bombs when a single mage could render them useless. Rumor was that their faith kept them safe, but Tenn had seen enough of faith to know it didn't keep the monsters from tearing out your bones and sucking them dry while you bled out on the concrete.

Instantly, he thought of Caius. *When you know the truth, you'll have the whole of the Church at your back.*

Tenn knew the Church had secrets. But what could they have to do with him?

"If there are any Inquisitors about..." Dreya muttered.

She didn't have to finish the thought.

Inquisitors stayed true to their ancient charge—wipe out witchcraft in all of its forms, from mages to necromancers, and anyone else they didn't like.

Tenn had heard enough horror stories of mages tortured by Inquisitors, had seen the bodies after they'd been hung up as examples. He had no clue how the hell Inquisitors were able to capture, let alone torture, mages when they themselves eschewed magic, but if he had to choose between a necromancer and an Inquisitor, he'd pick the necromancer. Necromancers weren't known for thumbscrews.

"This is bad," Dreya said. She kept sharing glances with her brother, who was staring at the glow on the horizon with narrowed eyes. Fire twitched on and off in his chest. "If the Witches are nearby... I do not want to think of what may have been done to them."

She didn't clarify, and Tenn didn't ask. He didn't need to wonder. If the sept was nearby, the Witches would be hunted down. If they were caught, they would be tortured. Just like he and the twins would be if they were found. Suddenly, he felt more exposed than he ever had in his life. If Matthias showed up, it would attract the Church and its Inquisitors. But whose side would they err on? The monsters from hell or those who opened the gateway? Or would they just wait until the battle was over and sweep up the remainders for "saving"?

He didn't want to find out either way.

Wherever the Witches were, he hoped they were safe. And close.

An hour or so later, the lights now somewhat behind them, Devon led them off the highway and into a field covered in freshly fallen snow. There were no tracks anywhere, not from deer or mice or anything else that might live out in the wilds. Just smooth, unbroken white.

The night air was far too quiet for his liking. Quiet always meant an attack. *Always*. Every few minutes, Dreya would open to Air and send a gust of wind behind them, effectively obscuring their own tracks. Tenn flinched every time—even that small amount of magic seemed like a beacon in the night. As if the lights that guided them weren't bad enough. A forest rose, tall and foreboding, on the far end of the field. Devon led them straight toward it.

They stopped near the edge of the trees. Devon stared into the undergrowth, his eyes set in concentration and Air pulsing in his throat.

"Are you sure?" Dreya asked softly.

Devon nodded. Nothing moved within the trees, nothing pulsed with life, not for miles, but Devon seemed dead set in his convictions and, frankly, there was nowhere else to go.

He opened to Fire, and then, before Tenn could say anything to stop him, he sent up a flare. It was like watching stars fall in reverse—tiny motes of light sparked into life around him and shot high into the air, blazing against the gray sky. Devon wove them together, lights streaking like white thread, forming intricate knots high above the tree line. Each was a symbol Tenn couldn't understand, and each flared bright as a strobe before being replaced by another whirling shape. The field around them flashed white and glaring.

Devon dropped the Sphere a moment later. The night seemed even heavier the moment the magical light vanished.

"What the hell was that?" Tenn hissed.

"It is the signal," Dreya said. "The Witches must be entreated. One cannot enter their territory without their express invitation."

Tenn pushed his senses into the forest, but that was still and silent, too. If anyone was living in there, they were miles away and far out of both his magic's reach and the sight of the flare.

This all seemed insane. And suicidal.

"So what do we do now?" he asked.

"We wait," Devon said. "And we hope they are still alive."

It was not the answer he was hoping for. The minutes seemed to stretch on forever. Tenn didn't let go of Earth, not once, but he didn't feel anything stirring within the forest. Devon and Dreya were both open to Air, scanning silently, their eyes practically glowing in the darkness. After using so much magic to send up a signal, using the Spheres to scout seemed pale in comparison.

Then a sound broke the air behind them.

A scream. A Howl.

In unison, their attention snapped to the way they'd come.

"They found us," Tenn whispered. He couldn't keep the fear from his voice.

"Did you expect anything less?" Dreya asked, her words biting.

"No, but I also didn't expect to hand out our location on a silver tray, either," he snapped, glaring at Devon.

Fire flickered in Devon's chest, and he bowed his head. Tenn wasn't certain where his own inner rage was coming from— hadn't he *wanted* to find Matthias? Hadn't he wanted to just end it all? And yet now, with the Howls approaching, he realized he didn't want to give in.

He wanted to fight. For Jarrett.

"How many?" he asked, because he knew she could sense farther than him. Although it was a vain hope, he was holding on to the idea that it was just a wandering pack of kravens. Something they could dispose of quickly and easily. Something that wouldn't require him to open to Water. He still had Earth, but until he strengthened that Sphere, a few uses would drain him completely and leave him broken and weak.

Dreya's hesitation told him more than enough.

"The full army," she said after a moment. "And it seems it has expanded."

"How?"

"There must be a Farm nearby," Dreya whispered. It made Tenn want to vomit. How many innocent lives had just been turned into Howls simply to come after him? How many more deaths were staining his soul?

"Great," Tenn whispered. He looked to Devon. "Any sign of your *friends?*"

Devon said nothing.

"It is not his fault," Dreya replied. "There is no other way to communicate with the clans. Not when they are in hiding."

"Tell that to my corpse," Tenn said. He gritted his teeth and stared into the horizon. He didn't want to die here. It wasn't self-preservation, but the need for revenge. He wasn't prepared to take on Matthias.

The army appeared like a black stain on the far edge of the field, darker and faster than shadow, and as it neared, Tenn could feel the army as the earth trembled beneath its feet. In any other situation, he would have forced them all to let go of the Spheres, to run and hide and vainly hope the army might pass them by. But they had already lost the element of surprise. The best they could do now was try to fend them off from a distance.

He opened his mouth to give the orders when a branch snapped behind him. He turned around, ready to kill any creature lurking in the shadows.

A little girl stepped out from the depths of the trees. She was in jeans and a wool sweater, her dark hair pulled to the sides in long pigtails. She couldn't have been older than twelve.

"Are you the ones who sent up the signal?" she asked. Her eyes surveyed them, then took in the approaching horde without even the mildest hint of concern.

Devon nodded.

"Follow me," she said. Then she headed back into the trees.

"But the army—" Tenn began, only to be cut off by her response.

"Won't be an issue if you do what I say. Stay close."

Tenn looked at the twins, but if there was any uncertainty between the two of them, they didn't show it. Without even glancing to the army behind them, they followed the girl into the woods.

Tenn spared the field a glance, just briefly. The horde was still a mile or so away, but it would arrive within minutes. They didn't have a chance against them no matter what, but in the forest, their probability of survival dropped dramatically. In here, the trees would hide friend and foe alike. He glanced back to the retreating forms of the twins, the white of their coats blending into the woods like ghosts.

"Fuck," he whispered. Then he bounded in after them.

CHAPTER TWENTY

"WHERE THE HELL ARE WE GOING?" HE WHISPERED to Dreya. The strange girl was only a few feet ahead of them, and she walked through the woods with a quick, assured step. He could barely see her in the deep shadows.

No one answered.

Even with Earth pulsing in his gut, he couldn't feel anyone else stirring in the woods. Just the four of them, moving deeper and deeper into the wilderness while the approaching army roared toward them.

"The first line is coming up," the girl said. She paused and held out a hand. "I suggest you hold on from here on out. It can be difficult to follow the path if you're not accustomed to the way."

Devon didn't hesitate. He took the girl's hand and Dreya took his. She held her hand out and raised an eyebrow at Tenn. If that wasn't an admonishing glance, he didn't know what was. He took her hand. His pulse was a panicked throb in his ears. Here they were, holding hands in the woods while their imminent death was minutes away. And yet, the girl was about as unconcerned as was humanly possible, and the twins weren't much different.

A few steps later, the girl disappeared. Devon appeared to be holding his arm out to thin air. Another step and Devon vanished into the night. Another step and Dreya was gone, though he still felt her hand in his. Something washed over him, a tingle that swept through his gut like vertigo and nausea and that sick feeling from spinning around too fast. It passed in an instant, leaving him feeling as though he'd just stepped off a ship to dry land. The girl and the twins were visible once more, the chain unbroken.

He glanced around as they moved forward. Something unsettled him, something in the very pit of his gut that just felt wrong. He looked behind him. Had they gotten turned around? He started to release Dreya's hand. Surely he'd left something behind...

"Don't be fooled by your instincts," the girl said. "We're approaching the second line. Just follow me."

Dreya gripped his hand even tighter.

This time, although he was prepared for it, he nearly yelped when the girl disappeared from sight. His grip on Dreya's hand was tighter than death as every fight-or-flight nerve in his body began to fire. He was going the wrong way. If he kept walking, he was going to die. The little girl wasn't one of the Witches—she had been sent to capture them. To kill them.

Devon disappeared.

Tenn knew if he stepped through that invisible wall, he'd

be torn apart. Fear welled up in his throat, fluttered in his chest as Dreya disappeared, as that blankness came for him.

Another step.

A wave of nausea rolled over him, stronger this time. The forest churned around him, sloshing from side to side as he stumbled. Even the twins were unsteady on their feet, staggering as the girl led them onward.

"Only one more," said the girl. She walked calmly, smoothly. "This is always the worst."

There was no mistaking it now. He needed to turn and run. He couldn't go another step, and yet the girl dragged them forward. On the other side of that invisible veil was Matthias, waiting to burn them alive. He could practically hear Jarrett's voice in his head, yelling at him to stop, to turn around, to flee. Dreya's nails dug into his skin.

The girl slipped from sight.

Then Devon.

No.

No.

No.

Dreya vanished.

He closed his eyes and bit his tongue to keep the screaming in, to keep his heart from exploding in its frantic beat.

Electricity rolled across his skin in a tingling wave. Pleasant, almost. And when it cleared, the panic was gone. He opened his eyes and gasped.

The trees had given way to a clearing roughly the size of a city block. A stream split it down the middle, and campers and trailers radiated out from a central bonfire like spokes on a wagon wheel. The crackle of fire and scent of wood smoke filled his head, along with the murmur of conversation. He paused. *How the hell is this possible?* He hadn't sensed any of this from the outside.

The girl didn't give them any time to ponder. She released Devon's hand and turned to them.

"Mother will see you now. You've kept us waiting."

Then she turned and walked toward the trailers.

The three of them paused. Dreya looked to Devon and took a deep breath. Devon nodded and squared his shoulders, looking for all the world like he was about to go into battle. They began to follow, but Tenn reached out and grabbed the sleeve of Dreya's coat. Although the panic from before was gone, there was still the gut-deep fear that came from knowing that, at any moment, the forest was going to be overrun by Howls and necromancers bent on their destruction.

"Are you sure we're safe here?" he asked. And the unspoken question: *Are they safe from what we've brought toward them?* He glanced back to the trees. He fully expected to see shadows darting through them, for people to start screaming as the nightmares leaped forth. But the woods were silent.

"We can trust their magic," Dreya said. She gestured to the trailers. "They have clearly been living here for some time."

And she was right. Camper wheels were covered in dead vines and weeds. Some trailers were propped up on cinder blocks or nestled in the earth.

"I guess," Tenn said, though he didn't really buy it. He kept a light touch on Earth, just in case, constantly scanning the woods for any sign of movement. He could feel the Howls and the rest of the army swarming against the edge of the trees, but they didn't come any farther. They just darted around it, swarming like ants around a stone. Was it true? Were they somehow magically hidden from the Howls and the necromancers? It seemed impossible. After the Academy, the illusion of safety set him on edge.

The girl led them over to a tan trailer that looked fairly generic—a few curtained windows, an awning slumped with snow. The only thing that set it apart was the amulet hung over the door: a seven-pointed star resting in the curve of a horned moon. She opened it without knocking and stepped inside, leaving Tenn and the twins to follow behind. The twins didn't move. After an awkward moment of standing there, being stared at by a few passersby, Tenn took the lead and stepped in.

Inside, the trailer was warm and cozy, filled with draped fabric and flickering candles. It was simple: a kitchen table in a small kitchenette, with a large tapestry hiding the rooms beyond. The girl was already sitting at the table, a mug of steaming tea in her hands. A woman stood by the stove, stirring a pot of soup that smelled like carrot and ginger. Everything in the trailer had the taste of home, and it was so perfect, so inviting, that Tenn's nerves immediately fired into defense mode.

Nothing in the world could feel this safe. Not unless it was all about to be torn away.

"We don't usually welcome Hunters in our midst," the woman said, not turning away from the soup. "Even if they do know our code."

She rested the spoon on top of the pot and wiped her hands on her apron. She was tall and slim, with long brown hair flecked with gray. Her gaze took in the twins and finally settled on Tenn. She didn't smile; she looked like she was appraising them, and for a split second he wondered if she would kick them out. He wondered if this was why the twins had been wary of the Witches: in the woman's eyes, Tenn felt his sins laid bare.

"Though perhaps we can make an exception for the ones the spirits told us to wait for." Her lips quirked into a small smile at Tenn's obvious shock. "You must be Tenn."

"How do you know my name?"

"I know much about you, young Hunter. But I'm getting ahead of myself. My name is Rhiannon. I'm the Mother of our clan. And we've been waiting for you for quite some time."

"How could you have been waiting for us?" Tenn asked.

Rhiannon just smiled again and went back over to the pot. She grabbed a ladle from the counter and began doling out soup into bowls. Tenn felt like he was stuck in one of those books he'd read as a kid—hanging out with a band of witches in the woods, eating soup in a caravan. Almost like the stories, if not for the dread that settled in his gut and the monsters looming on the horizon.

"You ask many questions, Tenn, but I'm afraid they aren't the right ones. At least, not for the moment." She handed a bowl to him with a smile. Even that felt storybook.

"Then what *is* the right question?" he asked. He couldn't keep the bite out of his words. Dreya noticed and shot him a glare.

"If we can help you in your quest, of course." She leaned back against the sink and nodded to the bowls in their hands. "Eat up before it gets cold. I suspect it's been a while since you've had a home-cooked meal. Mara, if you could make some room."

Quest. This wasn't a quest. He'd just lost the guy he'd been falling for and had been dragged through hell. That wasn't a quest. That was torture. That was life.

The girl at the table, Mara, slid to the side, allowing them space to sit and eat. Tenn couldn't help but notice that the twins were unusually silent. It didn't help his nerves.

What had they done to incur the wrath of someone so kind? Or was Rhiannon hiding a darker secret?

"Now," she said once a few minutes had passed. "We know you are here to learn about the runes. The spirits have told us of your need, and we know what rides on your shoulders. We will aid as we can."

The soup caught in his throat, but he swallowed it down. Was it that easy? She would just give them the information like that? Rage filled him, but was quickly suppressed. If they'd gone faster, if they'd gotten here sooner, Jarrett might still be alive. But that was dangerous thinking. There were a dozen things he could have done to save Jarrett, had he known. The first being dying during the Resurrection...

Then another, more bitter thought crossed his mind: if the Witches had shared this knowledge sooner, they could have prevented the deaths of millions.

"You have to teach us—" Tenn began, but she waved him off.

"You are too hasty," she said. "What do you know of the runes?"

Tenn glanced at the twins, since they were the ones who seemed to know more than anyone, but Dreya kept silent. She hid behind her hair, spinning her spoon idly in her soup.

He pulled back his sleeve to reveal his Hunter's mark.

"I know that the runes connect us to the elements," he said. He wasn't about to mention that he could hear them, in a way. "They're what let us use the Spheres. I know they're magical. That they can turn people into Howls."

"In a sense, but not quite," Rhiannon said. "The runes are an alphabet—they hold no power in themselves. Ages ago, man and the gods communicated freely. As time progressed, the communication turned into a written language. The gods granted mankind words to influence the world, the words the gods used to will creation into being. Because when humanity thrived, so did the gods humanity served. Every culture had its own alphabet and its own words, as the gods were as unique as the culture and land. In time, however, the languages changed. Became diluted. Humans lost sight of the gods and the origin of their words, and as they turned away from the source, the words lost their power. Eventually, magic bled from the words, and only the holiest of mortals were able to tap into the original power. Only a few remembered the original sigils of change. Runes, hieroglyphs, even the words we speak today, were all derived from the lost words of power.

"But the gods never stopped speaking. Years ago, when we learned how to tap into magic again, it was not because we stumbled upon the right symbols by accident. It was because we finally learned how to listen to the gods, and to the language they'd been speaking this entire time. When we use the runes, we tap into their power. We literally speak the language of the gods our Ancestors once served."

"So these runes," Tenn muttered, pulling back his sleeve to stare at his arm, "these were spoken by gods?"

Rhiannon nodded. "They are the words of creation. The words of the elements."

"And the necromancers..."

"Serve a darker god," Rhiannon said, her voice lowering. "They have tainted the sacred language, turned it against the very fabric of creation."

"The Dark Lady," he said.

"Yes," Rhiannon said. She pushed herself away from the counter and walked over to them, sidling onto the bench next to Devon. He seemed to shrink away from her, but if Rhiannon noticed, she didn't acknowledge it. "The Dark Lady was human once, but She wrapped herself up in the words of gods that were best left forgotten. That knowledge changed her into something more. She became a vessel for something darker, a power that had been lying in wait."

"But She's dead," Tenn said. "She died after creating the Kin. The Church killed her. Now, She's just a story."

"You can't kill a god, Tenn," Rhiannon said. "The mortal we know as the Dark Lady may have died, but the gods She served, the forces that worked through her—and perhaps even the consciousness She embodied—those live on."

He suppressed the shudder that wanted to rack him: he knew the Dark Lady lived on. He'd felt her, in his dreams, and in the runes he'd seen carved into her artifacts.

"What can you tell us about the runes?" he asked. The sooner he got what they were looking for, the sooner he could end this nightmare. "How do we use them to kill her minions?"

Rhiannon sighed.

"We do not use magic for violence, Tenn. That is what got us into this mess, and nonviolence is the core of our faith. In that regard, we cannot help you. But we can teach you what we *do* know of the runes. And perhaps, if the spirits wish to speak through you as they said, they will teach you themselves.

"Tomorrow," she said. "It is far too late to begin your studies. Besides, our translator is out in the woods right now, doubling our defenses. You three have brought quite an army our way. We must ensure our lines hold up."

"Sorry," Tenn said. The rage from before faltered in an instant, all under the reminder that now he was the reason people were dying. The Dark Lady wanted *him*.

Rhiannon reached out and patted his hand.

"Never apologize for being hunted," she said. "We have been on the lookout ever since we settled here last summer. The sept nearby has been very active lately. Inquisitors roaming the woods, children missing... These are dark days."

"Why would you put yourselves in danger by moving here?" he asked.

"Because the spirits told us this is where we would find you. We go where the gods will." She sighed and leaned back in her chair. "I'm sure you are tired, but I'm afraid we have no room in our trailers for guests. There's a tent by the fire. It should keep you warm enough."

Tenn wanted to demand more information. He didn't want to sleep. No, he didn't want to sleep *alone*. Not that he ever would, with Matthias or Tomás peering into his head. But he'd somehow eaten all the soup, and with every passing moment the warmth and exhaustion seeped through his limbs. Earth rumbled in his pelvis—he needed to rest. If he was to have any chance of killing Matthias, he needed to be at full strength.

"It's more than enough," Tenn said. He looked at the twins,

who were still staring at their bowls of soup. Neither had tasted a drop. Earth almost made him ask for their portions. "Thank you for the hospitality."

"Of course, Tenn," Rhiannon said. "In the morning, you'll find the answers you seek. Sleep well."

Tenn nodded and stood, the twins only a beat behind.

"Thank you again," he said.

"It is we who should be thanking you, Tenn," Rhiannon said. She watched them leave from the doorway.

He wanted to ask her what she meant.

The majority of him didn't want to know.

CHAPTER TWENTY-ONE

TENN WOKE EARLY, BUT A QUICK GLANCE AROUND the tent told him he wasn't the first to rise. Devon was missing, though Dreya was still fast asleep.

He slipped from the tent and stood by the edge of the fire, the snow drifting around his ankles in a breeze. It was a clear day, and fresh snow blazed white in the bright morning air. It looked beautiful—frost on the trailer windows, snow against tires and sloping on roofs. No Tomás in the night, no Matthias in his dreams—at least, not that he could remember. Even the weight of Jarrett's death seemed lighter, though that didn't actually make him feel any better.

He didn't want to forget. He wouldn't.

Devon sat on the opposite side of the fire pit, his legs crossed and body turned toward the rising sun. Fire flickered in his chest, and sparks danced about like motes of dust, the heat melting a perfect circle in the snow around him. A part of Tenn wanted to walk over and try to talk, but he had a feeling that would be a mistake. If meditating was the only thing keeping the rage of Fire in check, Tenn wouldn't do anything to interfere.

The door of the trailer behind him opened and Rhiannon stepped out, a thick quilt wrapped around her. She smiled when she saw him, then caught sight of Devon. The smile slipped as she walked up beside Tenn.

"He is deeply hurt," she whispered.

"Yeah," Tenn replied.

"Do you know why?" she asked.

He shook his head. Even though their voices were muted, they still carried in the thin morning air. If Devon heard them, he didn't show it.

"You hurt, as well," she said. "You, most of all."

Tenn shrugged. "We all do," he replied, but his words didn't carry the resoluteness he wanted. He was quickly growing tired of all these people seeing inside his head, speaking like they were from some other century. Rhiannon shuffled her quilt tighter around her. She smelled like wildflowers.

"You lost someone dear to you," she said. It wasn't a question, and the statement hung on the air like a specter.

"How do you know? Did the spirits tell you?"

She looked at him. He'd expected the bitterness to cut, but she just smiled softly. "No. It may as well be tattooed on your face. I know you don't fully trust us or our beliefs—not many do—but I have lived long enough to know one thing: pain is what lets us know we are alive. Without it, we are ghosts. Accept it as a gift. It will give you strength. Otherwise, pain will consume you, and then you risk losing sight of what life has granted you." She looked at her trailer briefly, then went back to staring at the trees. "I'll introduce you to Luke after breakfast. He's quite excited to meet the three the gods have been speaking of." She put a hand on his shoulder. "You, especially. Our Circle is soon. You are welcome to join if you'd like."

"What's a Circle?" he asked.

She smiled. "You will find out."

The rest of the community woke up shortly thereafter. The moment the first door cracked open, Devon started and stood, wiping invisible dust from his jeans and disappearing into the tent.

One by one, the Witches gathered around the fire, silent and solemn; unlike the citizens of Outer Chicago, the people didn't look ragged or run-down. Their clothes looked secondhand, sure, but they were colorful and upcycled, a little more vibrant and bohemian than he was used to in this dismal world. The twins appeared much later, neither making eye contact. Rhiannon walked into her trailer and brought out a large brass bowl. When she returned to Tenn's side, she struck the bowl with a mallet wrapped in leather, creating a low, ringing tone that echoed through the clearing. Immediately, the timbre of the morning changed. Silence grew, and even Tenn felt compelled to stand at attention. Rhiannon stepped forward with the bowl held before her.

"We give thanks," she said. "Today, we give thanks for warmth and shelter, for food and family. We give thanks for new friends," she said, glancing at him and the twins, "and we give thanks for old traditions." She struck the bowl. "We call to the ancient ones, to the spirits of the earth and air, the gods of fire and rain, and pray for guidance as we navigate this new world. We offer our prayers and our lives. Lead us back to balance, and we shall follow willingly." Another ring.

"We are your messengers." Her words were echoed by the group. Strike.

"We are your workers." Strike.

"We are your vessels." Strike.

"So mote it be," she whispered. The group repeated her words just as quietly, a whispered prayer.

She drew the mallet around the bowl in a slow, circular motion. At first Tenn couldn't hear anything; everyone and everything had gone completely silent. Then, low at first, he heard the tone of the bowl, the hum of metal as it vibrated in the chill morning air. Or maybe it wasn't the bowl. There was another sound, another pitch, as the people around him began to hum as well, matching their voices to the drone of the bowl. Devon and Dreya joined in. No magic was used, but the tone seemed to pull at his Spheres. Before he could wonder what was going on, he began to hum, as well.

In that instant, warmth spilled through him, an electric, comforting spark that made his skin tingle with life. Earth pulsed joyously in his gut; Water swirled in his stomach—for once without dredging up the horrors of his past. And even though he'd never been attuned to them, he could feel Fire and Air, the barest brush of their powers stirring in his body: a heat in his chest, a cool breath in his throat. There was even a tingle at the top of his scalp, the barest brush of energy where Maya rested in all its enigmatic power.

He couldn't tell how long he stood like that, swirling among the elements that pulsed in his veins like lifeblood, surrounded by others who surely felt it, too. Then the sound began to die down, slow and natural, a quiet fade into silence. He could still feel the tingle of the song.

Rhiannon struck the bowl again, softer this time. The Circle was over.

"What was that?" he asked as everyone began to go about their morning chores. Despite the horrors of the last few days, something about the Circle had lightened his mood, made the burden seem a little more bearable. "I've never felt anything like it."

Rhiannon smiled at him.

"That, dear Hunter, is the true magic of the Spheres." She turned and began walking back to the trailer. "Come on in, you three. It's time to learn."

The translator, Luke, wasn't what Tenn had expected. Somewhere along the way he figured the man who translated runes would be old, much older than him. That he'd have gray hair and wizard's robes, or else he'd look like some knockoff Norse god, all blond and muscular and mean. So when Rhiannon answered the door and welcomed in a guy not much older than Tenn, he was a little disappointed. Luke looked like every other hipster guy he'd seen—scruffy facial hair, messy brown hair pulled back in a man-bun and even the ubiquitous black-and-red check flannel. So much for a grand old wizard.

"So," Luke said. "You're here to learn about the runes."

Tenn nodded.

"Why?"

Tenn opened his mouth and realized quite quickly that he had no idea what to say. An answer to why he was being targeted. To how the runes could undo the undead. To why his magic was taking over, and the runes whispering in his head. Thankfully, Dreya chose that moment to step in.

"Our commander sent us," she said. She didn't meet anyone in the eye—strange, especially for her. She just stared at the table, one finger tracing nervous circles against the surface. "A jar covered in runes was found at the scene of our last battle. It's how the necromancers have been creating Howls. We believe…" She took a deep breath and glanced up, looking Rhiannon straight in the eye. "We believe that if the runes could be understood and reversed, so could the condition."

Silence filled the trailer. And for the first time since they'd been there, Tenn felt wholly unwelcome.

"Impossible," Luke finally said. His word broke the tension, but it didn't make Tenn feel any better. "We have known for years that the Howls were birthed using runes. How else could necromancers tap into such devastating power? But those runes won't help you. Nothing can."

"Why?"

Luke folded his hands and leaned back in his chair.

"To understand, you have to grasp the nature of magic. The runes are the language of the gods. They are, quite literally, the words that created our existence. This language is the magic that keeps the cosmos spinning, the threads and the loom on which everything is woven. The runes themselves are just markings, but they allow us to tap into that language, to harness its power." He reached over and pushed up the sleeve of Tenn's coat, revealing the twining Hunter's mark. "The runes of your mark allow you to use the elements, but you aren't really creating anything new. You're just using the powers that have already been built into the world. You're speaking a language spoken for centuries.

"And just as there are many races of man, there are many types of god. Each god has their own language. The language of the Dark Lady is as old as time and was spoken by countless other tainted souls before the Resurrection—the Dark Lady was merely the most recent, and perhaps the most successful. It is a language of evil gods, of forces that wish to rip the world apart. Every use of that power is another tear in the weave. You wish to reverse her work by twisting the words She used, but that will simply cause more destruction. The language of her gods is one geared entirely toward chaos. Any attempts to change it, to control or reverse it, will only unleash more evil. The repercussions could destroy the world."

"How do you know all this?" Tenn asked.

"Because we have tried," Rhiannon said. "In the beginning, when the Howls first formed, we begged the spirits for a solution. A cure. But not even the spirits we served were willing to delve into those darker mysteries. So we attempted on our own, tried to reverse or mute the language. It only made things worse. And, in our hubris, the spirits we served turned their backs on us." She sighed and stared out the window. "There was a time, years ago, when we could hear the gods in every sigh of wind, in every drop of rain. Now they have grown almost silent."

"Hearing the gods is my calling," Luke continued. "For some reason, the gods chose me to be their vessel. I've become the one person in all the clans who can hear their voices and translate those words into runes. That's how we learned to cloak ourselves from danger, how to purify water and grow food in barren soil. But it was like hearing a melody from far away. They were whispers from the past, old skills. The spirits refused to speak anything new. No matter how much I begged or tried to prove myself, they refused to speak the greater magics. I wasn't... I'm not a suitable vessel for their power. They refuse to help us do anything more than scrape by and survive."

"If that is true," Dreya said, "why did the spirits tell you to wait for us? Why do they want Tenn?"

And, Tenn wondered, *why didn't you tell anyone else? You could have saved millions!* The anger rose in his chest, but Rhiannon's words stamped it out.

"Because they need a host who can handle the power these words would carry. To speak the full language of the gods, one must be godlike." She looked at Tenn.

For a moment, his heart refused to beat.

"I'm not godlike," Tenn whispered. His words caught in his throat. If he had any special power, he would have been able to save Jarrett.

"So says the one toward whom the elements bend."

Tenn swallowed hard. Water seemed to curl in his stomach at the words; instantly, all he could think of was the battlefield only days ago, when the Sphere opened against his will. As if to keep him alive. As if the element itself was trying to protect him...

"How did—"

"I felt it the moment you stepped into our camp," she said. "The elements swirl around you like moths to the flame. You don't wield power. You attract it."

For a moment he envisioned Tomás and Matthias; he was attracting a great deal of power. Most of it, he wanted to avoid.

He shook his head and tried to keep the memories down. He didn't need them to be acting up. Not here. Not with everyone watching.

"Water..." he said, trying to stay in the present, "it's been acting up. Taking over. Sometimes it's almost like it wields itself. Like it's trying to survive."

"The greatest vanity of our time has been the belief that we can control nature," Rhiannon said. "We manipulate the elements, but they always fight back. Look at what has happened to the earth. Rivers boiled, mountains moved, forests turned to deserts and deserts crumbled to the seas. We don't control or wield the elements—only those who serve the Dark Lady would be so vain as to think we could truly change creation. No, the elements *allow* us to work with them. But humanity has always tried to claim dominance. The elements have been waiting for years to find someone that they could work not with, but through."

"Why me?"

She smiled, as though she'd been waiting for him to ask that question the entire time.

"Because you never asked for power. Power asked for you."

Tenn wanted to say that they were insane, that he wasn't special or chosen or anything like that, but before he could voice his concerns the trailer door slammed open. A boy burst in, his face bloody and a mangled arm held to his chest.

"Mother," he panted, gripping the doorframe. "We were attacked. Howls in the forest where we were playing. Near the final barrier. They took...they took Tori."

Rhiannon was there in a moment, her arms embracing the boy as he broke into sobs against her chest. Luke stood.

"I reinforced those runes myself," he said, shocked and staring out the window, as if waiting for the Howls to seep through. *It wasn't enough. It will never be enough.*

"We'll find her," Tenn said. He was on his feet and already heading toward the door, blood pounding in his ears and guilt riding his heart. It didn't matter how the Howls broke through, only that they had. "You don't know what you're dealing with. We do. We're the ones who brought him."

CHAPTER TWENTY-TWO

RHIANNON GRABBED HIS ARM BEFORE HE COULD make it out the door.

"We are not fighters, Tenn, so you are the only ones who can save Tori, but if you leave without an escort, you'll never find your way back. You'll need a tracking rune. Luke—I leave them in your care."

Luke pulled the brass singing bowl over to the table while Rhiannon left the camper, the boy held tight in her arms.

Tenn hovered by the door. Water was singing its siren song. It was time to kill. It was time to drown. He couldn't keep his agitation from his words.

"We don't have time—"

"Then learn fast!" Luke barked. He took a deep breath. "Runes are a language, yes? Each is a different word, a different purpose. But on the page, they're just marks. Letters. Same way a written word is just ink until read or spoken." He pointed into the brass singing bowl. A symbol was etched into

the center, a dark, deep groove that looked like the letter S,
with two strikes through it.

Just looking at it made Tenn's head ring, sent whispers of
waves and an arrow through the dark in his mind. "This is a
tracking rune. Most runes require elemental energy to work,
but this one runs on thought. Memorize it. Memorize the
rune and the object it is carved upon. Each clan has a unique
object—it's how we stay connected, no matter the distance
between us. I'm assuming that's how you found us."

Tenn barely noticed Devon nod. The rune took up his entire focus: it burned itself into his mind, humming in his head
as he memorized the curve of the bowl, the grain of the metal,
each individual hammer-mark of its forming. He felt heavy
with power, with a knowing that settled into his bones.

"When you have it memorized," Luke said, his voice barely
cutting through his thoughts. The rune seemed to be *calling*
to him. "Close your eyes and bring it to mind."

He did so. He could still see it, glowing in the dark of
his eyelids, orange and fiery like a lantern. The moment he
brought it to mind, he could *feel* it. Like an inner compass, he
could sense precisely where the bowl was in relation to him.
He turned and felt the proper direction slide around him, always calling him to the bowl.

When he opened his eyes, Luke was nodding.

"Good. Good. The rune is the same across the board—it's
the object it's drawn on that allows you to focus. It will help
you find us from anywhere in the world." He put a hand on

Tenn's shoulder. "Find Tori. And use the runes to bring her back to us."

"We'll find her," Tenn said. He looked to the twins. They were still avoiding his eyes. "I promise."

They left immediately.

A wave of energy washed over him a few yards from the clearing. The magic of the first barrier tingled over his skin and soaked into his bones, and for the briefest moment he swore he heard a whisper, felt the urging deep within his muscles: *run, run fast, run away*. Then it was over, a voice on the breeze. Apparently, the defenses didn't have so strong an effect when approached from behind.

A few yards on and he began to slow. Dreya cast him a glance, but she didn't speak as he scanned the trees. He could sense the next line of defense, the line of runes that somehow kept the clan safe. He could feel it in his gut. And he knew he needed to see the magic for himself.

Something glowed on the trunk of a nearby tree. He walked over and brushed the snow away. Green light shone beneath the flurry, glowing like a faerie fire. A long line of runes was etched down the tree, a sentence he could almost understand: the second barrier. Flashes burned through his mind the moment his fingers grazed the bark—being lost in the woods late at night, a wolf at your heels; spinning around at full force, never stopping; staring into the mouth of a ferocious beast; a chameleon, hiding in plain sight. In an instant the visions cleared, washed away with a whisper of dark promises. His fingertips tingled as he traced the runes over and over, trying to memorize the markings. Something about the language was familiar, like reading

Italian when versed in Spanish—there were traces of things he knew, patterns he could almost but not entirely piece together. If only he had more time to study them…

"Tenn," Dreya snapped. He looked up. "We must hurry."

He nodded, guilt doubling as he stood. Every time he blinked, he saw the runes burning in his mind, their whispered meaning nearly drowning out his thoughts. "Sorry. Let's keep going."

She led him onward—Devon had already disappeared from sight.

"How did they get through?" Tenn asked as they approached the third barrier—he could feel the buzz of its magic now, could see the faint glow of runes scattered throughout the trees.

"I do not know," Dreya whispered. "They should not have been able to find their way through. Not without the tracking rune."

Tenn didn't ask the other questions on his mind: if the Howls had broken through the first two barriers, why had they not penetrated the third? Why were they not out here, waiting, swarming? Why had they not attacked the rest of the Witches?

The field stretched out before them when they broke through the trees, snow freshly trampled. And on the ground, Tenn found his answer. Written in the same script as the desk in his dorm room, were words written in blood.

come out, come out, wherever you are

"He's toying with us," Tenn muttered. His gut writhed with anger and self-hate. He'd been right. The illusion of safety was just that: an illusion. He would never be safe. He would never feel at home. Not so long as Matthias was out there.

Or maybe even that was a lie. Maybe Tenn was the greatest danger to himself—death seemed to follow wherever he went.

"Correct," Dreya said. "And so, the question: Will you play his games?"

Dreya opened to Air beside him, her pale blue eyes fixed on a point far, far away.

"Anything?" Tenn asked. He didn't answer her question; mainly because he felt like, no matter what, he was a pawn in someone's game. Matthias or Tomás, the death following him seemed the same. His grip was tight on his staff, the point digging into the frozen earth. He refused to stare at the blood in the snow.

She nodded.

"Yes. I can feel them moving a few miles off. They have quite the start. I don't know how they moved so fast..." She shook her head and looked at him. "It is not the full army, of that I'm certain. Matthias must have split his forces."

"Where are they going? And where are the others?"

Dreya gestured to the horizon. "There is a town nearby. They are heading toward it. A few more Howls wait there. But not all. As for the rest, I cannot say."

This was a trap. They all knew it. But the alternative was waiting around and letting an innocent die. Jarrett's image flashed through his mind. He wasn't going to have any more deaths on his conscience. It was time to fight back. The Witches had their defenses—they would be safe. It was Tenn that Matthias was after.

"Well, then," he said. He opened to Earth and stretched the points of his staff into two wickedly curved blades. "Let's show these bastards what happens when they mess with our friends."

CHAPTER TWENTY-THREE

TENN AND DREYA SAT NESTLED IN THE RELATIVE safety of a pine grove, huddled under blankets and watching the town on the horizon. To the left of the town was the white light of the sept. Just the sight of it made Tenn shiver. Devon was out scouting. There was no chance they'd use magic and give themselves away, so they were forced to rely on their other senses. He wanted to attack, but Dreya advised waiting—if there were necromancers in the town, it would be best to attack when they were asleep.

It still felt like wasting time to him. The only consolation was the idea that Matthias would have expected them to rush in. That maybe, by biding their time for the proper moment to strike, the trio was turning the tables, playing a game Matthias wouldn't expect.

It was barely a consolation at all; every blink, and he saw Tori's blood in the snow. Every heartbeat, and he imagined hers stopping.

"Why didn't you tell me about the tracking rune?" Tenn asked.

Dreya glanced at him. There was a small fire between them, just enough to give a little light and warmth, but not enough to give them away. Her eyes went wide, then narrowed. It took her a long time to answer.

"What?"

"The tracking rune. Devon knew about it, so you did, too. Why didn't you tell me? Or show me?"

She opened her mouth to speak, then bit back her words and stared into the fire for a while.

"Because it was not my information to give," she whispered. "You must understand, Tenn. We have already broken so many vows. We had to hold on to those we could."

"If you had told me, we could have skipped coming here. Tori would still be alive."

She gasped. It sounded like she was biting back a sob.

"Yes," she finally said. "Yes, I know that. But they have magics we have never dreamed of. Runes we've never seen—like their defenses. We were ever only shown the tracking rune so we could find the clans. A small magic. Of no use to fighting the Dark Lady. That is why we brought you here—the Witches have access to so much more. They can teach you how to understand runes we've never seen. And when this is over... When this is over, you will learn everything they know. They will help you. I'm sure of it."

"If they're so helpful, why are you scared of them?"

He didn't care that it was mean. He couldn't even blame it on Water at the moment. He was tired of being the cause of so much pain. Especially when it seemed to be preventable.

"Devon and I...we grew up among them. Years ago, years before the Resurrection, we lived in an orphanage. We were five when Genevieve adopted us. She was smart, that woman. Most people believe that the Spheres were discovered only shortly before the Resurrection, when the first Academy was built, but the Witches, they've known about the Spheres for centuries. They just never told anyone or hid them under different names. Genevieve was one of those who knew the true power of the elements, how to attune to the Spheres and use their powers, and she guarded her knowledge with ferocious passion. She created one of the first clans after the Resurrection hit."

"I thought you said you grew up with a fashion designer?"

She gave him a small smile.

"I did cosplay growing up, and Genevieve loved her clothes and the ones I designed for her. The rest...it's an easier story to tell than the truth."

She took a deep breath and closed her eyes.

"Genevieve taught us everything she knew about the world and the nature of magic. She even attuned us to our first Spheres. When the Howls appeared, she kept us safe, taught us never to turn to violence. We stayed with her clan until... until we couldn't."

"What happened?"

She bit her lip. In that one, small action, she looked terribly young and impossibly vulnerable. "We killed them," she whispered.

"What?" Had he misheard? "You mean the Howls?"

"No. The clan. We killed them. All of them. That is how we repaid their kindness."

Tenn's stomach knotted.

"I don't understand…" he began. She held out her hand, and he fell into silence.

"It is better to show you," she whispered.

"I—"

"Open to Water," she said. "Open to Water and see."

He looked at her hand, at her delicate fingers. He had no clue what she was going on about, and a part of him didn't want to find out.

"Please," she said.

He nodded, took her hand and opened to Water.

Her memories flooded through him in a downpour…

"What's that?" she asks.

Devon sits bolt upright beside her, his shirt unbuttoned and his legs crossed before him, sweat dripping down his forehead and stubbled cheeks. The moon is full above them, the hum of cicadas around them almost deafening. She hadn't thought the insects lived this far up the mountain. Beyond the hum, the air is still and humid, with the bellow of thunder in the valley below.

"I don't know," he says, his words trailing like a question. They lock eyes.

We aren't supposed to use magic, she feels him say.

I don't care, she replies.

Trees rise up on all sides of them, blocking their view of everything for miles around. She stands and walks to the edge of the small stone circle they'd created—their sanctuary and sign to the gods that they were there to feel their voice, there to be granted a vision. She had locked away the hunger of the fast days ago, until it was nothing but a quiet murmur in the back of her mind. No food, no shelter, no magic—the ritual demanded such. Just water and meditation. Just waiting and praying and begging for a sign from the gods. The rumble comes again, and she closes her eyes. Something is wrong. Something is very, very wrong.

She breaks her vows.

She opens to Air, the first Sphere she'd ever been attuned to.

The power sends her flying, her senses soaring down the mountain like an eagle. Every leaf and blade of grass, every movement of every creature, all of it stands out like shadows in the light. She can see the outline of it all, can hear the rustle and staccato of breath. She pushes her magic farther, down into the valley where the rest of the clan camps, waiting for them and holding a vigil for their eventual return.

Smoke and fire fill the air, the scent of brimstone scoring the screams of men and women and children as flesh chars and snaps. But there is another taste that makes her skin crawl—the taint of twisted magic. She can feel energy sizzling as Witches try to fight back, feel shapes moving through the surrounding woods as kravens burst forth, searching for flesh. She senses necromancers using their evil magic to turn her friends and family into Howls.

As she stands there, everyone she knows is being slaughtered. Or worse.

She snaps back the power and opens her eyes. There's no need to tell Devon what she saw. Through their connection, he's seen it, too. He stands facing the direction of the clan. His fists clench, knuckles white. Sparks dance around him like fireflies while Fire burns in his chest, casting strange lights on the trees around them. It was the first Sphere he had attuned to, and that meant its hold on him was the greatest.

"Kill them," he says. "We have to."

"No," she gasps. The very thought makes her stomach churn.

Her mind swims from using Air, the aftereffect making her slow, her thoughts confused. She must have heard him wrong.

He looks at her, his eyes burning with hatred. It doesn't matter how many times she's seen Fire take him over—it still terrifies her. When the Sphere takes hold, he is no longer her brother. Not fully. He's something infinitely angrier, and infinitely more powerful.

"It's the only way," he says. "If we don't kill them, they'll come for us."

Then the Fire in him mellows, just for a moment.

"They would have wanted this, Dreya. They would rather die at our hands than be turned."

She bites back the tears that try to form in her eyes. Now isn't the time for emotion. Now is the time for clear thought, for action. Air screams in her throat like a gale, pushing away all weakness. She closes her eyes and feels the power surge between them.

"Night has fallen," she whispers, Air carrying her words, the funereal chant echoing down the cliff, piercing through the chaos below. "The Ancestors come to take us away, for we are but ghosts and form, ash and breath. We call to you, gods of water, earth, air and flame, protect us, shield us and carry us home again."

Fire blooms in the valley, sharp and hot, searing through the woods like the hands of a hundred gods. Devon's magic knows no bounds, holds no distinction between Witch or necromancer or Howl. Flesh is flesh, and flesh is food. She fuels his flames with Air, until the night sky grows white and bright as day. The roar of fire is deafening, a scream and hiss that pierces through her bones. The hell feels like it should burn and last forever, but the fight is over in an instant. She doesn't open her eyes. Not until she hears him sobbing beside her.

She turns and looks to her brother, tries to find some words to comfort him. But she can smell the smoke of flesh filtering through the air, can taste the dead. Air leaves her breathless, without thought, without words. She can only gasp as she puts a hand on his shoulder. He cries, his fingers clenching and unclenching in the dirt as if trying to tear the world apart. As if trying to make the world feel their pain.

Tenn snapped his hand back. His senses were on fire, every inch of his skin tingling and burning as the aftereffect of the vision faded. Dreya watched him, her expression carefully guarded. There was a look in her eyes, though, one he wasn't used to seeing. Expectant. Like she was waiting for him to cast his judgment.

"What was that?" he finally managed.

She held her hand to her chest and stared into the flames.

"That is why we avoid the Witches. Violence goes against the very core of their beliefs, and we killed our entire clan. We killed everyone we ever loved. They were innocent, and they died by our hands." She cradled her head in her hands. "I can still hear their screams."

Tenn closed his eyes. Her grief was fresh in his mind and heart, just as raw and nagging as his own. He felt her memories lingering with his, filling in cracks, becoming his own history.

"You had no choice," he whispered. *We've all done horrible things.* If it were his parents being turned, if he'd had that chance to save them from an agonizing death or an eternity of mindless devouring, would he have done any differently?

"We always have a choice, Tenn," she said. "Every day, I question ours. Every day, I try to convince myself we chose properly."

"You did," he said. His words sounded hollow.

A few beats passed in silence. He opened his eyes, but neither of them looked at each other. Finally, Dreya spoke.

"Do you remember when you asked us how to control the madness of the Spheres? How to stop the visions and nightmares?"

He nodded. Of course he remembered. Devon's words burned in his mind behind every thought: *you die.*

"I would give anything to silence them," she said, almost to herself. "But we cannot die. Not yet. Not until the necromancers are gone and the threat of this happening to anyone else is vanished. That is why we joined the guild, why Jarrett did us the greatest of services. We told him what we had done, yet he let us fight by his side. And that is why we will follow you to the very end.

"We cannot rest until we have destroyed every servant of the Dark Lady. Then, and only then, will our deeds be absolved. Until that day, we live knowing we killed our own family. We live with the madness, and we let it burn." She paused and looked at him, the fire glinting in her pale, wet eyes. "We let it burn until it burns us alive."

CHAPTER TWENTY-FOUR

DEVON ARRIVED A WHILE LATER. HIS SCARF WAS wrapped high over his ears and around his head to keep out the cold. He put a hand on Dreya's shoulder. Now that Tenn knew that they actually *could* read each other's thoughts, the exchange was, oddly, a little less strange.

"The humans are asleep," she said. "If we are to strike, we should do it now."

Tenn nodded. Adrenaline coursed through his veins at the thought of running headfirst into a town overrun with the undead. He stood and kicked some snow into the fire. They left before the last ember died out.

They kept to the highway as they made their way to the town. It was so dark and the wind so biting it was impossible to see more than a few feet in front of them. They made their way from car to abandoned car, finding brief solace against toppled semis. Every once in a while, Dreya would pulse a small flame between her hands, letting the faint light filter out between her fingertips to guide the way. Then darkness would swallow them again. What Tenn wouldn't give to once more live in a world with electricity. Or at least a flashlight.

It was the third or fourth time that Dreya opened to Air that she stiffened and halted them in their tracks. The flame in her hand burned longer than usual, but her eyes were focused on the road before them.

"Something is moving," she said.

Tenn's grip instinctively tightened on his staff. Even through the thick leather of his gloves, the metal was bitingly cold.

"Howl?" he asked.

"I do not think so," she whispered. "It is staggering." She sniffed. "Blood. I smell blood."

"Tori," Tenn said.

He opened to Earth and Water, a quick flash, just enough to let him sense the figure's approach. Sure enough, it was a young girl, maybe thirteen, maybe younger. He could feel her cooling flesh, taste the blood that sprinkled on the ground with every footstep. Every shivering, bare footstep.

"She's hurt," he said. Then instinct took over. He opened once more to Earth and ran, the power guiding him through the dark.

"Tenn, wait!" Dreya yelled, but it was too late. He had already taken off, the twins falling fast behind him. He knew it was a trap. He knew that he was running to his death. But Water and Earth told him all he needed to know: Tori's pulse was failing, her skin was bare. If he didn't reach her soon, she was as good as dead.

He wouldn't lose someone else because he was too slow, because he had hesitated. He wouldn't let someone die because he hadn't been there to help. Not again.

He couldn't get Jarrett's face out of his head.

He ran full speed, Earth fueling his muscles and numbing him to the wind and the snow that beat down in chunks of ice. A few hundred yards. A hundred. Fifty away, and he felt her stagger. She fell into the snow, shivering. He felt her heart skip.

He reached her seconds later, dropped to his knees in the snow and tried not to panic. Now that he was near, he could sense all the things he'd been too distanced to notice before. Like the way blood smeared over every inch of her flesh. Or the thousand cuts slashed across her bare skin. Not one inch of her was clothed, and not one inch was spared from the slices that slowly bled her dry.

When he placed a hand on her shoulder, she flinched away and screamed.

"Shh, shh," he whispered. "It's okay. I'm here to help."

But the girl was lost to him. Her screams split the air, and with every inch she tried to put between them, another ounce of blood was lost. If he didn't act fast, she'd bleed out before he even had a chance to start healing. If she didn't die of hypothermia first.

"I'm sorry," he said. He reached out and grabbed her arm, clamped it tight as a vise. Then he began pouring Earth into her body.

She screamed again at the pain he knew the process was inflicting. Her heart hammered fast. Stuttered. She fell silent.

He knew the cuts that crossed her skin. He'd seen them before. They weren't the casual, careless marks of a kraven or even a necromancer. They were made by a bloodling, one who knew how to prolong the pain and the bleeding, how to make the most from their victim. He'd felt himself make those same marks when consumed by Dmitri's past.

Devon and Dreya knelt by his side. Dreya put a hand on his shoulder. Cool light filtered down around them, but he didn't check to see which of them was using magic.

"Tenn, you must stop," she said. "The power you're using will give us away."

"Either help me or shut up," he snapped. He wouldn't lose her. Not like he lost his parents. And Katherine. And Jarrett. And countless others.

He poured his focus into the girl. The process was pain-stakingly slow, even though he worked as fast as he could. A small voice inside of him screamed that it wasn't fast enough— he could only heal one cut at a time. He didn't listen. He forced Water into her veins and Earth into her bones, tried to replenish the blood that was quickly seeping into the snow, staining it crimson.

There was only the slightest hesitation from Dreya.

"What can we do?" she asked.

"Heat," he replied. He could barely hear them through his concentration. "She'll freeze to death otherwise."

Devon knelt by the girl's side and placed his hands on the concrete. Fire opened in his chest, and the snow around them melted in moments. A small cocoon of warmth enveloped them and sweat burst across Tenn's skin.

"Tenn," Dreya whispered suddenly. Her grip on Tenn's shoulder tightened.

"What?" he asked.

"They're coming," was all she said.

Tenn glanced up, spared a half second to focus on something other than the girl quickly dying at his feet. The Howls within the town emerged like a swarm of vermin. In spite of the warmth Devon enveloped them in, the air grew colder, a chill that seeped and burned into his very bones. He didn't need to see them to know what was causing the sudden cold. Succubi. The town was harboring succubi.

"Fight them off," he said, then refocused on Tori. In that momentary distraction, she had slipped away even further. Her pulse was weak, so weak.

"But the sept—" Dreya began.

"I don't care about the fucking sept!" he yelled. He glared up at her. "I won't let her die."

Her jaw clenched, but she nodded and looked out to the city. Using all this magic would call the full wrath of the Church down upon them, that was for certain. He could only hope that if the Inquisitors appeared, they'd fight off the necromancers and Howls first.

Dreya opened to Air and opened her lips, a single, clear note ringing out into the wild night. The wind became a gale. But the necromancers were ready. Fire billowed up around Tenn and the others. Devon cursed and threw out a shield, the air around them whirling with flame and magic. The heat was suffocating. But it didn't block out the darker powers at work: Tenn's hands shook from the succubi's life-stealing cold.

"I said fight them off!" he yelled. Rage filled him. But it wasn't just anger, it was desperation. Tori's skin glistened red and bloody in the firelight, and now, when he looked at her, he couldn't help but imagine Jarrett lying there, slowly bleeding out. Every blink, and he saw Jarrett's face. Pleading. Waiting. Dying.

Dreya didn't answer in words. Instead, her song rose in volume as a blast of wind shot across the countryside, wailing like hungry wolves. Funnels broke down from the sky, but that didn't stop the oncoming Howls. He could hear their screams, could feel the necromancers' magic as they worked against him. But that knowledge was small and distant. Every ounce of attention he had he gave to the girl.

"Tenn," Dreya said, her song cut short. Her voice was strained, her breathing ragged; the twins were already holding each other for support. "I cannot hold them off. There are too many necromancers. And I think… I think they have a Breathless One. Some Howls are resisting my magic."

In spite of his focus, this made him halt. The Breathless Ones were hard to create and harder to kill and were thankfully rare—but just as Fire magic didn't harm a succubus, Air didn't harm the Breathless Ones. If anything, it gave them strength by feeding their hungering Sphere. Bloodlings, succubi, Breathless Ones… What other nightmares had been lying in wait for them?

"Devon," he said. "Help her."

Devon nodded. Power flashed through him as Fire billowed in his chest. The town erupted into flame.

Tori continued to slip from Tenn's fingers. She shivered uncontrollably in spite of the heat. He poured more power into her, more than he would have ever dared before. Her body shook as wound after wound sealed itself. The ground rumbled with latent magic.

More flames erupted on all sides, and the earth heaved violently as a fresh surge of dark Earth magic flew their way. Tenn lost his grip on Tori. Just for a moment, their connection severed. He stumbled back, hurried over to her side.

But it had been long enough.

When he placed his hands on her cold skin once more, he felt her heart beat for one, final time.

"No," he whispered. He shook her, gently, and flooded her limp limbs with magic. "No," he said, louder, over and over until he was screaming it at the top of his lungs and it wasn't Tori on the ground, but Jarrett, Jarrett staring up with those pleading blue eyes, Jarrett soaked in his own blood.

Blood, blood everywhere.

Tenn rocked back on his heels as another wave of magic rolled over them and sent the ground squirming. The twins screamed with power. With fear. It was too much. Too much.

Blood on his hands. Blood on his jeans. Blood seeping through his skin.

Red filled his vision.

He stood and Water was raging, raging red. Water filled him with power. All that red. All that blood. All that magic. Filling him.

He screamed.

It wasn't a scream of loss or desperation. This was the scream of Water, of rage and death and bloodlust. The Sphere howled in his gut as torrents of energy lashed through his body. The world seemed to pause with his heart. Everything slowed. Everything stopped.

Then his heart beat again, and it beat with power.

He reached out, latched on to the hearts and pulses of every creature in that town. He felt them, all of them—the Howls and the humans, the damned and the damning. He felt their hearts throb, the water pulse in their veins. Magic flooded through him in painful ecstasy. He felt their hearts beat. All of them, beating a rhythm of life. A rhythm neither Jarrett nor Tori would ever feel again.

He clenched his fingers, felt every muscle, every vein, a glowing, terrible lacework of fragile life.

And then he stopped their hearts.

The blowback was immediate and immense. His own heart screamed out as the hundred lives at the ends of his fingertips squirmed for life. He held on. His heart ached. Tears streamed down his face and he heard them screaming. Screaming, just as his parents had screamed, as his friends had screamed, as Jarrett had screamed. Water filled him, amplified the pain, the agony, the pure ecstasy of it all. His head whipped back and his arms stretched out from his sides as the power flooded through him, lifting him off the ground in a halo of blue. The enemy screamed. He screamed louder. Their pulses throbbed. Burned.

Stopped.

A snap.

The power vanished. And as he fell to the ground like a marionette cut from its strings, he felt the hundred others die with him.

He crumpled, along with his enemy. When darkness overtook him, he heard nothing but silence.

CHAPTER TWENTY-FIVE

TOMÁS STROKED THE SIDE OF TENN'S FACE.

"It's rare," Tomás said.

"What is?" Tenn asked.

He sat before Tomás on a fur rug while the incubus lounged in a large leather chair, a fire crackling in the hearth behind him.

"To meet one like you. You're a challenge."

"I don't know what you mean."

In the corner of the room, chains clinked together. Tenn looked over. Jarrett was there, chained to the wall like a dog, a thick collar around his neck. His naked body was smeared with blood.

"Let him go," Tenn said. He looked back, but it was no longer Tomás. It was the necromancer Matthias. He sneered, his dark eyes burning like coal fires.

"Of course. He doesn't matter. But you? You're mine forever."

Tenn glanced at the chains on his own wrists and ankles,

felt the large manacle around his neck. Matthias held the other end in his hand. Matthias opened to Fire; the chains glowed red. Tenn smelled his flesh burning before the pain arrived. When it hit, his whole world went white.

"You're still alive," Dreya said.

Her words cut through the haze of his dream. He couldn't tell if it was a statement or a question.

He tried to move, but every single joint in his body ached. It felt like he'd been filled with acid—his very blood seemed to beat against him. When he opened his eyes, he found that it was morning. At least, he thought it was morning. The sun sat on a cloudy horizon, the world a pinkish wash of white.

"What happened?" Tenn asked. His throat was dry. So dry. He needed to drink.

He couldn't remember anything, just pain. Then it began to come back to him in a haze. Heading out to the city, the army, the girl...

"Tori," he said. Despite the pain, he pushed himself up to sitting. The world swayed. "Where is she?"

Dreya looked down, then pointed to her side. He followed her finger and found a blanket-wrapped bundle sitting at the edge of the clearing they were in, nestled against the trunk of a pine. Tenn's heart sank and tears filled his eyes. How did he have moisture left for tears?

He couldn't help himself. He started to sob.

"You tried," Dreya responded. "What you did—"

"Didn't help," Tenn said through his tears. He wanted to believe the emotion was from Water, but he couldn't bring himself to buy it. *I failed. I failed. I will always fail.*

"You saved our lives," Dreya said. There was a note in her voice, something he'd not heard before. Awe. "I don't know how you did it. I've never seen so much power. You stopped their hearts—such magic should be impossible."

"But it was too late," he croaked. He could barely remember what he'd done after Tori died in his hands. He just knew he was paying for it dearly. And it hadn't even been enough. *If only you'd found that power sooner.*

Dreya slapped him.

And it wasn't gentle.

"Stop being a fool," she said. "Only an idiot mourns what he could not change. You saved our lives, and you tried to save hers. Let that be enough."

He didn't move, but he stared up at her, sniffing back his tears. His heart broke and he couldn't tell if it was the ache of Water or the realization that it would never, ever be enough. Her eyes were set, and there was an edge to her voice that told him she'd be more than happy to slap him again.

"Where's Devon?" he asked, rather than letting himself drown in images of what he'd failed to do.

"Searching," she said. "Looking for survivors."

"And?"

"None so far," she said. Again, that note of awe. "How did you channel so much power? You took out the entire army in a single swipe. It should have killed you."

"I don't know," Tenn said. Like so many things happening in his life right now, he didn't have a clue.

She shook her head in disbelief and stared at him for a while.

"Here, I thought the world was done with surprises," she said. Then she looked to the city on the horizon.

Smoke and red light curled up from the burning buildings. He swallowed harshly and shuffled over to a spot of untouched snow. With numb hands, he began scraping it up and putting it to his lips.

"Here," Dreya said. She moved to his side and took the snow in her own hands, opened to Fire and Water and both melted the snow and turned the ice below it into a bowl. A crystalline bowl filled with water, beautiful as fine china.

"How did you do that?" he asked. He'd never seen such delicate uses of magic, and maybe it was the rawness of Water, but he didn't think he'd ever seen something so beautiful.

Dreya gave a faint smile.

"I've had a lot of practice," she said. She handed him the bowl, water glittering against her pale, willowy fingers. He took it and drank. Dreya settled back and looked to the city.

"He will be back soon," she said. "When he is, we will leave. But I'm afraid…" She sighed. "We are going to have to leave her body here. We have no way of carrying her."

Again, the thought of driving crossed his mind, but there was no way, not in all this snow. They could melt it, sure, but even though he'd just alerted everything in a hundred miles of their location, he didn't want to use any more magic. Not if it meant drawing more eyes to the clan.

"I can't just leave her out like this," Tenn said. "Especially if I didn't get them all."

"We hoped that you could bury her. A pyre seems too… I don't know. It doesn't feel right."

He nodded, but he didn't answer. It wasn't a job he looked forward to. Especially since Earth would force him to feel everything.

Devon appeared a while later, as promised. A bag was slung over his back Tenn had never seen before. Tenn didn't have to ask. Although the Howls didn't need food, their human slave drivers did. The spoils of war were small, but they were spoils nonetheless. They didn't speak as they sorted through the bag and made a hasty breakfast. There was nothing else to say anymore.

They had tried, and they had failed. Even eating, his stomach turned against him. Matthias hadn't been in the city, that much was obvious, both from the lack of seeing him in the battle and Devon's scouting of the corpses. It felt like he'd sprung a trap. It felt like he was still being played. But he couldn't for the life of him imagine what the game could be.

Finally, they gathered their things and moved Tori to the center of the glade. Tenn's body hurt like hell and his blood burned with acid, but the water and food had helped. A bit.

The three of them stood over the wrapped body, the twins with their heads bowed. Tenn didn't know if they were praying or just being respectful. He closed his eyes and tried to pray for the girl he didn't know. But as much as he hated himself for it, he couldn't help but find himself praying for Jarrett and the funeral he would never receive.

He had wondered if there would be a cue, some perfect moment to pull the girl down into the earth. He figured the twins would say something, maybe the funeral chant he'd seen from Dreya's past, but they didn't. Instead, after a few moments of silence, they began to sing.

The song was just a melody, but it was deep and sorrowful and sent chills down his spine. The quiet woods seemed to go even more silent, as if every particle of creation had paused to listen in. And that, he knew, was the cue he was waiting for. He opened to Earth and reached deep.

The ground in front of them rumbled. Like quicksand, the snow and dirt became fluid. The body—no, *Tori*—sank into the soil. Tenn could feel her tiny, birdlike body drawn down into the depths of the earth from which she'd come. He wanted it to be beautiful, that final embrace. He wanted to block out the sensation of her bones snapping under the weight of stone, the fluid that spilled from her flesh. But he couldn't. Magic was a curse. Magic would always be a curse.

Finally, when she was at least six feet under, he cut himself from the power and the awareness of her twisted body. His limbs shook from emotion and Earth's drain, and he slumped against his staff. The twins finished their song. They gave him a solemn look, then bowed before the freshly turned dirt and walked off. Tenn hesitated.

"I'm sorry," he whispered into the snow.

He wasn't certain who he was apologizing to.

They gathered their things and began the long, slow walk back to the clan in silence. Tenn couldn't wash the feeling from his bones, the uncleanliness of the magic he had done. Even that small amount of magic made his legs shake and stomach rumble. At least, sometime during the night, one of the twins had pulled the blood from his clothes. Not that it made him feel any cleaner.

It was midday when they stopped for lunch. And it was midday when they realized something was wrong.

Devon stiffened, his chunk of bread forgotten.

"What is it?" Dreya asked.

He didn't respond at first. But then Devon's lips parted, and he whispered one, weighted word.

"Impossible."

"What?" Tenn asked. His heart began to race, and he opened to Earth, scanning the countryside for anything moving, any sign of Howls or Inquisitors or worse. He felt nothing.

"The rune," Devon said. He looked at Dreya, his eyes wide. A second passed, and then she hissed in a breath.

"It is moving," she whispered.

Tenn didn't ask more. He closed his eyes and visualized the tracking rune. He could feel its location. It was right in front of them, pulling them on. And that's when he felt the slight shift, the tug.

Devon was right. The rune was moving. Fast.

"What the hell?" he said.

They all shared a glance. Then, as one, they grabbed their things. When they started back down the highway, they were running.

Despite their haste, they didn't reach the woods until just before dusk. Tenn pushed his senses through the trees. For a moment, nothing seemed amiss. The woods were empty. Still. Except...

"I can feel the trailers," he said. He looked at Dreya.

"The runes," she said. "They must have been compromised."

They ran into the trees at full speed. They didn't hesitate to examine the marks on the trees that they passed, the lashings that seemed less than random. They all knew the marks of kravens when they saw them. And Tenn knew without a doubt that these slashes were cut across the runes themselves, rendering them useless. *No one should have even known about them.*

That's when it clicked. Matthias could follow his dreams, read his thoughts. And if that were true, Matthias had seen everything Luke had shown him. The runes on the trees. And the tracking rune that would have led him straight to the Witches.

"It's my fault," Tenn gasped. He nearly collapsed in disbelief. Matthias hadn't taken Tori to try and kill him. Matthias had taken her to lure him out and take the Witches. Matthias didn't want him learning more about the runes.

Either that, or Matthias just wanted to prove that no one was safe around Tenn. Not even those Tenn turned to for guidance.

Neither of the twins said anything. He knew they wouldn't lie. He knew they were drawing the same conclusions he was.

"There might be survivors," Dreya said instead. He could tell from the waver in her voice that she didn't quite believe it.

But when they reached the camp, the trailers were silent. Empty. Earth and Air told them as much.

The fire in the center had burned out, and more than one trailer door stood open, swaying gently in the wind. They stepped into the midst of the encampment, feeling for all the world like they were entering a ghost town.

"Search them," Tenn said. Even his words seemed too heavy in the emptiness of this place. "Maybe they fled. Or left a clue."

They split up and did precisely what he commanded, though he knew it was from protocol and not actual hope. He ducked inside Rhiannon's trailer. The curtains were drawn and bowls of cold porridge sat untouched on the table. The scene reminded him of the dining room, where he'd first encountered emotional transference, but no shades of the dead ran through him. He glanced to the cabinet holding the singing bowl. It was open, the door dangling from a single hinge. Empty. Whatever happened, Rhiannon had had the foresight to grab the bowl with the rune. She wanted to be followed.

Someone yelled. He bolted outside.

It was Devon.

Devon stumbled backward from a trailer, his hands over his face. He tripped, fell into the snow. Dreya was at his side in an instant. Tenn was right behind.

Dreya smoothed his hair, whispering soothing sounds into his ears. His eyes were wide and he gripped the arm she wrapped around him.

"What happened?" Tenn asked.

"Go..." Devon stammered. "Go look." He pointed a shaky finger at the trailer he'd just left.

Tenn looked at Dreya for support, but she was focused entirely on her brother.

He stood, doing his best to steel himself for whatever was waiting inside. If it had been enough to scare Devon...

He crept up to the trailer, Earth blazing in his stomach and his grip on the staff tight. The door opened with the screech of hinges.

The interior was dim, barely illuminated by the dying light outside. But it was enough.

The trailer was perfectly intact—the bed made, clothing folded on the nightstand, a cold mug of tea on the counter. Everything looked normal. Everything, save for the lump on the edge of the bed. At first glance, he'd thought it was a pillow. Only pillows didn't drip crimson.

It was a body.

Half of one.

And there, splattered on the wall in the corpse's blood, in Matthias's jagged script, were two words.

your move

CHAPTER TWENTY-SIX

TENN BURIED HIS SECOND BODY AT NIGHTFALL, THE only light coming from an orb of magic hovering in the air.

It was far less ceremonial than with Tori. Tenn didn't even try to be gentle as he pulled the body down into the earth.

There was no point.

They'd never found the other half of the corpse.

"What are we going to do?" Dreya asked.

There weren't any more bodies. Devon was still in shock, his arms crossed around himself tight. Tenn didn't blame him. After seeing what had happened in the twins' past, he knew another dead Witch was hitting far too close to home. Rage burned in his chest even as Earth ate at his insides, his limbs shaking from magic and anger.

Matthias would pay. For all of this, Matthias would pay.

"We follow them," Tenn said.

"Do you have a plan?" Dreya asked.

"Yeah," he said. And he did. Mostly. It had been forming

ever since he found the empty cabinet that once held the bowl. It was suicide, and it probably wouldn't work, but it was the only hope they had.

"What is it?"

"Runes," he said. "I'll explain on the way." He looked to Devon. "Do you think he's well enough to travel?"

She nodded.

"Don't worry about him. He has been through much worse."

They all had. Hopefully, after this, Matthias at least would be out of the picture.

They stopped atop a small hill overlooking a field. Tenn had a feeling the hill hadn't been there before, considering it was strewn with the rubble of toppled houses, and the base ringed with overturned cars. The necromancers had set up camp below—a few tents, a few campfires. It was, without a doubt, the rest of Matthias's army. It made Tenn's blood boil, made him want to burn the whole world down. But he had to stick to the plan. To get the Witches out alive, they had to be tactful.

"I know where they are taking them," Dreya whispered. Her words were tight. Clipped.

"Where?"

She nodded to the black horizon.

"There is a Farm ahead. A few miles. I can smell it."

Tenn's gut twisted. The Witches had been safe until he'd come along. Now, they were set to be food or new recruits to the Dark Lady's army. Matthias was definitely playing him: What worse fate was there for a bunch of pacifists than to be turned into bloodthirsty monsters, or food for them?

"Then we'll have to finish this tonight," he said.

As though there'd been another choice.

They set to work immediately. They gathered a handful of stones, and Tenn slowly carved the tracking rune into each of them. Then he flipped them over and carved in the symbols he'd memorized from the trees, runes of misdirection and hiding. He hoped he'd remembered correctly.

But the runes seemed to whisper in his head as he wrote them. The rest of the world fell away. It was like writing a language he'd always known, a string of runes that spelled a phrase that tingled on the tip of his tongue. It took only a few minutes, but it felt like hours—sweat dripped down his forehead and his thoughts spun in a haze. He felt high. If not for the weight of what he was about to do, he might have drifted off entirely.

Then, using the end of his staff, he traced a large circle in a space cleared of rubble, the line cutting through the frozen dirt. He traced more misdirection runes along the perimeter while the twins waited impatiently inside. When it was done, he stepped back and stared at the runes. They glowed faint and green, just like they had on the trees, the entire circle a dim neon.

Luke had said runes required energy to work. Tenn had assumed the energy from the earth powered the cloaking runes; it looked like he was correct.

"Do you see that?" he asked, his voice quiet with awe and not a small bit of...not pride...humility.

"See what?" Dreya asked.

"The runes," he said. "They're glowing."

Dreya raised an eyebrow but said nothing. It was Devon who spoke.

"They just look like chicken scratch to me," he said.

"Never mind," Tenn said. He held out a hand. "Give me your wrist," he said to Dreya.

She didn't even pause before holding her arm out. He took it gently, pulling back the layers of her coat and sweater. The skin beneath was pale porcelain, her veins just visible beneath the surface.

"This might sting," Tenn said. Then he opened to Earth and drew.

It was a cheap trick, one he'd learned early on as an easy way to practice his new Sphere. He changed the pigments in Dreya's wrist, tracing the tracking rune into her skin. It wasn't healing and it wasn't harming, but it still required him to touch her to make it work. It took only a few seconds. The rune stood out delicate and dark on her wrist. Devon was next, and this time Tenn changed the pigment to white, the rune glowing ghostly against Devon's dark flesh. Finally, he traced it into his own wrist.

"Memorize these," he said, holding out his wrist. "Once I'm outside of the circle, it's the only way we'll have of keeping track of each other."

Tenn took a deep breath and stared out at the encampment. What he was about to do was suicide, but there was no fear or anticipation. Coldness filled him with a dead resolution. Jarrett's face came to mind—is this how he had felt before leaping to his death? Is this how it felt to truly sacrifice yourself for something greater: the clarity, the stillness?

The absolute calm.

"Remember the signals?"

"Yes."

"Then...I guess I'll see you soon," he said, the words tasting horribly close to a lie. They nodded solemnly, and Dreya opened to Air.

The gathered stones hovered up and twisted a slow orbit around him. The moment they left the ground, he opened to Earth and siphoned energy into each stone. The runes glowed green with life. He could tell from the sudden glaze in Dreya's eyes that the runes had worked; he was invisible.

He jumped and dodged side to side, just to make sure, but the stones continued their rotation around him undisturbed. So long as Dreya stayed focused on the tracking runes, she should be able to keep the stones centered on him. So many *shoulds*, but it was the best he could hope for.

"I'll miss you guys," he said.

As expected, neither of the twins heard him.

He stepped out of the circle, and they vanished from sight.

For a moment, he stood there, staring down at the army, Earth fueling his senses as he sought out the huddle of Witches. He could feel them, just barely, congregated near the center of the encampment. He couldn't tell how many were left, but he had a feeling it was a smaller number than what they'd started with.

He stilled his thoughts, gripped the staff tighter.

Then he ran down into the mouth of hell.

CHAPTER TWENTY-SEVEN

HALFWAY DOWN THE HILL, TENN SENT A SURGE OF
Earth into the branches of the tree beside the twins, making
the limbs shudder. The first signal. A heartbeat later, chaos
broke out in the encampment.

Devon's work was quick and efficient, a vicious blend of
calculated destruction and artistic flourishes. The dozen or so
campfires blazed into life with a roar, searing the sky with pillars of flame. Fire spread in seconds, leaping to ignite flesh and
canvas. It was beautiful, in a way, the smear of orange against
the dark. Beautiful, save for the scent of burning Howls. Not
that Tenn had any time to admire from afar. Even though the
fires made sweat drip down his skin, he ran straight into the
heart of the army. Everything was sound and heat, screams
and cinders, and the madness slashed a grin across his face.

Finally, the monsters would know how it felt to fear the
night.

Kravens swarmed past him, but they edged around his runes

like water flowing around a stone. Up close, when he wasn't trying to kill them or dodge their blows, he saw them for their true monstrosity—graying flesh sagging or peeling off, strands of fat and blood and pus dripping from every open sore and orifice, bones broken and twisted and reshaped as talons and spikes, spines horribly bent and arms and fingers elongated. Even worse was the smell, the cloying sweetness of rot and blood that seemed to crawl into the recesses of his throat. He wanted to gag. Wanted to strike out and end their putrid existence.

He didn't.

He just ran, ducking and dodging and waiting for a monster to stumble past his runes, but they never did. The nightmares shoved around him unaware, and it wasn't just the kravens that sought out prey, but the more humanoid Howls—the pale bloodlings and deceptively beautiful succubi. They stood out from the throng, both crazed and aloof. But even they were repelled by Tenn's defenses, and he marveled at how well the runes were actually working. He just hoped he worked fast enough that Matthias couldn't read his thoughts—hopefully, it was something that could only be done when sleeping or passed out.

His luck held. He reached the Witches without being discovered. As he'd hoped, they were barely guarded—why should they be when Matthias's entire army surrounded them? Instead, there was a single necromancer, a man in an old ski coat and knit hat. Not exactly the most intimidating or dark choice in attire, but it *was* cold. The Sphere of Earth glowed bright in the man's pelvis, and he held a stone covered in pulsating runes. So that was why the guard was so loose—Tenn could feel the strands of magic twisting from the necromancer, twining into the Spheres of the entire clan.

Each of their Earth Spheres were being drained. Just enough to make them weak and tired, enough to make using magic an impossible chore. He remembered the feeling of being tapped well.

The Witches themselves gathered in a tight knot near the bonfire, the only group in the entire camp that hadn't moved. Only a few were dressed to be out in the cold; the rest had clearly been taken in their sleep. One man near the edge wore nothing but jeans, his feet bare and frostbitten, another kid—a few years younger than Tenn—was missing his arms. Just the sight made Tenn's blood boil. All of the Witches had a sort of stoicism to them, though, one that said this wasn't the worst they had undergone.

He didn't see Rhiannon. Fear shot through his chest. Was she held captive elsewhere? He didn't want to think of the alternative.

It was then that he noticed the smear of darkness on the ground by the fire, the few small mounds he wished he could mistake for rocks. But he knew precisely what those chunks were. The kravens had feasted, and they'd let the Witches watch. He wondered if they'd made the clan choose who died first.

That alone made Tenn want to prolong the necromancer's pain, but another burst of fire nearby brought him to his senses. While he was here deliberating, the twins were weaving their destruction and keeping him safe. And the army was trying to hunt them down. He had to act fast.

Even if the man did deserve to suffer.

Tenn stepped over to the necromancer. Then, holding his staff like a spear, he stabbed forward, right through the man's back. The necromancer yelled out, but Tenn was faster—he moved in as the man collapsed, so the man fell within the stones' orbit, and gave the staff another wrench. Blood sprayed over him as the necromancer gave his final cry. No one heard it through the magic of the runes. He yanked out his staff and refrained from kicking the corpse.

Tenn reached out with Earth and snapped a branch from the twins' tree.

Briefly, he stopped channeling Earth into the stones. Dreya responded to his signal, and the stones flew out another twenty feet, drawing the Witches into their orbit. Then he sent power to the stones once more, rendering them all invisible as the stones orbited the pack. Barely a murmur went through the Witches at his appearance.

"Where's Rhiannon?" he asked.

She wasn't there, and neither was Luke. He recognized a few of the faces from the camp, but none he'd spoken to. It was Rhiannon's daughter—Mara—who stepped forward.

"My mother is dead," she said.

It should have come as more of a shock than it did, but he'd already experienced too much death for it to register.

"I'm sorry," he said.

"We don't have time for sorry," she said. She looked out, to the necromancers and Howls that swarmed around them, clearly confused at the sudden disappearance. The runes might convince the lesser Howls to stay away, but if a necromancer took notice, they'd be screwed.

Tenn nodded. Swallowed hard.

"Stay close to me. If you can fight, stand to the outside. Let's go. And leave the singing bowl behind."

The fires ran wild now, and the world was a torrent of sparks and heat and chaos. Tenn and the Witches darted through the madness as fast as they could, which wasn't nearly fast enough for his comfort. He held his breath. Every single step and he expected disaster.

They were nearly to the edge of the encampment—hard to discern, as even the countryside had been set ablaze—when his good luck turned south. A man stumbled through the edge of the circle, blinking and clearly in shock from the runes and the sudden appearance of fleeing prisoners. His shock didn't last long. A moment later, his eyes narrowed, and he took a deep breath.

Immediately, the air was ripped from Tenn's lungs. He nearly dropped to his knees, nearly lost hold on the stream of Earth that was keeping them all hidden and alive as the Breathless One attacked.

For a brief, blinding moment, Fire flashed in Mara's chest. The Howl went up in flames, blazed bright as the sun. Then the light vanished. The man was gone in a puff of ash.

She caught Tenn's shocked gaze and raised an eyebrow. He said nothing. Of all the Spheres he'd expected her to be attuned to, Fire was probably the last. He didn't waste any more time. He ran. The clan followed at his heels.

They dodged the fires that spun out of control, or perhaps the fires dodged them, as they ran up the hill, the shouts and screams of the encampment fading behind them. Tenn kept the twins' tracking runes firmly in mind, let them guide him forward like a beacon. He kept waiting for Matthias to jump from the shadows and attack him, for a group of kravens to lunge and rip out their throats, but there was no one. Devon kept them all occupied.

When they broke through the line of runes and found the twins, he nearly sighed with relief. He dropped the connection to Earth and their camouflage winked out. The moment he stopped running, the clan crowded around, hugging him and the twins, showering them with kisses and gratitude. Not one of them asked about Tori or blamed him for what had become of them, but the guilt still gaped in his heart like a wound.

For the first time, the twins didn't look subdued, didn't look like they were waiting for the ax to fall. Dreya's back was straight, and even Devon seemed to soften under the hugs of the children that flocked around him. Tenn wondered if they felt they'd finally atoned for their sins.

But there was no time for congratulations; he looked to the twins and nodded.

"Be careful," Dreya whispered.

Tenn opened to Earth as he brought the whirling stones into a closer orbit, circling only a foot from his body. Runes flashed, ensconcing him in misdirection. He didn't offer any explanation to those he'd just saved.

He just ran, hunting down the man who would hunt *him* no more.

CHAPTER TWENTY-EIGHT

HE THOUGHT MATTHIAS WOULD BE DIFFICULT TO find. He couldn't have been more wrong. Seeking out the necromancer was as simple as finding a beacon in the night. Matthias stood at the edge of the encampment, staring out at the blazing fields, his eyes alight with anger. All three of his Spheres were churning within him, their combined light nearly as bright as the inferno. Tenn knew he was seeking him out. Tenn knew Matthias was on to their games. And he knew without doubt that Matthias would never find them. Not now. Not ever.

He slowed the moment he neared the man. Tenn's pulse was calm, his breathing slow. Earth was a steady hum in his pelvis, Water impatiently waiting to be unleashed. Just the sight of Matthias was enough to make the Sphere growl with hatred. Water churned, bubbling with memories of Jarrett's eyes, flashing traces of his touch. Over and over, with every blink,

Tenn watched Jarrett leap to his death. All at the hands of the man in front of him.

Tenn clenched his jaw. Studied his foe. He was so close he could see the fields reflected in Matthias's eyes, could watch every single bead of sweat drip down the man's forehead. Matthias was straining. And yes, there was a hint in his eyes of more than concentration. Matthias looked unnerved. Surprised. And that emotion clearly frightened him.

Tenn opened to Water.

The Sphere sang with bloodlust. There were a thousand ways to die, and Water wanted to inflict every single one—impale him on a tree and let him bleed, drain his magic and make him a Howl, slit his wrists and spike him to the ground... It showed Tenn other things, too—things besides Jarrett leaping into the night. It showed him his house, empty, blood smeared on the walls; it showed him his parents, a bloody mound in the back shed; it showed him endless days of nothingness, of waiting to die.

It showed him every single thing that was wrong with his life.

And all he had to do to rectify it was kill Matthias.

He slowly walked around, behind the necromancer. He knew it was cowardly. He was far past caring.

This is for Jarrett.

Tenn struck.

He slashed low with his staff, severing Matthias's heels. Matthias fell to his knees, his Spheres flickering from the shock.

Matthias gasped as Tenn stepped around him, bringing the man into the stones' orbit. But he was a man used to battle, and Tenn's appearance was a quick surprise.

Fire blossomed at his fingertips. Tenn was faster.

He pulled through Water, dragged every droplet of moisture into a shield of ice just inches in front of his skin. Power screamed within him. He tasted blood, but whether his own or his imagination, he couldn't tell. Fire billowed across the shield, white-hot and angry, but Tenn's power was stronger. *Your pain is your greatest strength,* Tomás had said. And Tenn had more than enough of that to spare.

Matthias's fire died out, and Water took its opportunity. The shield shattered, crystallized into a million tiny pieces that Tenn sent slashing across Matthias's skin.

This is for me.

The man had the decency to scream.

Water had taken control now, a torrent of rage and memory that wanted to destroy as much as it wanted to prolong the blissful agony. It felt the pulse in Matthias's veins, the beat of his heart, the blood trickling from his wounds. It delighted in the beauty of red, in the symmetry of every slash, each cut a testament to Rhiannon, to Jarrett, to everyone this man had killed. The man brought his hands up, wisps of flame swirling in his palms, but Tenn slashed off his hands and the magic faded. He fell backward on the ashen grass, staring up at Tenn with narrowed eyes.

Tenn stepped over him and raised his staff, then brought it down and speared the necromancer's stomach to the ground.

Matthias's back arched, blood spraying from his lips. Tenn could feel Matthias's life flickering, fading. But Tenn wasn't done just yet. Not by a long shot.

When Matthias sank back to the ground, he looked Tenn straight in the eyes and laughed.

The sound made Tenn's skin turn cold.

Blood trickled from Matthias's lips in streams, each heartbeat another spurt, each laugh a spray of crimson. Tenn twisted the staff. Matthias gasped, but he kept laughing.

"How does it feel?" Matthias asked. His voice came out in a rasp, but it was still strong, still had the power to chill Tenn to the bone.

"What?" Tenn asked through gritted teeth.

"Revenge," he said. "Is it everything you hoped for? Do you… do you feel vindicated?"

"I feel nothing. I just want you dead," Tenn said. Another twist of his staff. Matthias didn't look away or flinch.

"And what good will that do?" Matthias asked. "I am one man. As are you. Who can you hope to save? Everyone you love is doomed to die."

"I can at least keep you from killing again," Tenn said.

Matthias chuckled again, the noise only broken by a wheeze.

"Killing me will do nothing. It won't bring back your parents. It won't save you from falling into Leanna's clutches. My goddess is the Dark Lady. For me, death is a reward." Matthias's smile was a red slash across his face, one that dripped to the ground.

No, no, he has to see that he's losing.

"I've already won," Matthias continued. "Leanna was right. Take the man you love, and you would leap right into our hands."

"I'm not playing anymore. I have the Witches, and once I have the proper runes, I'll destroy her."

"No," Matthias said. He lifted his head off the ground and

smiled. "You won't. Because you have overlooked one key thing."

Tenn didn't say anything. He wasn't going to fall prey to this, not anymore.

"You'll seek out Leanna." Matthias chuckled. "You're still the mouse in our little game."

Tenn twisted the staff again. Water screamed, wanted the man to choke on his own blood.

Fire opened in Matthias's chest. Snakes of flame raced across Matthias's skin, twisted through his clothes. Tenn yanked out his staff as the fire swept higher, as Matthias burned himself alive.

Tenn wanted to scream, to cry out, but all he could do was watch Matthias self-immolate.

"She has him," Matthias yelled through the blaze. "Your lover's still alive."

"We have no way of fathoming
the evil these creatures possess, the malice
in their hearts. Our only hope
is the dying chance
that they retain a semblance of humanity."

—President's Final Address.
P.R., Week Two.

PART
3

BLOOD SINGS

CHAPTER TWENTY-NINE

TENN SCREAMED. WATER ROARED.

Matthias's body was a funeral pyre blazing in the night, and Tenn was blazing, too. Water raged in his chest, churned with such ferocity he had no doubt that the power would tear him apart. Matthias was burning, burning, and Tenn howled.

There was no thought. There was no questioning.

Water raged.

Water wanted everything to hurt as much as him.

He plunged his senses into the earth, reached deep to the aquifers running silently below. He dragged the water up, pushed it through rock and soil. The earth rumbled and split, a beast coming to life, and then it broke. Water burst from the cracks, lashed high into the night sky, flickering red and orange against the firelight. He held out his arms, power spiraling around him in blue waves. He felt his feet leave the ground, but the sensation was distant, his body barely an impression in the power flooding through him. Fire hissed and steamed

as he forced more water up, up, up into the night sky, twisting it like serpents. The tendrils hovered there, stared down
into the midst of the army horde. The screams of the army
cut short as even the kravens stared up in awe.

Then he brought the water down, brought it crashing against
the enemy camp, the flood devouring the beasts within. He
had no mercy. He gave no quarter. He felt bones shatter, felt
lungs fill as water crashed down like fists, pummeling into the
earth, churning snow and blood and earth to mud. The torrent
swirled in front of him, a wall of waves twenty feet high. The
sky went dark as flames hissed out. He could feel the bodies.
He could feel them float and kick and scream as they fought
to find air in the swirl of madness.

Then he twisted the power.

Water froze.

He dropped to his knees and stared up at the cathedral of
ice. Hundreds of Howls and necromancers were encased within
their glass prison, screams frozen on silent faces. But he could
hear them, all of them. He heard the tremor of their hearts and
the howls of their stilled lungs. Each second the cacophony
rose, until everything was pain and heartbeat, agonized ice.
Until, as one, the voices cut out and the monsters perished.

The power faded, dropped him to the ground. He fell on
hands and knees, felt Matthias's warm ashes beneath his
fingertips.

Everything fell to darkness.

"Well done, my prince."

Tomás's voice echoed through the shadows. Tenn felt a cool,
soft bed beneath him, felt Tomás's hand on his back. But he

couldn't open his eyes. Everything in him hurt like hell, as though he'd acquired every injury from everyone on the battlefield. Everything hurt except Tomás's touch.

"Your part of the bargain is nearly complete."

Tenn moved his head, winced. Pain filled him, and then he felt Tomás's lips on his neck, the chilled burn of his touch.

"Deliver me Leanna, and I will make you king."

Tomás bit his neck, and the darkness exploded in burning stars.

CHAPTER THIRTY

WAKING WAS LIKE SURFACING FROM AN ABYSS, PULL-
ing himself up from a void that wanted nothing more than to
suck him back down and devour him whole. He almost let it.
But Jarrett's face kept him struggling toward the surface. The
thin light streaming through cracks in the window shades
was enough to set his temples on fire, though the cool cloth
on his forehead kept the pain from raging. Mostly. Everything
smelled of musk and earth, woodland herbs and cool streams.
Comforting smells, but not enough to take the edge off the
ache in his bones. He'd pulled far too much from the Spheres;
this was their way of paying him back. He knew in the dark
corners of his mind that he should be dead—that much magic
would kill another man. Even the twins.

Moonlight streamed through the trailer, turned everything
the shade of dust and memory. Dreya sat in a chair across from
him. She was asleep, her eyes closed and her chin drooping

against her chest. Innocent. Tenn shifted, making the mattress creak. Dreya's eyes shot open.

"You are awake," was all she said.

"Where—" he began, but the moment the words left his mouth he had to fight back a gag.

"You are safe. We found you on the battlefield...after what you did... We are back with the Witches. In their camp."

He tried to sit up. The process was slow, but it didn't hurt nearly as much as it should have. Dreya watched him like a hawk and didn't speak again until Tenn was upright, the sheets gathered around his waist.

"You've been asleep for two days," she said. "We thought... we thought you might not make it. You'd drawn too much. I've never seen such power. Not even the Violet Sage could—"

"He's alive," Tenn interjected, his voice barely a whisper. Even voicing the words sent a fresh wave of memory through him, a surge of Water that burned with regret. With hope. He didn't care who or what the Violet Sage was. Jarrett was alive. Nothing else was important.

"Who's alive?" Dreya asked, suddenly tense. "The necromancer?"

"No," Tenn said. He forced aside the image of Matthias immolating himself. "No, Matthias is dead. But...he told me before he died. He said that Jarrett's alive. Leanna has him."

"Lying," Dreya said without hesitation. Her blue eyes seemed to flash in the candlelight. "He was lying to you. He had to have been."

Even as she said it, he knew it was probably true. Matthias just wanted him to fall into Leanna's clutches. He would do anything to deliver Tenn to his mistress. But the nagging doubt was too much to overlook.

"I don't think he was."

"He was."

"How do you know? What would you do? If they had Devon? Even if just a rumor?"

Her face darkened. She hesitated before answering.

"If there was a chance, *any* chance, I would try to save him."

Tenn nodded. Stupid move. It made his head spin.

"Now is not the time," she said. She stood and walked over to the nearby table. She opened to Fire, briefly, and steam began waving from the dishes.

"Eat," she said. "You have much recovering to do. We will speak of this in the morning."

"There's nothing to talk about," Tenn said. "I'm going to save him."

"Eat," she said again. "If…if what you say is true, there is much to discuss."

"There's nothing to discuss," Tenn said, but she was already out the door.

He stared down at the food, forced aside the nausea and tried to convince himself he had an appetite. It wasn't hard. When the first drop of broth touched his tongue, Earth and Water growled with hunger. They wanted to devour it all.

He ate. And while he did, he couldn't help but feed the tiny flame of hope that fluttered inside of him. Jarrett might still be alive. Jarrett might be waiting for him.

And Tenn was going to do anything he could to get him back.

CHAPTER THIRTY-ONE

DREYA CAME IN ONLY ONCE MORE, DEVON AT HER SIDE.

Tenn had drifted in and out of uneasy sleep. It wasn't night-mares that plagued him, but memories of Jarrett—some real, some imagined. Dreams that stuck with him even when he woke, so that every time he opened his eyes he felt the man beside him. In his cold sweat, he felt the absence like an ache.

Dreya had Tenn recount everything he'd seen and everything Matthias had said. Devon said nothing when Tenn was fin-ished, but he shared a look with his sister that spoke volumes.

It was clear that neither of them believed Matthias.

It was also clear that neither could risk the chance it was true.

"We've spoken with the Witches," Dreya said. "With Rhi-annon and Luke gone, there is no one else to teach about the runes."

Tenn's heart sank.

"So what do we do?" he asked.

Again, the twins shared a look, though brief.

"There is a way," Dreya said. She took a deep breath. "Rhiannon said the spirits wanted to speak through you. If that is the case, we should bring you to a place where you can meet them."

"How?"

"You can find out. Tonight."

The bonfire was ready at dusk.

Dreya came and helped him from his bed. He'd spent the afternoon sleeping fitfully, and every time he'd opened his eyes there had been fresh warm food on the bedside table. Every time, he'd eaten the whole meal. Even then, however, he leaned heavily on Dreya. His heart hammered in his chest as she led him out the trailer and into the cold evening air.

He was scared.

He didn't want to admit it, not even to himself, but his fear was a living thing, a rabbit chasing through his veins.

It was one thing to be at the mercy of Water, or to be told he was important. It was another thing entirely to be told you were going to speak to the powers that created you.

The world outside was quiet, save for the crackle of flames. Everyone in the clan had assembled around the bonfire, firelight making them all glow orange and red in the coming dusk. Their expressions were solemn, expectant. He wasn't the only one worried about what he'd find.

Dreya silently led him to a space beside the bonfire, to where a few blankets had been laid out on the ground. Room enough for one. For him. Dreya went and stood by her brother.

Mara stood beside the blanket. She gestured for Tenn to

lie down, and then picked up a bundle of herbs resting beside the blanket. She thrust them into the flames and, once they'd caught, blew out the fire. Heavy smoke wafted from the incense. It smelled of sage and cedar, and with it she began to walk around the fire, leaving Tenn to stand awkwardly on his own.

"We call to the spirits," she said as she walked, "to the Ancestors and gods. We call to the earth, to the sky, to the flame and the streams. We call to the Mystery that binds us all, hear us!" When she reached Tenn again, she wafted the fragrant smoke over him, from his toes to the top of his head. The scent made his head spin. Inside, he felt the Spheres flicker in response, the smoke pulling some magic out of him he hadn't known he possessed.

"With this smoke I purify you," she said. "In body, mind and spirit, you are clean."

If only it were that easy

She drew the smoke about her, smudging herself, and then raised her hands to the heavens.

"On this night, we call to you and beg for your guidance. Like a fire in the dark, we seek to bring light to this world. Let us be the flame, the star. Let us be the way to wholeness." She swept her arms down and looked at her clan, then gestured to the blanket on the ground. He just stared at her before realizing she wanted him to lie down. He did so, staring up at her as she continued waving the smoke over his body.

She knelt by his side and placed the herbs on a patch of dirt, then whispered in his ear, "Close your eyes, Tenn, and let the drums guide you. Delve deep into the earth, to where the Ancestors sleep. They will guide you from there."

For the briefest moment, she rested her hand on his temple, the lightest butterfly of a touch. Then she stood.

The drumming began.

It reverberated in his bones, made his whole body vibrate. It was a pulse, a heartbeat, the very hum of life. He had worried he wouldn't know what to do, that this was all some smoke-and-mirrors bullshit, but the moment the drumming started, he felt himself fall. His body became heavy. His Spheres flared into life. And like Alice tumbling down the rabbit hole, he felt his consciousness sliding into the soil.

Stars streaked across his closed eyes as the tunnel took him deeper, deeper, his mind or spirit or whatever it was riding the beat of the drums like a horse into the underworld.

The tunnel seemed to stretch on forever, and soon he forgot that he was actually lying on the ground beside a bonfire. It was like a dream, that world, and it slid from his mind as another reality woke him.

After an eternity, or no time at all, the tunnel opened before him. He stepped into a cavern that glowed white as snow, light coming from every crystalline surface. Water swirled at his feet, but it wasn't cold or warm or wet. It had a presence, a vibration like static, and it made his whole body hum. He looked around at the vast expanse, at the great stalactites dripping down from a ceiling that glowed the dull gray of a wintry night sky. Something splashed at his feet, a ripple that drew his gaze down to the shimmering waters.

A tiny fish swam against his calves, its scales glinting silver and light. He knelt down. The fish didn't swim away, and in that moment he realized the fish wasn't reflecting light, but creating it. The creature glowed like a platinum star.

He reached into the water. It felt like sifting through electrified smoke. He cupped his hands.

The fish swam between his fingertips. It tingled, sent chimes flurrying across his skin. Its light grew.

Light spiraled through his arms, twisted around his chest. He felt his skin dissolve, his body unraveling into tendrils of radiance as he floated, hovering above the water in a cave that was more than a cave. It was a body, a womb, a heart.

He looked down to the water that shone like a mirror, at the fish that was a constellation of stars. He saw his reflection as fluid as smoke, as luminescent as moonlight. It glimmered like a thousand dancing fireflies.

It changed.

The face that stared back was no longer his. The waters now showed a boy his age, a boy with burnt hair and rings in his lower lip. His eyes breathed galaxies, a thousand suns whirling like the lights that swam across the water's surface.

Tenn reached out to touch the boy and felt the entire earth hum with need. *Find him, find him*, and for a moment, he forgot himself, why he'd come there, all of it replaced by the one need to reach out and touch this boy he had never seen. But that movement caused the water to ripple, and the boy's face vanished in the dust of stars.

How do I find him? Tenn asked, or thought he asked.

The lights kept moving, tracing patterns over the water, tracing *a* pattern that burned into his mind. Over and over the lights moved, the runes glowing so bright it was blinding.

Nearly a dozen of them, each thick with meaning but becoming so much more in sequence. He could barely keep up with them. Could barely figure out their meaning as they flashed over and over—he caught only whispers, only traces of meaning, and he prayed that recognition was enough. They filled him, burst through his senses—the rush of vertigo, the thunder of hoofbeats, the exhilaration of wind in his hair and the horizon opening, opening, expanding and contracting as he sped to meet the rising sun. The sun burned through him, the runes seared to memory. Light was everything, everything, light and movement and an ecstatic, shimmering truth.

Find him, the spirits sang. *Find him and be whole. Find him and make the world whole.*

Then he felt the drumbeat change.

He didn't hear it, but he felt it. It tugged at his bones, pulled him up by the scruff of his neck. Like a puppet on a string, the drumbeat dragged him away, light fading as the tunnel reappeared, whirling around him in shadows and tremors of sound. All of it vibrating, vibrating, a second heart to echo his own. The tunnel went dark. And, like a diver bursting from the tide, Tenn broke back into the world of firelight and sound.

He sucked in a deep mouthful of air, his whole back arched as though possessed. One inhalation, and he fell back to the earth. His body was weak, spent, like it had been inhabited by something else, something that had used him up and left him lying in the dirt beside the fire. But he felt good. Ecstatic. The power was faint, but the light of the cave still hummed in his veins.

The drumming shook and fell apart, cascaded into a cavalcade of beats that faded to the hiss of rattles. Then silence. The crackle of fire.

Mara was at his side, one hand on his shoulder, the other holding a rattle of bone and rawhide. Her eyes were shadowed, expectant. He could only lie there, staring up at a sky that was uncannily clear, the stars above mirroring the cosmos in his mind.

"Welcome home," she said. Then she stood.

Tenn couldn't pay attention to the words she spoke next, only caught snippets of "thanks" and "gratitude." He spun with ecstasy, weighted to the world that slipped and swam beneath him. Holding on to the memory of the vision was harder than holding fast to a dream. Like the fish, it slipped between his fingertips, shining and beckoning and impossible to grasp.

The rest of the Witches dispersed. He knew it, dimly. But he was too busy spinning in the vision. The runes. And the boy. And the need.

"What did you see?" Dreya asked. When had she knelt beside him?

"Runes," he whispered. "For travel. They need Earth and Air to work, but they will take us..." He almost said *to Jarrett* but faltered. "They'll take us to Leanna. To wherever we need to go."

"That is all?" Dreya asked. She almost sounded disappointed.

He nodded. For some reason, he didn't want to mention the boy. Not out of shame or fear, but because something about the vision felt intensely private. Not even he understood it, and voicing it to the world felt sacrilegious. Besides, he already had a guy to search for. Jarrett was out there. Waiting for him.

"Then we should be off soon," Dreya said. "If you are strong enough."

"I have to be," Tenn said. He pushed himself to standing and did his best not to waver. "We leave tonight."

CHAPTER THIRTY-TWO

THEY WERE READY WITHIN THE HOUR. THERE WASN'T much to pack—just extra rations and layers of clothing. Tenn sat by the fire for most of the preparations, staring into the flames and watching the runes flash over and over again in his mind. With every trace, he felt his understanding shift deeper, as though it were slowly sifting away layers of confusion. He knew the runes would transport them wherever they desired. He knew they needed Earth for grounding, Air for speed. And he knew they were a power the world hadn't seen in hundreds of years, a language the gods had long ago stopped speaking. The weight of that knowledge settled on his shoulders with every crackle of the bonfire. Once more, he was entrusted with something he had no right to possess. What made *him* worthy of this knowledge? Why was *he* the one the spirits or gods were entrusting with their secrets?

And perhaps most important, *would it be enough to save Jarrett?*

One must be godlike...

At the moment, he felt terribly small.

"How does this work?" Dreya asked when they were ready. She had a small bag on her back, and wore a necklace with the symbol he'd seen above Rhiannon's door, the seven-pointed star within a horned moon. He didn't ask how she'd come across it.

Dreya's was a question he barely had an answer to. Each of the dozen or so runes and symbols from the vision had a meaning. Each layered atop each other to create a sentence, a spell. In a way, he had whispers of meaning from each rune. But he didn't know the individual powers, just as he didn't fully grasp the individual meanings of the runes he used in the protection circles. He just knew they worked as a whole.

Until he had time to experiment, that would have to be enough.

Thankfully, his time in the vision, or whatever it was, gave him enough of a hunch on how to use the runes.

"I need you to channel Air into the runes. Each of you. It will only carry someone using the magic that fuels it. That's it."

They nodded.

"Ready?"

Another nod. That was enough for him.

He knelt and traced the runes into the cooler ashes by the fire, let the grit sift around his fingertip. There was a small voice in the back of his head screaming that he was getting it wrong, that he needed to give up now, that there was no way he was the one meant to channel this power. But with every rune, the voice grew weaker and the hum of power in his head grew stronger. Every scratch of his finger, and resolution grew. When the runes were completed, he looked up to the twins. They stared at the runes with…trepidation? It didn't help his confidence.

He pressed his hand to the center of the runes and opened to Earth.

Magic swirled through him, blossomed from his fingertips and twined around the ash, billowing and fluttering like a butterfly, a fold in the fabric of the world.

"Now," he said. The twins opened to Air.

The runes exploded in light and ash, funneled up and around the three of them in a cocoon of soot and wind and brilliance. The world shifted, swirled, sank. Power was everything.

Then the cocoon collapsed around them, and the trailers vanished to light and the sound of hoofbeats.

When the dust cleared, they were no longer in the Midwest.

Mountains rose on all sides, peaks silhouetted in dark blue and starlight. The moon was hidden, but the stars were bright enough to see by, glittering off snow that blanketed every rise and sweep. Light bloomed in the valley below them. Violent. Orange. Electric.

Leanna's compound glowed and smoked in the night. The sight of it made Tenn's head whirl. It looked so…out of place. The streetlamps, the swept streets, the houses with their plumes of smoke. Exactly like before the Resurrection, save for the wall that surrounded the city and the warren of ramshackle houses splayed about just within the perimeter.

"It worked," Dreya said. Her voice was breathless, thin in the mountain air. Tenn glanced at her. She stared with wide eyes at the city below them. It looked like the way life once was, a city of life and energy and sound. Yet every human in there served the Dark Lady, willingly or not. It wasn't like the Farms he'd seen in the Midwest. Those had just been giant kennels for holding human livestock. This was almost worse. Here, the Howls and necromancers feeding on the innocent lived in the same pen.

"Yeah," Tenn whispered. "It worked." He had no other words. He still felt the magic swirling within him, the runes an after-trace in his vision. He was too preoccupied with finding Jarrett to be surprised by his own skill.

"What…what do we do now?" It wasn't Dreya who asked, but Devon. He stared down at the compound with narrowed eyes. His voice was tight, and even though he wasn't using Fire, Tenn could practically feel the impatience in him, the need to avenge. Tenn felt it, too.

"It could be a trap," Tenn said. "Matthias might have been lying, just trying to get me to come here. I don't want you two to be in danger if that's the case."

"But we are already here—" Dreya began.

Tenn shook his head and cut her off. "And I'm grateful for it. Leanna wants me. That's always been apparent. Chances are that means that, even if I'm caught, I'll make it to her alive. She'd kill you both in a heartbeat."

The twins shared a long, silent look. Fire flickered in Devon's chest, just the slightest flare, and Tenn fully expected him to speak out.

"Do you propose we just sit and watch you, then?" Dreya asked when she looked back to him.

"Of course not," Tenn said. "Once I get Jarrett, you're in

charge of getting us out. I'll need a distraction. And everyone down there is going to need a rescue."

"Just like with the Witches," Devon said. There was a level of hurt in his eyes. Tenn didn't blame him. They didn't want to sit around and watch the show. They wanted to be in the ring. He wasn't the only one trying to avenge his bloody past.

"I'm sorry," he said. "I can't risk you two getting hurt. You're more valuable alive and out here. Besides, I don't know anyone else whose magic can reach as far as yours."

He caught Dreya rolling her eyes, but she didn't fend off his lame attempt at pacifying them. There was logic in his words, even if their desire for revenge was stronger.

"What happens then?" Dreya asked. "When the prisoners are freed? No one has successfully overthrown a compound before. Ever. What chance do we three have?"

"No one has had the runes," Tenn said. He hoped it was the truth, that the small advantage was enough. If he thought about the fact that he only had a handful of runes, ones for hiding and travel, the task seemed even more dire. His plan had worked on the necromancers, but this? Matthias may have been powerful, but he didn't hold a candle to the Kin.

"How will we know you have succeeded?" Dreya asked.

Tenn shrugged. They were too far away for Earth to reach like last time. Which meant there was only one way to show that he had Jarrett, and was safe.

"Give me until dawn," he said. "I should be able to get in and back before then. If I need your help, I'll start an earthquake or something. If you don't hear from me, or if my tracking rune stops moving... Well, dawn at the latest."

"And if you haven't found him? If you are killed?"

"Then there are still hundreds of innocent lives down there for you to save. I'll create a protection circle around you, just like last time. You'll be safe to do your magic."

She gave him a look that said she wanted to argue. But there wasn't time.

He gritted his teeth, then got to work.

He walked a circle around the twins, melting the snow with a thin stream of Water and scratching the runes into the earth with his staff. Just like with the Witches. It had worked with them; it would work again here. He tried to ignore the fact that, barely a mile away, there was a town filled with necromancers and Howls and worse, all bent on finding him and killing anyone associated with him. This was the nexus from which all of his pain stemmed.

On the one hand, it meant the end of this fight.

On the other hand...it could mean a lot of other ends, as well.

"Why are you doing this?" Dreya's voice was quiet. It barely carried on the otherwise-silent night air, the town too far away to be heard.

"I'm setting up defenses—" Tenn began, but she cut him off.

"Not the runes," she said. *"This."* She gestured to the town, to the surrounding countryside. "This is suicide. Madness. Do you truly think Jarrett would *want* you to run headfirst into Leanna's hands? Alone?"

I'm not alone, he thought.

What he actually said was more biting.

"Are you telling me you wouldn't do the same?" he asked again. He pointed to Devon. "If he was in there? Would you?"

She dropped her gaze.

"Precisely," he said. He went back to scribing the runes into the earth.

"But you could *die*." The way she said it made her sound so small. "What about us?"

Tenn stopped, felt his whole world come to a grinding halt. "What do you mean?"

She looked back up to him. "I mean, what happens to us if you die in there?" She sighed, as though the words she was about to say were painful. "We can't do this without you."

"Of course you can," he said. He shrugged and looked back to his work.

"No." It was Devon, not Dreya, who continued the argument. He had pulled his scarf down, so his voice rang out in the night, low and deep like a mourning bell. "Rhiannon told us the spirits had chosen you. You are the one they will work through. You are the one who will change the world. If you die, that change dies, too. You are no longer responsible for just your own life. You never were."

Tenn wanted to punch him. He wanted to shut Devon up for saying all the things he'd been trying to ignore since the very beginning. The idea that he was different. Important. The sheer, crippling weight that he had the world riding on his shoulders. He knew without a doubt that, if he'd been a Fire mage, he would have exploded. Instead, Water filled him with doubt. *What if you fail?*

Tenn looked toward the compound and tried not to sink to his knees.

"Do you have a better idea?" he asked.

Silence.

"I'm doing this," Tenn continued. "With or without your

help. I'm saving Jarrett. And then I'll save anyone else in there. Why else were we sent on this mission if not to wipe out the Howls? Well, here's our chance to start. Leanna runs the Howls in America. We take her down, we're one step closer to freedom."

Dreya sighed. She looked at Devon, who looked both angry and bewildered.

"Dawn, then," she finally said. "If we do not hear from you, we will attack at dawn." She fingered her wrist, the spot where he had marked her with the tracking rune. "We will watch out for you. But come back to us before then."

Tenn nodded. "I will."

He scratched the last of the runes into the ground and watched his only friends wink out of sight.

CHAPTER THIRTY-THREE

TENN TOOK A FEW STEPS FROM THE CIRCLE, THE snow immediately enveloping his shins, nearly reaching his knees the farther down he stumbled. A few steps away, he used the one surprise he had left up his sleeve.

He opened to Earth, and just like he had with the tracking runes, he traced the runes of hiding into his skin.

The whispers that had accompanied the runes were louder this time, billowing through his senses like a whirlwind of smoke. He nearly toppled with vertigo. He propped himself up with his staff, watching the snow spin at his feet. Skin burned. But he kept going, kept tracing the runes over every inch of flesh even though it felt like dragging a knife across his skin. The completed marks tingled. Glowed.

After all, flesh was Earth. It should be enough to power the runes.

He hoped.

When the last rune was finished, he stood and waited for

the sensory overload to pass. It seemed to take ages. Even the stars above danced. He could still see his shaking hands and his clothes and his weapon. He just prayed no one else could. He prayed even that small amount of Earth hadn't weakened him too much.

I should have asked the twins. But he knew that was a terrible idea. If it hadn't worked, if they had known that this was his supposed ace, they never would have let him leave.

Finally, he felt well enough to continue on, even though his stomach rumbled with Earth's hunger. He did his best to run down the hill, shoving through snowdrifts and trying not to tumble. Every few yards he swept the snow behind him with Water. If he failed, he didn't want anyone tracing him back to the twins. Besides, with Water filling him, he could ignore the biting cold. It meant he had to force down the images playing on repeat in his head, but that had become habitual, images of his friends dying and burning, Jarrett's final kiss before leaping to his death, and worse—illusions of the life he thought he could have, him and Jarrett in a house together, cooking or laughing and completely numb to the horrors of the last few years. The ache of that loss filled him with need.

The slope eventually flattened out into a valley crossed by a highway. Farther on and past an exit ramp, the colony glowed orange and unawares.

The wall surrounding the city was easily three stories tall, made of earth and steel and concrete, a strange amalgamation of magic and rusting technology. Spikes jutted from the top, twisted iron spires preventing anyone from scaling the wall either within or without. Coal smoke filled his nostrils, combined with a nasty undercurrent of human refuse. The factories in

which the remaining humans were forced to work were mysteries at best; no one had been inside and escaped. But Tenn had
no doubt that the conditions were worse than the sweatshops
from before the Resurrection. If someone passed out or died
from poor work conditions, they just became the next meal
for the bloodlings and kravens waiting outside. Nothing lost.

He paused an arm's length away from the wall, staring up
at the structure. The rusted steel was the color of blood, and
the scent of inhumanity was stronger the closer he got. He
pressed his fingertips to a patch of wall that looked like it was
hewn from soil and stone. His Spheres stirred.

Earth and Water opened in his gut, and through them he
felt it all.

He felt the blood that had seeped its way to the bedrock of
the place, the tears that had salted the soil and made it barren.

He felt the warren of crumbling houses and makeshift lean-
tos that spread along the length of the wall. He felt the humans struggling to keep warm within.

Worse, he felt the kravens that patrolled the empty streets
or prowled within cages of steel and razor wire. He felt a few
kravens feeding.

And in the other houses, the ones closer to the center of
the city, he felt other human figures, sleeping in warm beds
with embers glowing in the fireplace. The necromancers and
higher-level Howls.

Deeper, and he felt what must surely have been Leanna's
house. It was a mansion, raised on a pedestal of magically
churned earth, and it overlooked everything. He could barely
sense the figures resting or patrolling the expansive corridors
of that place. A part of him had hoped that he would know

the form that must be Jarrett, that he would somehow lock on to the man's spark and know precisely where to go. But he just felt shapes, the blur of bodies. Jarrett could have been any of them.

Or none.

He half expected for a sentinel to call out, for lights to flash and his location to be discovered as he stood at the wall. Apparently, the runes were working; the guards patrolling the wall said nothing. Maybe it was the runes, or maybe he was just too tired to care, but he was remarkably calm for being this close to Leanna. Locked in the far corner of his mind was the knowledge that the only thing separating him from one of the most powerful Howls in existence, as well as the hub of the Dark Lady's forces in North America, was a few feet of earth and steel. He should have been quaking.

Instead, he felt at peace. He had been through and seen so much. This time, he wasn't just fighting for survival or to find some unknown weapon. He was fighting for Jarrett. He was fighting for home. There was no room for fear. His duty was more important.

A large door was set into the wall a few feet to his left, twenty feet tall and made of thick, riveted steel the color of old blood. Maybe it *was* old blood. How the hell was he going to get in there? Not for the first time, he wished he was attuned to Air, if only so he could fly. It would have made this so much easier.

He looked behind him, to the blank snow that swept against cars and coated everything a perfect, unbroken white. The fact that he was well-concealed was actually a hindrance. Well, that was easily changed.

He opened to Earth.

It began as a tremor, then a crack that struck through the air like a gunshot, like ice breaking in the Arctic. With one great tug, he pulled at the steel rods and concrete of the road. It reared from the ground like a serpent, the cracks and metallic screeches of its movements making Tenn's teeth clench. The concrete viper twisted. He pulled it higher, made it arc overhead, its mass raining mists of snow and gravel hail. Its silhouette blotted out the stars above him. He moved it like a marionette, his fingers twisting as he worked his magic. And then, with a roar that sounded like the heavens falling, he crashed the great weight into the wall.

The structure gave immediately.

Large chunks of earth and steel collapsed as he let his hold on Earth vanish. The road collapsed on the wall, sent the whole chunk crumbling in a plume of ash and snow. Earth rumbled hungrily in his stomach and his body shook hard enough to bring him to his knees. When he forced himself to standing, his skin cracked and his scalp tingled; he didn't rub his hair, for fear what would fall out. It had been too much magic, but it was too late for that worry now.

In a few hours, the twins would begin their attack, and he wanted this place to be in as much of a disheveled panic as possible before then. If that hadn't gotten the town's attention, nothing would. It would also make for an easy escape for the civilians.

Sure enough, only moments passed before he heard the first inhuman cries. Monsters swarmed over the felled wall, swelling into the otherwise-quiet night like a plague. Tenn pressed himself closer to the wall, didn't dare to breathe. Thousands of kravens flooded into the landscape. They ran toward the remaining highway, spread out toward the mountains. Tenn prayed the twins had stayed inside the circle. A huddle of kravens ran past him, so close he could have reached out and touched the decaying gray flesh. Their jaws drooled saliva and congealed blood, their teeth broken, their bloodshot eyes and sagging nostrils seeking out whoever had done this. Here he was, inches away from the monsters that had once made his hair stand on end. And they didn't even see him. He shot a pulse of Earth at the ground beneath a creature's feet, made it stagger. It fell, and he watched as the other kravens piled on top of it. The sound of ripping flesh filled the air, along with a putrid scent he didn't want to place.

Damn cannibals.

When the tide of kravens began to lessen, he edged along the opening and slipped into the town.

Guards huddled in a tight circle near the entrance, a few pointing at the wall and yelling. Tenn stayed far away, but he didn't need to be close to hear the anger in their voices. *What do you mean you couldn't sense any magic?* he could imagine them screaming.

Don't worry, he thought as he began racing through the streets. *Leanna will be dead before you can be held responsible.*

The place must have been a skiing village before Leanna turned it into her own personal prison and sweatshop. The buildings that lined the street had high A-framed roofs and Swiss latticework hanging from the eaves. Dead strings of lights still twined over the roofs and empty windows. In spite of the smoke rising over the city, no fires burned within these dwellings. Tenn could sense the people crowded inside, twenty or more to a house, all huddled together to stay warm. A few faces peeked timidly through the windows, drawn by the commotion outside, but not one of those gaunt figures stepped out. Tenn couldn't blame them. Kravens and necromancers roved the streets. He had no doubt that the citizens were only safe within their hovels, and even that wasn't guaranteed.

He ran straight up the main street.

The pedestal of earth towered above the center of the town, the château atop it glowing white with electricity. The closer he got, the nicer the houses looked. Smoke came from a few of these chimneys, smoke that didn't smell like coal or burning flesh. Wood smoke. If he closed his eyes and ignored the monsters running past him, he could have pretended he was camping in the woods, snow piling around his ankles... His eyes snapped open. The snow. He looked behind him, his heart hammering *stupid stupid stupid*, but the snow here was churned to hell and stained with dirt and...other things. Although his feet were making imprints, they were impossible to see in the churned-up muck. He sighed in relief. He might be invisible, but even a dumb kraven would notice footprints without a foot.

In minutes, he stood at the base of the earthen pedestal. It rose a good ten stories into the air, the sides sheer and glinting like granite. He considered what it would be like having to scale the thing—not impossible, not with the strength of Earth, but not something he wanted to try—when he heard the clomp of boots to his right. He followed the noise and found a ramp cut into the side of the mound. Guards ran down in tight formation. They wore armor and, of all things, carried assault rifles. The sight made him hesitate. Not out of fear—it was more the shock of seeing someone actually *using* a gun. Unless the guards had imbued each bullet with their own magic or blood, any mage could turn the projectiles against them.

When the guards passed by, heading the direction he had come, he made his way up the spiral ramp, keeping close to the wall lest another guard run past. He didn't meet any. Wind howled past him, eddying with scents of char and industry, bringing and hiding the cries of the Howls that scoured the city for whoever had dared breach their defenses. He smiled grimly. Oh, how pissed they would be when they learned he'd snuck in.

He reached the top of the rise and took a moment to stare in wonder at the house. It was grand—three stories tall with all-white siding and Roman columns, the great picture windows glowing with soft electric lights. The lawn was covered in snow, miniature topiaries dusted and glowing with inner lights. The sight made Tenn's stomach roil. Just a hundred feet away, the rest of the town was dark and freezing. And here was Leanna, warm and comfortable, using more electricity in an hour than most of the States had seen in a year. He pushed through with Earth and felt for the figures inside, ignoring the ache the Sphere spread through his bones. Figures crowded the labyrinthine corridors, but he still had no clue who was who. He walked up to the front door. It was wood, with diamond glass windows that glinted invitingly. All this place needed was a tree glimmering in the foyer and it would look like a fucking Christmas card.

But now what? Could he sneak inside like before? He fed his senses through the door. Locked. Easy to fix with a flick of Earth, but would they notice? There was a small group of people in the front hall. Guards, no doubt. He bit the inside of his lip and wondered if maybe there was another entrance, one less guarded.

Then one of the guards opened the door.

It was a woman. She wore a thick black dressing gown. Her hair was black and spiraled behind her in loose ringlets. She left one crimson-manicured hand on the doorknob and scanned the exterior. Light-blue eyes, nearly gray. Tenn stiffened the moment that gaze swept over him. She looked awfully unarmed to be a guard. A necromancer, then?

"What is it?" someone inside called.

The corner of the woman's lips curled into a tight grin.

"I do believe our guest has arrived," she said. Her nostrils flared. His grip on his staff tightened.

She stepped out onto the stoop and closed the door behind her. It latched, the sound like a gunshot in the night air. Then, before he could think to act, she took a deep breath.

It hit him like a punch to the chest.

He fell to the ground, staff skidding into a snowdrift. Stars flashed across his vision. Breath left his lungs. He tried to gasp, hands clenched to his burning chest. Then the stars spun, and he spiraled into darkness.

CHAPTER THIRTY-FOUR

COLD WATER FORCED HIM AWAKE.

Tenn's eyes snapped open, and he tried to turn away from the freezing current. He was facedown on the concrete, the world a harsh mix of fluorescent light and cold. He blinked, spluttered, rolled over to his side. His lungs burned and every breath was a ragged gasp. He tried to push himself up to standing, but that made his head swim.

That's when he saw his captors.

The woman from outside was there in front of him, still in the black dressing gown, the hem of which was getting soaked under the shower's jet. A man stood by her side. He was tall and lean, wearing a T-shirt and slim jeans, his blond hair slicked back loosely. Something about his appearance made Tenn think of all the old commercials for surfing in California— the defined features, the nonchalant pose with his hands in his pockets. But it was the woman who had his full attention.

Her eyes were fixed on him like a hawk. Which should have been impossible.

"Now," the woman said. "I will ask you nicely. Remove whatever enchantments you are wearing, and we will talk. Otherwise, I will have Justin remove your limbs one by one." The man at her side smiled even wider at the mention of his name.

Tenn glanced down at himself. Of course. They could see his shape in the spray. There was no doubt that they would follow through with the threat. He glanced around the room. He was in a basement. The water siphoned into a drain next to a dusty water heater, and the rafters above were covered in cobwebs. Even if he did manage to dodge these two, the woman could fell him in a moment. She was a Breathless One. She didn't even have to be able to see him to take him down.

So, against all his better judgment, he opened to Earth and bled out the runes, leaving only the tracking rune on his wrist. They didn't need to know about that one.

"Much better," the woman said. "Now we can talk."

She reached down and pulled him from the spray, yanking him up by the collar of his shirt. She looked willowy, but she nearly lifted him off his feet in that movement.

"Who...who are you?" he asked. He tried to will his voice not to shake. It worked—mostly.

"Who do you think?" she asked, leaning over to whisper in his ear. Then she did something that sent chills down his spine—she opened to Earth and shut off the tap.

"Leanna," he said. He didn't flinch back. There was no point—he wouldn't get an inch away from her. He had thought, coming in, that maybe he had some sort of divine purpose, that he'd be able to walk right up to her and kill her without breaking a sweat. He had the runes.

But the runes hadn't saved him. They'd just helped him walk straight into her clutches.

Leanna nodded.

"I take it this means you've killed him," she said.

It took a moment for it to click. Of course.

"Matthias," he said. "Yeah, I killed him." *To be fair, he killed himself.*

"Pity," she said. There was nothing in her flat blue eyes to hint at any such emotion. "He was my favorite of pets." She looked back to the man still lounging a few feet away. "We'll have to find a suitable replacement. Perhaps one a little less arrogant."

Justin nodded.

"What have you done with him?" Tenn asked.

"With whom?" Leanna said, turning her attention back to him. There was a hint of a grin at the corner of her mouth.

"You know who. Jarrett."

For half a heartbeat, he worried her eyes would glaze over, that she'd admit to not knowing what he was talking about. But then that little grin widened.

"Ah, yes," she said. "Of course. You're here for the boy."

"Where is he?" Tenn hissed. He was inches away from one of the Kin; he knew he wasn't in any condition to make demands. He didn't care.

"Alive," Leanna said. "For now."

"I want to see him," Tenn said. His teeth gritted together.

"Be careful what you ask for," Leanna said, though she was looking at Justin. He stepped forward. "Justin, take our guest to his room. He has surely had a long journey. I want to make sure he's comfortable."

Justin nodded and stepped over to Tenn, throwing him over his shoulder fireman-style. Tenn wanted to map the place out, but all he could see was the floor and he was too drained to fight for a better view.

A door opened, and Tenn was hit with a blast of warm air that smelled like cinnamon and fir as they went down a maze of white-carpeted hallways. He closed his eyes briefly. How long had he been unconscious in the basement? How long until sunrise and the twins started their attack? How the hell was he going to fight his way to Jarrett—and fight their way out—when he could barely move his head without being struck with pain? They already knew he could cloak himself, and it was clear even that magic was faulty.

He tried to think. He tried to race through the runes, to discover some deeper level of meaning, but his thoughts were thick, his mind slow from what Leanna had done to him.

They halted, and he heard the *click* of a door opening. All thoughts of fighting and escape were knocked from his head, along with the wind in his lungs, when Justin threw him to the ground. Tenn moaned.

"Don't be such a pussy," Justin said. He kicked Tenn in the side. Then he knelt down. "After all, you don't want to fuck up your heroic entrance."

He grabbed Tenn's chin and forced his face to the side.

The room was white and dimly lit. And there, in the shadows, was Jarrett.

"I'll let you two lovebirds reconnect," he said.

Then Justin stood and left, the lock latching behind him.

Jarrett's eyes were closed. He didn't register the noise of the door slamming. Tenn crawled over, his muscles screaming nearly as loudly as the hammer of his heart. *Please. Please. Please be alive.*

Jarrett's arms were twisted behind his back, his legs bound with rope in front of him, and his hair hung limp over a pale face. Bruises masked his eyes and a gag wrapped around his mouth. Jarrett was still. So, so still. Tenn reached out and put a hand to Jarrett's face, his fingers shaking. Jarrett's skin was warm. But not nearly warm enough. Tenn gently removed the gag, swept the strands of hair behind Jarrett's ear. More bruises. Jarrett didn't move. When his chest rose, Tenn gave a small cry of relief.

"Jarrett," he whispered. He brushed his forehead, touched his lips. Jarrett remained as still as the dead. "Please," he whispered. His words were salty with tears. "Please be okay."

He opened to Earth and tried to heal Jarrett's wounds.

Tenn gasped.

The force of it hit like a blow to the gut. The moment he pressed the magic to Jarrett's body, something took hold. A hunger so great, a void so vast, Tenn felt himself nearly swallowed by the pull. Earth screamed. He fell back, stared at his hands as though burned. Then he looked at Jarrett. *Really* looked.

The sallow skin, the bruises that had nothing to do with being beaten. Jarrett hadn't been attacked. His Earth Sphere had been tapped.

Tenn's breath caught in his lungs as he stared at the man he had hoped could be everything—home, safety, salvation. The man who was only minutes away from turning into a kraven.

Earth was dying in Jarrett's pelvis. It had been drained to the point of exhaustion, well past the point of replenishing itself. If it was pulled just a little bit more, it would implode and start the horrific process of turning Jarrett into a Howl. That hunger... That was more than Tenn's magic could fill.

He stared at Jarrett and felt a horrible vise clench at his heart.

He was going to have to watch Jarrett die.

Again.

The door opened behind him, but he was too stricken to even turn around. The door closed with a click. Tenn could feel the intruder's presence but wouldn't look. He couldn't tear his eyes off Jarrett. He reached out, touched Jarrett's shoulder. He didn't let go. *Maybe if I just give him a little. If I try.*

"This one, he has been such a charming guest. So polite." Tenn heard her step closer to them. "He's been waiting so long for you to arrive. Imagine his delight when we heard the wall crumble! We knew who it was, of course. And so, I had him specially *prepared* for your arrival."

"You did this to him," Tenn said. The vise tightened, but a new emotion tinged his hopelessness: rage.

"In a sense," Leanna said. "My necromancers have been practicing for *ages* to perfect it. Do you have any idea how difficult it is to pause the draining process right on the tip of conversion? Even the tiniest amount too much, and he would be nothing but a mindless kraven right now." The swish of fabric, and he saw her kneeling beside him from the corner of his eye. "You should be honored. I did all of this for you."

Tenn's gut churned. He spared her a glance.

"Why?" The word sounded so small. But in the face of this,

he didn't feel strong. He didn't know why he'd ever thought he could save anyone.

"Because," she said, "you are special. And I had to make sure you were the one before continuing."

"What?"

She placed something in his free hand. It was warm and heavy, and it seemed to press against his heart like oil. He glanced down. It was a stone, smooth and black, inscribed with tiny marks that caught the light like quicksilver. Just looking at the marks sent whispers through his thoughts, the Dark Lady echoing in the void: *be mine, be mine.*

Tenn tried to let go but she clenched his fingers around it. He felt bones grind.

"You know what this is, don't you?" she asked. "You've seen this before."

He didn't answer. He couldn't move. He couldn't look away from Jarrett as a slow realization dawned. It took everything he had to push the thought away.

"But I would bet there's something you don't know," she said. She turned his face to hers with her free hand.

Before he could ask what the hell she was talking about, she opened to Earth again.

He saw and felt her filter energy into the stone clasped in their hands. But that was it. The runes didn't glow. The stone didn't shiver with energy. She closed off to Earth and let go of his hand, settling back on her heels.

"As you see," she said, her voice tinged with bitterness, "although those are the words of the Dark Lady, one must be fully *alive* to use them." She glanced out the window. "The runes won't activate for the Kin, even though we wield the Spheres like any of our...minions." She nearly spat the word. "It's the only reason we put up with those idiots in the first place."

The implications made Tenn's head spin: the Kin couldn't use runes. That's why they needed living necromancers to turn the Howls. He had thought the Kin were all-powerful. *But why the hell is she telling me this?*

Leanna looked back to him, and there was something in her eyes that made him wonder if she could read his thoughts.

"That is where you come in."

"I don't—"

"You don't understand. Yes, I'm well aware." She gestured to the stone. "Why do you think there are only six Kin? Why do you think we've settled for creating lesser Howls since the Dark Lady died?"

Tenn shook his head. Jarrett was dying in front of him. He didn't have time for this. He should be healing Jarrett, not listening to this madwoman rant.

"She used special runes to bestow our abilities to use magic. Runes that let us keep our minds and our powers. But she took those secrets to her grave. We have tried. Oh, we have tried. No one has been able to replicate her runes. The words were never right. We needed someone who could speak the language the Dark Lady had tapped into. Someone who could hear and read the runes."

That made him look at her. His heart thudded. Did she truly think he'd...

"So this is your dilemma," she said. She stood. "Jarrett is well beyond healing, as I'm sure you've already discovered. He will die very soon unless you do something to change it. The stone in your hand will push your lover over the edge and turn him into a kraven. He will lose his mind and every inch of beauty in that well-defined body. It would be a terrible waste. The runes inscribed on that stone are too weak to do anything else. But if you are truly able to read the Dark Lady's language, if you can communicate with the gods, then you will be able to change that. You could turn him into one such as I—immortal, powerful, beautiful. And entirely in control of his Sphere's hunger. You could grant him that gift. You could have your future again."

She leaned down and whispered in his ear.

"Or he will die within the hour. The choice is yours."

Then she left, locking the door behind her.

CHAPTER THIRTY-FIVE

TENN HAD MENTALLY PREPARED HIMSELF FOR MANY things. He'd prepared to blow the house down, to face off against Leanna. He'd prepared to die in here, so long as Jarrett got out safe.

Nothing could have prepared him for this.

Leanna's locking the door behind her brought it all crashing down. The scene had been too horrible to take in. It felt like some awful dream. But now reality was dawning.

He dropped the stone and pressed closer to Jarrett. He placed his hands on Jarrett's cooling face, bit back the tears that were forcing themselves to the surface. He had to save him. He had to heal him. There had to be a way. There *had* to.

"I've come too far," he heard himself say. "I can't lose you. Not now. Not again." The last word came out as a sob.

He opened to Earth and gently, gently, pressed the power to Jarrett's skin. Maybe if he took it in doses...

Again, the power wrenched from his fingertips. It was like

catapulting into a whirlpool. He let go of the Sphere as Jarrett's starving center tried to suck him dry. Tenn closed his eyes and knew Leanna hadn't been lying. Jarrett was going to die; no amount of Tenn's power could replenish what had been stolen from him. And there was nothing Tenn could do about it.

Almost against his wishes, he looked to the stone that had rolled to Jarrett's hip.

Or is there?

He knew how the stone worked; it was the same as the markings on the jar they'd found, only attuned to Earth. Just a little bit of magic and the runes would activate, would start drawing out Jarrett's magic, just like Cassandra had demonstrated. The memory made his head swim. It felt like years had passed.

If Leanna was telling the truth, maybe he *could* do it. Maybe he could alter the runes and turn Jarrett into…into what? A Kin? Some sort of bastardized kraven? Rumor was not even the Dark Lady could create an Earth Howl that kept its sanity—the Kin were all bloodlings or higher. Earth was a hungry, mindless Sphere.

But what if he managed it?

He looked at Jarrett. He traced the curve of Jarrett's jaw with his fingers, delicately, not wanting to hurt the bruises that marred his gaunt face. The scars seemed to stick out even more now, made him look more battle-hardened. He looked older. Too old.

Tenn tried to imagine his world anew. A different future, where Jarrett was still alive but not quite human. He looked just like before, acted just like before, only now, every night, they didn't sit down to dinner, didn't drink wine before the fire while reading books. Jarrett would be out hunting. And Tenn would have to ignore the blood on his lover's clothes, would have to train himself never to ask what or whom Jarrett had had for supper.

It would be possible, that future. *He could feed off necromancers or maybe even cattle or kravens or...anything.* They could still be together. It wouldn't be any different from now, right? They still had to kill to survive. Jarrett would be in control of his urges. He'd be like the Kin. Like Tomás. He'd still be the man Tenn cared for. Only different.

There were tears in his eyes. They blurred Jarrett's sharp features, but Tenn didn't wipe them away. Only a few days ago, Tenn had thought Jarrett was dead. Gone. Seeing him here and now ripped that open, left Tenn bleeding in the gutter of memory. Tenn had hoped, in his rage to get here, that he could have his future again. He could have the home and the family, the reason to wake up in the morning.

Only now, he didn't. The man he loved would die no matter what. But maybe, if he really *was* chosen or important, he could have a semblance of Jarrett back. He could save him. Part of him.

Tenn shook as he leaned in and kissed Jarrett on the lips. He closed his eyes, wove his fingers gently through Jarrett's hair and prayed Jarrett could feel this. Jarrett needed to know he had fought for him. He had found him. He hadn't given up. In the end, Jarrett needed to know that Tenn had tried everything he could to save him. Even this.

Against his wishes, Water opened and flooded between them.

In the space of a heartbeat, his reality shattered.

"You have to let me go," Jarrett said.

The room was dark, so dark, but somehow Tenn could see Jarrett clearly, like he carried his own light. They stood in the darkness together, hands linked. Jarrett stood tall, his face warm and golden. Glowing. No sign of the damage Leanna had wrought. He looked whole. Tenn sobbed in relief and fell into his arms. Tears rained unchecked on Jarrett's shoulder.

"I can't," Tenn said. He knew what this was. He hadn't expected Jarrett to be conscious enough, but there it was. Emotional transference. He wanted to believe this was real, that this wasn't just a memory. He wanted more than anything to live that lie. But he knew the awful truth.

These were Jarrett's final thoughts.

Jarrett squeezed him tight, kissed the side of his neck.

"I can still do it," Tenn sobbed. "I can still save you."

Jarrett pulled back, his hands tight on Tenn's shoulders.

"You did save me," he said. His blue eyes sparkled like the sky, wet with tears.

"But I wanted us. Our future. I can give us that again. I can make you a Kin."

Jarrett smiled sadly.

"I wanted our future, too. But I can't let you do that. You know it wouldn't be right, for either of us. You have to let me go."

"But I told you I'd fight for you. I can't just—"

Jarrett pressed a finger to his lips.

"You *are* fighting," he said. "And you always will. For us. For our memory. Fight for that, if nothing else. Fight for a new future."

He removed his finger and leaned in, kissed Tenn with more

emotion and passion than Tenn had ever felt before. It made his heart sing and break, all in one gloriously painful moment.

"I love you," Jarrett said. "And I always will."

The vision faded.

Tenn sobbed, leaning against Jarrett's limp body. He wanted to slap him awake, wanted to see those blue eyes one last time, but he knew Jarrett had done all he could, had given Tenn more than he could have hoped. He'd had his goodbye. And now, Jarrett needed Tenn to say goodbye, as well.

Water was still alive in Tenn's gut. He reached out with hands and magic, touched the pulse of Jarrett's chest. It was so faint, so weak. It was barely there at all.

He could kill him. He could twist his power and stop the blood in Jarrett's veins. He could open to Earth and push Jarrett over the edge, pray that he would turn him into something resembling the man he wanted so badly to love.

Either way, he would lose the man he had fought for. The future he wanted to fight for. A life that went beyond revenge. A life worth living.

He closed his eyes.

He couldn't save Jarrett.

He couldn't save his family.

His family.

His family.

Water surged in his gut.

Mom? Dad?

He doesn't want to walk down the hall. He doesn't want to go back outside. He'd seen the shed door swinging in the wind, saw the way the grass had been trampled. But that isn't what makes him drag his feet toward the shed. It's a feeling in the pit of his stom-

ach, a resonance with Water that draws him forward. He couldn't have fought it if he tried.

But he's tired of trying. He'd already tried so hard. Fought so much. Across state lines and through hordes of the undead, past classmates fighting and dying and bleeding around him. And through all of it—all of it—Water had fought back. His only Sphere had pulled him forward, pressed him like a tidal wave through hell and high water. Just as it presses him now. Down the steps.

Out the back door.

Across the backyard.

His knees buckle the moment he opens the door.

They lay there. Pale. So pale. So hurt. Water hurts for them, feels the pull in their empty veins, feels the echoes of their life in the pools of crimson surrounding them. Tenn closes his eyes.

He hadn't been fast enough.

Water hadn't been strong enough.

He hadn't been strong enough.

Tears well in his eyes and power wells in his gut. Water blossoms. Water rages. Behind him, another scream roars. The monsters have found him. The monsters will always find him.

He needs to bury his parents. He needs to give them a proper, final rest. But he can't—there's no time. Just like he couldn't have saved them. Water bellows. This is unfair. So unfair. He's traveled so far, fought through so much. And it wasn't enough.

He turns. Lets the shed door close behind him, hiding them away.

"I'm sorry," he whispers as he stands. As he stands and turns to face the coming monsters.

They surround him. He can barely see the freshly decaying flesh, the putrid shades of red and pink and purple. Not through *the tears that shatter his vision in starlight. Not through the roar of Water in his gut, in his heart, in his head. He spent so many days fighting. Fighting the monsters. Fighting the other mages. Fighting the power within him.*

He's done fighting.

Not done fighting the monsters.

He's done fighting the power.

He screams, and the Sphere of Water screams through him, pulses out into the world like a tidal wave. It catches the blood in the veins of the monsters, both living and undead. Tosses them to the ground. Pulls the blood from their veins.

He doesn't stop screaming.

Water doesn't stop screaming.

He has all the pain in the world.

He has all the power.

Tenn gasped. Water still flooded his mind, but it relinquished his thoughts.

He stared at Jarrett. So close. So close to death. And so close to being forever far away.

"I wasn't there for them," Tenn whispered. "But I'm sure as hell going to be there for you."

How was he supposed to save the world if he couldn't even save another human? How was he supposed to change the language of runes if he couldn't even face the words he'd been given? He'd been given power. It was time he damn well used it.

Tenn grabbed the stone Leanna had left behind. It was wrong. He knew it in his bones, knew it in the way it seemed to sink into his flesh like oil, in the whispers of death and destruction the runes wrought in his mind, but he also knew it held power. So much power.

He traced the runes along the stone with a finger, let the grooves twist words and images through his mind.

The endless void; the teetering expanse; a black hole devouring the horizon; the pull of power.

It was made to drain its victims, yes. But he realized, as he read the runes over and over again, that it was more than that. It was a vessel.

And it was storing Jarrett's power.

He traced the runes again. Felt the surge of energy deep within the stone. Tenn couldn't channel enough Earth to mend Jarrett—maybe, if it had been Water, he would have stood a chance. But he'd only been attuned to Earth for a year or so. It wasn't nearly strong enough. But if he could rewrite these runes. If he could reverse the power...

He opened to Earth.

He opened to Water.

Water had always guided him. Water had always pulled him forward, connected him to something bigger than himself. Water, he realized, was how the gods spoke to him. Spoke *through* him. And he would give them that chance.

"Help me," he whispered and prayed. *Please help me save him.*

He poured a thin stream of energy into the stone. But not to activate it. To change it. He manipulated the runes. Changed the paths of the currents of power. His eyes were half-closed, his breathing soft, his thoughts no longer his.

Save him, he thought on repeat. His mantra. His lifeline.

The stone hummed. Grew hot with power as the runes slowly changed. As the runes became a different language. A lighter language. One not cursed by the Dark Lady's tongue.

He reached out, pressed the stone to Jarrett's belly. Pressed more power into the stone. Into the runes as he changed them: *release; the rising sun; a plant bursting to blossom.*

The stone glowed green, runes flared emerald.

And with a rush of energy that sounded like thunder, that shook the room like a windfall, the stone connected to Jarrett's dying Sphere. The stone and the runes stopped draining. The stone released its power and filled him.

Jarrett's body arched from the ground as wave upon wave of light and energy crashed through him, flares of green that nearly sent Tenn backward. But he kept holding on. Holding on to the power he poured into the stone. Holding on to Jarrett's arm even as he bucked away. Holding on to the hope that this had worked. This *had* to work.

Another rumble. Another wave of power. A lance of energy as the stone cracked, as light poured out and nearly blinded him.

Then Jarrett collapsed to the ground.

The stone fell to the side and shattered.

Tenn sat there. Staring. His heart hammering louder than thunder in his chest.

Come on. Come on. Come on.

"I believe," Jarrett whispered, his eyes quirking open, "my prince is supposed to kiss me awake."

CHAPTER THIRTY-SIX

HE DIDN'T KNOW HOW LONG THEY HUDDLED THERE, curled against one another. Jarrett was alive. *Jarrett was alive.* But weak. So weak. He fell asleep in Tenn's arms right after speaking, as though that act had been scaling a mountain. Tenn didn't care. He could have stayed there all night, holding Jarrett to his chest, until the twins began their attack and he had to kick his brain into gear.

He could have stayed there, if not for the hand that touched his shoulder. The hand that burned with fire and ice.

"Tomás," Tenn hissed, flinching away, shielding Jarrett from the incubus.

Tomás stood there, inches away, once more wearing nothing but skintight jeans and a smile, as though it weren't snowing outside. As though this were just another seduction. He burned like a sun. He must have been feeding. Tenn hated himself for not sensing the Kin's arrival. He should have known Tomás and Leanna would be together. Working together. And now, here he was to gloat.

"I am impressed," Tomás said. He was staring not at Tenn but at Jarrett. Jarrett, who could barely keep his eyes open. "You have done what no other could do."

"I didn't turn him," Tenn said.

"No. But you spoke the language of the runes. You heard the Dark Lady's call." His eyes trailed to Tenn as he spoke, the smile twisting into something else. Tenn didn't like that change in Tomás's demeanor.

Tomás was looking at him like an equal.

"I didn't hear anything," Tenn said. "What the hell do you want?"

"Touchy, touchy," Tomás muttered. He stroked the side of Tenn's face, sending chills down his spine. Then he reached for Jarrett. Tenn beat his hand away. Tomás actually chuckled. "She expects this one to be a monster, you know." He looked at Tenn. "What will you do when my sister arrives and finds him whole? Do you truly think you will leave here?"

"We'll fight."

Tomás laughed. Far too loudly. Tenn fully expected Leanna to come barging in right then. The fact that she didn't had him on edge. She had to have felt that much magic. Maybe she just thought it was him turning Jarrett into a Howl?

"You'll fight?" Tomás asked. "Adorable. And here I thought you had actually *learned* something in the last few days." Quick as a viper, Tomás had Tenn against the wall, feet away from Jarrett, a hand around his neck. "You forget your place, little mouse. You cannot kill Leanna. Just as you cannot kill me. At best, you are our plaything. At worst, a meal."

He leaned in and licked Tenn's jawline. Fire screamed inside

Tenn's chest as the incubus drew the heat from him, leaving him shuddering. A renegade sigh escaped his lips.

"You don't have it in you to fight her," Tomás said, his words tilting on bedroom huskiness. "And neither does your lover. If you want to get out of here alive, you are going to have to play by my rules."

Tenn wanted to say he wasn't playing. He wasn't going to be manipulated by Tomás—not after what he'd just done, not after he'd done the impossible. But he couldn't get the words out.

Tomás could be very commanding when he wanted to be.

"What...what do you want?" Tenn managed. He shuddered and his chest ached; Tomás was drawing heat from him even now, more than he ever had before.

Tomás chuckled. "You always ask that. My answer is always the same. I want everything, Tenn. And you have just proven that you can help me get it." He leaned in, and the little strength Tenn had left wanted to pull the Howl closer. "I am actually quite glad you restored your lover. He is going to make the coming days so much more interesting to watch."

"I don't—"

But Tomás put his free finger over Tenn's lips.

"You don't. But you will. If you follow my lead."

He let Tenn go. Tenn slumped to the floor.

Heat rushed back through Tenn's limbs, followed by a terrible tingling that made it impossible to move. He watched Tomás saunter toward Jarrett. Jarrett watched him approach with half-lidded eyes.

"Don't you dare—"

"I'm not going to hurt him, Tenn. I already told you, I look forward to the fun we will all have soon. Oh, so very soon."

He knelt down in front of Jarrett, studying him but not touching. "But he will die if you keep him here. And you are in no shape to protect him from what is about to come. I won't be able to, either."

He looked back to Tenn.

"I will take him from here. Bring him to your friends. We can tell Leanna you pushed your lover out the window or something."

Tenn wanted to ask a thousand questions, but the only one he could get out was "Why?"

Tomás's smile read every question.

"Do you truly believe there is a single moment where I am not watching you, Tenn? I observed you and your friends creating your little runic circle. How positively ancient of you, by the way. As for why... I have my reasons. Let's just say, it's much more fun to watch you struggle. Opposition breeds resilience, after all."

Tenn inched forward. He couldn't trust Tomás. Not when Tomás had kept this from him. He must have known Jarrett was alive this entire time. He couldn't trust him...

"I haven't lied to you once, Tenn," Tomás said as Tenn tried to move, his limbs barely working. "I told you from day one that I would keep you alive. And that I have. But you are right not to trust me. You shouldn't trust anyone. Not even your lover, who still hasn't admitted why he was sent to find you. Charming, if not a little convenient. Oh, yes, keeping him alive will make this so much more fun."

Before Tenn could ask what Tomás meant, the incubus and Jarrett were gone.

Tenn blinked. The room suddenly empty, as if it had all

been a dream. He could have almost believed it was a hallucination, too. If not for the shattered stone marking where Jarrett had lain.

Moments later, Tomás reappeared.

One day, Tenn would figure out how he was traveling like that.

Tenn opened his mouth, but Tomás was at his side before he could speak.

"Do not worry, little mouse. Your boyfriend is safe."

"Why are you doing this?" Tenn asked. "Why are you helping me?"

"I'm not," Tomás said. He gently caressed Tenn's face, once more sending chills and heat through Tenn's skin. Tenn's mind raced with the images of what other sensations the man could arouse, but his words cut the thoughts short. "*You* are helping *me*."

Tenn reached up and grabbed Tomás's hand. His mind was fluttering, but he had to stay focused. Had to draw the Howl closer. Had to...

The door opened.

Leanna stormed in, her lackey Justin right behind her. She took one look at the room before her eyes narrowed on Tomás. It was clear, seeing them in the same room, that their relation was only through being Kin. Leanna was pale to Tomás's tan, willowy to his muscle. Calm, to his crazy.

"Brother," she said. Her voice was flat.

"Sister," Tomás said. "How pleasant—"

"What are you doing here? And where is the boy?" she asked, staring at Tomás warily. It wasn't fear on her face. It was consideration. He was clearly a very unpleasant surprise.

Maybe Tomás was telling the truth, and they weren't working together, after all.

"Your captive is whole once more," Tomás said. "Our little wonder boy here came through—he didn't just read the runes, he *changed* them. And now, Jarrett is back outside your clutches, just waiting for this one's return. Tenn succeeded. Just as I knew he would. But not in the ways you thought."

Leanna didn't even spare Tenn a glance.

"Get him out of here," she said to Justin. "Lock him in the basement."

Justin stepped forward, but before he could wrest Tenn from Tomás's death grip on his arm, Tenn's thoughts coalesced. He was still open to Earth. And he wasn't going to lose track of Tomás again. He wasn't going to be watched from the shadows.

With a whip-quick lance of power, he seared the tracking rune onto Tomás's heart. Tomás cried out and yanked his hand away. He stared at Tenn with a snarl on his lips and rubbed his chest with a free hand. Was he actually shocked? Or just impressed that Tenn had bitten back?

"What the hell was that?" Tomás asked.

"A going-away present."

Justin gave Leanna a wary look, but she just nodded dismissively. Tenn closed off to Earth and let Justin haul him to his feet.

"Wait," Tenn said, just before they reached the door. The sky outside the window was starting to lighten.

"What?" Leanna asked.

But he wasn't looking at her. He was looking at Tomás.

"Why do this?" Tenn asked. "Why did you bring me here? If it was to kill her, why not just do it yourself?"

Tomás's look of indignation took on its usual elfish grin. "Oh," he said. "That."

Leanna's jaw was clenched, and Justin was clearly torn between following his mistress's orders and watching this play out. Tomás sighed dramatically and walked over to an armchair in the corner, settling himself down and crossing his ankles. Leanna looked ready to spit fire, but Tomás's grin was all comfortable mischief.

"I crave power," he said. He was looking straight at Leanna.

"I fail to see how this," she said, gesturing to Tenn, "is your path to power, brother. I have precisely what I sought: the one who can speak the language of the runes..." Tomás started miming her with his hand, rolling his eyes. Leanna snapped her jaw shut.

"Oh, yes, sister. You have the 'Chosen One,'" he said, making air quotes. "Too bad you're going to die before you can use him to create more of us."

Leanna actually laughed at this.

"What? You believe this boy can kill me?"

"No," Tomás said. "But having him here will make him the perfect scapegoat. After all, our brethren already know his name. They know to fear him, as much as they covet."

"Coward," Leanna said.

Tomás chuckled.

"I am many things, but a coward I am not. If *I* killed you, the rest of our brethren would be up in arms. What would our mother say? I'd have the entirety of the Dark Lady's army at my throat. But if the Chosen One kills you? Well, no harm, no foul, as they say."

"Get him out of here," Leanna growled. She didn't take her

eyes off Tomás, but the flick of her wrist toward Justin was in-dicator enough. "I'll deal with this traitor."

"Perhaps you will," Tomás said. "But, dear sister, there are two things about this boy I have come to expect."

"And what are those?" Leanna asked. Justin had already begun dragging Tenn away. They were nearly out the door when Tenn caught Tomás's final word.

"Twins."

Above them, on cue, thunder roared. Even Justin paused.

Leanna was at the window in a heartbeat, one hand pressed to the pane. Tomás didn't take his eyes off Tenn. His smile spoke volumes; it made Tenn's blood run hot and cold.

"How did they—" Leanna began.

"Go undetected?" Tomás asked. He winked at Tenn. "You'll have to ask our *weak* little friend over here. Apparently, he has a few tricks up his sleeve."

"The runes," Leanna hissed. She opened to Earth. Tenn knew without a doubt that she was trying to find the twins' hiding place. And he knew she would never succeed.

"Bingo," Tomás said.

"Why is he still here?" Leanna yelled.

Justin jolted and continued dragging Tenn back down the hall. Tenn tried to struggle, to break free, but Justin was much stron-ger. The whole world shuddered as the twins began their attack.

And Tenn was right in the center of their target.

He stopped struggling.

At least Jarrett was safe. At least one of them had made it out of here alive.

If Tomás had been telling the truth.

CHAPTER THIRTY-SEVEN

THUNDER.

The chair he was tied to nearly toppled. It probably would have, too, if Justin hadn't been there to hold it steady.

"Impressive," Justin said, staring up at the ceiling. It was the first thing he'd said since bringing Tenn down here, what felt like ages ago. The rafters rained down wafts of dust with every tremor, and the fluorescent lights swayed back and forth. Even from down here, he could feel the great amounts of energy being thrown around outside. Every Sphere—Air and Fire, Water and Earth—which meant Leanna was fighting back. Not that it would do much good. "Your friends are powerful."

Another explosion shook the house, this one echoed by a rumble that seemed to come from the pits of hell. A light in the corner exploded in a shower of sparks. Still, Justin didn't flinch, and his hand on the back of Tenn's chair kept him from moving. Justin was unnaturally strong; the guy was a Howl, that much was certain, but he definitely wasn't one of the Kin—not with how dismissive Tomás and Leanna had been of him. The question was, what type of Howl was he dealing with?

Tenn gritted his teeth and twisted his wrists behind him, hoping he could maybe loosen the bonds. Justin sniffed, and the air left Tenn's lungs in a gasp.

That answered that question.

"What did I say about cooperation?" He glanced down at Tenn before reverting to his skyward glance. He tapped his throat with his free hand. "I can sense every movement you make. Struggling will just make it worse."

A sick feeling settled itself in Tenn's gut. He closed his eyes and focused on the runes he had inked into his friends' wrists. Only Devon was still on the hillside. His heart sunk, though he'd known she would break command like this: Dreya was heading toward them. Barely a hundred yards away.

Tenn knew that Dreya was coming to find him. While Devon was throwing around as much magic as he could to distract the guards and Leanna, she was coming in for the rescue. He glanced up at Justin. Even if Dreya *did* make it into the house, there was no way she'd make it past him. Not if she was going for the element of surprise. Which left one shaky alternative.

"My friends are going to kill you. Again," he said. It wasn't much, but it did get Justin's attention. The guy looked at him with a bemused expression.

"Oh, really? How, precisely? This place is a bunker guarded by hundreds of necromancers. Even if they do get in, they'll have to deal with Leanna and me."

Tenn shrugged, as much as he could under restraint.

"Doesn't matter," he said. "They will. Tell me, what were you? You know, before you became Leanna's toy."

Justin laughed, his mouth curving into a smile.

"And why would you want to know?" he asked.

"Because you had a spine once. I can't imagine what that would have been like."

In the blink of an eye, Justin was hunched over Tenn, a finger jabbed between his clavicles. Tenn didn't gasp, even though it felt like Justin was about to collapse his throat.

"I was a fitness instructor in LA before my girlfriend joined the cult of the Dark Lady," he said. "She turned me. I was her first."

"So why are you with Leanna?" Tenn managed to ask.

Justin's eyes narrowed. "My maker was human. Humans. Die." His finger dug deeper. "So I came to serve Leanna, who is as close to my goddess as we can become."

"Then tell your Goddess of Death hello for me," Tenn whispered.

"What?"

The door at the top of the stairs blew open.

The force of the explosion made Tenn's ears ring, but in that one brief moment of Justin's distraction he pushed the chair over and opened to Earth. The bonds broke free. Tenn crashed to the side and scrambled away on shaking limbs. Justin didn't try to stop him. He didn't curse. He just stared up at the broken door with his arms crossed over his chest, a bored expression plastered on his face.

Dreya floated down the steps, her white coat fluttering in the windstorm. She looked like a goddess, her body laced with

an aura of yellow and blue, her Spheres blazing. Tenn ran toward Dreya's side. Her power roared in his ears.

"Go," Dreya said. There was a tightness in her eyes as she
stared at Justin, a recognition that bordered on madness. It
reminded him of when Devon let Fire take control.

"I'm fighting," Tenn replied.

She said nothing to this.

Justin didn't attack. He raised an eyebrow instead and looked
at them like they were mice toying with a cat. Tenn was still
horribly weak, and the very thought of fighting again made
him want to sink into the ground and never come up. But Jarrett was alive. He was alive. And that was worth fighting for.

"Who are you?" Justin asked.

"You wouldn't remember me," Dreya replied. "But I remember seeing you, running. You escaped me that once. You will
not do so again."

She struck. The air within the basement became a cyclone
of dust and rubble. It whipped around Tenn, slashed marks in
his skin, but he didn't flinch and he didn't close his eyes. He
might not have been any use in the fight, but he was going
to see this through.

Water sprayed from the wall as the water heater tore away,
crashing into storage boxes and scraping along the concrete
floor with the wail of banshees. Everything swept up in the
maelstrom—pipes burst, foundations cracked. Everything
thrashed about but Justin.

He stepped forward, appearing from the screen of flying debris in a halo of stillness, water sloshing around his feet. The
Sphere of Air burned in his throat, a bruised blue, a garish

yellow, and Tenn realized the awful truth: his inverted Sphere consumed the power Dreya whipped at him.

Justin grinned. "Dumb bitch."

Tenn had no idea how he could hear the guy over the roar of wind, but his voice carried like they were talking over a dinner table.

"You're making him stronger!" Tenn yelled, praying that Dreya would hear him. "He's a Breathless One!"

"He is," she replied. "And he was there, when our clan died. He was there, stealing their breath. For that, for all of this, he deserves a slow death. I will make him suffer."

Her face was a grimace, a mask of barely controlled rage. Then she opened her mouth and sang.

The burning light within her flashed bright as a strobe as the power inside the basement amplified. Wind howled. Tenn sank back against the wall behind her, trying to find shelter from the hell Dreya had unleashed. Through the blinding light and whirling debris, he saw Justin take a step forward. He was laughing now, and his twisted Sphere devoured the power. The water heater flew past, and he smashed it with a fist without even looking. His eyes were focused entirely on Dreya.

"I will eat you alive, little bug," he sneered. "I will drain you till your bones implode. And then I'll feed you to the kravens."

Dreya paused her singing, just long enough to call to Tenn, "Hold him!"

Tenn looked between the two of them, standing only feet apart. Then, before Justin could take another step, Tenn opened to Earth. The floor beneath Justin's feet turned to quicksand, sucked him down to his ankles. Then he let go of the power, and the concrete solidified in an instant. Even that was enough to drop Tenn to his knees. Shock turned to hate on Justin's face as he tried and failed to wrench a leg free.

"Oh, you are going to pay for that," he said.

He inhaled.

If it weren't for the sheer strength of Dreya's magic, Tenn knew they would have both died in that instant. Justin pulled the air from the room. Tenn's lungs burned, and even Dreya stumbled. But she didn't cease her song, and her power filled the void with everything Justin tried to steal. Her song became a scream, one that matched pitch with the howl of wind, but it only fed the monster. All Justin had to do was wait for Dreya to become used up; then, a small gasp and he would have them both.

"Dreya," Tenn said, hoping he could get them both out of there before she fainted. She glared at him, her eyes bright as azure stars, and he shut up. That was a look that said she knew precisely what she was doing. Whatever it was, it seemed insane.

He glanced back at Justin, still sunk in the concrete, still glaring at them as the wind whipped around him and his Sphere swallowed it whole. The water had risen, was now splashing around his calves. That's when Tenn noticed something...different.

The darkness of Justin's empty Sphere was lightening. The vortex of power that swirled around and into him flickered.

"I hear it hurts," Dreya said, the song cutting off, her words slicing through the maelstrom like a knife. "I hear that the hunger is unbearable. That this is why you kill the very people you once loved, because it hurts too much to do otherwise. Consider this your final blessing, then. No. More. Hunger."

She flung her hands forward, sending a blinding torrent of magic and wind at Justin's locked frame.

Justin gasped. His hands shot to his throat.

And in that instant, with a roar of magic that sent shivers through Tenn's very bones, Justin's Sphere...healed.

There was no other word for it. One moment, the Sphere was a vacuum in Justin's throat. The next, it was whole: shining, flickering, *exuding*. Dreya let go of her power. If Tenn hadn't been watching her, he would have missed the way she slouched and steadied herself on the stair banister. She quickly righted herself, her chest heaving with exertion and her eyes wild.

"You healed him," Tenn whispered.

He looked to Justin, who was just as shell-shocked as Tenn felt. The man had been cured of the incurable.

Dreya didn't give him time to question. She grabbed him by the sleeve and began pulling him up the stairs, her breath loud and ragged even against the roar of leaking water.

"Wait!" Justin called out.

Tenn looked back. He was still stuck in the concrete, water quickly rising past his knees. The basement was small. How long would it take to fill? Water sent a chill through him. What would it feel like to drown?

"Don't leave me like this!"

Dreya paused, perhaps from the panic in his voice, perhaps because she couldn't move any farther. Her eyes were pale, and her chest fluttered as fast as a rabbit's. She leaned against the wall and looked back to the Howl. She didn't speak. For a moment, Tenn wondered if she even could.

"You saved me," Justin said. He was frantic, struggling

against the concrete that was lodged around his legs. "You can't just leave me like this. I'll die."

"I did not save you," Dreya said. Her voice was flat, emotionless, but it also had a breathlessness that made Tenn fear the worst. She'd drawn way too much, and they still had to find a way out of here. "You are still a monster," she continued. "But you will die a human."

She turned and walked up the stairs. Justin screamed.

Tenn didn't move. There were tears in his eyes. Justin screamed at him, begged to be released. They couldn't let him die—not when he was no longer a Howl. Not when he was human, and scared.

Dreya grabbed Tenn by the collar, pulled his face close to hers.

"Move," she grated. "Before the Kin return."

"But you saved him! You made him human again."

Sure, Tenn had brought Jarrett back from the brink of becoming a Howl. But that wasn't reversing the process and that wasn't his power. That was the runes. Dreya had done the impossible, the task they'd come all this way to achieve.

Dreya squeezed her eyes shut. Her breath was fast, too fast, and when she spoke it was barely a whisper.

"It's impossible," she said. Another rumble shook the house, but neither of them flinched.

"But I just saw—"

"You saw nothing," she said, her eyes opening in a flash of blue. Her voice was tired. "You cannot cure the disease that ails him."

"But—"

Again, her eyes closed.

"One can only assuage the Sphere's hunger for a time. When the Sphere is damaged to that degree, it cannot be mended, not by any human hands. Soon, that Howl's Sphere will eat itself again. And when it does, he will be just as broken as before. He will always be a monster, Tenn. I just wanted him to remember how it felt to be a terrified human."

Tenn glanced back at the man who, only moments before, had threatened his life. He deserved to die. He deserved to die like this. *Right?*

What are you becoming?

What have you become?

The question made his heart sink. Dreya pulled him again, and he followed.

"I'm sorry," Tenn whispered. He doubted Justin heard it over his own, terrified screams.

CHAPTER THIRTY-EIGHT

THE SKY BURNED RED. NOT JUST THE RED OF FIRE, but the red of a wound, raw and bleeding. Clouds dripped fire like lava, and the once-picturesque mountain landscape now looked like the fangs of some broken beast. Flames roared on the hillside, weaving trails of smoke up into the air as lightning forked back and forth with strobe-like speed. Everything was heat and fury. Every hair on Tenn's body stood on end, his Spheres echoing the destruction around him. And yet, in spite of the havoc that wove like madness through the countryside, the town below was strangely untouched. Only a few fires leaped between buildings, snaring the dark shadows that raced through the streets. Tenn knew Devon was trying to avoid the innocent lives that swarmed near the outer wall. Trying, and probably failing. There were just too many to save.

Dreya paused in the doorway and turned to him. Her breath was still erratic, and she looked paler than usual, as though her skin was becoming translucent. She reached out a shaky hand and took Tenn's arm.

"I must go help my brother," she said.

"Is Jarrett...?"

"Alive. With Devon. Though we will speak of what happened later. You must finish this." She took a deep breath. Swayed. "I am no help. I should not have killed the Breathless One like that. Anger overtook..."

Tenn reached out, steadied her.

She shook him off. When she looked at him, her eyes were fierce, even if the rest of her seemed uncertain.

"Leanna cannot make it out alive," she said. "End this."

His legs were lead. He'd already run in here alone. But to be left amid the destruction?

"I can't—"

She shook her head.

"Your pain gives you strength," she said. Another chill swept through him. Did she know she was repeating Tomás's words? "And that will help you win this fight. Just don't let your pain consume you."

Air flickered in Dreya's throat. It was faint, barely a trace of its normal strength, but the wind still whipped around her and sent her white coat fluttering. She lifted herself up, hovered a few inches above the ground. "Good luck," she said. "We will see you on the other side."

And with that, she shot through the air like an arrow, speeding toward her brother.

It wasn't until he turned to find the Kin that he realized her parting words were far from comforting.

Tomás was near, that much was certain—the incubus's tracking rune glowed in Tenn's mind, a red lace against the fibers of the Howl's heart. Tenn ran around to the back of the house. His body screamed with protest, but he shut it down, deep in the recesses he usually reserved for silencing Water's screams. Those, he let loose. If ever there was a time to drown in the wrongs he had suffered, in the rage he wanted so badly to unleash on the world, it was now. He had Jarrett back, sure. But he was done with being used. It was time to use his power.

He found Tomás in the courtyard. The house formed a horseshoe around a cleared space that had, at one time, been beautiful. Now it was the scene of an eerily silent apocalypse.

Every window facing the yard was blown out and gaping, shards of glass sticking from the churned mud like incisors. Chunks of concrete jutted from the soil, along with toppled trees and statuary. The earth itself rippled like static waves in a black sea. In the center of it all was Tomás, standing on a dais of black marble.

And there, at his feet, lying in a circle of frost and snapped icicles, was Leanna. Tenn thought she was dead. He stopped in his tracks and stared at them. Tomás glared down at his sister, his chest heaving, his whole body shaking. For a moment, he thought the man was mourning. Then the sound of thunder faded, and he realized Tomás was laughing.

"Worthless, she said." His voice made Tenn take a step back. He'd seen Tomás upset. Now he seemed unhinged. "Who is worthless now? Dear, dear sister, how sweet you look like this." He knelt down, one knee crushing into her chest. She gasped, and Tenn felt his lungs expand. "Now who is helpless, sister dear? Now whose heart is made of ice?"

Tomás's hand snapped forward, quicker than lightning, and Leanna spasmed. His wrist sunk deep into her chest. She didn't bleed. Just arched against his hand, a soft cry escaping her lips. Another snap motion, and he pulled his arm back in a spray of broken bone and old blood. He held something up in the red twilight.

Her heart.

Tenn watched in horror as Tomás's fingers clenched the red muscle. It didn't beat, not like in the movies. Instead, the crimson flesh turned black under his fingertips. It was only when it began to crush in his grip, falling to the ground in sand-fine wisps, that Tenn realized Tomás had frozen it. Tomás let the last of the shards filter through his fingers before standing. He looked down at his sister, still writhing on her bed of ice. Then he turned his head, ever so slowly, and stared straight at Tenn.

"I had hoped," he said, hopping off the dais and taking a limping step toward him, "that you would arrive in time to see that." He snickered and his whole body convulsed. The air around him shivered red.

"She fought well, my sister. So very well. But she is not used to killing anymore. No, no, that never was her joy. She let others do it for her. That was her mistake. Her big mistake."

Tenn took a half step back. The roar in his head faltered, his heart thudding in his chest. With every step closer, the air around Tenn grew both colder and hotter, sending sweat and chills down his skin. He was weaponless, exhausted.

He was no match against Tomás.

"She's not *dead*, of course. I couldn't do that. What would they say? *Tomás, Tomás, youngest brother, what have you done?* Hah!" He did a little jump, and Tenn jumped back. "I saved the rest for you, little mouse. I saved you the best part."

Tenn looked past Tomás, to where Leanna lay frozen on the ground. How was she still alive? Could the Kin even be killed? "Ah, he wonders now." Tomás's voice was singsong. He paused a few feet away and cocked his head to the side. Tenn's heart raged with fear and revulsion and desire. The damn incubus was still toying with him. "He wonders why. Why why why me? Why must *I* be the one who kills the beast? And *how?*"

Tomás shuddered, and his next words were terrifyingly sane.

"Thou art the reaper," he said grimly, "and the world shall bleed at thy hands."

"I'm sick of playing your games," Tenn hissed.

"But we've only just started to play," Tomás replied. His grin widened.

The next moment, he was on Tenn, forcing him to the ground and pinning his arms to his sides. The ground was cold and wet, but Tenn's skin burned at Tomás's touch. The Howl's face loomed just inches from his own, only a few, delectable inches. Tenn gritted his teeth and looked to the side, to where Leanna was sprawled much like he was. In spite of the heat roaring off the incubus, the ground around them cracked with cold.

"Now he sees," Tomás said, half to himself. "Now he sees my power. Now they *all* will see my power!"

"You're insane," Tenn said.

"Those who hear not the music," Tomás replied, singsong. Another roar filled the sky and he chuckled, sitting back on Tenn's chest to look to the heavens. Somewhere out there, Tenn heard the unmistakable sound of tornadoes. At least Dreya had made it to her brother safely.

"If you're going to kill me, just do it," Tenn said. He forced himself to look Tomás in the face, forced down the whirl of emotions that the damned incubus stirred in his chest. Oh, how he wanted to rip the man apart, just as much as he wanted to rip off his few clothes and make him scream in other ways. Tenn's heart hurt as Tomás's empty Sphere tugged.

"Kill you?" Tomás said. His head tilted to the other side. "Why would I kill the man who will rule beside me as king?" His words were smooth, remarkably sane in spite of the madness in his glowing copper eyes. He reached down and gently placed his hand against Tenn's jaw. The movement was so intimate Tenn wanted to vomit. He wanted it to go further.

"We will be gods," Tomás said. "Can't you see? Consider this the day of your ascension."

Then, before Tenn could grasp what he was saying, Tomás bent down and kissed him.

The Howl's lips were cinnamon and fire, the bite of brimstone and ice. It sent ice through Tenn's skin, traced waves of blinding heat down his spine. He wanted to resist. Wanted to hate the monster that had torn his whole world apart. He wanted to, for what Tomás had done—to him, to the twins, to Jarrett. He told himself he wanted to hate Tomás. He told himself...

But under the magic of the incubus, his resolve gave way. Every pulse was a roar in his veins, every second a floating eternity. His back arched against his will, his whole body desiring to be closer, to lose itself in an embrace that tore everything else away. The world around them faded, everything distilled to their lips, to Tomás's burning hand on his face. The world was red and black and frosted like hell, and Tenn melted. The fear. The anger. The desire for revenge. All of it burned to ash.

When Tomás pulled back, he smiled down at Tenn with a smoldering light in his eyes. Tenn's head swam. His lips tingled. His chest burned and heart fluttered. Tomás stood in one smooth motion and reached down, helped Tenn to his feet. Tenn didn't resist. He floated in a world of static and heat. The ground beneath his feet was light as clouds. He let Tomás guide him over to where Leanna rested on her bed of ice. Her dark hair stuck to the ground, frosted around her head like dead veins. There was a hole in her rib cage, but it didn't bleed. It didn't repulse him. Her dull eyes flickered. They were skimmed over, cloudy, but they fixed on Tenn and widened.

"Do it," Tomás whispered, his lips brushing promises against Tenn's ear. Tenn's heart soared. "Her broken Sphere is the only thing keeping her alive. Rip it out."

Tenn knelt at Leanna's side, Tomás's hands on his shoulders. Leanna tried to open her mouth, but her lips were frosted shut. Her skin was dusted with white.

He could feel her twisted Sphere. Air still hungered in her throat, still tried to steal the breath from his lungs. He reached down in a haze. Her flesh was colder than ice beneath his grip, but he barely felt it, not with Tomás so near. The incubus burned like a sun, and Tenn floated in the heat.

Leanna didn't scream when Tenn dug his fingers into her throat. She couldn't.

Her flesh gave way as easily as burned paper, crisping and collapsing. He jerked his hands, and her throat caved in on itself as ash. Leanna's eyes fluttered wide. Then they rolled back in her head, and her body paled to ivory white.

"You have done well, my prince," Tomás whispered into his ear. The man knelt beside him, wrapping his arms around

Tenn's chest and stomach, holding him tight to the inferno. Tenn burned in bliss. "Now, to take care of your other half."

The monster kissed the back of Tenn's neck, made fire swell across his skin. Tenn shivered with sudden cold. His eyes shut on their own accord. *Other half?* Jarrett's face fluttered through his mind, along with the boy he'd seen in the vision.

His heart panicked as Tomás drained his heat with the press of his lips. But it was mild, distant. None of it mattered, not so long as Tomás was there. So long as he had the heat. The heat and the life and the power. Then his heart slowed. Stopped.

Before he could wonder if it would ever beat again, the world went dark and numb.

CHAPTER THIRTY-NINE

DARKNESS EVERYWHERE.

His ears filled with screams, with people calling his name. Pain, so distant. The constant jumble of motion.

He spun through it all, blind, blissful, floating in a torrent of fire that racked his body with cold. But he didn't mind. He barely noticed.

Because in that void, Tomás was ever at his side. And together, they ruled the nothingness as kings.

CHAPTER FORTY

"YOU'RE AWAKE," CAME A VOICE.

It cut through the haze of dreams like a knife. Tenn opened his eyes. Jarrett looked down at him.

"You're alive," Tenn whispered. His voice cracked. It hadn't been a dream. It hadn't been a delusion.

Tomás hadn't lied.

Jarrett smiled. "Thanks to you."

Tenn tried to sit up, but he was tired, so tired, and so damned cold. Blankets piled atop his body, and fires flickered magically in the air, but he still shivered.

"What happened?" he asked, remembering Tomás's embrace. "Where are we?"

"A guild," Dreya said. She stepped out from the shadows. "East of Leanna's compound. We brought you here, after you killed her."

Clearly time had passed. Dreya didn't look tired anymore. Neither did Devon, who was leaning against the wall, Fire smoldering in his chest as he fueled the flames dancing around the ceiling. But Tenn's gaze kept going back to Jarrett.

Jarrett, whose skin no longer looked bruised and sallow. Whose smile looked as natural as sunrise. Jarrett, whose eyes looked at Tenn the same way they had in Outer Chicago, when their shared history had knit itself into the present.

Jarrett, who felt like a part of him.

Who would always be a part of him.

"You did it," Jarrett said. "You saved me."

"Of course," Tenn replied. He smiled. "You still owe me a milk shake."

Jarrett laughed. Then he leaned over and kissed him.

It was warmth and light, gentle and strong, and it filled Tenn's chest with a sensation he hadn't felt in ages: love. He thought he would never use the word again, but there it was, gossamer and shining as Jarrett kissed him, deep and powerful, and the rest of the world melted away. For a while, he floated there, in Jarrett's kiss, in the embrace his whole body had ached for.

When Jarrett pulled back, reality inked in with a dreadful rush.

He had killed Leanna. He had saved Jarrett. He should have been floating. So why was his heart hammering? Why did it feel like a terrible setup?

Then he remembered Tomás's parting words.

Now, to take care of your other half.

He looked at Jarrett, who stood there, smiling, safe. He looked to the twins, who watched him with silent eyes.

His other half was here.

Tenn's heart pounded. He fully expected Tomás to appear

then, and murder them all. Right before his eyes. Just to prove a point. But the seconds ticked by, and the moment didn't shatter. It made everything worse. Jarrett ran a hand through Tenn's hair.

"You've been out for a while," Jarrett whispered. "But we'll let you rest. I'll be right outside. Always."

Tenn nodded. He wanted so badly to be happy right then. He wanted to feel like he had done something good. But Tomás's words were a curse: How could he celebrate when the incubus was still out there, pulling the threads of Tenn's life? Playing them all in a game he didn't understand? He wanted to tell Jarrett, but he knew Tomás would deliver on his threat. The Kin had just killed his own sister. He would have no problem killing Jarrett and the twins.

Tenn closed his eyes. Jarrett kissed him again, and although Tenn's heart fluttered, it wasn't enough to cut through the fear he prayed the others couldn't see.

They left.

The door closed behind them.

Tenn waited for the shadows to shift into Tomás.

They never did.

He thought of the tracking rune on Tomás's heart, felt the incubus's presence in the corners of his mind, but Tomás was far away. Very far away. So why did he feel like Tomás was a part of him? Inside of him? The Howl had somehow enchanted Tenn into killing Leanna. Tenn remembered so vividly how it felt to be manipulated like that. How easy it had been to give in.

He may have saved Jarrett. But who would save them from

him if Tomás ever came back, if he ever took over Tenn so easily again?

Tenn shuddered. Pulled the blankets tighter. This wasn't the happy ending he'd wanted. There was still a monster out there.

There was still a monster *in here*.

Sleep sidled in on him. He felt heavy, though his thoughts raced and drifted in half-slumber. Light flashed across his closed eyes. Silver flickers. Like stars. Like tiny silver fish.

And he was back in the cave. Back in the swirl of constellations. Back in the vision.

The stars coalesced. Became the face of the guy with rings in his lip and anger in his eyes. Became a voice. A feeling.

A fear.

The boy was in trouble.

The boy needed him.

Then the image shifted, and Tomás was there, his hands on the boy's shoulders, as around them the white stars burst into crimson flame. As the shadows laughed with the Dark Lady's voice.

Tenn snapped awake. His heart raced and the lamps flickered and all he could sense was the fire, the fire. The knowledge that the boy would burn the world to the ground.

Tenn visualized Tomás's tracking rune once more.

It was distant.

It was getting farther away.

He pushed himself from the bed and went to the door, stumbling in his weakness. The door opened before his hand was on the knob.

"What is it?" Jarrett asked.

"Tomás," Tenn said. "The incubus. He's after someone. And if we don't get there first…the end…it's just beginning."

The twins shared a look. Jarrett stared straight at Tenn, his eyes filled with questions Tenn knew he could never answer. Not if he wanted to keep his friends alive.

Dread settled in Tenn's gut. Water sloshed with regret and fear. Of what he'd done. Of what he'd do again.

He wanted so badly to have a future, one that wasn't filled with bloodshed and monsters and magic.

He knew, in that moment, that it wasn't the future he'd created.

* * * * *

ACKNOWLEDGMENTS

FIFTEEN YEARS.

That's how long the world of RUNEBINDER has been percolating in my brain. First as a story told at a lunch table, sophomore year of high school, featuring a very not-evil necromancer named Bob and his fluffy sidekick Bane. The plot has changed quite a bit since then. Then as the book that landed me my amazing agent, Laurie McLean, over six years ago. In the time since, the story has gone through many incarnations and three publishing houses, but RUNEBINDER is finally being (re)released into the world in all its diabolic glory.

As you could imagine, fifteen years means there are many people to thank.

First, my heartfelt thanks goes to Laurie McLean and Fuse Literary, for taking a chance on a queer apocalyptic story that—six years ago—seemed too outside the box to get published. She believed in me anyway.

Next, to Patricia Riley, who saw the spark in this book and

decided that, yes, the world was ready for a gay, magic-wielding protagonist. And an antagonist with "panty-dropping powers."

To Asja Parrish, for loving these characters as much as I did and helping them come alive.

To Michael Strother, for bringing this book into its latest form. And, obviously, a huge thank you for allowing most of our Important Business Emails to be relayed via RuPaul GIFs. Werk.

To the entire team at HarlequinTeen for putting their heart and soul into this book and making it a work of art, inside and out. With a special shout-out to T.S. Ferguson and Natashya Wilson, for being the latest to take the reins.

To my publicist Siena Koncsol, for always making me feel like a rock star.

To my family, who believed in me every step of the way. My mother, for letting me fly. My father, for sharing his love of words. My brother, for showing me perseverance.

To Beatrice Schares, for drafting the very first sketches of these characters, and being their number one supporter from the very beginning. Who doesn't want more half-naked images of Tomás?

To Will Taylor, for the countless hours spent brainstorming. And by that I mean listening to me whine. Sometimes about writing. Usually about boys (sorry not sorry).

To my Seattle writing friends, who kept me sane in the rainy city—Kristin Halbrook, Danielle Dreger, Lish McBride, and Mark Henry.

To my LA wives, for the rosé and writing dates—Kirsten Hubbard, Sarah Enni, and Maurene Goo. I couldn't ask for a stronger safety net in so strange a place.

To my Scottish family—Adam Wright and Julie Riddell—for being a home when home was far away.

To the countless readers and reviewers who have shared their love of this world and these characters, and kept me going when things got tough.

Never has a story been so close to my heart—a book in which a gay boy can be more than his sexuality, a book in which anyone can save the world. And this book has lived in my heart for a very long time.

So, my final thanks is to you, dear reader, for proving that the world isn't just ready for diverse YA. The world *needs* it. Thank you for supporting this and for leaping into a world of monsters and magic and queer love.

Everyone has a story worth sharing. Everyone is the protagonist in a great adventure.

You are the hero we've been waiting for.